DREAM FRAGMENTS

Book Four of the Dream Waters Series

Erin A. Jensen

Dream Fragments is a work of fiction. Names, characters, places and incidents are the products of the author's imagination or are used fictitiously. Any resemblance to actual events, locales or persons, living or dead, is entirely coincidental.

2020 Dream Fragments
Text copyright © 2020 Erin A. Jensen
All Rights Reserved
Dream Waters Publishing LLC
5"x8" Softcover
ISBN: 1-7336504-1-5
ISBN 13: 978-1-7336504-1-0

First and always, to Chris—for supporting my writing career from the get-go in every possible way. I would never have gotten this far without you.

To Missy, Phil, Christine, Jim, Yvonne, and John—for encouraging me on this journey, listening to me vent about the bumps in the road along the way, supplying me with peanut butter cups whenever possible, and making my life so much richer. I love you all dearly.

To Katie, Amy, Tara, Stacy, Sandy, and Emilie—for beta reading this story. You all hold a special place in my heart.

To my editor, Kathryn Kenyon—for your unique combination of speed and attention to detail. You are one of a kind, and I'm grateful to have you on my team.

To Jennie Landschoot from Evergreen Photography—for capturing my personality on film (while only capturing one of my chins).

And to my Wegmans family for supporting me in a million different ways.

Ah, dream too bright to last!
Ah, starry Hope, that didst arise
But to be overcast!
A voice from out the Future cries,
"On! on!"—but o'er the Past
…my spirit hovering lies
Mute, motionless, aghast.

–Edgar Allan Poe / To One in Paradise

1

CHARLIE

I shut the door to my room, shuffled to the armchair in the corner at an arthritic pace, and stifled a whimper as I lowered myself into it. As I dropped my head back against the headrest, I glanced out the window and instantly wished that I hadn't. Just minutes after wrapping up our self-defense torture session for the day, Benjamin was already in the backyard constructing an obstacle course from hell to torment us with as soon as the sun rose the next morning. Benjamin was enjoying this way too much. Rose was raised among royal dragons, so she'd basically been in training since birth. None of these sessions were beyond her, and the Darkness knew I'd push myself to no end to keep from looking like a weakling in front of my girlfriend.

I flexed a bicep and winced at the burn, although I couldn't help grinning at the results. There was no arguing the fact that I was in the best shape of my life. Don't get me wrong, I wasn't gonna beat Tristan or Brian in a flexing competition anytime soon. For a second, I wondered if the two of them had looked like regular guys before Benjamin got ahold of them, but I dismissed the notion just as quickly because they were never *regular guys*. No regular guy could ever match up to an incubus in the looks department. Still, I didn't look half bad for me. Then again, I wasn't exactly a regular guy either. I was a dragon, and so was my girlfriend and fellow trainee—which was why I was working so hard to kick ass during our training sessions.

I pushed myself out of the chair with a muffled groan, peeled off my t-shirt, and headed to my bathroom for a much-needed shower. Two steps into the bathroom, a knock on my bedroom door suggested someone had other plans for me.

I plastered my best I'm-not-in-excruciating-pain smile on my face as I tossed my shirt on the bathroom floor and headed to the door. For all I knew, somebody I didn't want to look like a wimp in front of was standing on the other side.

Tristan greeted me with a playful grin as I pulled the door open. Then he nudged the opening wider and barged his way into my room without waiting for an invite. "Damn," he muttered, wrinkling his nose as he looked me up and down, "you stink."

I plopped down on my bed with a sigh of frustration. "I was just about to take a shower before I was rudely interrupted. Can I help you with something?"

"Yeah." He tugged my aching arm, and a knowing grin spread across his face as he yanked me to my feet. "You're gonna end up giving yourself a hernia, dragon. I doubt Rose would think any less of you if you eased up a little during your training sessions."

I took a quick peek into the hall to make sure Rose hadn't been out there to overhear that. Satisfied that the hallway was empty, I shut the door and dropped my voice to a whisper, hoping he'd take the hint and do the same. "Whatever. I don't need relationship advice from a guy who looks like a Greek god. What the hell do you know about impressing a girl? For you, it's as easy as breathing."

A pained expression contorted Tristan's chiseled features, making me feel like a total jackass. "Not always."

"Sorry," I muttered, wincing at my stupidity. "I'm a real idiot when I'm tired."

His carefree smirk assuaged some of my guilt, but not all of it. "Huh. Guess I've never seen you well rested."

I flashed him a grin that was part apology for sticking my foot in my mouth and part gratitude for his forgiving nature. "Hilarious. So, what do you need my help with?"

"We've got a couple new residents to chauffeur to the house."

"Wow," I muttered as I grabbed a fresh t-shirt from the dresser and slipped it over my head. "This place is filling up fast."

When I first moved into the house on fifty-five Sycamore Lane to start my training, the only other occupants were Tristan's brother, Brian; and Benjamin, aka the Darkness, the Sarrum's bonded shadow. Rose and Doc had moved in after me. Rose came to visit Isa—her comatose birth mother—and Doc came to restore Isa's health. After Isa was healed, she resumed her duties as the royal sorceress and moved in with her soul mate, Benjamin. Tristan had moved into the house along with Mia, the changeling he rescued from the Purists' cabin in the woods. Those sick bastards had kidnapped Mia, forced her to take Emma's form, and tortured her to lure the Sarrum there after Godric abducted Emma from the clearing.

There were still plenty of empty rooms in the stately old brick house, but privacy was getting harder and harder to come by unless you wanted to be antisocial and hole up in your bedroom.

"Why do you need my help driving people to the house?" I muttered. "That kinda sounds like a one-man job."

A mischievous grin spread across Tristan's gorgeous face. "Well, there's a bit of a catch."

"Alright, I'll bite. What's the catch?"

"They haven't exactly consented to moving in with us yet."

I raked a hand through my hair as I mulled that over. "So, you need my help kidnapping a couple people?"

Tristan shrugged his broad shoulders, rippling muscles I was pretty sure I'd been born without. "I suppose you could look at it that way."

"Wouldn't Benjamin be better at helping with something like that?" Even as I said it, I marveled at the fact that my greatest concern was Tristan's choice of co-kidnapper, rather than the fact that he needed help with something like that at all.

Tristan let out a chuckle that was beyond sexy. "Not with these two."

"For that matter," I muttered, reminding myself that I didn't have to let Tristan's charm affect me, "can't you just charm them into hopping into your car?"

"That's a negative," he murmured. "Come on, dragon. Where's your sense of adventure?"

"In what universe is *kidnapping* an adventure?"

"It's not exactly kidnapping," Tristan murmured as he moved to the door. "It's more of an invitation that they have no choice but to accept."

"Yeah, that pretty much sounds like kidnapping to me."

Tristan shook his head as he wrapped his fingers around the doorknob, and for a split second, I couldn't help being jealous of my door. "It's just the start of their grand new adventure."

"Uh huh, and why exactly are we *insisting* that these people move in with us?"

"For their own safety," Tristan replied in a silky whisper as he opened the door. "If they're here, the Purists won't be able to get to them."

"Stop being so freaking mysterious," I grumbled as I followed him out the door and down the stairs. "Who the hell are these people?"

Tristan winked at me as he opened the front door and ushered me outside. "Old friends of yours."

"Okay?"

He sauntered to the sleek silver vehicle parked in the driveway and opened the driver's side door. "Just get in."

Against my better judgment, I opened the passenger side door, plopped into the leather seat, and buckled myself in nice and tight. This wasn't my first ride with Tristan, so I was painfully aware that the gas was his favorite pedal and he considered the brakes optional in most situations. When you looked like him, and could charm the pants off almost anyone, you didn't need to worry about traffic tickets. So he saw no reason to wait around for something like a pesky green light to give him permission to go. I braced myself as he started the engine. It purred like a freaking kitten, which meant that his sweet touch on the gas pedal would propel us to warp speed as soon as the tires hit the road. "Where the hell are we going, Tristan?"

"The boss thinks your favorite elderly couple would be safer with us than they are at the facility."

I let out a laugh at the thought of Unsighted old Bob snoring on the couch in the middle of one of Benjamin's training sessions. "One look at the monster flat screen television in the living room and Bob will be in his glory."

"See, that's why we need you," Tristan murmured as he eased the gas pedal closer to the floor. "You know how to coax that ornery old bastard off the couch and into the car of a total stranger."

I raised an eyebrow as I cinched my seatbelt a little tighter. "Have you already tried this without me?"

"Yeah," he muttered, shaking his head before adding, "it didn't go so well."

"Can't Nellie just convince Bob that it's for the best? She knows who you are, and she understands why they'd be safer with us."

"Nellie had him convinced before I showed up at the facility, just like we'd planned it with young Bob in Draumer. But when I got there, old Bob informed me that he had no intention of riding off into the sunset with some pretty boy who's liable to rape them and leave them for dead."

I tried to stifle a laugh, but it came bursting out of my nose in an obnoxious snort. "Seriously?"

"Nellie says he's into criminal detective shows lately. Apparently, there's a real danger of handsome young guys with elder-abuse fetishes stealing crotchety dementia patients from mental institutions."

"So Bob wouldn't listen to Nellie, but you think he'll listen to me?"

"He knows you, so he won't suspect you're there to rape them," Tristan muttered as he pulled into the facility parking lot. "That'll start you off on a better foot than me."

"Just when I thought old Bob couldn't get any crazier..." My voice trailed off as my eyes fixed on the massive stone sign on the front lawn. *Parker-Banks Mental Health Facility* was etched in big bold letters, assuring normal passersby that the scourge of society was safely locked away inside. How many times had I stared at the back of that sign from the other side of a break-proof pane of glass, like a fish staring out of his tank at a parallel reality he'd never be a part of? "Can't you just charm the doctor into letting you take Bob kicking and screaming?"

"As delightful as that sounds," Tristan murmured as he parked the car, "it'd be best if we got the pair of them to come willingly."

I battled the inevitable bouts of déjà vu as we crossed the parking lot and entered the building. Lost in an onslaught of memories, I moved alongside Tristan as he approached the front desk. Then we followed an unfamiliar woman in white down the sterile corridor to the double doors that could only be opened with a staff member's key. As we entered the locked ward and made our way down the hall, I scanned the faces—both painfully familiar and recently admitted. It was no shock that we found Bob and Nellie on the couch in front of the television in the main common room.

I walked in and did the unthinkable. I planted myself right in front of Bob, blocking his view of the screen. "Hey, Bob."

To my surprise, he grinned at me. "Hey, kid. Long time no see." But the grin slipped from his face as his eyes moved to Tristan. "What's this pretty boy doin here again? I oughta bust that perfect nose of yours for comin back."

Tristan crossed his arms over his chest as he stepped closer to Bob. "Good to see you too, Grandpa."

"Fuck off, pretty boy," Bob spat as his wrinkled hands balled into fists. "I ain't your damn Grandpa."

I touched a hand to my old friend's shoulder to recapture his attention. "Bob, Tristan is a friend of mine."

"A friend of yours?" Bob echoed as he narrowed his eyes at Tristan. "What the fuck've you gotten yourself into these days, kid?"

I glanced at Tristan out of the corner of my eye and spoke in a voice too low for old Bob's ears to pick up, "Why doesn't your charm work on him?"

"He's too deeply in love with this lovely woman beside him to be affected by my charm."

I shook my head as I watched Nellie's wrinkled cheeks blush at the compliment. It didn't exactly take a rocket scientist to figure out what the problem was. "Then stop flirting with his soul mate, you idiot."

"I'm not flirting," Tristan whispered. "It's called being polite. You should try it sometime."

"Trust me on this. When *you* are polite to the love of somebody else's life, it comes across as flirting whether you mean it to or not."

"What do you suggest I do," Tristan whispered, "be rude to her?"

"It always worked for me," I muttered, earning a scowl from Nellie. I scowled right back at her. "Do you have to smile at him like that?"

"I didn't realize I was smiling," she whispered. "I can't help it. My heart belongs to the old coot next to me, but my body's not dead. When I see an Adonis like this, what am I supposed to do?"

"I'd suggest the old picture-him-in-his-underwear trick," I muttered, "but that wouldn't exactly help in this situation."

Nellie blushed a shade deeper as she looked the incubus up and down. "No kidding."

Bob hopped to his feet faster than I'd have guessed he could. "Get this sick fuck away from us!"

"My friend's not a bad guy, Bob," I assured him as I planted myself between the two men. "He came here to help me bring you to your new home."

"New home?" Bob muttered. "Will this asshole be there?"

I deflected the question the best way I knew how. "There's a huge flat screen television there that's gonna knock your socks off."

Bob glanced over his shoulder at Nellie as he spoke the words I never would've expected him to utter, "There's more important things than television."

Tristan grinned at the look of adoration on the old man's face. "You and Nellie can share a room there."

I expected Bob to take a swing at him, but if Tristan knew how to read any situation, it was that one. "Can you promise that for sure?" Bob muttered as he eyed the incubus.

"Yes," Tristan murmured. "I promise you, Grandpa. You and Grandma can share a room, and anyone who says otherwise will have to answer to me."

Bob relaxed his stance the instant Tristan referred to Nellie as *Grandma*. "Charlie, you can vouch for this guy?"

"Yeah, Bob. This guy has a heart of gold."

Bob scrunched up his face as he mulled it over. "Huge fuckin television, and an angel in my bed every night."

That made Nellie's face light up ten times brighter than it had when Tristan smiled at her.

Bob grinned at her reaction as he nodded. "Well, what the fuck're we waitin for? I got a program to watch at eleven a'clock."

2

GODRIC

Satisfied that my new headquarters had been adequately warded, I concluded my tour of the grounds and sat down on a bench near the entrance to the garden. The property encased within my latest mirage was identical to my childhood home, right down to the plaque on the garden gate with *Godric Manor* etched in delicate gold filigree. As much as I desired to escape certain elements of my past, there were memories within this framework that I could never bear to part with. Followers of the dragon who currently occupied my throne believed me to be a monster, but there are two sides to every story. No man is the villain of his own tale.

The throne was *mine*. It had been promised to me since birth, and I had every intention of claiming what rightfully belonged to me. However, my story began long before the usurper who sat upon my throne drew his first breath.

I was six years old when my mother died giving birth to my sister, Lilly. She was a coldhearted dragon, as was my father, but I suppose that was to be expected.

After all, they had been bred for strength and power sufficient enough to conceive the child who would one day take the throne. Such things were plotted out decades in advance. Every royal marriage was precisely orchestrated to strengthen the genetic makeup of the royal dragon families. This ensured that when a family's designated time arose—to wed a child to the eldest Talbot son or daughter—suitable traits would be passed on to future generations of monarchs.

Any love that either of my coldhearted parents ever expressed was directed toward the other because they treasured each other above all else—an inane frivolity on my father's part, as the likelihood of my mother surviving childbirth was slim to none. She was strong enough to survive the birth of one child, but the second proved too much for my mother. It was my father's fault of course, for being reckless enough to impregnate her twice. Yet, in his grief-stricken insanity, my father blamed my infant sister for the death of his beloved treasure. His madness fostered a deep-seated need within me to protect the youngest member of the Godric family. Within hours of her birth, Lilly captured my heart and became the creature whom I treasured above all else.

Whatever warmth once dwelt in my father's heart was buried along with the woman who gave birth to us. Our father's apathy cemented our bond and inspired my vow to protect Lilly from ever suffering the same fate as our mother. It was a promise I had no doubt I could keep because I was the future Sarrum of Draumer. If I deemed Lilly untouchable, then it would be so...

DREAM FRAGMENTS

...I grinned from ear to ear as I walked away from my fencing lesson. Father would need to find me yet another new instructor. After besting this one, he'd scarcely return for more humiliation. However, I was confident that Father would have no problem with that. Although he expressed no affection toward either of his children, he always beamed with pride at my accomplishments. After all, his son was the future ruler of Draumer. All my victories were his to take credit for.

In his grief-maddened wisdom, Father reasoned that my achievements justified his rather unorthodox methods of parenting. Weakness was not to be tolerated in the Godric household. Thankfully, my strength was sufficient enough for him to pay little attention to Lilly. Cold as that may sound, our father's attention was nothing to covet. He was a bitter old dragon who had lost his precious treasure. Being six years Lilly's elder, I willingly endured any violent fits of rage that might otherwise have been directed at her. In my younger days, I simply stepped in his path whenever he went after Lilly. Void of any emotion, save blind fury, our father was easily swayed to take his frustrations out on me in her stead. In his rare moments of clarity, he would justify the violence by declaring that he was strengthening me into "a force to be reckoned with." As my sister and I grew older, my strength waxed whilst my father's waned. Once the balance of power reached its tipping point, it took surprisingly few retaliatory blows to convince him to abandon his old ways and keep his hands off both his children.

With my fencing lesson behind me, it was time to move on to the happiest hours of my day—guiding Lilly in her lessons. Since Father had shirked every responsibility after my mother passed, I'd taken it upon myself to act as my sister's guide. It was a tremendous task for a boy who was only six years her elder, but I had the finest teachers and my father saw no point in bothering to educate Lilly at all. In fact, had I not been around, I suspect Lilly might never have reached her first birthday. Now she was two days shy of her seventeenth, and thriving.

I swung the gate open and entered the garden beaming with pride. The smile slipped from my face the instant I saw Lilly sitting amidst the rose bushes with tears streaming down her cheeks.

I sat down on the ground beside her, kissed the top of her head, and waited for her to regain enough composure to provide an explanation.

She slouched against me and dropped her head to my shoulder as she wiped the tears from her cheeks. "The Grayson family is coming for a visit this weekend. Father has a business proposition for their patriarch."

I tipped my head to rest against hers. "And this bothers you?"

She nodded without lifting her head from my shoulder, and her hair brushed against my cheek, mingling her delicate spiced scent with the velvet sweetness of the roses. "Father believes a union between me and Mr. Grayson's eldest son would strengthen the ties between our families."

Flames filled my eyes, tinting the world around me in flickering shades of blue as I snarled, "What?"

"He came to tell me during your fencing lesson."

An infuriated growl rumbled in the base of my throat. "He has no right to arrange a marriage for you. I will provide an heir to the throne and continue the Godric bloodline. You needn't marry at all."

"Father doesn't agree. He sees no value to my life beyond a means to strengthen his business alliances."

"He sees no value to any life," I whispered. "You know that."

DREAM FRAGMENTS

She nodded and drew an unsteady breath, but said nothing.

I wrapped an arm around her shoulders, and my heart ached at the way her slender frame was trembling. "You have nothing to worry about, Lilly."

Her response was no more than a faint whisper, "How can you say that?"

"I promise you," I whispered, tightening my protective hold on her shoulders to emphasize my words, "I will fix this. There is no reason for an arranged marriage beyond Father's own selfish gains. I'll just point that out and convince him to call it off."

"Promise me I won't have to leave with the Graysons, Henry." Tears spilled from Lilly's crystal blue eyes as she looked up at me. "I want to stay here with you."

"I promise," I whispered. "You will always stay with me, and no man will ever touch you."

"How can you—"

"I am the future ruler of Draumer," I reminded her with a reassuring smile. "My say is the final say, and I promise you that no man will lay a hand on you—not now, not ever."

She wrapped her arms around my neck and pressed her cheek against mine as she whispered, "I love you."

A thin wisp of smoke escaped my flared nostrils as I allowed her affection to dampen the flames within me. Rage had no place in our lessons.

When I spoke to Father later that evening, I rekindled my fury and persuaded him to see things as I did. He left me little choice. Violence was the only means of communication the miserable old dragon could comprehend.

Monsters are rarely born as such. More often than not, they are created...

..."Godric," my demon informant rasped as he approached, shooing the memory back to the dusty recesses of my mind from whence it came. "The Sarrum had your estranged wife and her gentleman friend transported from the facility to a more secure location this morning."

I scowled at the bearer of this displeasing news. "Do *not* refer to him that way."

A perplexed grimace contorted the demon's gaunt features. "Who, the knight? Should I not call him her *gentleman friend?*"

I wrapped a hand around the mongrel's throat and lifted him off the ground by his neck. "I don't give a damn what you call Nellie's lover. I am talking about the man who sits on *my* throne. *I* am the rightful *Sarrum* of Draumer. Refer to him by my title again, and I will rip out your throat. Understood?"

I let the demon drop to the ground, and he coughed and sniffled like a child as he responded with an emphatic nod.

"Where has he taken the old couple?"

The demon winced and lowered his eyes to the ground. "Not sure. The incubus drove too fast for me to keep up."

3

DAVID

We sat on a cushioned lounge chair on the terrace in no particular hurry to dress for the day. Emma's sun-kissed legs were draped over mine and a blanket from our bed was wrapped around her shoulders like an oversized shawl as we sipped our coffee and watched the sun ascend to its rightful place in the sky. There was a faint tinge of dampness to the air that gave the early morning breeze a chilling bite. If it weren't for the heat radiating from the raging inferno inside her husband, the temperature might've been enough to drive Emma indoors—although, perhaps not. My wife's stubborn streak was not to be underestimated.

She cradled the coffee cup in her hands with an adoration that bordered on worship as she dropped her head to my shoulder. "I wish we could suspend time and just live in this moment for a few days."

I kissed the top of her head. "A few days? I would stay for a brief eternity."

"A brief eternity," she murmured, pausing to sip the precious liquid in her cup before adding, "that's quite a contradiction in terms."

I lowered my head, touching it to hers. "A bit like you and I—polar opposites that combine to form something unlikely, yet exquisitely delicious—all the better for the impossibility of their union."

Something between a contented purr and a chuckle escaped her throat in a velvet whisper. "Such deep thoughts for so early in the day."

"Alas," I whispered, nuzzling her ear as I spoke, "reality awaits. I'm afraid time stops for no man."

"But neither of us is a man," Emma murmured as she tilted her head to look up at me. "Wouldn't time consider stilling for a dragon and a fairy?"

I took the cup from her hand and smothered her groan of protest with a kiss as I placed it on the table beside us. She slid onto my lap and exhaled a much breathier groan when I broke the kiss. "Unfortunately, we cannot afford to still time this morning."

She spun around to face me and straddled my legs, hovering above me on her knees as she touched her forehead to mine. "Too bad for you."

I slid my fingers through the silken strands of her hair, cupped the base of her skull in my palm and drew her mouth toward mine. Her lips parted in response, but I stopped a few centimeters shy of a kiss. "I would burn both worlds to ash to still time for us if you asked me to."

She closed the gap between our mouths, brushing her lips against mine as she murmured, "I'm extremely tempted to take you up on that offer."

I drew her head closer and kissed her pouting lips.

This time, she broke the kiss. "I'm coming with you today."

I slid the blanket off her leg and traced a finger over the flesh above the house arrest ankle bracelet that confined her to our property. "And how would we explain that to the police?"

She tugged the blanket back over the offensive piece of jewelry, threaded her fingers through mine and pulled my hand away from it. "Conduct the meeting in the palace or have them meet you here at the house. I'm tired of being on the periphery of everything that's happening."

"You needn't rush your recovery," I murmured as I trailed our joined hands up her calf.

"I spent too much time living only half my life. I need to be a part of what's going on now that I'm whole again."

"Fair enough," I muttered as I slid our hands over her knee and continued up her outer thigh. "I'll have Benjamin bring them here."

"Thank you," she murmured as our fingers skirted beneath the hem of her nightgown.

I slipped my other hand beneath the thin fabric, gripped her waist and pulled her to my lap. "We've got a bit of time before that can be arranged. How shall we occupy ourselves?"

She tugged her fingers free from mine and retrieved her cup from the table with a sinful smirk. "More coffee."

"Coffee can wait," I whispered. "I cannot."

She feigned an innocent smile as she lifted the cup to her lips and took a sip. "Liar. You would wait for me forever. You're an incredibly patient man."

"Perhaps," I whispered, pausing to sip from her cup as she tipped it to my lips, "but I'm a miserably impatient dragon with an insatiable appetite that it's rather unwise to ignore."

She raised an eyebrow as she downed what was left in her cup. "Then I suppose we'll have to compromise."

"How so?"

"You'll just have to see to it that I'm thoroughly awake."

I took the empty cup from her hand, tossed it to the tiled floor of the terrace and watched her eyes darken as it shattered. "Challenge accepted." Crushing my lips against hers, I slid my hands beneath her nightgown. All sounds but her quickened heartbeat faded away as I hooked an index finger on either side of her panties, tore the fabric at the seams and tossed them aside. Such satisfying sounds—the tearing of lace and the resultant whimper of pleasure that followed.

She wrapped her blanket around my shoulders as she rose to her knees, allowing me to tug the waist of my pajama bottoms out of the way.

A low growl rumbled in the base of my throat as I took her by the waist, pulled her to my lap and buried myself deep inside her in one fluid movement. A hushed moan escaped her lips as I tilted my head toward the blanket she kept carefully wrapped around us. "Why so modest this morning, Princess?"

"It's cold out here," she groaned as her body began to undulate in perfect synchrony with the beating of my heart. "I'm freezing."

A wicked grin spread across my face as I shook my head. "Not for long."

Then spoken words escaped us both as the world around us stilled.

4

EMMA

After seeing to it that I was wide awake and blissfully warm, David headed downstairs to his office to call Benji and inform him that the meeting would take place in our lounge. While my husband orchestrated the change of plans, I took a long luxurious shower. Not long ago, the walls of our home had been my prison. Although I still wore the hideous ankle bracelet that confined me to our property, I'd never felt freer. I was finally whole again.

I'd spent so long blaming my husband for decisions I couldn't comprehend, and hating him for sins he hadn't even committed. With all that behind us, I was eager to move forward and get on with our life together. Fearing that I might push myself too hard and cause my memories to slip again, David had urged me to take things slow. I had no desire to ease back into my old life. I wanted to plunge right in and make up for all the time I'd lost, but I respected his concerns. I'd put David through hell while I was blind.

Eventually David and I had reached a compromise by agreeing to take a joint leave of absence from the firm. Although technically, I'd already been absent for months. After I lost my Sight, there were so many facets of my life that I just couldn't wrap my blinded brain around. My mind had compensated by blocking out the details I couldn't make heads nor tails of, and one of those details was that Talbot and Associates wasn't just David's law firm. I was the other senior partner, and the two of us tried the majority of our cases together.

When David and my father originally founded the firm, under the name Talbot and Reed, it consisted of two separate locations. Although he didn't know it, my father headed the division that represented Unsighted clients, while David headed the Sighted division. That was his reason for partnering with my Unsighted father. David couldn't very well advertise that his firm was strictly for Sighted clients, so the cases were discreetly sorted by his Sighted assistant, a young paralegal succubus named Sophie Turner. She routed the Unsighted clients who wandered in off the street to my father's office, while the Sighted clients were directed to David's branch of the firm. I interned at David's office as a teenager because David convinced my father it'd be more appropriate for me to do an internship with a partner rather than my own parent. I did end up falling in love with the field, but in those days the arrangement served as a convenient excuse for us to spend time together back when I was most vulnerable. After I forsook the Light and bound myself to the Darkness in Draumer, frequent physical contact in both worlds was needed to maintain David's protective scent-marking. We became a proper couple in every sense of the word in Draumer just before my seventeenth birthday—the night he claimed me as his own—but David insisted that we abide by the laws of the waking world and wait to consummate our waking relationship until I turned eighteen. It was a risky decision because it meant that his scent on my skin would be diluted in this world, but he wouldn't hear of doing things any other way. So we worked together almost every day, and his touch was frequent but appropriate. When David and I were apart in the waking world back then, Benji spent much of his time cloaked in shadow to watch over me so any potential threat could be detected and dealt with.

A smug grin tugged at the corners of my mouth as I turned off the water and stepped out of the shower, recalling the day temptation finally got the better of David. Since I saw no point in waiting till I turned eighteen, I made every attempt to thwart his noble intentions in the waking world. He may have been the most powerful creature in existence, but I was his weakness. I always had been. Compound that with the fact that I was his to touch in Draumer and his waking body was desperate to take me, and eventually I wore down his resolve.

Lost in the euphoria of the memory, I dried off haphazardly. Then I stepped out of the bathroom wrapped in a towel and was greeted by an amorous growl. There was no hiding my lustful train of thought—or my body's response to it—from David. He could feel it just as well as I could. I loosened the towel and let it fall to the floor as I moved toward him.

He put his hands on my waist as his fiery gaze traveled over me. "Warmer now?"

I leaned into him, crushing damp flesh against his freshly pressed dress shirt. "Yes, thank you."

A rush of heat blossomed inside me as he trailed a hand down my back. "You've no further need for my warmth then?" he murmured as his hand paused at the small of my back, pressing me tighter against him.

I rose up to my tiptoes with a sinful smile and planted a chaste kiss on his lips. "Now that you mention it, I think I might feel a chill coming on."

His deep-throated chuckle further stoked the fire inside me.

"You came in here to tell me they'll be arriving soon," I whispered, draping my arms around his neck.

"Yes," he replied in a hushed rasp as he lifted me off the floor and wrapped my legs around his waist, "but I'm afraid I got distracted and forgot why I came in."

I brushed my lips against his as he sauntered across the room and sat me down on top of his dresser. "Would you like me to remind you?"

"No," he murmured, kissing his way down my neck as I unbuttoned his shirt, "I'd much rather make you forget."

I wore my husband's spiced scent like a second skin as we descended the staircase and entered the lounge hand in hand. Rose and Benjamin were seated in the chairs by the fireplace. Across from them, Isa sat on the couch beside a long-legged man with a scruffy beard and dark wavy hair with hints of gray at the temples.

He was dressed in jeans and an unbuttoned flannel shirt over a fitted gray t-shirt that emphasized his well-toned physique. The man's primal masculine features suggested that he would've been ruggedly handsome if life had been kinder to him. As it was, there was a hollow emptiness in his eyes underscored by dark circles and more wrinkles than you'd expect to find on someone his age.

David and Benji had met this demon before, but I was blind at the time and wouldn't have understood the reason for his visit. Now that my Sight was restored, I was anxious to meet the first satori to ever cross my path. The satori demons' ability to observe and share memories through physical contact had always fascinated me during my childhood lessons, and I wasn't about to pass up an opportunity to experience what the satori could do firsthand.

Benji signaled for the satori to stand, and he hopped off the couch and moved toward us.

My husband greeted him with a polite nod. "You're looking well, Barker."

A spark of mischief flashed in the satori's eyes as he grinned at me. "So is your wife."

Blue smoke wafted from my husband's flared nostrils, scenting the air around us as he narrowed his eyes at the demon. "Excuse me?"

"Sorry, Sarrum." The satori's left eye twitched as he muttered, "I just meant...that I uh...I'm glad she got her Sight back."

A warning growl rumbled in my husband's throat as I grinned at our guest. "It's nice to meet you."

I extended a hand, and the satori turned to David with a raised eyebrow. When my husband nodded, the satori took my hand, gave it a polite shake then dropped it as fast as he could. "The pleasure's all mine, my Queen."

My grin widened at the formality. "You can call me Emma."

"*Queen* will do nicely," David interjected.

The satori nodded. "Queen it is, then. My name's Clay, by the way."

"Mr. Barker," David growled.

David's second growl seemed to rattle the satori. I could almost *feel* his internal struggle to stand his ground and resist taking a step back from the King. "Sorry," he muttered. "Call me Mr. Barker."

"Mr. Barker," I repeated, stifling a grin, "you are the first satori I've ever met. Would you be willing to demonstrate your ability to me?"

My husband tensed at the request, and Clay naturally hesitated. For a second, I thought it was the physical contact that the sharing of a memory required that David was taking issue with. Then it hit me. The Purists had tricked David into viewing a memory through a satori's eyes. The victim of the brutal abuse he witnessed was a changeling who'd been forced to take my form so he would think they'd hurt me. A twinge of guilt churned my stomach as David nodded, granting the satori permission to demonstrate what he could do.

As Clay Barker held a trembling hand out to me, I found myself wondering whether the tremor was due to nerves or a lifetime of drug use.

I took his hand and my stomach lurched as the room melted away. A new room immediately took its place, so real that I would've sworn I was actually there.

The dimly lit hovel stank of a nauseating mix of drug fumes, stale body fluids, and forgotten dreams. A mellow reggae tune wafted from the poor-quality speakers across the room, but not loud enough to drown out the guttural groans echoing through thin walls caked with layers of filth.

My heart raced as I looked around, searching the room for the satori who'd transported me to this place. Then I realized I wouldn't find him because I was seeing through his eyes. This was *his* memory I was viewing clear as day.

I didn't realize I was seated until two men walked in the door and sauntered across the room to tower above me. As they stepped into the light, I wanted to breathe a sigh of relief at the welcome sight of David and Benji's faces. Instead, my heart began to pound— *no, not my heart, Clay Barker's.* This was all part of the satori's astoundingly vivid memory.

David shook his head as he glared at me. "You are filthy."

"Sorry," a voice that wasn't mine croaked from my mouth. "I wasn't expecting a visit from royalty today."

Fear washed over me as Benji's deep voice thundered in my ears, "I told you to be ready when I came back for you."

"What can I say? I'm a procrastinator," the voice that wasn't mine slurred. "But don't worry, I'm great under pressure."

A puff of blue smoke wafted from David's nostrils as he grabbed me by the collar. "I haven't got time for this nonsense."

A rush of warmth trickled down my legs as he yanked me to my feet as if I weighed nothing. "My apologies, Sarrum," the voice that wasn't mine muttered. "I'm a coward. It ain't gonna be easy dredging up the past."

David's expression softened as he released my collar. "She would want you to do this."

Filthy man-sized fingers that didn't belong to me wiped a tear from a stubbled cheek that certainly wasn't mine. "Yeah, I know."

The hedonistic den dissolved just as rapidly as it'd appeared, and I almost lost my footing as the lounge reformed around me.

As Clay released my hand, David reached out to steady me. "Well, was it everything you dreamt it would be?"

"Yes," I whispered, too relieved to hear my own voice to concern myself with the sarcasm in David's. He clearly wasn't fond of Clay Barker, and after delving into the satori's memory, it wasn't difficult to guess why. "I can't believe how real that seemed. It felt like I was actually him."

My stomach turned as David winced at my words. All the horrible things he'd watched them do to the woman he thought was me, *did it feel like he was doing them himself?* A tear slid from my eye before I could blink it back.

David brushed it from my cheek with his fingertips as he shook his head. "Bygones."

I took his hand and squeezed it to let him know I understood. *Don't go there.*

Some memories were just too horrific to revisit.

5

MIA

Happiness lingered on the tip of my tongue,
like a verse from a fairytale
I once knew by heart
but had long since forgotten.
I could almost taste the words
that brought me such joy
once upon a time.
Now,
those words soured on my tongue
and no one understood my tears.
Perhaps happiness is best forgotten,
a childish fairytale
we're taught to search for
but will never find.

I'd been kicking the words around in my head for over an hour. As much as I tried to ignore them these days, words constantly filled my head and insisted that I arrange them into some sick semblance of beauty before they would drift away. It'd been years since I actually captured one of my poems on paper. That felt a bit too much like pinning a butterfly—mounting it with its wings outstretched, and leaving it to die—preserved in mint condition. Displaying your agony for the entertainment of voyeuristic souls was a perverse fetish. I preferred to release my words and let them soar unhindered into the void of space and time, never to be uttered aloud or read by any eyes.

I couldn't tell you what was playing on the television across the room. There could have been a news report announcing the end of the world on that massive screen, and I doubt I would've noticed. My focus was on giving my poem a proper send-off, and attempting to banish the memories that came flooding back whenever the house was too quiet. I normally kept to my room to avoid the looks of pity everyone gave me when Tristan wasn't around, but even pity seemed preferable to the flashbacks that refused to subside this morning.

The metallic click of the lock on the front door slipping out of place startled me from my thoughts, and I bit my lip as I watched the doorknob turn. I took a deep breath, reminded myself that I was safe, and prayed that it was Tristan returning home. I didn't have the energy to deal with anyone else, and I needed to see the kindness in those beautiful green eyes of his. After everything I'd been through, the incubus's physical perfection no longer affected me the way it used to. Now, it was the understanding without a trace of pity that made him the only person in the world I wanted to interact with.

I breathed a sigh of relief as Tristan stepped into the foyer and flashed me a brilliant smile, but the tension seeped back into me as a parade of misfits followed him inside.

"Well, shit," muttered an old man with slicked back salt-and-pepper hair as he shuffled around the foyer, taking in his surroundings.

A shriveled old woman dressed in a faded housecoat stepped in after the foul-mouthed man, smoothing a hand over her frizzy white hair. "Damn, this place is classy."

Charlie stepped in after her and to my relief, he closed the front door. Two senior citizens with potty mouths wasn't too horrible, especially since neither of them was really a stranger. I'd met Nellie and Bob in Draumer, but it was always interesting to see how someone's alternate form stacked up against the familiar.

Charlie grinned at me as he kicked off his shoes and stepped into the living room. "Hey, Mia. Is Rose around?"

"No," I muttered, eyeing the old couple as they followed him into the room, "I haven't seen her yet this morning."

"Holy fuckin jackpot," old Bob muttered as he shuffled toward the big screen television at the other end of the room. A middle-aged woman with a figure that suggested she enjoyed sampling her own creations was dicing up vegetables on-screen. *A cooking show.* That's what I'd settled on, or at least zoned out during. The old man muttered something under his breath as he turned and headed toward the couch. He plopped down on the opposite end from me and gestured toward the remote on the coffee table. "Mind if I surf a little?"

I shook my head and whispered, "Go ahead."

As Bob grabbed the remote, Nellie settled down beside him.

Charlie stood there grinning at them for a moment before asking, "You guys want a tour of the house?"

"Maybe later," Bob muttered as he started flipping through the channels.

Amusement glinted in Tristan's eyes as he sat down between me and Nellie.

That definitely got Bob's attention. He immediately dropped the remote and hopped off the couch. "Are we gonna have a problem, pretty boy?"

"Easy, Bob," Charlie muttered, putting a hand on the old man's shoulder. "Tristan isn't a threat to Nellie."

Bob narrowed his eyes at Tristan as he shook his head. Then his gaze shifted to me. "Who the fuck's this?"

Even with Tristan beside me, I couldn't help flinching at the harshness of the old man's tone. I knew he was just confused and disoriented by his unfamiliar surroundings, but it'd been a rough enough morning already. I didn't have the energy to deal with old Bob's temper, even if it was nothing more than an involuntary spasm of senile dementia.

As he watched Tristan wrap a protective arm around my shoulders, the old man's expression softened. His apologetic eyes drifted to my tear-filled gaze and he cleared his throat, visibly changing gears. Then he dropped to one arthritic knee with a muffled grunt and held a hand out to me. "Sorry, Miss. I uh…think I mighta misread the situation here. I promise, I'm not as big a jackass as I come across."

"Don't let him fool you, honey," old Nellie muttered. "He is that big of a jackass, but he's my jackass, and he's harmless."

The concerned grimace on Charlie's face morphed into a faint smile at that. "Bob's an ornery old jackass with a heart of gold," he assured me in a whisper too low for the old man's ears to pick up. "His mind's not all there in this world, but his heart still is."

I considered the sorrow in old Bob's eyes. There was no trace of sympathy or pity in them. It was genuine heartache that shimmered in his age-weary eyes. Moved by the raw emotion staring back at me, I reached a tentative hand across the coffee table and shook the old man's outstretched hand.

A groan of exertion escaped Bob's throat as he pushed himself to his feet using the coffee table for leverage. "What's your name, dear?"

"Her name is Mia," Tristan answered for me before I could open my mouth to respond. An uncharacteristic hint of malice crept into his tone as he added, "You can be as much of an ass to me as you like, old man. But if you so much as look at her with a cross expression, we're gonna have a *big* problem."

"We got no problem," Bob muttered as he settled back in his spot on the couch beside Nellie. "You got my word."

"Good," Tristan growled. "Because as much as I like you in Draumer, I'll have no problem kicking your wrinkled old ass to the curb if you make Mia even the slightest bit uncomfortable. Are we clear?"

Bob pursed his lips and furrowed his brow, then muttered, "Yeah, kid. We're good."

Tristan nodded, but his expression didn't soften. I almost felt bad for old Bob and yet, I appreciated the intensity of Tristan's reaction. There was a reason he was the one person who made me feel safe. Tristan turned to me and smiled. "Wanna get some air?"

"Yeah," I whispered, "that sounds good."

He stood up from the couch and helped me to my feet like a perfect gentleman. I was perfectly capable of standing on my own, but I appreciated the chivalry of the gesture. As we started toward the foyer, Tristan put his arm around my shoulders and narrowed his eyes at Bob. "Watch yourself, Grandpa."

"Yes, sir," Bob muttered without a trace of sarcasm.

We moved down the hall to the back of the house in silence. Tristan opened the french doors and motioned for me to step out first. Then he followed me out onto the deck and shut the doors. As we headed toward the cushioned furniture on the other side of the deck, I was pleasantly surprised to see that we had the backyard to ourselves.

I sat down on a loveseat, and Tristan sat down beside me. "You okay?"

"I'm fine," I muttered. "Bob seems harmless enough."

"I'm not just talking about Bob," Tristan whispered as he took my hand and gave it an affectionate squeeze. "You had another rough night last night."

I tucked a flyaway strand of hair behind my ear and shrugged. "No big deal."

"Don't forget who you're talking to."

"How could I?" I muttered with a shy smile. "You're the only person I feel safe with."

"It's gonna get easier," he whispered as he touched the side of his head to mine. "I promise. It just takes time."

I turned my head to look him in the eye. "What happened to you, Tristan? Are you ever going to open up to me?"

"Doesn't matter," he whispered as his eyes moved to the obstacle course Benjamin had constructed in the yard. "It was another lifetime."

"But the scars never completely healed," I muttered. "I can see it in your eyes."

Tristan shook his head without taking his eyes off the obstacle course. "Dredging up the past won't do anyone any good."

"I think you're wrong," I muttered. "You've helped me a lot by listening to me."

"That's different," he replied in a hoarse whisper.

I dropped my head to his broad shoulder. "How so?"

"What happened to you isn't ancient history. Those scars are still fresh, and you still have trouble falling asleep."

I closed my eyes and drew a deep breath of the fresh morning air, content to feel completely safe in that moment. "I wish I could go back in time and hurt whoever hurt you."

"No one is gonna hurt either of us ever again," he murmured, turning his head to look at me. "I promise you that, Mia."

Finally able to let go of the tension, I yawned and drifted off to sleep...

...And when I woke in Draumer, Tristan was waiting for me.

6

TRISTAN

I knew exactly how to time it so Mia could fall asleep while I was still awake beside her and wake to find me waiting for her in the other world. It was a trick I mastered a lifetime ago, the only valuable lesson my worthless excuse for a father had ever taught me.

Most creatures misjudged the amount of time it took them to pass between worlds. The transport that felt like mere seconds to them actually took about thirty to forty-five minutes. The Water creatures just messed with their perception of time. Even among the Sighted, the Water creatures were a mysterious entity because the majority of us couldn't see them or detect them in any way. They fed off the memories of almost every creature as they passed between worlds, but they did it to differing degrees depending on what type of creature they were preying on. It goes without saying that Unsighted minds were the easiest for them to manipulate, but their process was always the same no matter what type of creature they were toying with. First, they devoured most—if not all—memories of whichever world the creature was departing. Any stray memories they happened to leave behind were interpreted as vivid dreams by the Unsighted mind. Next, the Water creatures filled their victim's head with a myriad of bizarre visions, fragmented thoughts, and hazy false memories. That was the majority of jumbled garbage the Unsighted mind thought of as dreams. Lastly, the Water creatures regurgitated their victim's memories of the world they were about to reenter, the memories they'd gorged on during the creature's last passage between worlds. Nobody knew exactly *how* the Water creatures accomplished that. Maybe each of them was responsible for a particular bunch of souls, or maybe they shared some sort of collective consciousness that allowed them access to the erased memories of any creature they happened upon in the Waters.

Fortunately for me, an incubus's charms didn't escape him in the Waters. With proper training, it was possible for an incubus or succubus to charm the Water creatures into leaving their mind untouched and speeding up their passage between worlds. I really shouldn't give my father much credit for teaching me to do it. He was the one who first introduced me to the concept, but it was my older brother who taught me how to master the technique.

We were just kids when Brian took over as my guide. To this day, I'm still stunned by my big brother's selflessness during our earliest years together. He had so many reasons to hate me and yet, he welcomed me into his home with open arms. I probably should've hated Brian's mother for the way she treated him, but God help me, I just couldn't. Her harsh treatment of Brian—her own flesh and blood, who she'd carried in her womb—paled in comparison to my birth mother's treatment of me during the first seven years of my life.

As I watched Mia's eyelids flutter while she drifted toward consciousness, the day I first met my brother came to mind...

...I watched with wide-eyed amazement as the scenery outside the car window gradually morphed from the dirty streets of my urban neighborhood to the manicured lawns of suburbia.

I glanced up at the woman in the fancy suit sitting next to me in the backseat, and she shot me a reassuring smile. I wanted her to tell me that it would all be okay, that my dad would be happy to see me. Instead, she blushed and turned her head to watch the world go by through the window on her side of the car. I swallowed the lump in my throat and blinked the tears from my eyes as I turned toward my window. At seven years old, my ability to control people's reactions to me was pretty hit-or-miss. I knew how to turn up the charm, but I couldn't always use it to manipulate people into doing what I wanted them to.

I guess you could say that my dad was my guide for my first seven years of life, except that he never had much interest in teaching me anything. He was usually too busy with my mom, and she was usually busy wishing I'd never been born. I tied her down too much. She was always reminding me how hard it was to sell enough "favors" to earn money for the medicine she needed with a snot-nosed brat to look after—her words, not mine. I only knew the terms she'd taught me, but I wasn't stupid. Real medicine wasn't powder you snorted up your nose or stuff you melted in a spoon and injected into your veins, and real mommies didn't let strange men do things to them in trade for money or "medicine." My mom was Unsighted, so she had no idea what kind of monsters she was constantly bringing into our home.

My dad was just a stranger who came around every once in a while when he "needed a break from his wife and kid," but I'd overheard him telling my mom that she shouldn't do the things she did in front of me. Sometimes it made me wonder. If he knew the whole story, would he have gotten me out of there? Probably not, since he didn't seem to care enough about the stuff he did know about to do anything to stop it. He was just another man who came to my mom for things he couldn't get at home, and I was just a mistake that neither of them wanted.

I looked away from the fancy houses with perfect lawns and bright colored flowers lining the walkways, and stared at the lady in the suit until she turned back to me. Did she know my dad called me his little mistake? That's how he'd greet me whenever he showed up on our doorstep with a pack of gum or a cheap plastic toy for me. He'd ruffle my hair and say, "How's my little mistake today?"

What was my dad going to say when I turned up on his doorstep with the lady in the suit telling him that my mom took too much medicine and would never wake up again? The lady said my mom put his name on my birth certificate, so that's where they had to take me first. If he turned me away, I wasn't sure where they'd take me. What did they do with mistakes whose parents didn't want them? I had no idea, but my mind constructed all sorts of scenarios as I stared at the lady in the suit.

Could I charm her into taking me home with her, so I wouldn't have to live on the street selling favors to strangers to survive? My mom used to say that was the only thing people like us were good for, and she hated me for being even better suited for it than her. Sometimes I picked up stray thoughts from her mind along those lines after she took her medicine. She hated me for being prettier than she was, and she resented me for making her less pretty and less free than she used to be.

I wiped a tear from my cheek as the car pulled into the driveway of a white house with a big front porch and a freshly mowed lawn. There was a boy sitting on the bottom step of the porch reading a book. He looked a little older than me, and a lot like my dad. He looked up from his book as the lady in the suit opened my door and took me by the hand, but he didn't say anything. He just watched us walk toward him.

The lady in the suit smiled at him as we reached the porch steps. "Hello."

He frowned at her without standing up. "Hi."

The lady cleared her throat and eyed the front door to the house. "Is your father home?"

"No."

Color rushed to the lady's cheeks as she nodded and cleared her throat again. "Well, is your mother home?"

The boy closed his book and sat it on the step beside him. "Yeah."

"Well..." The lady cleared her throat again. "Could you please go get her for me?"

The boy stood up and narrowed his eyes at her. "Who should I say is here?"

The longer this dragged on, the redder the lady's face got and the worse my stomach ached. I slipped my hand out of her clammy grip and hid behind her. "Tell her I work for the state," the lady replied, "and I'm here because we need to get in touch with her husband."

The boy let out an irritated huff as he marched up the steps, but he didn't have to go inside. His mother stepped out the front door just as he reached the porch.

She moved toward the edge of the porch and scowled at the lady in the suit. "Can I help you with something?"

"Yes," the lady in the suit muttered as she fumbled to dig a business card out of her pocket and hand it to the boy's mother. "I'm from Child Protective Services, and I'm here because we need to get in touch with your husband as soon as possible."

For some strange reason, the woman frowned at her son. "What the hell does CPS want with my husband?"

The lady cleared her throat for about the hundredth time. "Mrs. Mason, are you aware that your husband fathered a son with another woman seven years ago?"

"No," the boy's mother muttered, "but it doesn't really shock me. My husband isn't exactly a saint. Why the hell are you coming here to tell me this?"

"The boy's mother overdosed on heroin last night, and your husband is listed as his father on the birth certificate. She intended for the boy to go to him in the event of her death."

The woman let out a bark of laughter that made both me and the lady jump. "You've got to be kidding! You expect me to take in his little bastard and give myself another mouth to feed? I've got my hands full enough taking care of this one with no help from him, so you can just march right back to your car and take him wherever you take orphans with no place else to go. He's not my problem."

The lady in the suit stiffened at the woman's brusqueness, but she responded in a gentle tone, "Why don't you meet the boy before you turn him away to get lost in the system? Don't you think your husband deserves the chance to decide what becomes of his son for himself?"

"What my husband deserves is forced castration."

I tuned out their conversation and focused on cranking up my charm as much as I possibly could. Even while she was biting the lady in the suit's head off, this woman seemed nicer than my mom ever did. If I could just charm her into letting me stay until my dad got back, maybe she'd decide I wasn't so bad. I could help her around the house and try my best to make her life easier. Even if she hated me, it'd be better than getting lost in the system—whatever that meant.

I cranked up the charm as high as I ever had as I peeked out from behind the lady in the suit.

"You can just..." the boy's mom trailed off mid-sentence as I caught her eye. She put a hand to her mouth as she stepped toward me, then whispered, "What's your name?"

Smiling didn't seem like the right thing to do, so I just blinked up at her with my big green lost puppy dog eyes. "Tristan."

"Well," the woman muttered as she knelt down to my level, "I'm Beverly and this is my son, Brian. I guess that would make him your brother, wouldn't it?"

I looked at the older boy standing on the porch steps and nodded.

"I suppose," Brian's mom muttered, "it wouldn't hurt to let you come in and join us for supper. Do you like shepherd's pie?"

"I don't know," I whispered as I cranked the charm up even more, willing her to let me stay. "I've never had it."

She smiled at me, not just with her mouth, but with her glistening eyes. "Well, what did your mother cook for you?"

I shrugged. "I know how to cook for myself."

"Oh," she muttered. "Well...would it be alright if I cooked for you tonight?"

I could tell it was working. Beverly's cheeks were getting all rosy and her smile kept widening. "Yeah," I whispered, "I'd like that."

Beverly stood up and smiled at the lady in the suit. "Why don't you come back and check on us tomorrow night? My husband should be back by then."

The lady in the suit nodded. Then Beverly asked Brian to take me inside and show me around the house while the two of them talked some more.

Brian nodded and headed for the door without saying a word.

I followed him into the house and found myself standing in a kitchen that looked like something straight out of a TV sitcom. Everything was so neat and clean, and whatever shepherd's pie was, it smelled better than anything I'd ever eaten.

Brian walked through a doorway into a room with a big long table surrounded by lots of chairs that all matched. Bright cheery paintings of people eating picnics by the lake and fields full of flowers hung in big wooden frames on the walls. Just like the kitchen, everything was neat and clean. It even smelled clean.

Brian marched into an adjoining room with a couch and two matching chairs and a big TV on a fancy wooden stand. He moved to the couch and plopped down on one end, so I followed his lead and sat down on the opposite end.

Brian just sat there and watched me for a minute. Then he glanced out the window at the two women talking out front. "Your mom was a succubus, wasn't she?"

"Yeah," I muttered. "How did you—"

DREAM FRAGMENTS

"Because you're as good at charming my mom as my dad is."

My eyes wandered over the quaint details of the room—decorative pillows with clever sayings stitched onto them, more colorful paintings of beachgoers and wildflowers, blankets that matched the pillows neatly folded and draped over the arms of matching chairs. "What is your mom?"

"She's an Unsighted elf."

"But you're half incubus," *I muttered,* "so you can charm her too. Can't you?"

"Sure," he agreed with a nod, *"but I don't."*

"Why not?"

"Because then I'd be like him, and I don't want to be anything like our dad." Brian glanced out the window as he whispered, "It isn't right to charm somebody into loving you."

I had to stop and think about that for a minute. "If I don't charm her," *I muttered, blinking back tears,* "she'll send me away."

"I know."

I wasn't so sure I liked my new brother. A tear slipped down my cheek as I whispered, "So, do you want me to stop?"

"No. I get why you have to do it." Instead of mocking me, like I was afraid he might, Brian's eyes filled with tears as he whispered, "She's gonna love you just like she loves him."

I wiped another tear off my cheek. "It doesn't sound like she loves him."

My big brother shook his head. "Just wait till he gets here. He'll have her charmed in under five minutes, and she'll forgive him for every wrong he's ever done. She only realizes what an ass he is while he's gone. Then she takes it out on me because she says I'm just like him."

"But you're not."

There was an almost grin on his face as he muttered, "No."

"Am I?"

"You don't have to be," he whispered as he watched his mother climb the porch steps.

I smiled at my brother as Beverly walked into the living room.

Then the three of us sat down to eat the most delicious meal of my young life...

..."Tristan?" Mia whispered as she sat up and rubbed her eyes.

I sat up beside her on the blanket we'd fallen asleep beneath the stars on the night before. "Yeah?"

"Can we walk a little farther into the garden today?"

"Sure," I whispered as we both got to our feet, "if you're feeling up to it."

She flashed me a sweet smile as she helped me fold the blanket. "With you beside me, I'm up for almost anything."

I wasn't sure I had the heart to tell her I'd be taking off soon.

7

CHARLIE

After my thorough search of the house failed to turn up any trace of Rose, I decided she must've gone to the Talbots' estate with Benjamin and Isa while I was helping Tristan abduct our new housemates. Tristan and Mia had retreated to the backyard for a little privacy. Bob and Nellie had made themselves right at home on the couch in the living room, and I was still in desperate need of a shower. So I headed upstairs to my room and beelined it to the bathroom. This time, I managed to strip off all my clothes before somebody knocked on my bedroom door. I considered ignoring whoever it was and hopping into the shower. But if it was Rose, I wanted to talk to her about our argument the night before; and if it was Benjamin, Brian or Tristan, they'd probably barge in anyway because they needed my help with another kidnapping or some other equally sketchy venture.

I tugged my towel off the hook with an aggravated sigh, wrapped it around my waist, and stomped across my room to the door. As I turned the knob, it occurred to me that I probably shouldn't pout like a toddler who hadn't gotten his way, just in case it was Rose on the other side of the door. I took a deep breath, then yanked the door open.

Brian shook his head as he looked me up and down. Unlike Tristan, his stare wasn't the least bit suggestive. "You haven't showered yet? We need to hit the road. The boss is waiting for us to join him at his place."

"Tell that to your brother," I muttered. "He was the one who barged in here this morning when I was about to shower and dragged me off to the facility to help him coax Bob into coming here."

Brian's clenched jaw was the only telltale sign that he was irritated. "No one's gonna want you showing up to the meeting smelling like a gym locker. Go take your shower."

"Finally," I muttered. "Thank you."

"Make it quick," Brian grumbled with a nod. "The boss won't appreciate us making him sit around and wait."

Now it was my turn to clench my jaw. The last thing I wanted to do was piss off the Dragon King now that we'd finally reached a point in our relationship where he didn't glare at me like he was contemplating ripping out my larynx with his teeth. "Why don't they just start without us?"

"Because you're gonna be a crucial participant at this meeting."

"I am?"

"Yeah. Now stop talking and get showering, or I'll take a separate car and let you take all the blame for being late."

"You mean, you aren't gonna throw me under the bus?"

"Does that sound like something I'd do? It wasn't your fault Tristan couldn't handle a simple task on his own."

"In all fairness," I muttered, "Tristan tried bringing them here on his own. But old Bob hates him because of the way Nellie blushes whenever he opens his mouth. Bob was convinced Tristan planned to drag them off somewhere to rape and kill them."

Brian's scowl dissipated in a burst of laughter. "Sorry I missed that." Then he nodded toward my bathroom. "Go. Shower."

"Yes, sir," I muttered as I closed the door.

While I took the fastest shower of my life, I wondered what the heck this mysterious meeting was about. Why the heck would I be a crucial participant? I pondered every possible scenario I could come up with as I slipped into a pair of jeans and a button-down shirt.

Brian was waiting for me in the foyer with his keys in hand as I came down the stairs. "What took you so long?"

"What are you talking about?" I muttered as I slipped on my shoes. "I showered in record time."

Brian yanked the front door open with a bit more force than he needed to. "We're still late."

I started toward the door, but a shout from the living room stopped me. "Hey! You're just gonna fuckin leave us here? How do I know we're safe alone with that pretty boy friend of yours?

"You won't be alone with him," I reminded Bob. "Mia's here too."

"Mia?" Bob muttered as he studied me with wary eyes. "Who the fuck's Mia?"

"She's that sweet young girl we just met," Nellie reminded him as she gave his wrinkled hand a squeeze, "the pretty boy's girlfriend or something."

"I don't remember meetin anybody," Bob muttered, "except that pervert with the tight shirt and the bulgin muscles."

Nellie blushed at Bob's description of Tristan as she grinned at him. "She seemed like a nice girl. Tristan, the pretty boy with the muscles, seemed very protective of her. He threatened to kick your wrinkled ass to the curb if you didn't treat her nice, remember?"

"Yeah," Bob muttered as his vacant eyes searched the room. "Sure, I remember..." But it was painfully obvious that he didn't remember any of that. Judging by his dazed expression, I wasn't even sure he remembered leaving the facility.

I met Nellie's gaze as I stepped into the living room. "Has his memory gotten worse?"

"Not that I've noticed," she replied in a barely audible squeak, "but sometimes, it does take him a while to remember new faces when somebody first starts working at the facility or gets admitted as a patient."

I nodded, but it didn't sit right with me. I'd never noticed anything like that when I was their fellow patient at the facility, and it really hadn't been all that long since I left.

"I guess...we're good here," Bob muttered. "I can defend us if that pretty boy tries anything while you're gone."

"He's *not* gonna try anything," I reminded him. "Tristan is a *friend*."

Bob's jaw muscles tensed at that. "He ain't *my* friend."

"I..." Not quite sure how to finish my sentence, I raked a hand through my shower-damp hair with a sigh of frustration.

"Tristan's a big boy," Brian grumbled as he stepped out the door. "He can handle things here."

"It isn't Tristan I'm worried about," I whispered as I touched a hand to Bob's shoulder. "Behave yourself, Bob. We're all on the same side here."

Bob nodded, but the scowl on his face wasn't exactly reassuring.

"We'll be fine," Nellie whispered as she dropped her head to Bob's shoulder. "Go on, get out of here."

"Finally, a voice of reason," Brian muttered from the porch. "Charlie, get your ass out here, or you're on your own getting to the meeting."

I clapped Bob on the shoulder, then followed Brian out the front door.

It didn't take us long to reach the boss's house because Brian's driving was just as lead footed as Tristan's, which wasn't the norm for him. *What the heck was the hurry to get to this meeting?* I kept mulling over possibilities, paying little attention as Brian nodded to the security guard at the gate, drove toward the Talbots' palatial waterfront estate and parked the car in the garage amidst all the other shiny jaw-droppingly expensive vehicles.

In fact, I didn't even notice when he shut off the engine and opened his door. "Charlie?" There was a note of concern in his voice as Brian tapped me on the shoulder. "You alright?"

"Yeah," I muttered with a forced grin. "Just tired from Benjamin's torture session this morning."

Brian nodded, but he didn't look convinced.

I followed him to the door of the house and stepped into the grand foyer after him. The instant I shut the door, Brian booked it toward the lounge with me following close on his heels. Whatever the hurry was, I didn't want to delay things any longer than I already had.

The door to the lounge was shut. But as we approached, I could hear muffled voices conversing behind it—several familiar ones, and one gravelly male voice I was sure I'd never heard before.

Before Brian's hand even touched the doorknob, the boss's voice sounded loud and clear inside the room. "Well, it's about time the two of you joined us." As I followed Brian into the room, the Sarrum narrowed his eyes at Brian. "What took you so long?"

"It took us a while to coax Bob into letting us leave him and Nellie alone with Tristan," Brian replied without missing a beat.

You had to love Brian for pinning it on the senile Unsighted guy who couldn't contradict our story.

The boss's cunning blue eyes shifted to me. "Yes, blame it on the one fellow who cannot defend himself. That seems fair."

Sometimes I wondered why the Sarrum even bothered asking us questions, since he already seemed to know all the answers. It was a skill he'd possessed since the day I met him, but now that Emma was safe and whole again, his abilities seemed sharper than ever. I shrugged off his stare with a muttered, "Sorry."

Benjamin shook his head as he stood from his seat and motioned for me to follow him to a door at the far end of the room that I'd never noticed before. I followed the Darkness through the door into a neatly organized storage room stocked with extra chairs, crates of liquor, and various other entertainment supplies.

Benjamin shut the door behind me. "Did Brian tell you why you're here?"

"No," I muttered as my eyes wandered over the contents of the room. "He just said we were late for a meeting, and that I was gonna be a crucial participant."

Benjamin shook his head. "Not exactly a thorough debriefing."

I kinda agreed with Benjamin, but I still felt the need to defend Brian—especially since he'd just shuffled the blame for our tardiness to cover for me. "We were kinda in a hurry. So, what's up?"

"We're gonna wrap up your training quicker than we normally would because we're organizing an intel-gathering mission that's set to embark in the very near future."

I raked a hand through my hair as I dropped into one of the spare chairs. "Why does that mean you have to finish my training early? Will *all of you* be going on this mission?"

"No," Benjamin replied as he sank into the chair facing mine, "but you will be."

"I will?"

"We'll fill you in on the details soon enough," Benjamin assured me, "but Brian was supposed to brief you on what the speedy wrap-up of your training would entail."

"It's not just more of the same?"

A grin spread across Benjamin's face as he shook his head. "Hardly. You're gonna begin training with the boss."

An involuntary shiver raced down my spine. "Are you sure I'm ready for that?"

"Yeah, I am," Benjamin replied without hesitation. "It's time for us to push you out of the nest, so he can teach you how to fly."

"Do you mean that *literally*?"

Benjamin nodded. "I do."

It was all I could do to suppress my kid-in-a-candy-store grin. "That's awesome, but why did you need to pull me aside to tell me that?"

"I didn't," Benjamin muttered as he glanced at the closed door. "It's the other final step that I wanted to prepare you for."

"Which is?"

"A history lesson."

Why the hell was everybody being so mysterious? "What's the big deal about a history lesson?"

"It's your history," he replied, leaning closer to me, "the story of where you came from."

"You mean..."

"It's time for you to learn who your mother was."

I couldn't even manage to form a response. They'd been vague about my roots for so long that I'd sorta given up hope that I'd ever learn the details about where I came from and who gave birth to me.

"The man in the lounge who you've never met before is a satori."

I'd learned a lot about the various creatures who inhabited Draumer since joining the royal guard. I knew all about the satori demons' ability to view and share the memories of others, but I'd never actually met one. "And?"

"And," Benjamin echoed in a much deeper voice than I could ever hope to produce, "he was your mother's best friend. He was also her guide."

8

GODRIC

I wandered somewhat aimlessly down the empty halls of my childhood home, eyeing each detail. It was a flawless replica of Godric manor, right down to the scuff marks we'd worn into the hardwood floors and the scents that hung heavy in the dwelling place of my youth. I had constructed enough of these mirages to have perfected its re-creation by now. Yet, I still felt the need to inspect each one to make certain everything was as it should be.

I stilled as I reached the doorway to our mother's bedroom. My parents had maintained separate rooms for as long as I could remember. They held firm to the belief that every respectable creature deserved a private space to retreat to when they wanted to be alone.

With each subsequent resurrection of my childhood home, it became harder to separate myself from the barrage of memories that came flooding back as I moved within its walls. Perhaps it would have been wiser to choose a less sentimental design for my

DREAM FRAGMENTS

headquarters. Yet, however painful the memories were, I couldn't bear to part with the memories of my Lilly. Each unbearable ache I suffered was a piece of her that I'd managed to keep alive. She had been gone for far more years than she'd been with me, but those were the only years that truly mattered—the only years that afforded me a modicum of joy.

I stepped into Mother's room, careful not to make a sound. My stealth was unnecessary, since she was long since dead and this was merely a replica of the room Father had preserved as a shrine to her. However, tethered as I was to my past, I couldn't quite shake the fear that I might get caught where I wasn't permitted to be.

Tears stung my eyes as I stepped toward Mother's dresser with my gaze fixed on her decorative perfume bottle...

...Finished with my lessons for the day, I strolled through the house with a joyous sense of purpose as I searched for my five-year-old sister. I was a young man of eleven, practically an adult compared to her. Yet, she never failed to bring out the giddy child within me. Searching the house for her was an unspoken game, akin to hide-and-seek or a treasure hunt, and her gleeful laughter and brilliant smile were the prizes I aimed to win.

I moved down the upstairs hallway without making a sound, partly to maintain the element of surprise so I could sneak up on Lilly, and partly to avoid aggravating Father. I had searched all her usual spots and turned up no trace of her. At age five, she wasn't nearly as stealthy as she believed herself to be. Her hiding places were usually quite predictable, but today she had stumped me thus far. She'd obviously discovered a new corner to tuck away in.

As I passed the closed door to our dead mother's room, soft footfalls sounded within and my stomach dropped. Father was in the parlor downstairs, and no one else was allowed in there—except the maid on occasion, when he decided the shrine to his wife needed cleaning.

I held my breath as I turned the doorknob and prayed that it wasn't the maid tidying up Mother's room. If it was, there would be no explaining why I'd set foot in the forbidden space. However, if it was Lilly, I had to get her out of there undetected. That possibility was well worth the risk, especially considering the fact that I hadn't found her in any of the usual spots.

I opened the door and cringed at the sight of my little sister. All of Mother's necklaces were draped around her neck and her small hands were clutching a bottle of Mother's perfume. Careful not to make a sound, I slipped inside the room and shut the door, and my heart nearly burst at the smile she greeted me with. The jewels were utterly unnecessary. A beauty like her needed no adornments to make her look radiant.

"What are you doing in here?" I whispered as I tiptoed toward her, painfully aware that Father was in the room below us.

A sheepish grin lit up her angelic face. "I wanted to feel closer to Mother."

"Mother was a cruel woman," I replied in a panicked whisper. "She would've been furious to find you rummaging through her things."

"Well," Lilly paused a moment to consider my words, "she's not around to get mad at me anymore."

"No," I whispered as I took a cautious step closer, "but Father is."

"I wanted to know what it felt like to be her," she whispered, her lovely blue eyes swimming with tears, "and I wondered what she smelled like."

As far as I knew, Mother was the only mated dragon who ever bothered with perfume. Father used to give her grief about it all the time. He constantly questioned why she felt the need to mask their collective scent. She always answered him the same way. With a coy smile that stunned him speechless, she'd reply that the scent merely enhanced their own. She was right. Their natural scent was Dark and deliciously spicy in a harsh sort of way, but her perfume mingled with the scent, enhancing it into something powerful, and dangerous, and entirely unforgettable. That scent was the only pleasant memory I associated with her. But Mother was nothing more than a memory now, and Father would be furious to find Lilly anywhere near that priceless bottled scent of hers.

"Come on, Lilly," I pleaded in a whisper, "let's get out of here before we get caught."

Even at a whisper, the severity of my tone was enough to convince her. She nodded with an apologetic frown as she moved to the dresser to set the decorative glass bottle back where she'd found it. But as she reached up, it slipped from her small hands and fell to the floor with a horrifying crash, shattering into a thousand pieces, and filling the room with the scent of a woman long since deceased. The heady fragrance hung in the air like the ghost of her, stinging my eyes for more reasons than one.

Lilly's tear-filled eyes widened with terror as our father's shout echoed up through the floorboards. The frantic pounding of her heart deafened me as her trembling hands fumbled to pull off the necklaces and hang them back on the mirror atop Mother's dresser.

Tears stung my eyes as I rushed to her and yanked them all off in one desperate handful of pearls and precious gems. An instant after I draped the glittering strands over the mirror, the door flew open. Father's Dark scent wafted into the enclosed space and mingled with Mother's, just as I remembered. Only now, his was soured by the foul stench of liquor that polluted his breath. Heartache visibly gripped the bitter old dragon as he stared at the shattered remnants of his beloved treasure's perfume bottle.

His growl echoed off the walls, feral and mad, making Lilly jump as tears began spilling down her cheeks.

Ribbons of blue smoke wafted from his flared nostrils, intensifying his contribution to the scent that now choked the air around us as he snarled, "Who did this?"

Lilly's bottom lip trembled as she opened her mouth to confess.

But I cut her off before she could utter so much as a self-condemning syllable, "I did. I wanted to remember what Mother smelled like. Lilly didn't want to come in with me, but I made her come anyway."

A sob escaped Lilly's lips as she shook her head and mouthed the words, "That's not true."

Thankfully, Father's flame-filled eyes were too fixed on me to notice...

...A harsh growl suggested that the demon in the doorway had already made several attempts to capture my attention.

Lost in the past as I was, it took a moment for my eyes to register the reality that surrounded me as I turned from the dresser, making no attempt to conceal my irritation. "What is it?"

"Apologies, my King," the skeletal creature growled through jagged teeth. "I was told to inform you that a

DREAM FRAGMENTS

meeting appears to be taking place at the Sarr... uh...your *nephew's* home in the waking world."

I narrowed my eyes at him, but otherwise ignored the slip. "Who is attending this meeting?"

"Your son," the demon muttered, "and the King...uh...*imposter* King, his fairy bride, the Darkness, the sorceress, their dragon child, that incubus-elven mutt who commands his troops, and a new fellow we couldn't identify."

"And," I snarled as I stepped toward him, "do you plan to give up so easily?"

The demon cringed as I narrowed the gap between us. "What?"

"Keep *trying* to identify him. Is that so difficult a concept? Do not report to me with failure. Make certain you succeed before you waste my time again."

"Right," the demon muttered. The fear in his eyes brought to mind those pathetic pets that animal shelter commercials always show to play upon the heartstrings of soft-hearted fools.

"For fuck's sake," I growled. "Cower as though you expect me to beat you, and you'll convince me to do just that. Grow a damn spine."

The demon nodded as he dropped his eyes to the floor.

I moved back to the dresser and picked up the perfume bottle. "Do not bother me again until you have something other than failure to report."

"Apologies, my King," the demon muttered as he slunk from the room.

"Apology not accepted," I growled as I removed the stopper and breathed in the aroma that evoked such visceral memories...

...I ignored the faint knock on my bedroom door the first three times, but not because I was angry with her or didn't want to see her. I always wanted to see her. She was the one light in my otherwise dark childhood. It was the pink welts on my pale skin and my swollen cheek and lip that I didn't want her to see. I knew I couldn't hide the marks for as long as it'd take them to fade, but it felt important to keep them from her till at least the next day. Even as the bruises darkened and purpled, the memory would grow stale so she wouldn't blame herself quite as much. Today, the marks were fresh and the sound of his fists striking my flesh still echoed in our ears.

Normally, Father at least had the decency to wait until Lilly was out of the room before hitting me. However, this infraction was so unforgiveable that blind fury had compelled him to act the moment I confessed to the crime. He'd hesitated for an instant, searching Lilly's eyes as if he suspected the blame wasn't mine. But I grabbed his arm as he stepped toward her and tugged on it with every ounce of strength my eleven-year-old body possessed.

That was enough to tip him over the edge of rational thought. I watched in stunned terror as he plummeted off the brink of sanity, morphing into something mindless and feral. His eyes filled with flames and smoke billowed from his nostrils as his fingers wrapped around my throat.

I spared no concern for myself and prayed with all my heart that Lilly would flee the room before his fists began to fly. She was only five. An innocent creature should never have to witness something so brutal, as the beating of her brother at their own father's hand—when the fault was her own, no less. My eyes drifted to her as his iron grip tightened around my neck, but no sound would pass beyond his chokehold. And my sweet Lilly stood there frozen in place, horrified as she watched each swing of his fist. She witnessed far too much before he finally had the decency to drag me from the room and dole out the rest of my punishment in private.

A few hours had passed since our father's fists had stilled. I had spent each minute lying on my bed, imagining an older version of myself beating him senseless for traumatizing his daughter like that. It was only when her knock came at my door that I gave any thought to the marks he'd left on my flesh. She didn't need to see those.

I buried my face in my pillow as she opened my bedroom door, stepped inside the room, and shut the door. Her stockinged feet barely made a sound as she approached my bed.

"Henry," she whispered.

I didn't answer, hoping perhaps if I ignored her, she'd take the hint and go back to her own room.

"Henry, please look at me."

It was the desperation in her voice that crumbled my resolve and made me look up.

She let out a sob as she touched my cheek with a gentleness that almost moved me to tears. "I'm so sorry, Henry. Please don't hate me."

I placed my hand over hers with as much of a smile as I could manage with my swollen lip. "I could never hate you. You're my treasure, Lilly. Do you know what that means?"

A tear slid down her cheek as she blinked at me.

"It means that you are everything to me," I whispered as she sat down on my bed. "I would do anything to protect you from harm. What happened wasn't your fault. It was mine. If I'd found you sooner... I should have stopped you from touching that bottle."

"That doesn't make any sense," she sobbed. *"It was all my fault, and you should hate me because I'm the reason Father hurt you."*

I slid closer and wrapped my bruised arms around her as she dropped her small head against my chest. "Nothing can hurt me as long as I have you," I whispered, "and when I'm big enough, no one will ever hurt either of us."

She tipped her head back to look me in the eye. "You can't promise a thing like that."

"Yes, I can," I whispered as I brushed her hair back from her face and wiped the tears from her cheeks, "because one day, I'll be King. My say will be the final say, and I will execute anyone who ever even considered hurting us."

Her lovely blue eyes widened as she whispered, "Even Father?"

I hugged her a bit tighter, as if he were an immediate threat in the room. "Especially Father."

9

DAVID

Emma's eyes had been glued to the door of the storage room at the other end of the lounge since the moment Benjamin took Charlie in there to speak with him in private. Tenderhearted creature that she was, my wife was worried about the effects unearthing the past might have on her friend, and witnessing the satori's ability firsthand had only amplified her concerns.

As the rest of our party chatted and waited for Benjamin and Charlie to join us, I remained seated on the couch beside my wife, but I heard every word of the conversation behind that closed door across the room. Charlie wasn't the least bit hesitant to learn his birth mother's story, which didn't surprise me. He had wanted answers since the moment I informed him that the heartless woman who had raised him wasn't his birth mother. In fact, I suspect he had craved those answers long before anyone offered him a shred of proof. Whether or not he consciously realized it, it was obvious that he'd sensed it.

Benjamin and Brian had taught Charlie much in the months since he'd pledged his allegiance to us. However, eager as the young dragon was to move forward, he still lacked confidence in his own abilities. Deep down he still felt like an imposter amongst us, but that would change once he grasped what it truly meant to be dragon.

Beside me on the couch, Emma exhaled a tense breath as the door to the storage room swung open.

I took her hand in mine. *He is ready, Princess. I have no doubt, and neither does Benjamin.*

She flashed me a radiant smile and slid a bit closer. *I know. I trust you. I just…*

All is well. I promise you.

Her eyes fixed on Charlie as she nodded. Brow furrowed with concern, she studied his facial expression as he helped Benjamin and Brian carry more chairs into the lounge.

Charlie felt her watching as he helped Brian fill in the gaps between the leather couch and chairs to form an imperfect circle. Sensing her concern, he winked at her with a carefree smile.

Her delicate hand twitched in mine as she smiled back at him.

I waited until everyone was seated, then cleared my throat. "Shall we begin? I believe we've wasted quite enough time already this morning." I narrowed my eyes at Charlie, and his face flushed. I certainly had my work cut out for me. Dragons—especially royal ones—did not apologize, nor did they allow anyone to intimidate them. I found it almost comical that Charlie believed he had fully tapped into his dragon instincts, when in truth he'd barely scratched the surface.

I locked eyes with each person in the circle until I reached my bride. My heart skipped a beat at the look of adoration in her eyes. I could gaze upon her face for a thousand years and never tire of the way she watched me beneath those hooded eyelids. Proper as her behavior was, there was always something wicked in those magnificent green eyes of hers, taunting me to shirk every responsibility, toss her over my shoulder, carry her to the nearest vacant space and drench her in my scent. There was nothing I would rather do, but there was much to be done in preparation for the impending war. Flames flared in my eyes as I held her gaze for a moment, and her body's response flooded my senses as I reluctantly looked away. "Most of you know why we've convened here today," I paused a moment, clearing my throat to rid my voice of the gravel my wife's arousal had evoked, "but I ask that you indulge me whilst I explain it to those who do not. First off," I continued with a nod toward the satori, "for those of you who have not yet met our guest, this is Clay Barker."

Uncomfortable with everyone's attention focused on him, Barker lowered his gaze to the coffee table at the center of the circle as he nodded.

"Mr. Barker is a satori, and he has volunteered his talents in order to fill in some gaps in our long-lost dragon's past."

Barker looked up at Charlie, and they exchanged a brief nod then returned their attention to me.

"Now," I continued, "I believe it's time to move on to the primary reason that I brought you all here today. We are planning to send a select team on a mission to gather intelligence as to the whereabouts of Godric's top supporters and with any luck, the whereabouts of Godric himself. Participation will be strictly on a voluntary basis. The journey will be arduous, as it will involve travel from the Dark Forest through No Man's Land, then on to the Light realm to confirm their allegiance to us before the fighting begins. In order to gather the necessary information on the first leg of their journey, the members of this mission shall pose as a group of Purists and the captive souls whom they intend to sell at the next slavers' auction. If they are successful in determining where the auction is to be held, they will attempt to infiltrate the Purists' slave trade. It rather goes without saying that we need unknown faces for this mission so they will not be recognized as my supporters. Thus far, the team consists of Tristan; Bob; and his pint-sized sidekick, Pip."

A perplexed frown replaced Charlie's carefree grin as he raised his hand.

"This is not kindergarten, Mr. Oliver. You needn't raise your hand to speak or ask permission to visit the restroom."

"Right," Charlie muttered as his face reddened at my words. "Sorry, but I don't get it. How is *Tristan* an unknown face? He tends bar at The Dragon's Lair where almost every creature in Draumer goes to unwind, and he's pretty unforgettable."

I shook my head at the way his blush deepened at the mention of Tristan. A dragon had no reason to be affected by the charms of an incubus, even one as powerful as Tristan. "Yes, that perfect face and muscular physique of his are quite memorable," I replied, arching an eyebrow as Charlie squirmed in his seat. "However, Tristan is the most powerful incubus I have ever encountered. Charming anyone who recognizes him into a lust-drunken stupor, and convincing them that they've never set eyes on the likes of him before—save in their wildest fantasies—would be child's play for him."

"Yeah, right," Charlie muttered under his breath.

"There's really not much to it," Brian chimed in. The half-incubus had never been one to flaunt his charms. In fact, the elven side of him deemed it improper to use his charm in most situations. However, there was much to be done in preparation for this mission and if demonstrating the accuracy of my statement could speed things along, he considered it entirely appropriate. Brian straightened in his chair as he locked eyes with Charlie. "Hello there, dragon."

Beads of sweat erupted on Charlie's brow as his face turned crimson.

To my left, I felt Benjamin suppress a snicker so as not to break the spell.

Eyes glued to Brian, Charlie wiped the sweat from his brow. "Hey."

"I've never seen you around here before," Brian murmured, dialing up the charm to a level that most creatures in the room couldn't help but react to in subtle physiological ways. "Are you new here?"

"No," Charlie replied in a throaty whisper as he slid to the edge of his chair, as if Brian's body had some sort of magnetic pull on him. "I've been here for months. I guess our paths just never crossed."

"What a shame," Brian murmured, grinning as Charlie nodded in agreement. Brian's voice took on a silkier tone as he added, "I guess we'll just have to make an effort to cross paths from now on."

"Yeah, I'd like that," Charlie rasped. "What did you say your name was?"

Emma's eyes widened with amusement as she turned toward me.

Unable to resist touching her, I flashed a wicked grin and placed a hand on her knee. *Brian has made them a rather captive audience. I suspect I could do just about anything to you whilst they're under his spell, and they'd be none the wiser.*

Benji and Brian would notice.

My hand ventured a bit further up the petal-soft flesh of her outer thigh. *Let them stare. I've nothing to hide.*

Mischief glinted in her eyes as she wrapped a hand around my wrist as if she meant to stop me but shifted on the couch, tilting her crossed legs to provide easier access beneath her skirt. *Shouldn't you put a stop to Brian's demonstration at some point?*

Her grip on my wrist offered no resistance as I slid my hand a bit higher. *I have complete faith in Brian's judgment. He merely intends to make his point crystal clear.*

Emma exhaled a ragged breath as the tips of my fingers skated beneath the hem of her skirt. *This isn't the time or place.*

Come now, Princess. You've known me long enough to realize that doesn't concern me in the slightest.

Brian stood from his seat across the circle from Charlie and extended an inked arm over the coffee table. "I'm Brian."

Charlie hopped to attention in more ways than one as he stood and reached across the table to take Brian's hand. A sigh that bordered on a moan escaped his throat as Brian's firm grip tightened around his hand and shook it. Utterly entranced by the physical contact, the young dragon nodded and muttered, "I'm Charlie."

Charmed as he was, Charlie gave no indication that the chuckle Benjamin could no longer hold back even reached his ears.

"Why don't you and I find an excuse to ditch this meeting," Brian murmured, "and find a quiet place to get to know each other?"

Charlie licked his lips as his eyes traveled over Brian's muscular torso. "Okay."

Oblivious to everyone else in the room, Charlie rounded the coffee table without letting go of Brian's hand.

Brian released his hand and outstretched his arms, and Charlie all but dove into his embrace. As Brian drew the young dragon into a hug, he brought his mouth to Charlie's ear. "Like I said, there's really nothing to it." With that, Brian dialed back his charm and the spell was broken.

I withdrew my hand from beneath my wife's skirt and winked at her as I wrapped an arm around her shoulders.

"Holy shit," Charlie muttered, shaking his head as if he couldn't quite comprehend how he'd ended up in Brian's arms. He raked a hand through his sweat-dampened hair as he backed away from Brian and rounded the coffee table, returning to his seat in the circle. "That was more intense than anything I've ever felt radiating from Tristan…and all this time, I didn't think you could charm people the way he does."

"I can," Brian replied, his tone all-business as he sat back down. "I just choose not to."

"Well, damn," Charlie muttered as he dropped into his chair. "Color me impressed."

10

EMMA

When Brian, Tristan, and I were in college together, the three of us once attended a hypnotist's show on campus. Impressive as his act was, I hadn't thought about it in ages. But as I watched Brian charm the heck out of everyone in the room—minus David, myself, and Benji—that hypnotist's show came to mind. Brian had them all practically drooling over him—especially Charlie, who was the recipient of the brunt of his charm.

David's fiery stare had a far greater effect on me than Brian's charm had on the others in the room. As his hand moved beneath my skirt, everything else slipped out of focus. Dragon alpha male that he was, my husband wouldn't hesitate to stake his claim in a room full of people. It was basic primal jungle behavior, and he was the king of the jungle. Maybe that brazenness should have bothered me, but it didn't. His absolute disregard for time or place aroused me to no end, and just when I thought he couldn't get any bolder, he'd find a new way to shock me.

It took me a minute to realize Brian had dropped the charm because it had no effect on me. My pulse was racing for a different reason, and I no longer cared who was watching.

Fully aware of the fire he'd ignited inside me, David withdrew his hand and winked at me as he wrapped an arm around my shoulders.

I concentrated on steadying my breathing and slowing my heart rate as Charlie and Brian returned to their seats. The two of them exchanged a few words, but they were lost on me.

As David drew me closer to him, each point of contact between us added fuel to the fire raging inside me. "Now that we've established what Brian and Tristan are capable of, I would like to invite Charlie and Rose to take part in the mission. There are very few creatures outside the palace walls who would recognize either of you, and you are both skilled members of the royal guard. I believe you would be valuable members of the team. Of course, it is strictly up to you whether you wish to take part in such a dangerous venture."

Charlie started to raise his hand, then thought better of it and cleared his throat instead. "I'd be honored to be part of the team, but I'm not sure I love the idea of Rose posing as a captive."

Rose scowled at Charlie as her fiery gaze locked with his. "Why do you assume I would be a captive?"

"Sorry," Charlie muttered. "I didn't mean anything by it. I just assumed, since the Purists are such chauvinistic pigs, the slavers' auction was for the buying and selling of female captives."

"Your assumption is correct," David confirmed with a nod. "We certainly don't condone such beliefs," he added as he turned to Rose, "but our intent is to blend in amongst the barbaric masses of Purists."

Isa straightened in her seat. "I'm not thrilled with the idea of using my daughter as bait either. She is a gifted sorceress and a skilled fighter. Couldn't her talents be put to better use here at the palace?"

Benji reached out and took Isa's hand in his. "There would be no better use of her talents. Including her in this mission is by no means an insult to her worth. She is unrecognizable as a dragon when she takes human form. The Purists wouldn't expect her to be a skilled fighter, and they sure as hell wouldn't expect a dragon to be among the captives. Sending a weaker female in her place would be unwise. If things go south on this mission, we need the women posing as captives to be capable of defending themselves and fighting their way out of there."

Isa shook her head as she shifted toward Benji. "How are you alright with this? You're incredibly protective of Rose, and you won't be able to look out for her because you won't be going on this mission. Your face and your aura are far too recognizable."

"You're right," Benji agreed in the hushed tone that he reserved for me, Isa, and Rose. "I won't be going, but Charlie will."

No one looked more surprised by that than Charlie. "Are you *actually* saying you trust me with Rose's life?"

"I am," Benji replied, "so you'd better not fuck it up."

"Right," Charlie muttered. "No pressure, as usual."

Benji leveled Charlie with a terror-inducing scowl. "This is no laughing matter, dragon. I'm placing my trust in Rose's abilities, and in your devotion to her because I'm pretty damn sure you'd die before you'd let any harm come to her."

"I would," Charlie whispered, "but I still don't like this—"

"I realize you see Tristan as a devil-may-care pleasure seeker," David interrupted. "But I assure you his skills on the battlefield are exemplary, and I'm sure I don't have to remind you that the same can be said of Bob. Do you doubt for one second that any one of you would hesitate to lay down your life for Rose if the situation called for it?"

Charlie dropped his gaze to the floor as he shook his head.

"More importantly," David continued, "Rose is a dragon who was raised amongst the royals. She is more than capable of protecting herself. In fact, she may well be the one who must come to your rescue."

"This discussion is pointless," Rose growled. "I want to be part of this. My mother was attacked by one of those monsters, and I'm the result of that vile shadow's violence. I owe it to my mother to do everything in my power to help take down those filthy creatures."

"You owe me nothing, Rose," Isa whispered. "I can't imagine a world without you in it. What brought you here is ancient history. I'm glad you're here, and I wouldn't want it any other way."

Benji squeezed Isa's hand. "I think it's safe to say Rose's decision is made, and nobody is gonna talk her out of it."

Rose put the discussion to rest with a nod.

David hugged me a bit closer as he cleared his throat. "There's still the matter of recruiting a few more females for the mission. I am open to suggestions if anyone has one."

11

MIA

We'd barely covered more than a few blocks' worth of ground on our stroll through the palace gardens. Tristan was distracted, and he wasn't exactly doing a stellar job of hiding it. I stopped walking and touched a hand to his arm. "What's on your mind?"

A tired sigh escaped him as he met my eyes. "There's a meeting taking place at the boss's house in the waking world right now. They're discussing the details of an upcoming mission to gather intel on the Purists."

"And you wish you were there to hear the details?"

"No," he whispered as he glanced down at my hand on his arm and placed his own hand on top of it. "I know all about the details." When he looked back up at me, his eyes were distant.

I searched those beautiful green eyes and waited for him to say more. When he didn't, I muttered, "Then why does it seem like your mind is a million miles away?"

"Because I'm trying to work up the courage to share those details with you."

The hesitation in his normally smooth-as-silk voice made my stomach drop. "Why do you need courage to tell me about a mission?"

"Because," he replied in a rough whisper, "I'm gonna be leading the mission."

I pulled my hand away from his as my eyes filled with tears. "Oh."

"I don't want to leave you, Mia," he muttered under his breath, almost as if he were talking to himself, "but this is something I need to do."

"Where are you going on this mission?"

Tristan exhaled an unsteady breath. "We plan to start in the Dark Forest, move on to No Man's Land, and then head to the Forest of Light."

"And?"

"And..." His whispered word lingered in the silence between us until he worked up the courage to mutter, "We'll be posing as a band of Purists traveling with their captives to gather information on Godric and hopefully find out where the next slavers' auction will be held."

A nightmarish rush of images came flooding back to me, unearthing all the sensations I'd been desperately fighting to keep buried. I knew what the Purists did to their slaves. *I'd been one of those captives*, and I was damaged beyond repair because of what they did to me. Tristan was my savior. He carried my broken body out of the Purists' cabin in the woods after the Dragon King stormed in to rescue his precious princess, but it wasn't the princess who'd suffered at the hands of those monsters. *It was me*—clothed in her likeness, and driven far beyond the breaking point—just to throw the Sarrum off the trail to his wife.

I didn't realize my legs were giving out until Tristan caught me in his arms. "I wasn't sure if I should share the details of the mission with you," he murmured as he steadied me. "Maybe I should've kept them to myself, but I didn't want to lie to you or mislead you. I wanted you to understand *why* I need to be a part of this."

"Why do you have to be part of it?" I asked in a faint whisper.

He reached up and touched my cheek with a tenderness that made my heart ache. "Because I need to make them pay for what they did to you."

"I'd rather have you stay here with me."

"I know," he whispered, touching his forehead to mine, "but I can't allow them to continue hurting people. I have to help put an end to it."

I swiped at the tears on my cheeks, frustrated that I'd failed to keep them from falling. "Why does it have to be you?"

"Because," he whispered, wiping a fresh tear from my cheek with his thumb, "I need it to be me."

"Tristan…" I needed him near me. Without him, I'd shrivel up and die. I pulled my head back so our foreheads no longer touched. "What am I supposed to do without you?"

The heartache in his eyes mirrored my own as he whispered, "Help prepare for this war in whatever way you can. We all need to play a part in ending those monsters."

DREAM FRAGMENTS

I dropped my eyes to his feet because it hurt too much to look at that beautiful face and imagine going a single day without seeing it.

Tristan exhaled an apologetic sigh as he took my hand in his. "We need to get back to the waking world. Bob is going on the mission with us, and I'm supposed to get him to the palace for the second half of the meeting." With that, he led me toward the nearest Waterfall.

Despite the panic churning my stomach, I almost laughed at the thought of that miserable old man on the couch in the waking world battling the Purists alongside Tristan. "Bob?"

Tristan nodded as he stopped in front of the Waterfall. "I know you haven't spent much time with him, but Bob is a warrior in this world. He's nothing like that old guy you met at the house."

Odd as the visual of that crotchety old man on a covert mission for the crown was, I wasn't surprised. Bob was a member of the royal guard in Draumer, and I'd suspected there was a significant reason they brought him to the house for safe keeping. "Yeah, I figured as much."

Tristan stepped through the Waterfall without letting go of my hand, leaving me little choice but to follow him...

...When I opened my eyes, Tristan and I were still on the loveseat on the back deck, but the sun was much higher in the sky than it was when we drifted off.

Tristan smiled at me and kissed the top of my head. "Let's go see if I can get that ornery old bastard to follow me through the Waters without pitching a fit."

A melancholy smile tugged at the corners of my mouth as I stood up and followed Tristan into the house and down the hall to the living room. Nellie and Bob were on the couch right where we'd left them. The only thing that'd changed was the show on the television across the room. An obnoxious game show had replaced the quiet talk show Bob had been watching earlier. Nellie looked up from Bob's shoulder as we stepped in the room, but Bob's heavy eyelids and deep grumbling breaths told us that Tristan had wasted his time returning to the waking world. Bob was already in Draumer.

Tristan and I started toward them, but a knock on the front door stopped us a few paces short of the couch. Ever the protector, Tristan motioned for me to wait in the living room with our elderly housemates.

He didn't need to tell me twice. I dropped into the recliner beside the couch as I watched Tristan walk to the front door, open it, and frown at whoever had knocked. "Can I help you?"

"Actually," a confident female voice replied, "I'm hoping I can help you."

Tristan tipped his head to rest against the door frame. "Okay?"

The woman on the front porch expelled an impatient breath. "May I come in?"

"That depends," Tristan replied as he shifted, blocking the doorway with his muscular frame. "Who are you, and why are you here?"

"My name is Addison Fletcher," the woman replied matter-of-factly, "and I'm here because I went to Parker-Banks Mental Health Facility to visit Bob and was told that he'd been moved here."

Tristan made no attempt to hide his displeasure. "They just *gave* you this address?"

"Yes."

"That's confidential information," Tristan growled. "Why the hell would they show it to you?"

"Because I showed them my badge."

Tristan leaned out the door, no doubt to examine the badge in question.

"Why don't I introduce myself again?" the woman suggested with quiet confidence. "I'm *Detective* Addison Fletcher, and I'd like to come in and have a word with you."

Tristan nodded, but by no means did he let down his guard as he ushered her into the foyer and shut the door. "Bob's asleep at the moment. Why don't you follow me out back so we can talk without waking him?"

The detective was attractive in a no-nonsense sort of way—short wavy reddish-brown hair tucked behind her ears, minimal makeup, and cunning pale green eyes. If I had to guess, I'd say she was probably in her early thirties. She was dressed in a simple cream-colored button-down blouse, beige pants, and sensible shoes that were fit for chasing after criminals, or whatever it was that detectives did. As she took a step toward the living room, her eyes fixed on the old man snoring on the couch.

"Follow me," Tristan repeated in a harsh whisper.

The detective's eyes shifted to me as she nodded. "Will you be joining us?"

Her abrupt demeanor made me take an instant disliking to her. "Why would I?"

"Because you're obviously curious about what I have to say to your boyfriend."

A bit taken aback, I muttered, "He's not—"

"Sure he isn't," Detective Fletcher interrupted, pretty much cinching my opinion of her. "I'm sure you look at every visitor who walks in the front door like you want to rip out her hair."

I stared at her like a deer caught in headlights, desperate to flee but frozen in place by a disorienting sense of dread.

Looking just as baffled as I felt, Tristan opened his mouth to defend me.

But Addison Fletcher held up a hand, wordlessly shushing him in the most obnoxious way. "Listen, incubus. I came here to help, and I don't really give a damn about any of your relationships or living arrangements. I'm only here because of Bob."

Nellie lifted her head off Bob's shoulder and glared at the detective. "Isn't he a little old for you, honey?"

Addison responded with a polite grin that did nothing to diminish her harsh demeanor. "Yeah. He is, but I'm *literally* only here because of him. I owe this man everything. I owe him *my life*."

Nellie studied her through narrowed eyes. "You're not…"

Addison's gaze shifted to Bob, and her smile grew far more genuine. "I am."

Feeling as if I'd missed something, I turned my attention to Tristan. But he looked just as confused as me.

"Why don't we all go out and talk in the backyard while Bob naps?" Addison whispered, as if she was suddenly concerned about waking him.

"He'd get flustered if he woke up in a strange place all alone," Nellie muttered. "Why don't you kids go out back while I stay here with him?"

Tristan cocked an eyebrow as he stared at Nellie. "What changed your tune?"

"She's on our side," Nellie muttered, "and she's obviously Sighted because she called you *incubus*. You can trust her, pretty boy. I'm sure of it." Then Nellie turned to me. "You should go too, dear."

Feeling more curious than wary, I shrugged and stood up from my chair. Then I followed Tristan and Addison to the back door.

12

TRISTAN

Godric's followers had all sorts of impressive titles and respectable professions in the waking world. There was no badge that proved a person in law enforcement wasn't a Purist. So I'm not sure what possessed me to invite Detective Addison Fletcher into our house and then out to the backyard for a chat—actually, that's not true. The tears in her eyes when she said Bob's name convinced me to let her in the door, and the look on Nellie's face convinced me to hear her out. This woman had a story to tell, and it was obvious that she and Bob had a history, one significant enough to melt Nellie's crusty old heart. I opened the french doors to the backyard, waited for Addison and Mia to step out onto the deck, then joined them and shut the doors.

Without waiting for anyone to invite her to, Addison marched across the deck and plopped herself down in a chair. Something about this woman's no-nonsense business attire and abrupt demeanor yanked me back in time and made me feel like that seven-year-old boy—in the backseat of a strange car—on his way to see a father who wanted nothing to do with him. I shook my head, banishing the past from my thoughts as I took Mia's hand and walked with her to the loveseat we'd woken up on a few minutes earlier.

As we sat down, I narrowed my eyes at Detective Addison. "Why are you here?"

She shot me a phony grin as she leaned back in her chair and crossed her legs. "Do you welcome all your guests like this? So much for that charm you incubi are famous for."

"Listen, Detective." I cleared my throat to rid some of the harshness from my tone. There was no need to let this woman know how much she ruffled me. "I could charm the pants off you in under a minute if I wanted to, but I'm a busy guy and I'm not interested. So cut to the chase and tell me what you want."

"I told you," Addison retorted as the grin slipped from her face. "I came here to help."

I shot her a glare that made it clear I was in no mood for games. "Can you elaborate on that?"

"Bob is family," Addison replied in a rough whisper. "I'm Sighted. I know about the war you're gearing up for, and I want to volunteer to fight alongside him."

Her timing seemed just a little too convenient. We moved Bob and Nellie from the facility for safe keeping, and the very same day this woman just happens to show up out of the blue for a visit? As far as I knew, the crotchety old bastard didn't have any family. We'd checked things out before making the decision to move him and Nellie to the house. "So, tell me your story. Why exactly do you think you owe Bob your life, or that he'd even want to fight beside you?"

"Wow," Addison muttered as she swiped a tear from the corner of her eye. "You really are an ass."

"I'm not trying to be." The detective's tears added a whole new level of discomfort to this exchange. I tightened my hold on Mia's hand, and in that instant, I realized she was my security blanket just as much as I was hers. Drawing strength from her, I added, "We're kind of under a time crunch. Bob and I are late for a meeting in Draumer."

"With the Sarrum?" Addison muttered. "Take me with you."

Everything about this woman's presumptuous attitude rubbed me the wrong way. "Why would I do that?"

Addison's jaw clenched as she shook her head. "You'd be a fool to ignore my offer to join the fight. Take me with you, so I can volunteer to help."

A voice in the back of my head was urging me to end this conversation and get this woman off our property. She'd shown up out of nowhere claiming to be family, and she was just too damn eager to jump in and join the cause. Nothing she'd said so far had convinced me otherwise. "What makes you think the Sarrum needs your help?"

Addison's clenched jaw relaxed into a sardonic smile. "I'm a good detective."

Feeling too pent-up to keep still, I started drumming my fingers on the arm of the loveseat. "And I'm just supposed to take you at your word? How do I know you're not spying for the Purists?"

"Because, you stubborn idiot," Addison growled, "I owe my life to that old man who's snoring on the couch in your living room. I'd wake him up and ask him to confirm my story, but he kinda can't because he ended up with some major holes in his memory after taking a bullet in the head for me. If you don't believe me, do some digging—police records, newspaper articles. You'll find that Detective Robert Cassleman was critically injured in the line of duty twenty-two years ago while saving two abducted siblings from the sons of bitches who kidnapped, assaulted, and tortured them in a shitty old abandoned house outside the city."

My throat constricted as I listened to Addison's story because I could feel Mia trembling beside me. It wasn't just my old scars the detective was poking at, and Mia's wounds were just beginning to heal.

"And you want to know the best part of it all?" Addison's eyes were fixed somewhere in the distance as she muttered, "Those two monsters—who kidnapped me and my brother—were *literally* monsters. The sick bastards were Sighted and when they realized I was too, they abducted me in both worlds. In the waking world, they forced me to unmask for them because they liked my pointy ears." The detective unmasked as she shared that detail of her story, and I couldn't quite tell whether revealing her elven form was a subconscious act or an intentional one to emphasize her words. "It was nonstop torture for me in both worlds. There wasn't a doubt in my mind that I was going to die in that filthy house, broken, and terrified, and stripped of my innocence."

I choked back the bile that was rising up my throat. "I'm sorry. I had no idea—"

"No, you didn't. But since you asked, let me finish my story," Addison growled. "Bob found us just as the two monsters were getting ready to move us to a new spot. He managed to get us both to his car, but one of the kidnappers snuck up behind him while he was setting me down next to my brother in the backseat. Bob looked so calm in that moment. When the monster pressed the gun to the back of his head, he actually *smiled* at me, and he whispered that everything was gonna be okay. Then he jerked back and shot that son of a bitch in the chest, but the kidnapper's gun went off and shot Bob in the head. I slumped toward the open door and watched Bob fall to the ground clutching his head. There was blood everywhere—soaking into his hair, seeping through his fingers, pooling on the ground around his head. But, excruciating as the pain must've been, his eyes never left mine. He just kept whispering that everything was gonna be okay...help was on the way...we were safe. Even after his eyes drooped shut, he kept muttering under his breath that everything was okay." Addison stopped speaking for a moment, her eyes still fixed on that point in the distance.

I felt like I ought to offer some words of comfort or at least a glass of water.

Before I could get my mouth to form the words, she cleared her throat and went on with her story. "I had to stay in the hospital for almost a month while my injuries healed, and Bob was right down the hall in the same hospital—comatose and all alone—the whole time. My first night in that hospital bed, I was terrified the Waters would take me back to the cave in Draumer that those monsters had kept me in. I stayed awake for as long as I could. But when I couldn't fight sleep off any longer, I squeezed my eyes shut and begged the

Waters to take me to that man with the kind eyes who'd saved my life. The Water creatures must've taken pity on me because I woke up on Bob's shore in Draumer. Bob had no idea who I was because he's not Sighted, but it didn't matter. I knew who he was. He was the only man in the world that I trusted—and I was a broken, frightened little girl all alone in a world full of monsters—that was all he needed to know. He watched over me and kept me safe. When I was ready to talk, he listened. Then he taught me how to fight so that no monster could ever hurt me again. If it wasn't for him, I doubt I would've made it past everything that happened to me. I stayed with Bob for years in Draumer, long after I went home from the hospital and he woke up from the coma and got transferred to a long-term care facility."

Addison drew an unsteady breath as her eyes returned to the present. "Bob doesn't remember any of that, but I still pay him a visit every year in the waking world when we come back to town for Thanksgiving. He never seems to have any idea who I am. But I like to think some buried part of him still senses it because, ornery as he is to everybody else in the waking world, he always talks to me in that same soft voice he used to lull me to sleep every night on his shore."

Once again, as the detective paused to clear her throat, I felt like I should offer some sort of comfort.

Again, she continued before I could find my voice. "When I grew old enough, I said my goodbyes to Bob in Draumer, and I set out to put what he'd taught me to good use and make the world a safer place. I owed that to him after everything he'd sacrificed for me. Honestly, I never would have left his shore if he hadn't nudged me to. He knew I needed to go out and make a difference. He also knew that he'd deteriorate without me there to keep him sharp, but he told me not to worry about that, and he made me promise to go out and live my life to the fullest. He said there was no better thank you I could give him than that."

Mia and I were both dead silent as Addison dropped her eyes to her lap and wiped the tears from her cheeks. After a moment, she looked up toward the doors to the house—and the man beyond those doors who'd sacrificed everything for her—and a nostalgic smile spread across her face. "I made good on my promise. I'm a detective in the waking world and a member of the nomadic knighthood in Draumer. When I heard about the Unsighted knight who helped rescue the Princess, something in my gut told me it was Bob. So I went to the ceremony in Draumer, and I watched the man who saved my life join the royal guard." Eyes still fixed on the doors to the house, Addison exhaled a slow deliberate breath. "In this world, I just wrapped up an out-of-town case, and I decided to take a detour on the trip back home to visit Bob and see how he's doing. So, here I am. I heard the Sarrum's speech in Draumer. I know there's a war coming and he needs everybody's help to defeat Godric. I want to do my part, and I want to fight beside Bob just once, even if he has no idea who I am."

13

CHARLIE

I missed at least half of what was said during the meeting at the boss's house. Everything felt a bit out of focus after Benjamin informed me that the new guy at the meeting was my mother's best friend and guide—my *real* mother, not the heartless woman who'd raised me to believe I wasn't good for much of anything and I wasn't even worth keeping around.

As soon as the first half of the meeting wrapped up, Rose kissed me on the cheek and told me to go talk to Clay. Rose was amazing. She always seemed to know exactly what I needed, but I guess that's what we dragons do; we sense and fulfill the needs of our treasures. As Rose headed across the room to talk to Isa, I left the lounge and took a right because that's the direction my mother's best friend had headed the instant the meeting disbanded.

It didn't take long to catch up to Clay at his unhurried pace, but I didn't approach him right away. I hung back and watched him step out the backdoor, cross the deck, walk down the steps and head for the beach. Then I slipped out the door and took a deep breath to steady my nerves, which was stupid. It wasn't like he was gonna tell me to take a hike. The man had come here to tell me about my mother. He was her best friend. I let that sink in for a minute as I moved toward the steps. I was *his best friend's son*.

My pulse quickened as I walked down the steps and headed toward Clay.

He had pulled out a cigarette and lighter in the time it'd taken me to work up the courage to approach him. Now, he smoked it as he meandered down the beach just inches beyond the water's reach. Clay felt me coming and turned around before I said a word. As I stepped toward him, his gaze was so intent that it almost felt like he was staring straight through me. He pulled the cigarette from his lips and expelled a lazy puff of smoke. "You look like her."

"Yeah?" It was all I could think to say. This stranger knew more about my beginning than I did.

"Yeah," he muttered, grinning to himself as he took another drag. Then he shook his head as if something had just occurred to him. He reached into a shirt pocket and pulled out a pack of cigarettes. "You smoke?"

"No," I muttered, shaking my head. "Thanks though."

He nodded and tucked the pack back in his pocket. "This is weird, huh?"

A rush of tension escaped me in a burst of laughter. "Yeah."

He nodded and took another puff of his cigarette. Then he started strolling along the water's edge again. "Wanna walk with me?"

"Yeah, sure," I muttered as I moved alongside him.

"Walking the beach has always calmed me," he muttered with a crooked grin. "There's just something about being near the water."

I cleared my throat. "So, uh…how did you and my mother meet?"

A wistful grin spread across his face as he stopped moving and looked out over the water. "Angel and I met our junior year of high school. It was one of those friendships where we felt like we'd known each other forever ten minutes after we met. It was just easy, you know? We just fit."

"My mother's name was Angel?"

He looked away from the water and smiled at me. "Sorry. I forgot you don't know anything about her. Her name was Angela, but I called her Angel. She was my angel, and I guess I was hers—although, I was sort of a dark one."

I nodded, soaking in every word this man shared about the stranger who'd given birth to me. "Were you two a couple?"

He let out a rough chuckle, the indisputable by-product of years of smoking. "No. We were never a couple."

I nodded. Although, I wasn't sure why that was such a funny question. This guy was good looking in a rough, *I've been taking shitty care of my body for decades* sort of way. It was easy to imagine how handsome he must've been as a teen. *Was my mother not pretty enough for him?* It was a bizarre sensation to feel offended on behalf of a woman I'd never even met.

Clay must've sensed what I felt because he frowned at me. Then he surveyed the landscape and started toward a nearby guesthouse. He sat down on the steps and motioned for me to join him. "No offense meant by that, Charlie. Your mother was a beautiful girl."

I sat down a step below him and stared at our footprints in the sand as I cleared my throat and nodded, feeling like a moron for caring about something so pointless.

Clay's rough voice drew my attention back to him, "Have you ever experienced a memory through a satori's eyes?"

"No," I muttered, "but I know what you can do."

He nodded. "Knowing it and experiencing it are two very different things."

"I'm pretty sure I can handle it."

Clay nodded and put his hand on my shoulder. "Then why don't I show you how we met? It'll tell you a hell of a lot more than my words could."

"Okay." As soon as I consented, the world around me grew fuzzy.

Clay's voice sounded distant as he set the stage, "I'd just transferred to your mom's school, and I was having some trouble with the jocks. I never had any interest in that athletic shit."

The world around me vanished, and a new one seamlessly took its place. I was standing in a parking lot behind the school with five buff meatheads surrounding me.

I could smell the ripe breath of the closest one as he yanked me toward him by the fistful of my shirt that he gripped in his beefy hand. "What the fuck are you smiling at Barker? I saw you staring at me in the locker room, you fucking faggot."

Was I smiling? I didn't feel like I was.

"I was just wondering if you realized that those steroids you're using are the reason your dick is so small," mused a younger, healthier version of Clay's gravelly voice.

Right. *I wasn't smiling.* I was experiencing Clay's memory, glimpsing the moment through his eyes just as he'd seen it years ago.

A blinding burst of pain exploded at my jaw as the jock he'd just insulted punched me in the mouth. *Fuck.* I hoped Clay's smart mouth would quit while he was behind because that felt as real as if I were actually there.

I wiped the blood from my chin with the back of my hand as the goon shoved me to the pavement. "I'm just trying to help you," Clay's voice muttered from my mouth.

The meathead shot me a death glare as he stepped closer. "You just don't know when to shut the fuck—"

"You should listen to Clay," a young female voice chimed in behind him.

He spun around and grabbed her by the collar. She was beautiful. Her hair—a mix of blond, copper, and red, just like mine—was cropped just below her chin with wisps sticking out all over the place. Her heavy makeup did nothing to hide the fact that the face beneath was sweet, and innocent, and full of life. I wanted to beat that bastard senseless for putting his hands on her.

Seemingly unfazed, she slapped him across the face, and he shoved her to the pavement beside me.

Rage coursed through my veins as I pushed myself to my feet, but I couldn't sort out whether it was Clay's rage or mine. As I suppressed the rage, I realized it must be his because I was still furious at this piece of crap for manhandling my mother. "Do that again," Clay's voice growled from my mouth, "and I'll kill you."

"Right," the jock chuckled, but the look on my face stopped him from saying more.

"Listen, fucktard," Clay's voice grumbled, "I'm trying to help you, but you're really making me think twice about it."

The goon just stared at me with his fat mouth hanging open.

"The dickweed who's selling you those steroids obviously doesn't know chemistry like I do. My stuff is pure. It'll pump you up without shriveling your junk and turning you into a mindless rage-monster. I'll give you a free sample if you stop acting like such an asshole. In fact, I can supply you and your buddies with whatever drugs you like. My stuff is pure, not like that shit you've been buying off some two-bit junky in a dark alley."

"Why should I believe you?" the meathead muttered.

"Because I make it myself, and I'm fucking brilliant at what I do. You want the best, you buy from me."

The bully narrowed his beady eyes at me. "How do you know how to do that?"

"It's my talent," Clay's voice replied as he reached into a pocket in his jacket. "You boys are good at sports, and I'm good at cooking up chemicals that'll rock your fucking world." I pulled out a handful of packets and held them out to the head bully.

He cocked his head to the side as he stared at the baggies in my hand. "How do I know that's not ex-lax, or birth control pills, or some shit?"

DREAM FRAGMENTS

"You try it, and you see for yourself how amazing it is."

"What is it?" one of the other jocks muttered as he took one of the packets from my hand.

"Ecstasy," I replied, turning toward him. "Try it, on the house. Then come back to me after you've seen what I can do."

The rest of them hesitantly stepped closer and took the other packets from my hand.

"There's just one condition," I growled as the main bully took the last packet. "I've got a boss, and he won't take kindly to you assholes roughing up his top supplier. I'll keep quiet about it this time. But if you touch me again, his goons are gonna make you regret it. So, are we good now?"

They exchanged baffled looks, then all of them nodded.

"Great," I muttered. "I look forward to doing business with you guys." As they stuffed their goody bags into pockets and backpacks, I added, "Oh, there's just one more thing."

No longer sure what the hell to make of me, they just stared at me with their mouths hanging open.

"If any of you lays a hand on Angela," I growled as I extended a hand and helped her to her feet, "I'll make sure my boss's men hunt you down and gut you."

They responded with a collective gulp as they backed away from Angela as if she were poison.

"It's been fun, guys," I growled as they slunk away. "Come find me when you need more." Then I turned to Angela with a shit-eating grin. "Nice to meet you, Angel."

She giggled and blushed. "Yeah. You too."

I looked her over. She was dressed in skintight jeans, her button-down shirt displayed a naughty glimpse of cleavage, and there was a bit too much makeup on her face for my taste—or, *for Clay's*. "You know, you'd be just as pretty without trying so hard."

That earned me a scowl. "Thanks for the advice, Mr. Hot-stuff. The other boys seem to like the way I look."

"The other boys want to get in your pants," I muttered, "and the way you make yourself up just encourages them."

"Fuck off," she muttered as she spun around to leave me standing alone in the parking lot like a putz.

I touched her arm as she started to walk away. "Hang on. I'm just looking out for you."

"Well, thank you very much," she muttered without turning around to look at me, "but I can look out for myself."

"You just picked a fight with a pack of meatheads." I gently nudged her to turn around and smiled at her when she did. "I think you need somebody to look out for you if you're gonna act that stupid."

She opened her mouth to yell at me.

But I shook my head and grinned at her. "You're just taking offense because I don't want to jump you in the parking lot."

"Who says—"

"Relax," I whispered. "I think you're gorgeous."

"Well," she muttered. "Thank you…I guess."

"You just aren't my type."

She opened her mouth to bite my head off again, which I found downright adorable.

"That bunch of dickwads I just scared off are more my type than you are, unfortunately."

She snapped her mouth shut, and judging by the look on her face, I figured she was about to say something rotten. I braced myself for the inevitable degrading remark, regretting my honesty for what felt like forever until she muttered, "Damn."

I cleared my throat, still bracing myself. It sure as hell wouldn't be the first time somebody judged me just for being who I was.

Before I could come up with a fitting way to tell her off, she muttered, "You have *shitty* taste in men."

The protective wall around my heart crumbled away in a fit of laughter as I pulled her into a hug, loving her more in that instant than I'd ever loved anybody. I dropped my mouth to her ear and whispered, "Don't I know it."

She looked up at me and giggled. "I guess you need somebody to look after you just as much as I do." Then she dropped her head to my shoulder like it was the most natural thing in the world, as if we'd been friends forever. And I felt more at home than I'd ever felt in my life.

Her laughter rang in my ears as the parking lot faded away and the Talbots' private beach reappeared. I raked a hand through my hair, thankful that I was sitting down. The fading in and out was dizzying. It took me a second to remember Clay was sitting on the stairs behind me.

I looked up at him, and saw the same expression on his face that I'd felt him make in the memory. He was bracing himself for a homophobic reaction.

I grinned at him, thankful as hell that he loved my mom enough to share such a personal memory with me. "It was an instantaneous connection, wasn't it?"

Having just looked at the world through his eyes, I could practically feel him relax as he answered with an easy grin. "It was pure magic."

"You were a drug dealer," I muttered, trying my best not to sound judgmental.

He nodded and took another drag of his cigarette. "Still am."

"Did you get my mom involved in that?"

"It wasn't how it seems," he muttered as he stood up from the steps.

I stood and followed him toward the water. "How was it then?"

"She was meant for it," he muttered, "just like me."

"What does that mean?"

"We were both potion-makers, Charlie," he muttered. "Do you think just any idiot can slap a bunch of ingredients together and whip up a batch of mind-altering chemicals?"

"Not any idiot," I muttered, "just any chemist."

"And what do you think those chemists are?"

I stopped moving and narrowed my eyes at him when he stopped beside me. "Are you telling me that all drug dealers are potion-makers?"

"No. Not all dealers, just all producers. That sorta recipe requires a hefty dose of magic."

"What about Unsighted drug producers?"

"Still potion-makers," he muttered, "they just don't know it."

"And the chemists who work for pharmaceutical companies?"

He nodded and grinned. "Potion-makers and sorcerers."

"Did the two of you use drugs?"

"Not back then." He cleared his throat and looked toward the water as he muttered, "That came later."

I shook my head.

He dropped his cigarette to the sand and ground it beneath his boot. "Don't judge what you don't understand."

I nodded and reminded myself that it was all ancient history. Good or bad, I wanted this glimpse into my mother's past. "Are you going to show me all of it?"

He looked up and studied me for a second before whispering, "Everything you wanna see."

"I want to see all of it," I muttered.

Brian tapped me on the shoulder as I finished my sentence, startling the hell out of me. "Break time's over. It's time for part two of the meeting."

Clay nodded and grinned at Brian. "Am I welcome to join part two?"

Some of the tension that Brian had been carrying for months visibly slipped away as he smiled at my mother's old friend. "As welcome as I am."

14

GODRIC

The mystery guest attending the meeting at the Talbots' estate turned out to be a drug dealer by the name of Clay Barker. The demon I'd tasked with identifying him had gone to work straightaway after I sent him off. Once he put some proper effort into it, he identified the newcomer rather quickly. It's remarkable, the results a hefty dose of fear can produce. I knew exactly who Barker was and why my nephew had taken him in, but it was no matter. Digging up the past would not change the future. In fact, I considered it a somewhat desperate attempt on my nephew's part.

Whilst David was busy unearthing the past, I was readying my troops for the future. He may have started gearing up for war, but I had been preparing for decades. All of my chess pieces were set in place, exactly where I wanted them. There was nothing that David could do to change that.

I slid my chair back from the table with my supper still untouched. Sitting at my childhood dining room table did nothing for my appetite. As I took the linen napkin from my lap and tossed it to the table, a memory struck without warning...

...Lilly grinned at me from across the table, studying my expression as I looked at the cherry pie she had baked for my birthday. It was just the two of us. Father had gone away on business, the best birthday gift he could've possibly given me. With him gone, the house felt uncharacteristically cheery and full of life.

Lilly almost seemed to take it as a personal offense that no one planned to buy me a present or bake me a cake. When she'd mentioned it weeks earlier, I told her it was fine because I never cared much for cake anyway. At which point, she announced that she was going to bake me a pie. Although I appreciated the sentiment, my nine-year-old sister had never prepared any portion of a meal in her life. Since she hadn't said another word about it in weeks, I had almost forgotten the entire conversation.

Imagine my surprise on the evening of my fifteenth birthday, when we finished the supper the cook had prepared and Lilly scrambled into the kitchen, instructing me to stay in my seat while she brought out a cherry pie, my absolute favorite.

Touched by the gesture, I cut myself a massive slice as she watched expectantly. Even if it tasted god-awful, I would swallow every last crumb and rave about how fabulous it was for months to come.

I smiled at my sister's rosy-cheeked grin as I lifted a forkful of pie to my mouth, expecting little but moved beyond words by her enthusiasm. As my teeth sank into the flaky crust and punctured the succulent fruit within, a groan of pleasure rumbled in my throat. I took my time chewing that first bite, savoring its delicate sweetness as my sister's grin widened. After I swallowed, I leaned across the table and planted a kiss on the top of her head.

She watched me carefully as I dropped back into my seat. "Do you like it?"

"No," I whispered, grinning as her face fell, "I absolutely love it. It's the most delicious thing I've ever tasted."

A hopeful grin replaced her frown. "You're not just saying that?"

"It's remarkable," I gushed with the utmost sincerity. "How did you learn to bake like this?"

"I've been taking lessons from the cook during your fencing practice."

"Well," I murmured, touched by the time and effort she'd devoted to surprising me, "it was certainly time well spent. I'm touched that you did all that for me, my sweet girl."

Her angelic face was positively radiant as her eyes welled with tears. "I would do anything for you, Henry. I love you more than anything else in the whole world."

I reached across the table and took her small hand in mine. "You are everything to me too. I treasure you more than you could ever know."

"You're wrong," she whispered. "I do know because I treasure you just as much."

A fullness blossomed in my chest as she spoke those words, as if my heart had swollen to twice its size. I lifted our joined hands to my lips and planted a kiss on the back of hers. "This is without a doubt the best birthday I've ever celebrated."

As I lowered our hands to the table, the cuff of my sleeve rose just enough to reveal the edge of a bruise on my wrist. The grin slipped from her face as her eyes fixed on the splotch of discolored skin, and a tear slid down her cheek as she looked up at me. "Henry..."

I smiled at her and shook my head, dismissing her concern. "It's nothing. It doesn't even hurt."

She pushed up my sleeve with a tenderness that spoke volumes of her love for me, and a sob burst from her mouth as she realized how large the bruise actually was. "Was this my fault?"

I tugged my sleeve back in place, then took hold of her chin and tilted her head upward. "Why would you ask that?"

"Because," she sobbed, refusing to lift her eyes from my wrist, "I forgot to mend the tear on Father's shirt like he asked me to before he left town."

I shook my head, but apparently not with enough conviction.

She jumped up from her chair, rounded the table, wrapped her slender arms around my neck, and hugged me with all her might. "I'm sorry, Henry. I'm so...so... sorry."

"Shhh," I whispered in her ear as I hugged her back. "It wasn't your fault. It's never your fault."

"How can you say that?" she sobbed. "It's my fault all the time."

"No, my Lilly," I whispered as I stroked a hand over her hair, "it isn't. Children forget, they make mistakes, but that's no excuse for their parents to beat them. I will never let him lay a hand on you. I don't want you to waste a second of your time blaming yourself for things that aren't your fault, especially not on my birthday. Alright?"

"Alright," she muttered as she buried her face against my neck.

"Good girl," I whispered. "Now, sit down and help me eat this delicious pie."

She loosened her grip and tilted her head so that our faces were close enough for me to smell her sweet cinnamon-scented breath. "I love you so much, Henry. But I'll never understand why you love me back."

"It's simple," I whispered as I tucked a strand of hair behind her ear. "You are the only thing in this world worth loving."

Another sob escaped her small mouth as she buried her face against my neck again.

I hugged her close and promised her that I'd love her more than anything with every breath I took until the day I died...

...And that's exactly what I intended to do.

15

DAVID

The meeting in the lounge concluded with me granting everyone a brief recess, after which we would reconvene at the palace. Whilst everyone else was dispersing, I drew Emma into my arms. "Your presence is making it quite difficult for me to focus this morning, Princess."

"Good," she replied in an amorous whisper. "That's what you get for distracting me during Brian's little demonstration."

"I suggest we pick up where we left off," I murmured in her ear, "so that we may better focus during the second half of the meeting."

She bit her lip and nodded in agreement.

Flames filled my eyes as I released her from my arms and escorted her from the room with a hand on the small of her back.

A playful grin spread across her face as I marched her past the staircase. "You really are distracted this morning. We just missed the turn to our room."

"That's too far," I murmured as I spun her and backed her up against the door to my office.

She gripped the doorknob, turning it as I crushed my lips against hers, and I backed her into my office as the door swung inward.

The sunlight spilling in through the windows across the room captured her attention as I shut the door. Charlie and Barker were outside walking along the beach together, and the sight of them conversing clearly put her mind at ease.

Emma took a step toward the windows, and I stepped up behind her, drew her into my arms and kissed the side of her neck.

"We should shut the curtains," she rasped as I slid my hand down her stomach, pressing her backside flush against me.

"The lights are off," I whispered as my hand slipped down the front of her skirt. "They can't see in here from the beach."

Her heartbeat quickened as my fingers ventured lower, slipping inside her panties and teasing her with the slightest whisper of my touch. She moaned in protest when I withdrew my hand, and a wicked grin spread across my face as I spun her around and backed her across the room.

A rush of breath escaped her as her backside collided with the edge of my desk. "What if they walk closer?"

"I could care less where anyone else goes," I murmured as I hoisted her to my desktop. With no time to waste, I yanked up her skirt, peeled off her panties with her breathless assistance, and tossed them to the floor. "We've little time, Princess. The second half of our meeting will be starting soon."

Hunger glinted in her gorgeous green eyes as they locked with mine. Then she dropped her gaze to my waistband as she unbuckled my belt, unbuttoned my pants and tugged down the zipper. "Then what are you waiting for?"

A puff of smoke wafted from my nostrils as I nudged her legs apart and positioned myself between them, and her pupils widened as my scent hit the air. I planted a firm hand on the small of her back, drawing her closer, and she moved toward me with such eagerness that she slipped off the edge of my desk just as I thrust forward, impaling her in place. Her lips parted on a carnal moan as her arms wrapped around my neck, pulling me closer. I pressed her tighter against me, and my breath caught in my throat as I sunk deeper inside her.

All else in either world faded to nothing as I moved inside her, drawing guttural groans of pleasure from her lips, each whimpered note pure music to my ears. We rose to the pinnacle of bliss, melded together as one, and plummeted over its edge, freefalling back to reality—each heartbeat, each breath, each tremor of pleasure—perfectly in synch.

I lowered her to my desktop, cushioning her descent with my arms as I dropped forward, covering her body with my mine. "How on earth did I go all those months without touching you?"

"I don't know," she whispered as she reached up and touched my cheek, "but I never want to endure a single day without you again."

"I'd go mad if you did," I murmured, caressing her bottom lip with my thumb. A groan of regret rumbled in my throat as her lips parted in response. "I suppose it's time to act like responsible adults and get back to ruling the world." I pushed myself upright and froze for a moment to appreciate the exquisite beauty of the creature beneath me. Although I wanted to keep her there all day, I held out a hand to help her up as I whispered, "My God, how you toy with my heart."

She took my hand, and brought her mouth to my ear as I tugged her upright. "I don't toy," she murmured. "You've never been a game to me. You're the sun, the moon, the earth, and the stars all wrapped into one. I'm so sorry I forgot that for a while. It doesn't seem possible now that I could've doubted your love for me. The way you look at me, how could I not see it?"

"You were blinded by a monster through no fault of your own."

"It wasn't your fault either," she whispered, pressing her palm to my chest. "This heart belongs to me. You've proven that a million times over. The past is best left in the past."

I placed a tender kiss on her lips, then glanced out the window over my shoulder. Charlie and Barker were beginning to make their way back toward the house. "For us perhaps, but for some the surest way to the future is through the past."

DREAM FRAGMENTS

As our brief intermission neared its end, the participants of the meeting began to funnel into the sitting room at the palace. I'd chosen the small gathering space because it would raise less eyebrows than a meeting in the great hall. I wasn't a fool. It was more than likely that Godric had planted spies within our midst. I had allowed the first part of our meeting to be obvious, just as I'd allowed prying eyes to witness Bob and Nellie's release from the facility. Directing the Purists' energy toward deciphering the intent behind those actions would distract them from discovering other moves that they had no knowledge of.

Benjamin and Isa entered the room, and my shadow wasted no time approaching my chair whilst Isa took her seat. "We may have found another female volunteer for the mission."

I raised an eyebrow. "How did you accomplish that when you haven't left the grounds?"

Benjamin's gaze drifted to the door. "Tristan brought her here."

As if on cue, Tristan stepped in the room accompanied by Mia and a female elf whose face was unfamiliar.

Tristan grinned at Emma, then turned his attention to me as they approached us. "Sarrum, this is Addison Fletcher."

The elf met my stare with unwavering confidence. "Hello, Sarrum."

"It's a pleasure to meet you," I murmured.

My focus drifted to the door, and the elf followed my gaze as Bob entered the room with Nellie at his side and Pip in his shirt pocket. There was a look of adoration on her face as she watched Bob cross the room and sit down between Nellie and Charlie.

"Why don't you take a seat?" I suggested, making the elf jump as my voice recaptured her attention. "We'll make the introductions soon enough."

Addison nodded, then crossed the room and took the empty seat next to Tristan. Mia cast her a wary glance from Tristan's other side, and the elf responded with an untroubled grin. Then she turned her head and fixed her eyes on the Unsighted knight, watching him with rapt attention until Brian and Barker filed into the room and took the last two seats.

"We might as well begin," I announced, silencing all peripheral chatter. "Am I correct in assuming that Tristan has filled in those of you who were not present for the first half of this meeting?"

"Yes, Sarrum," Tristan replied with a nod. "Everybody's up to speed."

"Good," I replied as my gaze shifted to the unexpected visitor beside him. "Would you care to introduce yourself, Ms. Fletcher?"

"My name is Addison," she announced, standing from her chair, "and I came to volunteer for the upcoming mission."

I narrowed my eyes at her. "And how exactly did you come to hear about the mission?"

"Tristan told me about it," she replied in a steady voice that didn't mesh with the racing of her heart, "after I showed up at the house to check on Bob."

Nellie and Tristan both smiled at that.

"I'm sorry," Bob muttered, squinting at the elf as if it might help him place her. "Do I know you?"

Color rushed to Addison's cheeks as her eyes met his. "You used to."

"In which world?" Bob muttered, clearly bothered by the fact that he couldn't place her.

Tears swam in her eyes as she whispered, "Both."

Bob stood from his seat and moved toward her. "Then why can't I place you?"

"Because it was another lifetime. I didn't expect you to remember me," Addison murmured. She paused to clear her throat before adding, "But I'll never forget you."

Recognition flickered in Bob's eyes as he stepped closer to her. "You aren't..."

"I am," she whispered. "I came here to show you that I kept my promise and made something of myself. It would be my absolute honor to fight beside you, just once."

"Addie?" Bob muttered under his breath.

A tear slid down her cheek as she nodded. "You remember me?"

"Of course," Bob whispered. "Not a day went by that I didn't think of you and wonder what had become of you."

The elf raised a hand to her mouth to muffle a sob.

Tears filled Bob's eyes as he wrapped his arms around her with tentative familiarity. "It's good to see you again, child."

She dropped her head to his shoulder and hugged him back, speechless for a moment—as were the rest of us. Then she stepped back and looked up at me as she wiped the tears from her cheeks. "Sarrum, with your permission, I would like to accompany Bob on the upcoming mission. I'm a police detective in the waking world and a member of the nomadic knighthood in this one. Let me put my skills to work aiding your cause."

16

EMMA

I don't imagine there was a dry eye in the room as we watched Bob reunite with the elf from his past, but I couldn't say for sure because I couldn't take my eyes off the two of them. There wasn't a doubt in my mind that Addison was the girl Bob rescued from the kidnappers in the waking world all those years ago, the girl he took the bullet for. When Charlie, Bob, Nellie and I were all patients at the facility, Dr. Spenser had shared Bob's story during a group therapy session one night because old Bob couldn't remember his own past. Getting shot in the head had decimated the former police officer's memory, along with his ability to filter what came out of his mouth.

"Well," Benji's deep Dark voice murmured, bringing everyone's focus back to the mission we'd gathered to discuss, "that's two females we've got to pose as captives. I suppose it'll do, but three or four would be a hell of a lot more convincing. A pack of slave traders wouldn't normally waste their time at an auction with only two captives among them."

"True," Brian agreed with a contemplative nod, "but bringing in others would increase the risk of tipping off one of Godric's spies. I'm not even entirely comfortable bringing in Addison." He leaned forward in his chair, eyeing the elf as he added, "No offense, but we can't be too careful. If the Purists figure out what we're up to, we'll be sending our team into a deathtrap."

Tristan shook his head as he glared at Brian. "I checked Addison's story out before bringing her here. I'm not a complete moron."

Always the more levelheaded of the two, Brian met his younger brother's stare with an apologetic frown. "I'm not saying you're a moron. I'm just saying we need to be cautious. Nobody outside these walls can know about this mission."

Across the room, Nellie cleared her throat. "I'd like to volunteer to go on the mission too."

The words were barely out of her mouth before Bob was voicing his objection. "No, it's too dangerous."

"So it's okay for your elf friend to go," Nellie replied, shifting in her chair to face her soul mate, "but not me?"

"She's a warrior," Bob muttered as he glanced at Addison. "I trained her myself, so I know how capable she is."

"Then train me," Nellie whispered as she took Bob's hand in hers. "You heard the Sarrum's speech when you joined the royal guard. Everybody needs to do their part to stop Godric, so let me do mine."

"Isn't Nellie too recognizable for this mission?" There was a slight tremor to the knight's normally confidant voice as his eyes locked with David's. "You said you needed unknown souls. Nellie is the dragon mother. Everyone knows her story."

"Everyone knows her *story*," David agreed with a sympathetic frown, "but few souls know what she actually looks like. All the Purists who were present when Godric was holding Nellie captive were killed when we rescued her and Emma. Aside from that, her entire adult life has been spent alone in the mirage Godric created for her."

The knight's posture wilted at David's words as he cursed under his breath.

Nellie squared her shoulders as if she'd somehow absorbed the confidence that had seeped out of Bob. "Godric has hurt me more than most. It makes sense for me to help bring him down."

"And if something goes wrong," Bob muttered, anguish contorting his handsome features, "what then?"

"Then I'll fight like you teach me to," Nellie replied without missing a beat, "or I'll die doing something good for once in my life."

Bob shook his head as he searched her eyes. "You make it sound as though your life is worthless."

A sorrowful smile spread across Nellie's face as her eyes filled with tears. "Isn't it?"

"You're my soul mate," Bob muttered. "That's worth everything to me."

Nellie's eyes dropped to their joined hands. "What other options do we have?"

Addison slid to the edge of her seat as if the question had been directed at her. She eyed Mia in silence for a few seconds before asking, "What about the changeling?"

Tristan's glare shifted from his brother to the elf sitting next to him. "What about her?"

"She can take any form she chooses," Addison replied, unfazed by Tristan's death glare. "Who could be less recognizable than that?"

Tears shimmered in Mia's eyes as she dropped her gaze to the floor without a word.

Tristan turned in his seat, blocking Mia from Addison's view as if she were an immediate threat to Mia's safety. "Mia doesn't have to join this fight."

"I thought everybody needed to do their part," Addison countered in a condescendingly sugary tone.

"She's sacrificed enough," Tristan growled, punctuating the end of his sentence by reaching back to take Mia's hand in his.

Addison threw her arms up in frustration. "Sorry. I didn't realize your girlfriend was exempt from the fight."

Beside me, David cleared his throat. As every set of eyes in the room shifted to him, he narrowed his eyes at Addison. "Let's move on, shall we?"

The elf nodded, but her expression didn't soften.

"Mia has nothing to prove," David stated with authoritative finality, "*ever.*"

"So," Charlie muttered, clearly uncomfortable with the tension in the air, "when do we start the mission?"

Brian looked equally eager to change the subject. "As soon as everyone's prepared."

Charlie nodded, then frowned at Brian. "What exactly does that mean?"

"For you, Mr. Oliver," David replied in a hushed tone that commanded his listeners' undivided attention, "it means that before departing, you shall spend time with both Mr. Barker and myself."

Charlie's face lit up like a kid on Christmas morning. As soon as he realized that, he straightened in his chair and responded with a businesslike nod.

"And apparently," Bob muttered, "it means I need to start training my soul mate."

"We also need to make sure everybody knows how to act in order to convince the Purists that we are who we say we are," Tristan added from the other side of the circle.

David nodded in agreement. "I think we've discussed this enough for today. We will meet again soon. For the time being, I believe everyone has a solid grasp of what must be done to prepare for the mission."

After a few closing remarks, the meeting disbanded. Rose left with Isa to tend to a potion they'd been working on for days, and I took the opportunity to go over and talk to Charlie.

He grinned at me as I sat down in the chair next to his. "Hey, Em. This new dynamic still feels kinda strange. I'm not used to you being a part of all this."

I gave his arm a playful nudge with my elbow. "Is me being a part of it a bad thing?"

"No," he whispered. "It's fantastic. I love seeing you this happy. I mean, you're practically glowing."

I felt my cheeks flame as a grin spread across my face. "I'm not sure whether that's because I've got my Sight back or because my faith in my husband has been restored."

Charlie glanced across the room at David. "I'm guessing the two go hand in hand."

"I suppose you're right," I whispered as my eyes drifted to Clay and Brian on the far side of the room. I watched their conversation for a few seconds before I worked up the courage to ask, "How did your first conversation with the satori go?"

An ear to ear grin spread across Charlie's face as he followed my gaze. "Pretty great actually. Clay already shared a memory with me. I got to see how he and my mom met. How weird is that? This guy knows more about my mother and my past than I do."

"It's no weirder than my past," I whispered as my gaze shifted to David.

As soon as my husband felt my eyes on him, he excused himself from his conversation with Benjamin and Tristan and crossed the room to us. David greeted Charlie with a polite nod as he sat down on my other side. "Hello, Charlie."

"Hey," Charlie whispered, grinning as his eyes drifted back to the satori. "I can't thank you enough for bringing Clay here."

"It was always my intention," David murmured with a dip of his head.

"So," Charlie muttered as his attention shifted to David, "when do I start my lessons with you?"

My husband shrugged his broad shoulders. "I'm free right now."

Charlie's eyes widened as he whispered, "Seriously?"

David raised an eyebrow and leveled Charlie with his signature don't-be-an-idiot stare. "Have you ever known me to be anything but serious?"

"Well...no," Charlie muttered. "I, uh... I'm free now too."

"Yes, I know," David replied without easing up on the stare. "Even if you weren't, do you suppose I must ask permission to steal you away?"

Charlie's face turned beet red. "No. I guess not."

I was dying to tell Charlie that David was testing him—because dragons don't let others intimidate them *ever*—but even if I directed the thought right to Charlie, David would hear it. He wouldn't do it intentionally. Most thoughts were just impossible for him to ignore. He could no sooner block them out than anyone else could stop themselves from hearing something that was shouted in their ear. So I directed my thought to David. *Go easy on him.*

The proper training of dragons is not accomplished by "going easy" on them, Princess. David flashed Charlie a smile that would ice the blood in an enemy's veins. "My wife thinks I ought to go easier on you, Mr. Oliver. Do you agree?"

Charlie's eyes darted between the two of us. "Is that a trick question?"

David arched an eyebrow. "I don't do tricks either. Honestly, are you sure you're ready for this?"

"Yeah, I'm sure," Charlie replied, a little louder than I was guessing he meant to. "I've been ready for ages. Just point out the hoops you want me to jump through, so we can get on with my training."

At that, David cracked a smile. "Better.

Charlie wiped the sweat from his brow with a shirtsleeve as he muttered, "What?"

"Dragons do not allow anyone to intimidate them," David replied, "not even other dragons."

Charlie pondered that for a few seconds before replying, "But you aren't just another dragon. You're the Dragon King. Isn't everyone supposed to be intimidated by you?"

"I do not rule by fear," David replied in a softer tone. "That has merely been your perception of me since the moment we met. It is far from the truth."

Charlie raked a hand through his hair as he muttered, "Then...what do you rule by?"

"The laws, as I interpret them. A monarch who rules his kingdom by instilling fear in the hearts of his subjects is destined for disaster." David paused a moment to let Charlie process that before adding, "You would do well to remember that."

Charlie's brows knit together in confusion. "Okay?"

"Royal blood flows through your veins," David murmured. "You should carry yourself accordingly."

"Right," Charlie muttered with a hesitant nod. "So, is that my lesson for today?"

"No, it is merely a word of wisdom to tuck away for future consideration. I assume you would like to learn more than a bit of fortune cookie wisdom."

"Yeah, I would," Charlie muttered. "What did you have in mind?"

"It's a lovely day," David murmured as he eyed the Waterfall across the room, "perfect weather for flying. Let's start there, shall we?"

Charlie made a marked attempt to hide his enthusiasm, but it was obvious he was all but bursting at the seams as he nodded. "Yeah."

David took my hand in his as he turned to me. "Would you care to join us, Princess?"

"If Charlie doesn't mind," I whispered, turning toward my friend. "I wouldn't want to make you uncomfortable."

"Nonsense," David replied without giving Charlie a chance to answer. "Dragons do not allow others to make them feel uncomfortable."

"Dragons kinda sound like arrogant assholes," Charlie muttered. "No offense."

"None taken," David replied without a trace of irritation in his voice, "but whom do you suppose would submit to the rule of a king who was less than certain of himself? No one expects a dragon to cower or ask permission to act. They expect us to do as we see fit."

"So, you want me to swagger around like you?"

"I do not *swagger*, Mr. Oliver. That implies a lack of innate confidence. I do as I please, and I am out to impress no one."

A smug grin spread across Charlie's face as he looked at me. "Not even Emma?"

"Treasures are an entirely different matter," David murmured as he winked at me. "But since you mentioned mine, why don't we invite Rose to join us for your lesson?"

The color drained from Charlie's face. "I'd kinda rather not have her watch me fumble around like an idiot."

David raised an eyebrow. "There you go again."

Poor Charlie just looked flustered and confused. "What?"

"You are operating under the assumption that you will perform poorly when you first attempt to fly. You are not exactly brimming with self-confidence."

Charlie's eyes wandered to the Waterfall across the room. "Can't we skip the lessons on confidence and treasures, and just focus on flying today?"

"Absolutely not. You will most assuredly fail with that outlook."

Charlie shot me a wordless plea for help. "What outlook?"

"That those are all separate lessons." David's piercing blue eyes darkened as his gaze shifted to me, and the room suddenly felt a bit too warm. "A dragon's ability to harness his power stems from his unshakable self-confidence and a deep-seated need to please and protect his most beloved treasure."

"Fabulous," Charlie muttered, dropping his eyes to the floor. "Does that mean Rose has to join my lesson today?"

"No," David replied with a sympathetic frown, which was lost on Charlie since he was staring at the floor. "But you mustn't compartmentalize your actions. You must always keep your treasure in mind, in all that you do. To behave otherwise is to court madness."

Charlie nodded without looking up.

David cleared his throat, prompting Charlie to meet his eyes. "Shall we head out to the balcony?"

"The balcony?" Charlie parroted in a hoarse whisper. "Shouldn't I start off trying from the ground?"

David shook his head as he stood from his chair, still holding onto my hand. When Charlie and I followed suit and stood up, David headed toward the Waterfall across the room without another word.

Charlie raised a questioning eyebrow as we moved along with David. No more certain of my husband's intentions than Charlie, all I could do was shrug as I followed my husband through the Waterfall.

Charlie stepped out into the sweltering heat right after me. It was pitch-dark out, without a single star to illuminate the sky. David and Charlie had no trouble seeing in utter darkness, but I might as well have been blind for all I could see. David dropped a hand to my waist, pulled me close and placed a tender kiss on my lips, enhancing my night vision. Then he lifted the hand he was still holding to his mouth, kissed it, and let it drop. Motioning for Charlie to follow, he moved to the railing.

I took a seat on a nearby bench as Charlie walked across the balcony to my husband's side. He leaned over the railing, and his eyes widened at the sight of the massive Waterfall entrance to the palace several stories below. "What am I supposed to do now?"

"Step up onto the railing for starters," David replied matter-of-factly, as if he were instructing him to do something mundane like wait in a line or sit on a chair.

Charlie stared at him for a few seconds before responding in an unsteady whisper, "If I unmask up there, my weight will collapse the railing."

"You are forgetting that you carry the weight of a dragon even in your human form," David murmured as he stepped up on a nearby chair, then stepped onto the railing as if it were the easiest thing in the world to do. "It really isn't difficult, and I believe you assured me just moments ago that you are quite ready for this.

In fact, you informed me that you've been ready for ages."

"Well," Charlie muttered, eyeing the chair David had used to boost himself onto the railing without holding onto anything to steady himself, "maybe I was wrong."

"I don't believe you were, Mr. Oliver." David sidestepped on the railing with the effortless grace of a ballroom dancer, making room for Charlie to step up beside him.

Charlie drew a shaky breath as he stared at the empty spot next to David. "What happens if I just plummet off the railing?"

David stuffed his hands in his pockets with a nonchalant shrug. "If you expect that to be the outcome, you most assuredly will."

"So, is it…it's uh…like in Peter Pan or something?" Charlie rambled, his voice nearing a borderline hysterical pitch. "I just have to believe?"

In stark contrast to Charlie's terrified squeak, David's voice was Dark and potent, "Don't be an imbecile."

As much as I knew I shouldn't, I couldn't help chuckling.

David raised a disapproving eyebrow as he met my eyes, scolding me for interrupting their lesson. "You must be confident that you are capable of taking flight."

I bit my lip, in a useless attempt to douse the fire my husband's smoldering stare ignited inside me.

"What if I'm not capable?" Charlie muttered. "Will you catch me…or just let me plunge to my death?"

DREAM FRAGMENTS

"If you rely on me to be your safety net," David murmured in an even Darker tone, "you won't have the proper motivation to take flight on your own."

His disciplinary tone was meant for me—because David knew exactly how it affected me—but in Charlie's panicked state, he seemed oblivious to the erotic undercurrent scorching beneath his lesson. "So," Charlie muttered, "you're just gonna watch me splatter on the rocks?"

"What if Rose were down there in your enemy's clutches?" David murmured, the Darkness in his tone nothing shy of venomous. "Would you allow fear to keep you weighted to the ground and just stand back and watch whilst they harmed her?"

"Jeez," Charlie muttered, looking down at the rocks. "Lighten up."

"This is no laughing matter, Mr. Oliver." With that, David stepped off the railing and dropped out of sight.

A startled yelp sprang from Charlie's throat as he jumped onto the chair.

A second later David soared back into view, regal and majestic in his dragon form.

"Okay," Charlie muttered, "that was impressive."

"Your turn," my husband roared in his thunderous dragon voice.

Charlie stared at him for a moment before muttering, "What?"

"Step off," David roared, "or would you rather I push you?"

Charlie raked a hand through his hair as he shook his head.

Without the slightest hesitation, David's massive shimmering wing swung out and swept Charlie up and over the railing in one broad elegant stroke.

Confident as I was that David wouldn't allow any harm to come to Charlie, I leapt to my feet with a reflexive cry of alarm. My heart hammered in my chest as I suppressed the urge to call out my friend's name. Fingers trembling, I wiped a tear from my cheek as I approached the railing.

David's voice thundered inside my head before I got close enough to see over the rail. *Do you doubt me, Princess?*

Never. But I doubt Charlie's confidence in himself.
You feel a dire need to help your friend?
Yes.
Then jump.

A smile spread across my face as I scrambled up onto the railing.

For a split second, the memory of my blinded-self—poised on the railing of our balcony in the waking world—paralyzed me as I looked down at the rocks. But I wasn't blind anymore. I might've had doubts about Charlie's confidence, but I trusted my husband without question.

As I stepped off the edge and plunged into Darkness, a thunderous roar shook the ground far below.

17

CHARLIE

Time seemed to still as I plummeted toward the rocks at the base of the Waterfall entrance to the palace, too petrified to move a muscle or make a sound. How many times had the Sarrum and his family of Sighted lunatics forced me into a death trap like this? There were more occasions than I could count—or at least, more than I could recall in my terrified stupor. I should've been focused on figuring out how to fly so I could save my ass from a Watery grave. Instead, my thoughts drifted to the day Benjamin drove us off that bridge in the waking world. No, that wasn't right. I *thought* we were still in the waking world, but Benjamin had tricked me and dragged me to Draumer without me realizing it. *Damn these Sighted maniacs and their reckless tricks.* How many times were they going to toy with my life just to prove a point or speed up a lesson I wasn't mastering fast enough to suit them? Did I really want to stick around and find out? Actually, that was kind of a moot point since I was currently plunging toward my death.

I struggled to suppress the fear that was paralyzing me until I managed to gain enough control to look up at the pitch-dark sky. The Sarrum was still up there, soaring just below the balcony railing, watching me fall to my death without a care in the world. *Well, fuck him.* Fuck all of them. This was the last straw.

A high-pitched cry from above snapped me back to my senses. *Emma's cry.* I craned my neck to look up again, half expecting to find that her heartless husband had pushed her off the balcony too. The rest of the world around me dimmed as I caught sight of Emma teetering on the railing, looking down at the rocks I was falling toward.

The pounding of my heart hammered in my ears as her scream reverberated inside my head. *That son of a bitch.* It was one thing to shove me to my death, but it was unforgivable for him to kick back and do nothing while his wife witnessed the death of her friend.

All of this took place in a matter of seconds—at least, I figured it must have—because I still hadn't hit the rocks. *Did time move differently in the Dream World?* The logical rules of the waking world didn't always apply in Draumer. You couldn't necessarily get from point A to point B by moving in a straight line.

As I was pondering that question, Emma stepped off the railing.

A thunderous roar deafened me as I fought to free myself from my terror-induced paralysis. *Where the hell did that roar come from?* It sounded too close to be the Sarrum. As I broke free from immobility, I caught sight of a massive wing—*my massive wing*—and realized the roar had come from me. The next thing I knew, I was moving upward, *flying upward.*

Before I had time to process how I'd done it, Emma was in my arms and I was soaring through the starless sky at a fevered pace. My eyes widened in amazement as I looked down at her.

Emma smiled at me, and my heart ached with an all-encompassing need to fly as far away as my wings would take us. The Sarrum didn't deserve her. That son of a bitch had just watched her step off the railing, and he hadn't done a damn thing to stop her.

I flapped my monstrous wings with every ounce of strength in me, and we soared through the air, picking up speed as the pool of Water at the base of the Waterfall grew small and distant.

"Charlie," Emma muttered, "where are you going?"

"I'm taking you someplace safe," I roared, "where that monster won't be able to sit back and watch you risk your life for no reason."

"Charlie," she whimpered as her trembling hands clutched my arm, "this isn't funny. Take me back. *Please.*"

That heartless bastard had her so brainwashed that she was shaking with fear at the thought of escaping his clutches. "You don't know what you're saying," I snarled, tightening my hold on her.

A tear slid down Emma's cheek as she opened her mouth to speak, but a massive blow to the back of my head brought our conversation to an abrupt end. A desperate desire to hear what Emma was about to say gnawed at me as the world went dark.

Then I was falling again...

...A blinding ache flared in my head as I opened my eyes.

"What the fuck were you thinking?" Benjamin's deep voice echoed, as if he was hollering at me from the other end of a tunnel.

I blinked a few times to bring the Darkness's features into focus, but the scowl on his face made me wish he was still a blur. Tempted as I was to shut my eyes and slip back into oblivion, I sat up and looked around.

Benjamin and I were sitting on the leather couch in the lounge. Everyone else who'd been at the meeting was gone—at least, I thought they were. It took me a few seconds to get my bearings enough to realize Brian and Clay were sitting on stools at the bar across the room, watching me.

Brian shook his head. "What the hell is wrong with you?"

I raked a hand through my hair, and realized the ache in my head was almost gone already. "Where should I start?"

Clay cracked a smile at that as he stood from his bar stool, crossed the room, and dropped into one of the leather chairs across the coffee table from me and Benjamin. Brian didn't look the least bit amused as he walked over, placed a glass of water on the coffee table in front of me, and settled into the other chair facing the couch. "What the hell happened up there, Charlie?"

I shook my head because I didn't have a clue. I'd acted like a mindless psychopath. I pictured Emma's face, flushed with fear as she clutched my arm, begging me to turn back. My erratic behavior had terrified her. *Why the hell hadn't I been able to see that?*

Brian narrowed his eyes at me as he gestured for me to drink the water. "It's like everything we ever taught you went flying out the window the second you took flight."

"It kinda did," I muttered, leaning forward to pick the glass up with an unsteady hand.

Benjamin scowled at me as he watched me down half the water in the glass. "You reverted to pure bestial dragon mode up there."

"Yeah, but why?" I muttered as I sat the glass down on the table. Then a thought occurred to me. "Shit. The Sarrum must want to kill me."

"No," David's Dark voice thundered louder than it should have in the waking world, "but I have no regrets about knocking you out."

I twisted sideways on the couch and watched David approach with a tumbler of expensive scotch in hand. To my astonishment, he looked less pissed at me than Brian and Benjamin.

"Why don't you look like you want to rip out my heart?" A lump formed in my throat as another thought occurred to me. "Emma? Is she…"

"She's fine," David replied as he sat down in one of the extra chairs left behind from our meeting. "Do you suppose I would look this calm if she wasn't?"

A vague sense of panic washed over me as I muttered, "Where is she?"

"She is elsewhere," David replied in that quiet authoritative tone of his that demanded his listeners' absolute attention. "But that's not really your concern, is it?"

"No," I muttered. "I guess not. I don't know what came over me."

David eyed me as he took a leisurely sip of his drink, in no particular hurry to respond. "Fortunately, I do."

"You do?"

"Your dragon form has been submerged for so long that you are having trouble controlling your bestial impulses when you allow it to surface," David replied as he swirled the glass in his hand with aloof elegance.

Transfixed by the perfect vortex of caramel-colored liquid swirling in his glass, I muttered, "I thought I was over that."

"Yeah," Benjamin muttered, "so did we."

"Flying requires a certain measure of savagery," David murmured as his gaze shifted to his shadow. "It is not a tame action. You must be more beast than man to achieve flight, and in that feral state your behavior is less rational. It takes a great deal of time and practice to learn to control your impulses and keep your composure whilst in flight. I did not expect you to be entirely in control of your actions on your first attempt. In fact, suppressed as your dragon tendencies have been all these years, a primal dose of fear and fury was likely the only way to get you in the air."

"Then," I muttered as I looked from face to face, "why does everybody else look so disappointed in me?"

"Because they are not dragons," David murmured, calling to mind a conversation we had back when Emma was blind and I hadn't even figured out how to unmask. "No other creature is fully capable of understanding what it truly means to be dragon."

"I thought you and Benjamin shared the same traits."

"Do you see a pair of wings on my back?" Benjamin growled. "I can't fucking fly, dumb ass."

I shook my head and leaned forward to pick up my glass, mostly just to give my hands something to do. "Why are you so disappointed in me if the King isn't?"

"I thought we'd brought you farther than this." The disappointment in Benjamin's voice hurt far worse than a crippling dose of his projected fear ever had.

"I guess you thought wrong," I muttered, fighting like hell to keep from tearing up. Benjamin would probably slap me if he saw tears in my eyes, and I couldn't take any more disappointed scowls. I turned back to the only man who didn't look like he'd lost faith in me, the one who had the most reason to hate me. "How did you stop me?"

"I stunned you with a blow to the head," David murmured. "Then I retrieved my wife from your arms, dragged your ass to the Waters at the entrance to the palace, and tossed you back to the waking world so you'd come to your senses."

How was that even possible? I weighed a ton in my dragon form, and I'd been so far below him, moving fast as hell *way* ahead of him. It took me a second to realize my mouth was hanging open. "How?"

David eyed me like I was the biggest idiot he'd ever laid eyes on.

"Okay..." The Sarrum was a magnificent beast capable of miraculous deeds. There was no questioning the fact that David Talbot was a total badass. *Was training a hopeless case like me even worth the trouble to him?* "So, am I banned from the mission now?"

David raised an eyebrow. "Why on earth would you be banned from the mission?"

"Because I have the self-control of a toddler," I muttered with a shrug, "and I can't fly unless my life and the life of a dear friend are in mortal jeopardy."

I almost could've sworn I glimpsed a hint of a grin on his face. "That will all change in time."

Nodding, I dropped my eyes to the glass in my hand. I tried to swirl my drink like him, but I just looked like a spastic idiot twirling my cup. "How much time do we have?"

The boss's eyes drifted to the clock on the mantle. "Very little."

I let out a frustrated sigh as I sat my glass down on the table. "So, what now?"

I was almost positive there was a hint of amusement in David's eyes as he twirled his glass. *He didn't need to show off.* Everybody in the room knew he was better than me, at pretty much everything. "Now you go sleep it off."

I dropped my eyes to my drink, and had to suppress an inexplicable urge to pick up the glass and try to swirl it again. "And what do I do in Draumer when I go back?"

"You come with me," Clay replied in a rough whisper.

I lifted my eyes to his. "Where?"

"Doesn't matter where," Clay muttered as he stood up and stretched. "The question isn't, *where* are we heading to? It's *when* are we heading to?"

18

MIA

I was on my own after the meeting at the palace wrapped up because Tristan had to discuss the details of the mission with the Sarrum and Benjamin. I would've given anything to talk him out of going on that mission. I honestly wasn't sure if I could survive without him. Compound that with the fact that Addison seemed intent on bullying me, and I felt like I was headed toward a colossal meltdown.

Isa must have sensed how lost I felt because she invited me to join her and Rose while they worked on the potion they'd been concocting for the past several days. I didn't know the first thing about potion-making. All that math, chemistry, and magic was beyond me, but I was grateful for the opportunity to hide myself away in a quiet spot while Tristan was busy.

"Could you grab me that jar of wolfsbane on the second shelf to your left please?"

Lost in my own thoughts, it took me a few seconds to realize Isa was talking to me. "Of course," I muttered as I stood up and perused the jars filled with dried plants, and tree bark, and God only knew what other ingredients. Fairly confident I'd found the right jar, I took it off the shelf and carried it across the room to the Sarrum's sorceress.

"Thank you, dear," Isa murmured as she took the jar from me and unscrewed the lid. "If you're not feeling up to company right now, I could step away and escort you to a peaceful spot where you could wait for Tristan."

I was about to shake my head, but I really didn't want to be around anyone other than Tristan. I blinked back the tears that filled my eyes at the thought of him—or rather, the thought of his absence. "Yeah," I muttered, "I'd appreciate that."

Isa smiled at me as she set the jar in her hands down next to a dusty leather-bound book of potions and spells. "Rose is more than capable of tending to this potion without me."

Rose looked up and grinned at the two of us. A second later, she was lost in her work again.

I envied Rose. She was a fierce warrior and a skilled potion-maker with a loving boyfriend and a set of parents who would lay down their lives for her without giving it a moment's thought. I had Tristan, and that was it. If something happened to him on this mission, I'd have no reason to keep breathing. My eyes welled with tears as I followed Isa across the room and stepped into the Waterfall after her.

I stepped out into a massive atrium filled with lush greenery and a brilliant assortment of exotic flowers. Iridescent butterflies in every imaginable hue flitted about the open space, their gossamer wings shimmering as they hovered above the pool of crystal blue water at the center of the room. The atrium appeared to be open to the sky above, but the sunlight spilling into the airy space told me that was an illusion. Sunlight didn't exist in the Dark Forest. The Sarrum had no doubt constructed this cheery sanctuary for his fairy Princess. Just the thought of her made my hands clench into fists at my sides.

The Princess was the reason for all the wrongs I had suffered. I hated her, but I couldn't hate the King. The agony on his face as he walked toward me, while I was tied to the bed in that godforsaken cabin, would stick with me forever. It'd destroyed him to see me like that. Of course, he only reacted that way because I was clothed in his wife's likeness, but when he realized I wasn't her, he treated me with no less kindness.

I bit my lip to quell the tears that were starting to blur my vision as I moved to the circular bench surrounding the pool at the center of the atrium.

Isa followed me and sat down beside me. "I'm always here to listen," she whispered, "day or night. You don't have to suffer through this alone, Mia."

A tear slid down my cheek as she spoke. Angry with myself for letting it spill, I shook my head. "I'm fine."

"No, you aren't," she whispered, placing her hand on top of mine, "but you will be in time."

Unlike most people's attempts to comfort me, Isa's contained no trace of pity. She understood what I was going through, as only another victim could. She'd tried to open up to me when I first moved into the house on Sycamore. I suppose she figured telling me about the shadow who attacked her would give me the strength to open up to her. I appreciated her efforts more than she would ever know, but she didn't really understand how I felt. Her attacker had forced himself on her in a dark corner of the park on her walk home from work one night. Horrible as I'm sure that was, he left her there when he was done with her, and she went back home to her family. I was kept bound for days, tied to a bed in that nightmarish cabin in the middle of nowhere. So many creatures hurt me that I lost count of how many there were, or how many times it happened. I wished I had died on that bed. Part of me *did* die in that room. Now I was just a walking shell of the person I used to be, a shallow husk who felt nothing but a dull echo of the pain I'd been forced to endure.

I mentally chastised myself for letting another tear slip down my cheek as I looked up at Isa. "I'm not going to make it without Tristan."

"Then go with him," Addison's voice echoed across the airy space as she stepped from the Waterfall.

I balled my hands into fists and dug my fingernails into my palms as I stood up to leave. But Addison stopped right in front of me, blocking my only means of escape. I couldn't get to the Waterfall unless I pushed her over—and believe me, I was tempted to.

Addison studied me through narrowed eyes as she stood there, blocking my path. "How long do you plan to sulk and play the victim card?"

I didn't want to have a conversation with this abrasive woman, especially not *that* conversation. I just wanted to get the hell out of there, slink off to an empty corner of the palace, and wallow in misery until Tristan came to find me. "Please move," I muttered in a feeble whisper.

Addison crossed her arms over her chest as she shook her head. "Would you like to know why you hate me so much?"

"Because you're a bully and you won't get out of my way," I muttered, blinking back more tears.

Isa stood up beside me and met Addison's gaze with a forced smile. "Perhaps it would be better if you found another spot to settle in, dear."

"You hate me," Addison continued, as if she hadn't heard Isa, "because I'm everything that you're afraid to be."

Too furious to stop myself, I growled, "What makes you think I want to be a bitch like you?"

"Go ahead. Call me a bitch," Addison replied in a harsh whisper. "Call me a bully, call me whatever you'd like. But you can never accuse me of being a victim."

Rage coursed through my veins as I snarled, "Do you think I *chose* this?"

"Of course not." Addison's entire demeanor softened as she whispered, "Nobody *chooses* to be a victim."

I swiped another tear from my cheek as I muttered, "Then why are you picking on me?"

"Because you're choosing to remain a victim," Addison whispered, "and I can't stand by and watch that."

"What?"

"Continue to act like a victim, and your abusers win," Addison whispered. "I get it. Damn it, I get it. You heard my story. I was just a *child* when I was kidnapped. Those monsters did things to me that I never could've imagined in my worst childhood nightmares. It went on forever, but *I survived*. And so did you, so start acting like it. Stop letting them have so much power over you. They can't hurt you anymore unless you allow them to."

"You don't understand..." My voice trailed off as I looked into Addison's eyes for the first time. There was a hollowness deep within them that mirrored my own. She *did* understand. Maybe I just wasn't as strong as her.

"I *do* understand," she whispered. "I just want you to fucking stick up for yourself."

"I'm not strong," I replied in a trembling whisper.

A somber smile spread across Addison's face as her pale green eyes filled with tears. "Do I look like a bodybuilder to you? You don't have to be a monster to fight like one."

"I..."

"I am where I am today because Bob took the time to get me there. He gave me a shoulder to cry on. Then he taught me how to fight so I'd never have to be a victim again."

"I don't..."

"You're surrounded by royal guards on a daily basis," Addison continued. "The people who protect you aren't just the fiercest warriors in Draumer. They're the people who *train* all the warriors who fight for the King."

I turned my head to look at Isa, and she nodded in agreement. "Benji and Brian would be happy to teach you to defend yourself, and do you doubt for a second that Tristan would spend every spare moment of his day training you to fight?"

"I don't know..."

"I've known Tristan for years," Isa whispered with a knowing grin, "and I've never seen him look at anyone the way he looks at you."

I shook my head. *Tristan just felt sorry for me.* He felt guilty because he saw me at The Dragon's Lair the night I was taken, and he hadn't been able to prevent my abduction. In my desperation, I took advantage of his guilt because he made me feel safe. That was all there was to it. "He just feels guilty because he saw me right before I was taken, and he wasn't able to stop them from…"

Isa's eyes widened at my words. "Is that what you think?"

More tears streamed down my cheeks, but my hands were shaking too badly to wipe them away. "It's what I *know*."

"You're wrong," Tristan whispered as he stepped from the Waterfall.

I locked eyes with the only man I truly trusted as he moved toward us. How much of that had he heard?

Tears glistened in his beautiful green eyes as he stopped beside Addison. "I'll teach you to fight, and I'll take you anywhere you want to go. If you're with me, I won't have to worry about how you're holding up without me."

A lump formed in my throat as I searched his eyes. "What if I'm just too damaged?"

"You're no more damaged than anyone else in this room," Tristan whispered as he wiped the tears from my cheeks.

Wiping my tears away was pointless because I couldn't stop more from falling. "How do you get past it?"

"You fight," Addison whispered, "and you keep on fighting until every fucking monster has been taken down. That's what this war is all about. If the Purists win, those monsters will take *us* down."

"And there's no way we're gonna let that happen," Tristan growled.

Addison smiled at him as she nodded in agreement. "I guess we found some common ground after all, incubus."

19

TRISTAN

I hated to walk away from Mia right after our breakthrough conversation with Isa and Addison, but I had work to do. So I left her with *Addison*, of all people. My thoughts were a million miles away as I headed down the dimly lit stone corridor toward the nearest Waterfall, and I needed to snap the hell out of it before my distraction jeopardized the mission. I stopped a few paces short of the Waterfall and took a deep breath to clear my head, but it didn't do any good. My thoughts were still stuck on Mia as I stepped through.

I emerged from the Water at the edge of the forest a bit on the damp side because I'd been too distracted to charm the Water creatures when I passed through. I shook my head as I started making my way toward the trees. Although, I had no intention of taking the path to the village tonight. I planned to take a roundabout route—making my way through a tangle of brambles, and roots, and rotting trees—to be sure I arrived undetected. It was dark enough inside the forest that most creatures would never notice me, especially if they stuck to the path like any sane soul would.

My mind was still on Mia as I stepped inside the trees, and I only trudged a few feet through the underbrush before a low hanging branch smacked me in the face. Damn it, what the hell was wrong with me? I needed to focus on where I was going. *How could Mia have spent all this time with me and still think I was only by her side out of guilt?* I guess I shouldn't have been all that shocked. The souls I cared about the most had always doubted my sincerity. They never believed they were good enough for me because they based their worth on the image that stared back at them in the mirror.

Beauty was a fucking curse. Anyone who thought otherwise had never been compartmentalized into nothing but a pretty face and a spectacular set of washboard abs. People made a lot of assumptions about you when you were beautiful. They assumed you were brainless. They assumed you were shallow. They assumed you thought ordinary-looking people were beneath you, and they *believed* you were better than people with average faces. My mother was beautiful. The woman looked like a freaking Nigerian Goddess. She was also a coldhearted whore. I went hungry all the time when I was a kid. She left me home alone before I was anywhere near old enough to be left unsupervised. I constantly had to fend for myself whenever she slipped into a drug-induced stupor. She sold her beautiful body to men for money or drugs, and if they paid enough—well, let's just say nothing was off the table if the price was right. Thanks to her, beauty meant nothing to me. I judged a person's worth by the essence of the being inside the meaningless package of flesh and bone. Beauty fades, skin wrinkles, but a good heart is priceless until its last beat. Inner beauty was all that mattered to me.

Awful as it sounds, I was drawn to broken souls, but it wasn't for any twisted reason. It was because I'd discovered as a teen that broken people were immune to my charm. Damaged souls shied away from physical perfection. Hell, they shied away from everything. But when I was lucky enough to find one, they saw me for *me*—not the pretty package, or the charm—the kindred damaged being inside.

Damaged souls are always the most beautiful because there's nothing shallow about them. They're deep because the pain that they've endured gouged its way through their insides—hollowing out bottomless depths of compassion—as it twisted them into living, breathing works of art. Those are the creatures I find beautiful, the broken misfits desperately fighting to claw their way through one more day.

I raised an arm to protect my face as another branch smacked me upside the head, jarring my mind back to the present. Shaking my head, I outstretched my arms and let my thoughts drift back to the past as I fought my way through the untamed forest.

My childhood therapist said it took years of therapy for him to undo all the damage my birth mother had done, but that smug son of a bitch had no idea what he was talking about. It was Brian who got me through it, not that self-righteous fool who had no idea what it was actually like to suffer. I could unearth years of angst—issues, and incidents, and outbursts at school—but who the fuck wanted to rehash all that?

So, fast forward to my life at age sixteen. Brian had moved out of our house two weeks after graduating from high school. He felt guilty leaving me behind, but I told him to worry about himself for once in his life. I would be fine because I had Beverly. *How fucked up was that?* Brian was the son she gave birth to, her own flesh and blood, and she practically kicked him to the curb the day he got his diploma. I, on the other hand, was the bastard son of her husband and his whore mistress. Beverly had every reason in the world to despise me, but she treated me like the crowned prince of castle Mason. I could do no wrong in that woman's eyes.

Selfless as he was, Brian never blamed me for charming his mom. He knew it was the only thing keeping me from growing up in an orphanage or foster care, and I was his kid brother. He wasn't about to let that happen. I can't tell you how many times I tried to talk Brian into using a little bit of charm on Beverly, just enough to make his life easier. But my older brother was a man of principle. I wasn't sure where the hell he'd gotten it from, but I was glad some of it had rubbed off on me.

Lost in thought once again, I snagged the toe of my boot on a root jutting out of the ground. The damn thing caught me off guard and tripped me up. Bracing my fall with outstretched arms, I smashed into a rotting tree trunk and gouged a nasty scrape up the side of my forearm. Grumbling to myself, I trudged on as my thoughts drifted to the day I met *her*...

...Summer had flown by fast like it always did, but I didn't care. It'd been a lonely summer without my big brother around. We were new in town, so I didn't have any friends to pass the time with. After Brian moved out,

Mom had decided it was time for a fresh start. Dad didn't give a crap since he was gone half the time anyway. His job as a salesman conveniently required him to spend a lot of time on the road. In his own selfish way, he loved Beverly, but he was never satisfied with just one woman. He rationalized his infidelity by telling himself that what Mom didn't know wouldn't hurt her. But she did know—long before I ever showed up on her doorstep as living, breathing proof—she'd have to be an idiot not to.

Mom insisted the move was for her because she needed a change, but I wasn't an idiot either. The change was for me. I was going into my sophomore year of high school, and Beverly hoped a fresh start would do me good after all the fights I'd gotten into at my last school. It was a new town, but it'd be the same story—jocks, cheerleaders, geeks, stoners. The new school was just another brick building full of raging hormones and stifling labels. If it wasn't for my brother keeping me in line, I probably would've dropped out.

A tightness gripped my chest as I approached the new brick building. For a minute, I considered turning around and ditching. I knew Beverly would forgive me, but Brian would give me hell when he found out about it.

As I was walking past the teachers' parking lot, a young teacher hopped out of her car with her arms piled high with books. She nudged the door shut with her hip, and the books tumbled out of her arms and scattered all over the pavement. She cursed under her breath then raised a hand to her mouth at the slipup.

I couldn't help grinning as she looked up at me. She blushed a deep shade of pink as our eyes met—embarrassment, coupled with the inevitable reaction to my charm. I dropped my backpack to the pavement and stooped to help her retrieve the books.

"Thanks," she murmured, a bit more breathless than a healthy young teacher should've been from crouching to pick up a few books.

"Don't mention it," I whispered, dialing down the charm as much as I could. The last thing I needed was a teacher with a crush on me.

"You don't look familiar," the teacher muttered as we stood up. *"Are you new here?"*

"Yep." I started to hand her the books I'd gathered, but stopped when she outstretched her already full arms to take them. *"Can I carry these in for you? There's kind of a lot of them."*

"That's very sweet of you," she muttered as her blush deepened, *"but I wouldn't want to make you late on your first day."*

I scooped up my backpack and started walking beside her. *"Doesn't matter. I don't know where the fuck I'm going anyway."*

As she grinned at me, I realized that probably wasn't the most appropriate thing to say to a teacher.

"Sorry," I muttered.

"You just heard me swear a minute ago," she whispered with a shrug. *"I won't tell if you don't. Why don't we dump these in my room? Then I can walk you to the office, and we can find out where you're supposed to go."*

"Sure," I muttered, still trying like hell to dampen my charm.

She grinned at me as we headed up the steps to the front doors. *"I'm Mrs. Barton, by the way. What's your name?"*

"Tristan Mason." I winced as we entered the building and merged into hallway traffic. If the school system only knew how many migraines corralling an incubus in with

so many virgins caused, they'd all be blushing a deep shade of scarlet. A virgin's scent was a blatant odor. It was heavenly in smaller doses, but the concentration in a building full of teens was overwhelming.

Mrs. Barton noticed my reaction as I followed her into her classroom. "Are you feeling alright, Tristan?"

I shut the door, thankful that the room was empty and even more thankful that Mrs. Barton was a Missus. "Yeah," I muttered, "just a migraine. It's no big deal. I get them all the time."

Mrs. Barton set the books in her arms down on her desk with a concerned frown. "Would you like me to show you to the nurse's office?"

"Nah," I muttered as I added the books in my arms to the pile. "I'm good. Just point me toward the office."

By the time we got Mrs. Barton's books squared away, she finished debating whether I needed to see the nurse, and we finally made it to the office to get my schedule, I was late for homeroom. She offered to show me to the room and explain why I was tardy, but I told her I'd be fine. Then I parted ways with her, hoping my homeroom teacher would go easy on me after a tiny dose of charm.

The teacher—Mr. Shoemaker, according to the schedule in my hand—was standing at the front of the classroom speaking to his students as I slipped in. He raised an eyebrow as he pointed to an empty desk at the back of the room. "You can take a seat back there..."

I shot him a dazzling smile before he could ask why I was late, and his eyes glazed over in response.

After taking a moment to massage his temples, he muttered, "You must be our new student, Mr. Mason?"

I nodded as I took my seat in the back row.

"Welcome," Mr. Shoemaker rasped. He cleared his throat and blinked his eyes a few times. Then he went back to talking about his expectations for the year.

A massive blast of female pheromones hit me as the girl in front of me turned in her chair and shot me a sinful grin. Cheerleader.

Muting my charm as best I could, I smiled back at her and turned my attention to Mr. Shoemaker, hoping she'd take the hint and turn around.

She did, not so subtly inching her skirt a little higher as she crossed her legs.

As I bit down on my tongue, a whopping dose of testosterone hit me. I turned in the direction it'd come from, and a thick specimen of adrenaline and steroids narrowed his beady eyes at me. Jock. *Fuck, high school was predictable. Never one to back down from a fight, I sat up a little straighter and scowled at him.*

You could practically see the steam spewing from his ears as he looked away and kicked the chair of the girl in front of him, forcing her a little closer to her desk as he snagged her backpack and knocked it on the floor.

She was a timid wisp of a girl. No makeup, dark hair sloppily twisted up with a simple elastic, she was dressed in modest clothes that hung a little too loose, like they were either hand-me-downs or she wasn't comfortable enough with her body to let her curves show. She didn't even turn around to look at the bastard.

Now I was pissed off. Like I said, thanks to my older brother, I was a man of principle. Even if it wasn't for Brian, I'd like to think I wouldn't be okay with a bully like that ass-wipe taking his frustration out on a shyer creature. I wanted to stand up and punch that dick right in his fucking face, but I'd promised my mom I would try to behave myself. A call from the principal on the first day of school wouldn't exactly put her mind at ease. So instead, I stuck out my leg and snaked the leg of the asshole's chair with my foot. Then I jerked the chair toward me hard and fast.

The asshole went toppling out of his seat with his arms flailing and a scowl that suggested he was ready to kill. As he righted himself, he kicked the girl's bag farther away from her desk in frustration and sent its contents spilling across the floor.

Mr. Shoemaker stopped talking and raised an eyebrow. "Mr. Henderson, is there a problem with your chair?"

"No," the jock muttered as he glared at me, "just lost my balance."

"Well then, perhaps we should send you back to elementary school for a lesson on sitting still and listening."

As the room filled with muffled snickering, the bell signaled the end of homeroom.

I stood up and winked at the jock, and he growled at me under his breath. Ignoring him, I bent down, collected the girl's backpack, scooped the things that'd fallen out back inside and handed it to her. She took the bag without meeting my eyes and whispered, "Thanks," so softly that I barely heard it standing right next to her.

"Don't mention it," I whispered. "I'm Tristan, by the way."

She answered with an awkward nod, then walked away without ever looking me in the eye or telling me her name. That was it—no blushing, no seductive smile, no indication that she'd felt any hint of my charm. She reacted just as I imagined she reacted to every other kid at school, like she wished she was invisible and she hoped they'd leave her the hell alone.

It was the first time in my life that anyone other than my dad or brother had ever treated me like I was just a normal guy, and it stunned me speechless...

...Distracted as I was the whole time, it was a wonder I made it to the other side of the forest without seriously injuring myself. I exhaled a tense breath as I stepped from the trees and kept to the shadows as I moved to the back door of The Dragon's Lair. I pulled out my key, unlocked the door, and slipped in without ever setting foot in the moonlight. Shutting the door as noiselessly as I could, I turned and found Aubrey waiting for me in the back hall.

"Hey, love," my favorite troll murmured as she pulled me into a bear hug. "Feels like it's been ages. How're you doing?"

"I'm alright," I whispered as I squeezed her back. "How about you? How are the renovations going?"

"It's been exhausting," she muttered as she broke the hug and took a step back, "but I'm loving every second of it. The Sarrum has really spared no expense. Whatever I want, he's generously offered to foot the bill."

"It's the least he can do after tearing the place to pieces."

"I'm just glad he got her back," she muttered. "How's Emma doing?"

"She's fantastic. They both are. Perpetual newlyweds, just like they were before the Princess lost her Sight."

Aubrey let out a dramatic sigh as she wiped her chubby hands on her grease-stained apron. "What I wouldn't give for a fairytale ending like that."

I grinned at her and shook my head. "I have no doubt that you'll find your warty prince charming someday."

She raised an eyebrow. "I seem to recall you loving me plenty, warts and all."

"I'll always love you," I whispered. "You know that."

"Yeah, but something's different about you now," she muttered as she looked me up and down. When her eyes reached my arm, she frowned at the gash I got when I collided with the tree trunk. "What the heck happened to you?"

"It's nothing," I whispered, glancing at the door to the main room of the tavern. "Is he here yet?"

"It's *not* nothing," she scolded. "I'm not letting you leave here till I tend to that cut. You don't want it to get all infected."

I cocked an eyebrow because she'd neglected to answer my question, and I was anxious to finish up and get back to Mia.

"Yeah, he's here," she muttered, "and it's about time you showed up. The big guy has already eaten and drank up half my profits for the night."

"Put it on the Sarrum's tab," I muttered with a shrug.

She opened her mouth, then closed it for a second before muttering, "Really?"

"Yeah," I whispered with a sly grin. "He's so damn happy to have his wife back, he'd probably agree to pay for you to take ballroom dance lessons."

She let out an un-ladylike snort. "Can you picture me twirling around a dance floor?"

"Sure," I whispered, "you'd look spectacular."

"I'd be a *spectacle*," she muttered. "I think I'll stick to running the tavern."

"So," I muttered as I stole another glance at the door to the main room, "where is he?"

"Backroom," Aubrey whispered as if it was top secret information. It kinda was, but we were the only ones there to hear it.

I gave her a peck on the cheek. "Thanks. I'll be sure to save a spot on my dance card for you."

"For you," she muttered, "I might consider the dance lessons."

I winked at her as I headed toward the meeting room at the back of the tavern. She giggled and headed out front as I grabbed the doorknob, finally focused on the reason I'd come.

A robust blend of liquor fumes and cigar smoke came wafting out as I opened the door. It was so damn smoky in there that it took a few blinks for my eyes to adjust and realize he wasn't alone. A high-pitched feminine giggle bounced off the walls as I shut the door, followed by another, and another. Behind the table—littered with stacks of empty plates and enough liquor bottles to serve an army—three doe-eyed fairies were seated on a cushioned bench. Each of them was doing their best to get as close as physically possible to the man in the middle. I couldn't say as I blamed them. The half-incubus-half-giant was a hulking specimen of male perfection. His bulging muscles were adorned with tribal tattoos. His strong gorgeous features were framed by a head of long dark hair, a full beard and a set of perfectly arched masculine eyebrows—one of which had a strip of missing hair where a knife scar sliced through it, but that only added to his dangerous appeal. He winked at me as he downed the shot in his hand. Then he slammed it down on the table and refilled his glass.

I shook my head as I grinned at my old friend. "Hello, Zeke. It's been a while."

A slight sway as he stood up from the table suggested he'd downed enough shots to intoxicate a small army. He leaned over the table, dragging clingy fairies and the edge of the tablecloth right along with him. I lunged forward, ready to catch whatever went toppling as he pulled me into a massive bear hug and grumbled, "Too long."

I glanced at the doe-eyed fairies as they sat back down beside him. "I'm sorry, ladies. I need to talk to this handsome fellow in private."

A collective moan rose from the bench at the thought of leaving the stallion seated between them.

"Awww," he echoed back as he shot them each a seductive frown. "My friend won't steal me away for long. Why don't you beauties go save us a seat out front, huh?"

He beamed at me as the fairies filed out of the room, each stopping to look me over and grumbling a bit more when I didn't respond to their pouty lips and batting eyelashes. As the last one left and pulled the door shut, he let out a boisterous chuckle. "There must be someone new in your life," he murmured, slurring his words just enough to be noticeable. "Who's the lucky woman?" When I just grinned at him, he let out another deep belly laugh. "The lucky man then, or four-legged lover? Something is different about you."

"I'm just so damned happy to set eyes on you, you sexy beast."

He let out another laugh as he picked up his cigar and took a long seductive drag while I slid onto the bench beside him. "Likewise," he muttered as he winked at me. Then he downed another shot and poured one for me. "You know, I always thought you and I would make big beautiful babies together."

I let out a laugh. "I don't think it works that way, big guy."

"Well, you couldn't blame us for trying," he muttered with another wink. He picked up my glass and tipped it to my lips. "Drink with me, brother. It's been too long."

I knocked back the liquor and took the cup from his hand with a dazzling smile. "So, what've you got for me?"

"No location yet," he grumbled with a frown that did nothing to diminish his attractiveness. "I can't appear too eager to get the information. Don't want to raise any flags."

"Then where do we go from here?" I murmured with a nod, doing my best to mask my disappointment.

"There's a disreputable inn and tavern at the center of No Man's Land," he muttered as he refilled both our glasses. "It's a popular stopping point for slavers on their way to or from capturing slaves. It's been some time since the cabin was burnt down. I don't imagine it'll be long till the next auction. That's the place to go if you want information on where to trade."

"Will you be there?"

"Of course." He stopped to down his drink before adding, "If all goes well, I'll meet you at the tavern and we can travel to the auction together. Safety in numbers."

"And if all goes to hell?" I whispered as I glanced at the closed door. "Your cover could get blown. Are you willing to risk that?"

"Fuck yes," he growled, pounding his fist on the table to emphasize his words. "The time has come to step out of the shadows and fight, my friend."

"What about Davina and the others? Aren't you worried about what might happen to them if you don't return?"

"Davina's strong," he growled. "They're all strong. We put an end to all this, and they'll have no need to take refuge with me."

I picked up my shot and downed it. "No argument here."

He nodded and took another puff of his cigar. "How many have you gathered?"

"Four to pose as captives and three and a half of us to pose as slavers."

He arched an eyebrow as he took another drag. "A half?"

"One's a mutt," I murmured with a grin, "half-troll-half-imp. He got the imp's size."

"Too bad for him," Zeke muttered, "but you've gotta admire his courage for one so small."

"For sure," I muttered. "Who're you bringing with you?"

He smoothed a hand over his beard as he thought about it for a second. "It might be best if I make this journey alone."

I nodded. "Do you plan to bid on any of the captives?"

"If it doesn't all go to shit," he muttered under his breath, "yeah. I'll purchase as many as I can afford."

"What's the name of the inn and tavern in the middle of No Man's Land?"

A wicked grin spread across his face. "Hell's Gate."

"It's fitting," I muttered, "since all hell's about to break loose."

"Let it," he growled. "It's long overdue, and I have no doubt that we'll be victorious. It's high time we took back the shadows."

"Amen, brother," I muttered as I watched him pour us both another drink.

We downed our drinks and slammed our glasses down on the table in unison. Then I smiled at him as I stood from the table. "It's time for me to slink out the back, my friend."

"Never thought I'd see the day when The Dragon's Lair's golden boy had to slink out the back of anywhere," he muttered with a melancholy grin.

"We do whatever has to be done," I whispered as I held out my hand.

He clasped my hand in both of his massive hands and shook it with vigor. "See you on the other side, brother. Tread carefully."

I nodded as he let go of my hand. Then I headed toward the door. "You too."

20

GODRIC

I downed the last sip of my tea, sat the empty cup on the table in front of me, and pulled the blanket a bit tighter around my shoulders. The early morning breeze coming off the water chilled me right down to my bones. Spending time in the waking world always made me feel weak and unsettled. I was a fierce and powerful ruler in Draumer, but in this world, a decrepit old man stared back at me from the other side of the looking glass.

It was melancholy mornings such as this that made me wonder why the hell I even bothered to keep going. Perhaps it would be best if I just gave in to time. Why not let my old bones rest and my tired heart give out, and move on to whatever came after this? I sure as hell hoped there was an *after*. Which begged the question, why not leave this deplorable world behind and slip away to my sweet Lilly in the great beyond? If there was an *after*, she'd surely be waiting to greet me when I crossed over.

The sound of the back door opening jarred my thoughts back to the present. I was fairly safe hidden away in this remote little corner of the world, but there was always the risk that someone would spot me and recognize me. My fugitive status made it difficult to ever fully let down my guard in the waking world.

The youngest daughter of my current host smiled at me as she slipped out the back door onto the balcony. "Would you care for another cup of tea, sir?"

I smiled politely at her as I placed a hand over the mouth of my cup. "No, thank you. I am quite good out here just enjoying the sunlight. Even an old Dark creature like me needs to feel the sun on his face every now and then."

My words brought a grin to her sweet lips, the sort of grin a child might give her kindly old grandfather.

If she only knew the desires that lurked in my cold Dark heart. What I wouldn't give to be fifty years younger. I gestured toward the chair beside mine. "Would you care to join me?"

"Yes," she whispered as she dropped into the seat and smoothed out her skirt.

Unfortunately, my oafish bodyguard came barreling out the door before any more pleasantries could be exchanged. He looked at me, then his beady eyes shifted to the girl.

"It's alright," I growled. "You may speak in front of her."

"Your guest should be arriving shortly in Draumer, my King," the oaf muttered, his eyes lingering on the girl for just a bit too long. "I thought you'd like to know, so you could be there to greet her."

"Yes, I suppose I should." I turned my attention back to the girl. "Would you care to accompany me to Draumer and keep an old man company whilst I wait?"

An eager grin spread across her face as she nodded, and my cold dead heart grew a bit warmer. Spending all my time sulking alone in my old homestead was beginning to take its toll on me, more than it normally did. I wasn't quite sure why this time was different, and I didn't care to dwell on it. This fresh-faced creature's golden hair reminded me of my sister's. Her presence in the house would provide a welcome distraction. I held my hand out to her and she placed her smooth hand in mine. A grin spread across my wrinkled face as I waved a hand to summon the Waters.

Her smile grew wider as we stood from our chairs and stepped into the tunnel in the center where the Waters dared not seep. A few seconds later, we stepped out into the parlor of my childhood home. She turned her head to look back at the tunnel, and her eyes widened as she realized it was no longer there.

My heart thawed a bit more at the wonder in her lovely blue eyes, so like my Lilly's. "Have you never traveled in such a manner before?"

"No," she replied in a breathless whisper.

My grin widened as I murmured, "I take it you enjoyed it?"

"Yes, I..." Her words died off as she turned to face me and realized a younger, fitter version of me now held onto her delicate hand.

I couldn't help but chuckle at her reaction. "I prefer to take this form in Draumer, I hope it doesn't throw you off too much."

She shook her head, still gripping my hand—a bit tighter than the loose hold she'd used to grip my wrinkled old hand.

I raised her hand to my lips, planted a chaste kiss on the back of it and let it drop to her side. "Have I rendered you speechless?"

"No," she muttered with a shake of her head. "I'm just...surprised."

"I presume you don't mind my younger self entertaining you for a while?"

Her cheeks blushed a lovely shade of pink as she whispered, "No, sir."

"Excellent," I murmured. "Shall I give you a tour then?"

"Yes, please."

I extended an arm crooked at the elbow, wordlessly inviting her to take it. And her blush deepened as she looped her slender arm around mine.

I shut my eyes for a moment, focused on her warmth, and tried to imagine my Lilly standing in her place. There was no mistaking the look she gave me when I opened my eyes.

Her eyes were ablaze with mischief without the slightest trace of familial affection. I held her gaze, toying with her as I considered what to take from her.

Once again, my oafish guard interrupted us before I could make up my mind. He flung the door open and stomped into the room without bothering to knock or await permission to enter. "Your guest is here, my King."

Flames flared in my eyes as I glared at him. "Didn't anyone ever teach you that it's impolite to barge into a room without knocking?"

The oaf's mouth dropped open as he nodded. When he turned and glanced back at the door, it wasn't difficult to surmise what was going on inside his pea-sized brain.

"Do *not* go back out and knock now," I snarled through gritted teeth.

The girl beside me flinched at the harshness of my tone.

Bored with playing nice, I turned to her with an icy grin. "Don't worry, my dear. You've nothing to fear...unless you displease me."

Her eyes widened, but she didn't say a word.

"Have them bring in our guest," I growled as I turned to the oaf, "and show this girl to the dining room. See that she's offered food and drink."

A perverse grin spread across his face as his eyes wandered over the girl. "Yes, my King."

"Lay a hand on her," I snarled, "and I'll make certain you regret it."

The grin slipped from his face as he took the girl by the arm.

I settled onto the couch and watched him lead her out of the room and close the door behind him. Then I sunk back against the velvet cushions with a tired sigh.

It was difficult to find good help these days. My nephew had done away with more than a few of my best men over the years. It started back when his little fairy Princess gave herself up to the Darkness. My bonded shadow had been stationed at the front of the pack, waiting for the mirage to crumble for months. We could have crippled David then and there, had my shadow been fast enough to tear the girl apart before he reached her. Then there were the raids along the fringe. I lost hordes of warriors during those bloody battles, which would have been worth it if the Princess's father had destroyed her before David got to her. But once again, he put a stop to it before her father even had time to violate her. Then David and the Darkness destroyed the warriors I'd sent to lead her dear father to the mirage. Lastly, when they stormed my stronghold to rescue his Princess and my former wife, David and his troop destroyed every damn demon I had positioned to guard the mirage. My numbers were still plentiful, but the droves of demons who remained loyal to me were no longer my first choices. They were fierce, and lethal, and would fight to the death alright, but dealing with the mongrels on a daily basis grated on my nerves. They weren't the best soldiers I had left, of course. I was reserving them for the war to come, and putting up with these incompetent buffoons in the meantime was a worthwhile sacrifice. As my patience wore thin, I felt the need to remind myself of that more and more frequently.

I squeezed my eyes shut and pressed my index fingers to my temples, and for a good ten minutes I was left in peace.

As the doorknob across the room turned, I opened my eyes and watched the door swing open. Two mixed breed demons of moderate size and minimal intelligence came stomping into the room carrying a woman between them. Her wrists and ankles were bound by metal cuffs and a cloth sack covered her head. The morons were clearly struggling to bring her into the room as she twisted in their grip. I shook my head as they dropped her onto the opposite end of the couch from me and left the room without uttering a syllable. Apparently, word had spread amongst the ranks of my dim-witted minions that I had no more patience for their idiocy.

I watched the door shut, then turned my attention to my guest. "I am sorry your travel accommodations were so lacking, but we can't be too careful these days."

She let out a muffled snarl. "Take this damn cloth off my head."

"Gladly," I murmured as I removed the sack, "as long as you agree to be civil."

"Civil?" she shrieked, her eyes wild and her dark hair a tangled mess from the cloth. "Do you consider sending your little demons to cuff me and drag me here *civil?*"

"I consider it necessary."

"You could've just invited me here," she growled. "Did that ever occur to you?"

"Correspondence is a dangerous thing these days, Louise," I murmured as I removed the chains from my former fiancé's wrists and ankles. "You must realize that."

Her eyes were ablaze with sapphire flames as she looked down at her wrists. "That's bound to leave marks."

"My apologies," I murmured as I took her right hand in mine and brushed my fingers over her wrist.

"Don't act all sweet now," she snarled. "It's too late for that."

"You know, you're beautiful when you're angry," I murmured. "I can only imagine what gorgeous children we would've made."

The flames in her eyes leapt higher. "There's no need to dig up the past. You know I'm on your side."

I nodded and released her hand. "Did it occur to you that being bound and masked would make it appear as if you'd been captured by the enemy, should someone have witnessed your departure?"

"I suppose you're right, damn it." The flames in her eyes died off as she exhaled a tired sigh. "I hate it when you're right."

A wicked grin spread across my face. "Have you missed me?"

"That ship sailed a lifetime ago, Henry—"

"Godric," I corrected. "I no longer answer to that name. I'll thank you not to call me that again."

"Fair enough," she grumbled, "as long as you refrain from binding me in the future."

I looked her over with a sinful smile. "Well, you're no fun at all."

"Lucky for you, you never had to find out," she muttered.

I took her hand in mine again with a regretful sigh. "We were robbed, you and I."

"That we were," she whispered.

"We will make them pay for it," I promised. "The Talbot reign is approaching its end."

"Not soon enough," she muttered as she pulled her hand away.

"I could still make you my Queen," I murmured, dropping back against the cushions, "just as it was always meant to be."

"I'm too old and barren for that," she growled, her words dripping with bitterness.

I took hold of her chin and tilted her head so she'd look at me. "I already have an heir."

"Yes," she grumbled, "but he stands with our nephew."

"For now," I murmured. "Your tireless efforts weren't for naught, Louise. All those thankless years of raising the Talbot children whose mothers didn't survive their births, it was all leading up to this. We will have our revenge on the lot of them."

"Some days I wonder if I should be grateful for what my family did," Louise muttered as her eyes focused somewhere in the distance. "If they hadn't sterilized me to justify passing you over for the throne and wedding my brother to your sister instead, I'd most likely be dead now."

Tears stung my eyes as I whispered, "And my sister would be alive."

She cocked her head to the side and studied me through narrowed eyes. "I am thankful for one thing."

"And what's that?"

"That I never had to marry you, you coldhearted bastard."

"I would have treated you like the Queen that you were, you know. They shattered my heart when they killed my sister."

"But you never would've loved me," she muttered to herself.

"What does love have to do with any of it?"

"I don't know," she whispered, "but my bed has been cold and empty all these years."

"We can fix that," I murmured. "I have hordes of soldiers who would gladly warm your bed."

She let out a laugh. "I'm too old for that now."

"Not in this world."

She shook her head and muttered, "None of that matters now."

I nodded because I couldn't care less who shared the old hag's bed. "Were you able to get them all?"

"Most," she muttered. "There was no opportunity to get to a few of them."

"Most will do nicely," I assured her with a satisfied smile. "You must be tired after your journey. Why don't you come dine with me? Then I'll see what we can do about warming your bed."

"Perhaps my family was right," she replied with a sinful smile. "We would have been a wicked King and Queen."

"We still can be."

21

CHARLIE

I'd expelled too much energy during my flying lesson/kidnapping attempt to summon the Waters and jump back to Draumer. Anxious as I was to meet up with Clay and learn more about my mom, I didn't have much choice but to drift off to sleep the old-fashioned way. I punched at my pillow with a frustrated sigh, rolled onto my back and fixed my eyes on the ceiling of the guestroom at the Talbots' estate. Going back to my room at the house on Sycamore to drift off to dreamland would've been a pointless waste of time, and there was no time to waste now. I needed to finish up my training and graduate from the dragon academy pronto, so I'd be ready to take part in the upcoming mission.

I raked a hand through my hair and grimaced as I rolled onto my stomach. I'd acted like a total psycho during my first flying lesson. Thank God Rose hadn't been there to witness it. I could only imagine what must've been going through Emma's mind as I tried to fly off into the proverbial sunset with her. The shocking thing was that David hadn't seemed the least bit angry with me—no jealous rage, no menacing display of superior strength, nothing. There was a time in the not so distant past, when it seemed like he'd rather rip out my larynx than talk to me. Now, he wasn't even pissed at me for trying to run off with his beloved treasure. The only explanation I could fathom was that he no longer saw me as any threat whatsoever to their relationship. Emma remembered who she was now. She remembered their history. She was his, and there wasn't a single cell in her body that wanted it any other way. Unfortunately, my dragon self didn't seem to have gotten that memo.

There were too many thoughts running through my head to let go and drift off to dreamland, and I didn't have the patience to lie in bed like a useless lump. So I tossed off the covers with a growl of frustration, moved to the door and stood there in the dark, staring at the knob. If I ran into Brian or Benjamin, they'd probably be pissed to find me wandering around the house instead of trying to fall asleep so I could meet up with Clay in Draumer. A rumbling in my stomach made me grin as I stood there with my hand on the doorknob. I could tell whoever I bumped into that I couldn't fall asleep on an empty stomach. It wasn't a total lie. Okay, in all honesty I was too nervous about the upcoming mission to be hungry, but it was the best excuse I could come up with. I opened the door, tiptoed down the hall and managed to make it all the way downstairs without running into anyone. The house was so quiet, I figured I was golden by the time I stepped into the kitchen.

"Can't sleep?" Brian's voice nearly startled me out of my skin. He was sitting on a kitchen stool on the opposite side of the counter across the room. His suit jacket was draped over the back of the stool beside his. The top two buttons of his dress shirt were undone, the cuffs were rolled up and his tie hung loose around his neck as he cradled a glass of liquor in his hands.

"No," I muttered, deciding I didn't have the energy to deliver a convincing lie. "You?"

He shook his head. "Too much on my mind tonight."

I nodded as I ventured a bit farther into the room. "I know the feeling." I opened a couple of cupboards and peeked in the fridge. When nothing grabbed my interest, I moved to the counter Brian was seated behind and hoisted myself up to sit on the adjacent countertop so I could face him while we talked.

Brian took a slow sip of his drink before muttering, "Isa would kick your ass if she knew you were sitting on the countertop."

"So don't tell her." Clay's rough voice drew my attention to the door as he stepped in the kitchen. He was dressed in sweatpants and a well-worn t-shirt that was snug enough to prove he was no stranger to the gym—which was probably a good thing, considering all the chemical damage he did to his body. A white bakery box was tucked under one of his sculpted arms. He held the box out to me as he walked toward us. "Heard you rummaging through the cupboards. Figured you might want something from my stash. Too much healthy organic stuff in this house."

As Clay lifted the lid of the box, golden light spilled out and a chorus of angels burst into song. Okay. That might be a slight exaggeration, but as I peeked at the assortment of fresh baked cookies in the box it felt pretty damn close to the truth.

"I think I love you," I whispered as I helped myself to a half-moon cookie.

"Cheap date," Clay muttered with a smirk as he sat the box down on the counter in front of Brian. "How about you, pretty boy? Can I buy your love with a cookie?"

The smoldering look that Brian shot Clay as he reached in the box and grabbed a monstrous chocolate chip cookie made me feel like a third wheel.

I cleared my throat. "Would you two like to be alone?"

With unflinching eye contact, Clay leaned across the counter and broke off half the cookie in Brian's hand as his teeth were sinking into the other side. "No time for pleasure," he muttered. Then he extended his tongue and drew the entire half of the giant cookie into his mouth in one impressive, extremely suggestive mouthful.

Yeah, I was definitely a third wheel. Heat rushed to my cheeks as I recalled Brian's drool-inducing demonstration of his charm at the morning meeting. "Maybe I'll just bring my cookie up to bed and take another shot at nodding off to sleep."

"What the hell for?" Brian murmured in a velvet tone that clearly wasn't meant for me. As he spoke, he reached across the counter and brushed a crumb from the corner of Clay's mouth with his thumb. "You've got nobody to meet up with in Draumer. Your dream date is standing right here in the kitchen."

DREAM FRAGMENTS

As Brian licked the crumb off his thumb, I hopped down from the counter and took a few steps back. "Yeah, I don't think I'm the dream date in this scenario."

"Sit your ass back down," Brian grumbled. "There's no time for any other scenarios. We're working under a deadline." As I hopped back up on the counter, Brian stood from his stool. "I'm gonna head off to bed. Tristan and I are supposed to meet up in Draumer."

"Can I ask something before you go?" I mumbled around a mouthful of sugary decadence.

"Shoot," Brian whispered as he flung his jacket over one shoulder and rounded the counter to join us in the kitchen.

"What will you, Benjamin, and the Sarrum be doing while we're on the mission?"

"Preparing for war," Brian muttered as he reached in the bakery box and grabbed another cookie for the road.

I nodded and turned to Clay. "What about you?"

"I'll be cooking up potions with Isa," Clay muttered as he watched Brian break the cookie he'd just taken from the box in half. He took the half in Brian's outstretched hand, then looked up at me. "In fact, we've started working on a pretty complex one already."

I opened the lid of the box as I swallowed my last bite of cookie. "What's it for?"

"It's for your buddy Bob," Clay muttered with a crooked grin.

My hand froze above the cookies as I looked up at him. "Bob?"

"Yeah," Clay muttered as he opened the cupboard behind my head and took out a glass. "It's a damn good potion too. Haven't cooked any up in years though." A wistful smile spread across his face as he opened the fridge, pulled out a jug of milk, and filled up his glass. "Last batch I made was for your mom."

I let the lid of the bakery box drop from my hand. "Now that sounds like a story."

"It is," Clay whispered, "but it's kinda out of order if you want to know everything."

Brian stole the glass from Clay's hand and downed a swig of his milk. As he handed it back, he muttered, "You might have to hit the highlights of her story and fill in the gaps down the road when the fate of the world isn't hanging in the balance."

Clay took a sip of milk, then wiped his mouth with the back of his hand. "Noted."

"I'm gonna go track down my baby brother," Brian murmured. "Thanks for the cookies."

Clay's face was all business as he motioned for me to follow him out of the room. "You want more later," he muttered to Brian as we parted ways in the hall, "you know where to find me."

The expression on Brian's face was unreadable as he nodded and whispered, "I do."

I followed Clay down the hall to the living room as Brian headed for the stairs. "Why do I get the feeling you'd rather be going upstairs?"

Clay smirked at me as we walked into the living room. "Cause you're so damn perceptive."

"I didn't realize Brian was gay," I muttered as I plopped down on the couch.

Clay shrugged as he sat down next to me. "He's an incubus."

"Which means?"

"Means their tastes don't discriminate," he muttered.

I nodded and whispered, "Tristan refers to himself as omni-sexual."

Clay's all-business expression softened into a lopsided grin. "Well, what in the fuck does that mean?"

"He said something about participating...and watching and...I don't know...farm animals, maybe?"

"Incubi," Clay muttered with a shake of his head. "If they weren't so damn pretty, that might be a turnoff."

"I don't know. I don't think there's any degree of pretty that makes hooking up with donkeys overlookable."

"Donkeys? Can't picture that." Clay shifted sideways as he pulled a pack of cigarettes and a lighter from his pocket. "I imagine something more along the lines of exotic jungle cats." He glanced at the doorway across the room, then down at his pack of cigarettes and up at me. "Shit. We probably aren't supposed to smoke in the Sarrum's place, are we?"

"Don't know. I don't smoke, but *no* is probably a good bet," I muttered with a shrug, "and I don't think jungle cats make it any less freaky."

Clay stuffed the cigarettes and lighter back in his pocket with a hoarse chuckle. "Why don't we just leave weird enough alone and take a trip down memory lane?"

"Works for me," I agreed as I slid a little closer to him and propped my arm on the pillow between us.

He put his hand on my arm, and I dropped my head back against the couch as the room went fuzzy.

"I'd love to share every detail of our story with you," Clay's gravelly voice assured me as our surroundings dissolved, "but I suppose Brian's got a point. We're running short on time. When this war is all over, I'll fill in all the gaps you want me to."

I nodded as a new backdrop solidified around me. It was night and I was sitting in a car, staring at a house across the street, feeling pissed as hell.

"Angel and I became best friends almost instantly," a gruff voice in my head whispered. Still a bit disoriented, it took me a few seconds to realize it was Clay talking in my ear, filling in some of the details he was skipping over. "It didn't take long for us to realize we were both Sighted. Her parents and older brother were Unsighted. Technically her uncle was her guide, but they weren't close. He didn't seem to care a hell of a lot about teaching her anything beyond the basics. I took over as her guide and taught her everything I knew, including everything I knew about potion-making. Most people don't have a knack for it, but it didn't take long to figure out that Angel did. She was a natural potion-maker, and a damn good one too. After we realized that, she started taking part in my business, but all she did was help me cook the stuff. She didn't have anything to do with selling it, and neither of us used it. Everything was going great till Angel's big brother died in a car crash. After that, she slipped into a deep depression. I tried like hell to get her out of it, but she started to pull away from everybody, including me. That's when my boss swooped in to invite her to a party. He'd seen pictures of her at my place, and he'd asked me to set them up lots of times. When he got tired of me saying no, he decided to introduce himself while she was at her most vulnerable and I wasn't around to stop him. I found out through one of his distributors that he'd taken her to a party, and that's where we are now. I'd just pulled up to the house."

The rough voice in my ear faded away as my mom came stumbling out the side door of the house, leaning on a shady-looking douchebag wearing a baseball cap and sunglasses, despite the fact that it was dark out. I hopped out of the car and slammed the door shut. Then I crossed the street and picked up speed as I headed toward the two of them.

Angel flashed me a drunken smile when she saw me coming. "Clay, I didn't know you were gonna be here tonight."

"I'm not supposed to be," I growled, "and neither are you."

"Back off," the douchebag with the hat and sunglasses slurred. "She's fine. I'm taking real good care of her."

Menace rolled off of me in waves as I growled, "Get your fucking hands off her." When he let out a laugh, I lost it. I hauled off and punched him square in the nose. As his hands flew up to his bleeding nose, Angel lost her balance. I caught her and threw her over my shoulder. "I'm taking you home now, Angel."

"I don't want to go home," she sobbed. "It's too depressing there. I'd rather be dead than go back to that place."

I marched across the street, sat her down in the passenger seat, and hopped in the driver's side without a word. As I pulled the door shut, I leaned over and kissed the top of her head. "If you died, I might as well go right along with you."

Tears streamed down her cheeks as she looked up at me. "It's too hard, Clay. I don't want to do it anymore."

"I know, Angel, but you don't have to go through this alone," I whispered as I wrapped my arms around her and pulled her against my chest, ignoring the commotion across the street as my boss's buddies filed out of the house…

Tears filled my eyes as that scene dissolved and another took its place.

…I was standing outside the door to an apartment with a key in my hand. As I unlocked the door and stepped inside, somehow I knew this was Clay's apartment. A growing sense of dread gripped me as I walked through the empty rooms. Nausea crept up my throat as I reached the bathroom door. It was closed, and I was positive I'd left it open. I heard a faint whimper inside the room and yanked the door open. My heart sank when I saw Angel lying on the floor next to the toilet. The room stunk of vomit and she was curled up in a ball, shivering like it was the dead of winter.

"I'm gonna kill that son of a bitch," I muttered as I rushed to her, shrugged out of my flannel and wrapped it around her.

She didn't say anything as I pulled her into my arms. She just dropped her head against my chest while I stroked a hand over her hair. "You don't belong here, Angel. You're better than this. Damn it. You're so freaking smart…and so talented. You could do anything…go anywhere. I could go with you. Just let me help you through this."

She didn't say a word. She just sobbed against my chest as I stroked her hair.

Her sobs echoed in my ears as the bathroom melted away, and I couldn't tell if the tears streaming down my cheeks were my own or a memory of the ones Clay had shed all those years ago…

"I tried everything short of locking her up," Clay's voice whispered in my head. "Hell, I even tried that. But it's damn near impossible to help a loved one when they don't want your help. I felt so fucking useless…"

…Clay's voice trailed off as a new scene formed around me. I was inside a police station, shouting at the scrawny cop behind the front desk. That vision faded almost as fast as it'd formed, but I got the gist. Angel had been arrested for dealing, and they were holding her in a cell. Her parents had arranged for them to stick her in rehab in the morning, and they'd left strict instructions not to let me anywhere near her…

"They knew just enough about me to assume I was the source of her problems," Clay's voice explained. "If I'd been able to get her out of there, maybe things would've ended different."

…My stomach balked as a new scene formed around me. All this fading in and out was making me dizzy as hell. I was sitting at a table in a rowdy tavern. The room was full of all sorts of degenerate Dark creatures, too many to be glimpses of souls in the waking world. This place was obviously in Draumer.

I took a swig of my ale as a nasty bloated creature sat down across the table from me. "What the hell do you want?"

The demon—who looked like he was half-troll-half-sorrow-eater—looked taken aback. "I'm just trying to help," he muttered as he looked around the room, his shifty eyes sizing up the other patrons. He leaned closer to me and whispered, "Angela's in danger."

I slammed my mug down on the table. "What the fuck do you know about Angela?"

He leaned closer and dropped his voice a little lower. "I work at the rehab clinic she was admitted to."

I narrowed my eyes at him. "And?"

"And Henry Godric is the psychiatrist at the clinic," he muttered. "He's been searching for the perfect incubator. He wants to have another go at making an heir, and he figures a girl from that place isn't likely to be missed."

Rage swelled inside me as I growled, "What the fuck are you talking about?"

"She's talented and smart with loads of untapped potential," he muttered. "Godric seems to think she's the one."

I reached across the table, grabbed him by the shirt, and pulled him toward me. "Are you honestly telling me *Godric* wants to make a baby with my best friend?"

"Yeah," he muttered, "I mean..."

"I've got no patience left," I growled. "Give me details."

"Godric released her from the clinic yesterday."

My stomach dropped. "No...she would've called me to come get her if that was true."

"Maybe she would have," the beady-eyed demon whispered, "if he'd given her the chance. He released her just before nightfall without allowing her a phone call or returning her belongings."

I choked back the urge to vomit as I let go of him. "Where the hell is she now?"

"His men nabbed her off the street right after he released her," the ugly bastard whimpered.

I choked back my own need to vomit as the tavern disappeared…

…The small apartment from Clay's previous memory reformed around me. I was sitting on the couch, staring at the wall. There was a beer in my hand and several empties were scattered on the floor. A faint knock at my door made me jump to my feet. I rushed across the room and peeked through the peephole, and a sob escaped my throat when I saw her face.

As soon as I yanked the door open, she fell into my arms. "I thought I'd never see you again," I whispered as I swept her into the apartment. I shut and locked the door then pulled her into my arms again. "I looked everywhere for you. How did you get away?"

"I made a run for it when there was only one thug watching me," she muttered as I led her to the couch.

I sat down on the couch, pulling her down beside me. "How'd you get past him?"

"They were keeping me drugged," she muttered. "So he figured I was incapacitated, and he didn't pay much attention to me. Turns out, the tolerance I'd built up came in pretty handy."

A sorrowful smile spread across my face as I wrapped my arms around her. "God, it's good to see you again."

"They're going to come looking for me," she whispered, "and this will be the first place they look."

"Shit." My heart was in my throat as I jumped to my feet, pulling her up with me. "We need to get the hell out of here."

"Clay," she muttered, tugging my hand to get my attention, "I'm pregnant."

I kissed the top of her head then pulled her into a hug. "I know."

"How?" she whispered.

"One of the clinic employees approached me at a tavern in Draumer and told me Godric was there and he meant to..." I looked at the tears in her eyes and didn't have the heart to finish the sentence, but there wasn't any need to. "Let's get the hell out of here before somebody comes looking for you."

I was heading toward the kitchen to grab my car keys as the room grew blurry...

As the apartment faded away, I whispered, "Why would they drug my mom if she was carrying Godric's child?" A lump formed in my throat as it occurred to me that *the child* I was talking about *was me*. "Weren't they worried about hurting the baby?" *Maybe that explained what was wrong with me.*

"Dragons are pretty much immune to the effects of chemical substances," Clay's voice echoed in my head as a new scene began to form around me. "Think about it. Have you ever gotten drunk, or been drugged out of your mind, or even felt dulled by any of the drugs they gave you at the facility?"

I tried to think back to a time in my life when I'd felt chemically altered as I muttered, "No, I always spit the pills out."

"How did you know to do that?"

"Common sense, I guess."

"Come on, Charlie," Clay's voice muttered in my head as I found myself sitting beside Angel in the backseat of a taxi that was pulling up to a brick building with an immaculately landscaped front yard. "Are you sure you always spit the pills out? Weren't there times when you forgot to spit them out, or you drank too much alcohol and you never felt the effects you should have?"

"Maybe," I muttered as I hopped out of the taxi with Angel clutching my hand.

We marched up the front steps and I gave her hand a squeeze as I pulled the front door open. A knockout beauty grinned at us as we moved toward her desk. Her sleek dark hair was neatly pinned up. Her lipstick was a tasteful shade of red that matched her manicured fingernails, and her low-cut blouse offered a teasing glimpse of her perfect breasts. I licked my lips as my heartbeat quickened, and wondered why I was so disturbed by the fact that I was attracted to her, until I remembered this was Clay's memory. I felt what *he felt*, and she wasn't exactly his type. There wasn't a single part of his body that seemed to remember that, apart from his dumbfounded brain. There was only one logical explanation for his reaction. This drop-dead gorgeous woman was a succubus.

I glanced at the nameplate on her desk—*Sophie Turner, Paralegal Assistant*—and immediately felt guilty for reacting to her charm, even if it was just the unavoidable memory of Clay's reaction.

Before I could dwell on that, a menacing wave of fear crashed over me. I turned toward the door and watched a younger version of Benjamin enter the building and narrow his eyes at me. The dread in the pit of my stomach told me Clay knew exactly who the Darkness was.

Benjamin approached us at the unhurried pace of a predator, who was well aware that his prey had no chance of escaping him. I watched his cold Dark eyes, transfixed as he moved closer to us.

His expression softened as his eyes met Angel's. "What brings you two here today?"

"We need to speak to the Sarrum," I muttered—or, *Clay* muttered.

Benjamin narrowed his eyes at me as he motioned for us to follow him.

My feet didn't want to budge, but I forced myself to walk forward and squeezed Angel's hand to reassure her. We followed the Darkness through a heavy oak door that he shut behind us.

He motioned for us to sit at a long conference table. As we did, he sat himself down across from us. "Who the hell are you, and why are you using titles that should never be uttered aloud in this world?"

"We're sorry," Angel whispered. "Fear got the better of us, I guess."

A sympathetic frown spread across Benjamin's face as his Dark eyes locked with my mother's. "Fear of what?"

"Isn't fear of *you* enough?" Clay muttered.

"It would be," Benjamin mused as his gaze shifted to me, "if I was projecting it toward you."

"This is you *not* projecting fear?" I muttered under my breath.

DREAM FRAGMENTS

"Yeah," Benjamin whispered, "it is. Now answer my question."

"We're nobodies," Angela whispered. When Benjamin met her eyes again, she added, "but I'm carrying Godric's child."

With that, the scenery dissolved...

I'm not gonna lie, I was a little relieved to find myself back on the couch in the Talbots' living room.

"That's all I've got in me tonight," Clay muttered, his voice rougher than just the usual smoker's rasp.

"Good," I muttered. "I'm not sure I could handle much more."

22

EMMA

David had gone back to the waking world to check on Charlie after his first flying lesson, but I figured my time would be better spent at the palace. The upcoming mission was our best chance of locating the Purists' new meeting place—and if we got really lucky, determining the whereabouts of Godric. If I could, I would've volunteered to go on the mission and pose as one of the captives, but my face was too recognizable and it was common knowledge that I was the Sarrum's only weakness. The Purists would do anything to get their hands on me because ending me would deliver the death blow to him. Still, I wasn't about to sit back and do nothing while the fate of our world hung in the balance.

I suppressed a shiver as I made my way down the drafty stone corridor. As much as I trusted David, Charlie's crazed attempt to fly off with me during his flying lesson had rattled me a little. If I was a drinker, I probably would've downed a drink or two to calm my nerves before heading to the courtyard. Unfortunately, unlike dragons—who barely felt the effects of obscene amounts of alcohol or drugs—fairies had almost no tolerance to mind-altering substances in either world. Forgetting that vital piece of information had gotten me into trouble on more than one occasion while I was blind. I drank too much at the Christmas party the night Sophie filled my head with lies about her and David. In my fractured mental state, the alcohol clouded my blinded brain enough to make me believe Sophie's lies, enough to attempt suicide and lash out at Isa when she tried to stop me. Lacking a better explanation to offer me for the psychotic episode caused by my alcohol consumption, my Sighted doctor told me the alcohol didn't mix well with the antidepressant I was taking to cope with my father's death. In truth, there never was any antidepressant. My fairy metabolism couldn't handle that sort of medication, but it only took a bit of Tristan's charm to convince me that I'd been taking an antidepressant all along. The anti-anxiety medication Dr. Spenser prescribed for me at the facility had also wreaked havoc on my fairy body chemistry, but I suspected that was unintentional on his part. As much of a monster as the sorrow-eater was, I doubted he would've risked his license by drugging me to the brink of unconsciousness. Then again, he was Sighted and he knew I was a fairy. He'd have to be completely incompetent to be unaware of the differences in tolerance that existed between different creatures. Either way, that was all water under the bridge, and I didn't care enough about Dr. Spenser's motives to dwell on it any longer.

I shook my head as I reached the silent spill of Water at the corridor's end. None of that mattered anymore. I was back home where I belonged now, and I didn't need chemicals to get through any of this.

I stepped through the Waterfall and stepped out onto a cobblestone path. Beneath the vast expanse of starless sky, the darkness in the palace courtyard was so absolute that I almost walked right into the shadow standing guard at the entrance.

He dipped his head in a respectful nod that I could only see because he touched my arm, enhancing my night vision as he greeted me with a cordial, "Good evening, Princess."

"Good evening," I muttered, squinting in a useless attempt to acclimate my eyes. "Would you mind?"

"Of course." The shadow touched my arm again, and the darkness lessened enough for me to make out the outlines of my surroundings.

"Thank you," I whispered.

"My pleasure," the shadow replied with a nod.

I made my way down the stone path that traversed the courtyard at a meandering pace, immersing myself in the inky darkness as I surveyed the grounds. The melancholy song of a lonely night bird echoed through the yard as he called for his mate from a hidden perch within the treetops. A widespread chorus of insects added their hushed lullaby notes to the song, enhancing the tranquility of the night melody. Now and then, a burst of scampering steps and rustling leaves would punctuate the tune as nocturnal creatures roamed the grounds in search of their next meal.

A warm breeze blew across my skin, welcoming me with a ghostly caress. I shut my eyes and breathed the night air deep into my lungs as I tucked a flyaway wisp of hair behind my ear.

I heard Nellie and Bob before I got close enough to see them. They were too far away to catch their words, but the emphatic rise and fall of their voices made it obvious they were in the middle of a heated discussion. I bit my lip as I inched closer, debating whether to approach them or leave them be.

"I'd give them some distance if I were you," a small but confident voice mused from the shadows.

I grinned at the familiar voice as I searched the darkness for the creature it belonged to.

"Up here," Pip whispered.

I squinted in the direction his voice was coming from and found him perched on a low hanging branch of a wisteria tree a few paces from the path. "How did you get up there?"

A grin spread across his wrinkled face as his eyes darted to Bob at the other end of the yard. "With a little help from a friend."

I smiled at Bob's tiny sidekick as I stepped toward his branch. "I came out here to offer my help with Nellie's training."

"No offense," Pip muttered, peering down at me from his lofty perch, "but I think Bob is more qualified to train somebody in the art of combat."

"He's more qualified to train a knight," I agreed as my eyes drifted toward the silhouettes bickering in the shadows across the lawn, "but Nellie is a fairy like me. Our methods of defense are quite different."

"Forgive me for saying so, Princess," Pip muttered, "but your methods didn't seem too effective against the Purists when Godric was holding you captive."

"That's because I didn't remember who *or what* I was at the time. My blinded brain forgot the sort of tricks I was capable of."

"I'm guessing we'll need plenty of tricks if it comes down to a fight," Addison mused as she stepped up behind me.

I turned toward her and was shocked to find Mia at her side. Isa, Brian and Tristan reached us a few seconds later.

"Training for the mission starts tomorrow," Brian murmured as his gaze drifted to Bob and Nellie's conversation across the yard. As his focus shifted back to us, his keen eyes met mine.

I smiled at him with a comfortable familiarity forged by years of shared history. "I'd like to lend a hand with Nellie's training."

Brian nodded. "Benjamin put together a pretty jam-packed agenda for the pre-mission boot camp, but I'll ask him to add giving Nellie some pointers on charming her enemy to the schedule. Tristan can help you with that."

I smiled at Tristan with the same familial tenderness I regarded his brother with.

My display of affection prompted a scowl from Mia, but Tristan winked at me as he wrapped a muscular arm around her shoulders. "I look forward to working with you, sunshine."

Brian stepped up to Pip's tree branch, plucked him from it without warning, and placed him on his broad shoulder. "Let's go get the lovebirds and discuss what we've got planned for tomorrow."

With that, Brian started toward Bob and Nellie, and the rest of us fell into step behind him. Their bickering died off as they heard us approaching.

"Sorry to interrupt," Brian murmured, although he didn't look at all apologetic, "but I came out here to inform everybody that training for the mission starts tomorrow morning at seven sharp."

A sigh of resignation hissed from Bob's lips as he nodded. "We'll be there."

"Nellie," Brian muttered, "Emma and Tristan have volunteered to give you some pointers on charming your enemy."

Nellie's brow furrowed as her eyes darted to Tristan. "I already know how to charm."

"You've got the basics down," Brian agreed, "but you were taught by Godric. Do you honestly think he gave you all the tools you'd need to charm someone like him?"

"I guess, I never really…" Nellie's face fell as her voice trailed off.

"I'll gladly teach you everything I know," Tristan murmured with a dazzling grin, "and Emma can show you how to modify my techniques to a fairy's abilities."

Ignoring the death glare that Bob shot Tristan, Nellie nodded. "Thanks. I'd appreciate that."

⁓

I smiled at David as we approached the Waterfall at the end of the stone corridor. He responded with a sinful grin that made me ache to veer off to an empty cell and forget all about the meeting we were headed to, but there was no more time for delays. If everything proceeded according to plan, the intel-gathering team would be setting out for No Man's Land in the morning. Brian and Benjamin had assured us that every member of the team would be ready by then, and neither of them were likely to miss a deadline, especially when the stakes were this high.

As we stopped in front of the Waterfall, I rose up to my tiptoes to kiss my husband's pursed lips. "They're ready."

A melancholy smile spread across his face as he stroked my cheek with his fingertips. "Perhaps most of them are. However, I am not entirely sure about Charlie."

"He won't disappoint you," I whispered. "You'll see."

"I suppose I will soon enough."

We stepped through the Waterfall hand in hand and stepped out into the palace courtyard, squinting at the light that bombarded our unadjusted eyes. Thanks to a clever incantation that Clay had developed for training purposes, a false sun now burned bright as day in the eternal night sky, temporarily eradicating the absolute darkness that ought to be there. The satori was a miracle worker when it came to potions and spells. It was such a shame that he squandered his talents, spending most of his life in a chemically induced stupor, but we tried not to judge him for it. Some losses are just too monumental for certain souls to bare without the aid of mind-numbing chemicals.

David and I strolled through the courtyard side by side, observing the trainees without comment so as not to distract them while we evaluated their progress.

Nellie's group was closest to the entrance. She was training with Bob and Demetri, the warrior elf in charge of the dungeons. The two men were attempting to attack Nellie, and she was doing an impressive job of fending both of them off with her charm. Neither man was moving, but the tension coiling their muscles as they fought to break free from her spell was palpable. The proud smile on Nellie's face paled in comparison to Bob's. There could be no better confirmation of her readiness for battle.

A satisfied grin tugged at the corners of David's mouth as we ventured a bit farther into the courtyard where Addison was sparring with Rose. It was no small accomplishment to match a dragon's moves blow for blow—especially one who had trained with the royals—but Addison anticipated Rose's every move. She blocked them all with apparent ease and delivered more than one jab to her dragon opponent. Bob had obviously trained her well.

David's grin widened as we approached Mia's group. He and I had both balked at the idea of Mia joining the mission when Tristan and Addison first suggested it. Mia had suffered unthinkable horrors at the hands of the Purists while she was cloaked in my likeness. Asking her to sacrifice anything more for us didn't seem right, but Tristan and Addison insisted that helping bring the monsters who'd harmed her to justice would be far more therapeutic than sitting on any therapist's couch. According to Brian, once Mia decided she wanted to be a part of the mission, she'd focused on her training as if it was as vital to her survival as breathing. She'd even squeezed extra self-defense lessons with Addison into what little free time they had. It hadn't taken her long to develop impressive accuracy with every weapon they introduced her to. She stood between Tristan and Brian, who were taking turns handing her weapons. Brian handed her a bow and arrow, and her arrow landed a few centimeters shy of dead center on the bull's-eye across the yard. The knife that Tristan handed her landed even closer. Focused as she was on her training, Mia gave no indication that she noticed us watching. When the second knife Tristan handed her landed dead center, David's deep chuckle of approval finally captured her attention. A victorious grin lit up her face as she nodded to us.

Thankful she no longer looked at me with hatred in her eyes, I responded with an even wider smile.

Charlie and Benjamin were a fair distance beyond Mia and the incubus brothers. They were both masked in human form, but the fight they were locked in was beyond anything humans were capable of. Benjamin blasted Charlie with a terror-inducing wave of energy that made my skin crawl even at a safe distance, but Charlie blocked its effect without even breaking a sweat. Then he retaliated by breathing a monstrous gust of orange flames from his human mouth. As the flames enveloped him, Benjamin grinned at Charlie like a proud papa. Being the Dragon King's shadow did have its perks. Most shadows' flesh would melt from their bones if dragon fire engulfed them like that, but the Darkness was entirely fireproof.

Shall we begin our meeting?

All eyes in the courtyard fixed on David as his deep Dark voice thundered inside our heads. Then every member of the team placed their weapons on the ground and moved toward us in such a unified manner that it almost seemed choreographed.

David and I headed for the chairs Isa and Clay had set up on the other side of the yard, and every soul in the courtyard fell into step behind us.

As the rest of us settled into our seats, Clay stood from his. He cleared his throat as his eyes wandered over the occupants of our circle. When his eyes met David's, he muttered, "Guess it's my turn to take the floor, huh?" David nodded, and Clay cleared his throat again. "While you folks have been training for this mission, Isa and I have been cooking up a potion that should help you all communicate better in the waking world from now on." Although he said *you all*, his eyes were fixed on Bob.

"Alright, I'll bite," Bob muttered. "What is this potion?"

Clay grinned at Bob as he pulled a vial of violet-colored liquid from his shirt pocket. "It's pretty rare stuff. Not many potion-makers have succeeded in mastering the elaborate brewing process this potion requires, but I perfected the technique for Charlie's mom when she was pregnant with him."

Charlie's raised eyebrow suggested this was the first he'd heard of that. "What is it?"

"A memory potion," Clay muttered as his gaze fixed on the elixir in his hand. "It allows an Unsighted creature to remember both worlds at once, basically granting them temporary Sight."

Bob leaned forward in his seat and squinted at the vile in Clay's hand with renewed interest. "Are you saying that if I drink that, I'll remember what happens here when I'm in the waking world?"

"Yeah," Clay muttered without taking his eyes off the vial, "that's exactly what I'm saying."

"But my mom was Sighted," Charlie muttered. "Why would she need that?"

A sorrowful smile spread across Clay's face as his gaze shifted to Charlie. "She didn't use it on herself. It was for your dad."

"Godric?" Charlie muttered with a perplexed frown. "He's a dragon—"

"I'm not talking about that son of a bitch," Clay growled, hatred glinting in his eyes at the mention of the would-be-king. "I'm talking about the man you knew as your dad."

Charlie opened his mouth to respond but closed it without saying a word.

Clay's expression softened as he muttered, "You and I are gonna go over the rest of your mom's story later today."

Apparently satisfied with Clay's answer to the question he hadn't asked, Charlie nodded.

Clay shot him an apologetic grin as he tucked the vial back in his pocket. Then he sat down and gestured for Doc to take over.

The corners of the witch doctor's bony mouth lifted into a demonic skeletal grin as he rose to his feet. "As most of you already know," he began, his soft soothing voice utterly at odds with his disconcerting appearance, "I will be watching over you in the waking world whilst you are on this mission. You will all be staying at the Talbots' estate for the duration of this venture. We have fashioned the ballroom into a temporary hospital ward, and I will be keeping you sedated there while monitoring your vitals and feeding you intravenously. That way, none of you will drift off to sleep in this world and return to the waking world at a time when it would be perilous to do so. Of course, it rather goes without saying that it would be unwise to sedate *all* of you. Someone must maintain the ability to return to the waking world and inform us if your team is in need of assistance. Pip has agreed to remain unsedated, since his presence would be the least crucial during a battle." Doc flashed Bob's pocket-sized partner a nightmarish grin. "I believe you and Brian have already worked out your travel arrangements."

Pip nodded from his perch in Bob's shirt pocket. "Yup, I'm actually on a plane in the waking world as we speak. In a few hours, Benjamin will be picking me up at the airport and driving me to the Sarrum's house."

"What about you, Addison?" Charlie muttered, turning toward her as if he'd just remembered she was there. "You've got an Unsighted family and a job in the waking world. How are you going to explain being gone for so long?"

Addison smiled at Charlie as she leaned forward in her seat. "I've taken a leave of absence from work, and I told my family I'd be out of town on an undercover operation for a while. It's not entirely untrue. It's just not an undercover operation in the waking world."

As Doc took his seat, Tristan stood from his. "We'll be departing tomorrow morning. If anybody's gonna have a change of heart, now would be the time. Once we set out, there'll be no turning back." He paused a moment, giving anyone who might be having second thoughts the opportunity to speak up. When no one did, he nodded and continued. "I'm not gonna lie. This trip isn't going to be a walk in the park. There's no telling where Godric might have spies in place, so forming temporary portals or traveling through the Waters is out of the question. The Purists could detect that and we don't want to do anything that might tip them off and let them know what we're up to, so we'll be traveling the old-fashioned way. Trekking across Draumer on foot sure as hell won't be the easiest way to get where we're going, but it will be the safest."

"But don't let that fool any of you into thinking there's no danger," Brian added.

Tristan nodded in agreement with his brother as he continued, "We'll be starting out by the Waterfall entrance to the palace and traveling through the Dark Forest to No Man's Land."

"Which is what, exactly?" Charlie muttered, sitting up a little straighter.

"It's the territory that lies between the Dark Forest and the Forest of Light," Benjamin's Dark voice interjected, "and the souls who dwell there are a venomous bunch."

Charlie swallowed back whatever clever remark he was about to make. "Do you mean that *literally*?"

"In some cases, yes," Benjamin replied in an even Darker tone. "The in-between space is populated by creatures who don't appreciate being disturbed. They'll sense that you don't belong there, and they'll do their damndest to convince you to turn the fuck back."

"Awesome," Charlie muttered under his breath.

"Venomous though they may be," David murmured beside me, "they are no match for a pair of dragons from the royal guard and the fierce warriors with whom they are traveling."

Once again, Charlie opened his mouth to speak but closed it without uttering a word. Instead, he responded with a nod of his head.

"Our first stop will be an inn and tavern in the middle of No Man's Land," Tristan continued, "a place called Hell's Gate."

"Fantastic," Pip muttered in a hoarse squeak. "That doesn't sound ominous at all."

"It's just a name," Tristan replied with a shrug. "The establishment is a popular spot for slavers to stop between trades because nobody's likely to come looking for them there, and nobody pokes around asking questions."

"How exactly are we supposed to gather intelignece if we can't ask questions?" Bob interrupted.

Mischief glinted in Tristan's gorgeous green eyes. "We hook up with somebody who doesn't need to ask questions because he's already in the know."

Bob narrowed his eyes at Tristan. "And who might that be?"

"An old friend of mine," Tristan murmured. "The Purists believe he stands with them, but he's on our side."

"How can you be so sure that we're the ones he's really loyal to," Pip chimed in from Bob's pocket, "and not the fools he's supposedly pumping for information?"

"He's with us," Brian stated in a rough whisper as he folded his muscular arms across his chest. "There's no doubt about that."

"And we're just supposed to blindly trust that?" Charlie muttered. "No offense, but that's kinda unnerving when we're putting our lives on the line. Can you tell us anything else about this guy?"

"That's really more up to him than me. It's not my story to tell." A faint grin tugged at the corners of Tristan's perfect mouth. "All I can tell you is that he and I go way back, and I trust him with all our lives without question."

"What do we hope to learn from this old friend of yours?" Bob asked.

"The location of the Purists' new meeting place," Tristan muttered as the smile slipped from his face, "where they'll be holding the next slavers' auction. If all goes according to plan, we'll be traveling to the auction with my friend."

Charlie's gaze drifted toward Mia. "What exactly do we hope to accomplish at the auction?"

"If we get lucky, Godric might be there," Tristan murmured, "but that's a hell of a long shot. We're more likely to get clues as to where he's hiding after we shut the place down and interrogate the Purists who showed up for the auction."

Charlie raised an eyebrow. "How is our little band going to shut them down?"

"That's when Pip would come back and pay us a visit in the waking world," Benjamin chimed in. "We'll be ready and waiting to charge in and shut that operation down for good. But even without reinforcements, you'd stand a decent chance."

"We would?" Charlie muttered.

"You've got two dragons, a couple of badass knights and a few women who are not to be trifled with," Benjamin murmured, "not to mention the fact that

Tristan's pal could take down at least half of them without any backup."

Charlie's eyes widened at that. "Is this guy a dragon?"

"No, but he's half giant," Tristan murmured with a grin. "I've seen him rip a man in half without even breaking a sweat."

"Shit," Pip muttered, "and he's only *half* giant? What's the other half?"

"Incubus," Tristan and Brian answered in unison.

"Damn," Pip muttered. "I'm not sure I can handle a giant-sized version of Tristan."

"There's no handling Ezekiel," Tristan replied with a sinful grin. "That boy marches to the beat of his own drum. You pretty much just have to smile and go with it."

Pip swallowed a gulp of air before asking, "Go with *what*?"

Tristan leveled Pip with a swoon-worthy grin. "Whatever the big guy decides to do."

"Not sure I like the sound of that," Charlie muttered under his breath.

"It'll be fine," Tristan answered. "The man's just a big muscular teddy bear. You're gonna love him."

"Yeah," Pip muttered. "That's kinda what I'm afraid of."

23

DAVID

After all the details of the mission had been discussed and all questions had been answered, the members of our assembled group parted ways to spend one last night with their loved ones before Tristan and his team departed for No Man's Land.

Charlie remained in his chair whilst the others disbanded because he knew his own debriefing was still far from over. I kissed my wife goodbye and watched her depart from the courtyard with Benjamin and Brian. Then I stood from my chair, crossed the circle and took the empty seat beside Charlie's.

He met my eyes with an uneasy grin and a whispered, "Hello."

I responded to his tentative greeting with a nod. "I trust you are ready for one last session with me?"

"Sure," he muttered. "One last session to cover the umpteen-thousand things on the list of what I still need to learn. That oughta cover it."

I raised an eyebrow and leveled him with the sort of glare that my Aunt Louise used to give me and my cousins whenever we acted like dolts during a lesson. "I suggest you put learning to drop the sarcasm at the top of that list of yours."

"Right," he muttered as he lowered his eyes to the ground. "Sorry. Guess I'm a little nervous about what we might be walking into on this mission."

"You would be a fool not to be nervous," I replied as I stood from my chair. "Shall we go start that lesson? Time is of the essence after all."

"Sure," Charlie muttered as he stood up. "Where are we going?"

I pointed toward the highest balcony on the far side of the palace. "Let's begin up there, shall we?" I unmasked and took to the sky without waiting for whatever sarcastic remark was sure to follow my words.

"What the hell?" Charlie grumbled from the ground. "This isn't exactly the time to play games, is it?"

I circled back and swooped down to the airspace directly above his head. *I do not play games, Mr. Oliver.* With that, I sped through the air toward the balcony at the far side of the palace, descending just low enough to grip Rose's slender waist and lift her into the air along with me.

She let out a startled shriek as we ascended toward the tower.

I grinned at her as she looked up at me. *You don't mind assisting me with Charlie's lesson this evening, do you?*

No, I guess not.

Even telepathically, there was a slight waver to her voice because I'd caught her so off guard. *I do apologize for the lack of warning, Rose. This needed to appear spontaneous in order to sufficiently rattle your boyfriend.*

Of course. I understand. I'm happy to help Charlie however I can.

She sounded calmer already, and her heart rate had almost returned to normal. *Excellent.*

A roar of frustration shook the ground far below, and Rose shook her head as she looked down at Charlie. *Why isn't he following us?*

Didn't he tell you? He has not yet mastered the art of flying. A massive dose of adrenaline is still required to get him off the ground.

No, he didn't tell me. But I overheard Benji telling my mother that his first lesson didn't go so well.

Actually, it went just as I suspected it would. When push comes to shove, I have no doubt that Charlie's instincts will take over. We just need to help him realize that on a primal level. How far are you willing to take this little charade of ours?

As far as you need me to, boss.

That's exactly what I was hoping you'd say. Just know that I would never actually harm you. Do you trust me?

Yes, without question, she replied as we reached the balcony.

I set her on her feet, landed beside her without a sound and masked myself in human form. We moved to the rail and stood side by side in silence, watching for several minutes as Charlie's composure unraveled. His breathing was shallow and furious, his heart was racing, and smoke billowed from his flared nostrils in sporadic gusts.

Training you has been a hopeless waste of time, Mr. Oliver. You are unworthy of a partner as noble and skilled as Rose.

Charlie unmasked as he stomped across the courtyard toward our end of the palace on foot, compacting the ground beneath him several feet with each point of contact. As he raced toward us, he growled his response telepathically. *What's that supposed to mean?*

I am claiming her for myself, I replied in a nonchalant tone that was guaranteed to infuriate my young apprentice. *She deserves a dragon who is capable of rescuing her, should the need arise. You are far more likely to need her help escaping your own capture.*

The hell I am! A deafening crack of thunder punctuated the end of Charlie's sentence. An instant later, the ground shook as a bolt of lightning streaked the sky.

Rose turned her head toward me to conceal a grin that she couldn't entirely suppress.

I resisted the urge to smile back as I eyed my young cousin through flame-filled eyes. *Is that meant to intimidate me? I have seen more impressive effects produced by a toddler in the throes of a temper tantrum.*

Another growl from below shook the palace as a massive streak of lightning lit the sky. Yet Charlie remained on the ground, pacing back and forth several stories below us. *Don't you dare lay a finger on her!*

Or what, hmm? I grinned at him as I wrapped an arm around Rose's waist and drew her closer to my side. *What will you do, Mr. Oliver?*

I'll tear you apart, Charlie growled as another clap of thunder shook the ground.

Please. We both know you haven't got the means to stop me from doing anything. If I choose to claim this female, there is little you could do to stop me.

His rage-fueled bellow produced another deafening crack of thunder, followed by a series of lightning bolts in quick succession. *I will destroy you, you arrogant son of a bitch!*

I filled Charlie's head with the sound of my laughter. Then I lifted his girlfriend off her feet and tossed her over my shoulder with no semblance of gentleness, confidant that Rose was onboard with this charade and tough enough to withstand any minor discomfort it might cause her. She was a warrior—a dragon trained by the royals—capable of besting the dragon below who so desperately desired to protect her from harm.

If I'd had any doubts about Rose's consent, her agonized shriek might have given me pause. Draped over my shoulder with her back to Charlie, she winked at me to alleviate any qualms I might have.

I directed my next thought to her. *I take it you do not fear that we might be pushing him too far?*

No, this is necessary. Charlie needs to be ready by tomorrow. There's no time for coddling at this point.

An involuntary grin spread across my face at Rose's use of Benjamin's catchphrase.

Charlie misinterpreted my smile as a venomous display of pleasure in overpowering his girlfriend. His roar of protest shook every stone in the palace and every fixture within its walls as he took to the sky with one massive beat of his wings. Gaining momentum with each wing stroke, he reached us mere seconds after his feet left the ground.

I turned my back to him and headed toward the Waterfall at the other end of the balcony with Rose still draped over my shoulder.

Charlie's growl died in his throat as Rose crossed her arms over my shoulder blade and propped her head up with her hands, the playful grin on her face telling him all he needed to know. He unmasked with a grunt of frustration as I stepped into the Waterfall without looking back. I didn't want the proud grin on my face to go to his head. Where they were headed, Charlie needed to keep his head out of the clouds.

24

CHARLIE

Embarrassed that I'd gotten so riled up over the King's little ruse, and pissed that Rose had gone along with it, I unmasked and followed the two of them off the balcony through the Waterfall. It took my eyes a minute to adapt to the room I stepped into because the lighting was so dim—actually, *dim* doesn't adequately describe it. Somehow, the room was both blindingly bright and pitch-dark at the same time. I realize that makes no sense, but there's no logical way to explain what my eyes were experiencing. Although, if I'd learned anything during my time with the Sarrum and his handpicked family of Sighted individuals, it was that things didn't always have to make logical sense in Draumer, and they quite often didn't. By the time my eyes had adjusted enough to make out my surroundings, the Sarrum and Rose were seated in sumptuous black velvet cushioned chairs in front of a roaring fire. There was no grate to contain the raging inferno that burned a deep brilliant blue within the massive stone fireplace. I imagine it was those sapphire flames that gave the room its inexplicable mood lighting, as well as a room temperature that felt hot enough to roast a turkey. *And damned if I didn't feel like the turkey.*

I mopped the sweat from my brow with a shirtsleeve, and did my best to expunge the visual of my sizzling flesh roasting on my bones as I moved toward them, surveying our extravagant surroundings. Describing the dome-ceilinged stone hall as *beyond humongous* would still be a gross understatement. The medieval style sitting room was downright colossal. A gigantic plush black rug adorned with elaborate silver embroidery covered most of the polished stone floor, and the portion of the floor that was showing appeared to be made of moonstone. Its gleaming white surface reflected the sapphire flames dancing in the fireplace, magnifying their effect and giving the room an otherworldly glow. The stone walls were adorned with ancient-looking tapestries that were all in mint condition and looked like they should be hanging on the walls of a museum. Each impressive work of art depicted a fairytale-type scene, the majority of them not surprisingly featuring dragons and fairies. The tapestries were evenly spaced between hefty silver wall sconces that held azure-flamed candles burning much brighter than any fire ought to. Across the room, a second noiseless Waterfall spilled from ceiling to floor. The cavernous space between the two Waterfall entrances was furnished with an array of haphazard groupings of couches and chairs, all of which were upholstered in sumptuous black velvet, and silver and black silk.

I took a seat in a chair with an elaborately carved ebony frame and overstuffed black silk cushions. Although, I thought better of it as soon as I realized sitting directly across from the Sarrum and Rose wasn't exactly ideal. I was still trying to suppress my red-faced reaction to Rose having witnessed my utter lack of prowess in flight. But standing up again to choose another seat would only emphasize my discomfort and make me seem even more pathetic.

Sensing my embarrassment, Rose flashed me a sheepish grin as she stood from her chair and crossed the empty space between us. She bent to kiss my cheek, then crossed the room and stepped out through the Waterfall without saying a word.

Awesome. Now I looked like an incompetent fool and a jackass.

"She thinks no less of you," the King murmured as he shifted in his seat to cross his legs, somehow managing to make even that simple movement seem regal and elegant.

My eyes drifted to the Waterfall my girlfriend had just stepped through. "How could she not?"

"Because she loves you," he replied matter-of-factly, "and she understands all too well how overwhelming a dragon's bestial impulses can be."

I nodded, then dropped my eyes to the floor to escape the Sarrum's astute gaze.

"You must learn to hold onto the rage that you felt when I flew off with Rose," the Sarrum murmured in that soft-spoken voice of his that commanded his listeners' absolute attention.

The suggestion prompted me to look up at him. "Why the hell would I want to hold onto that?"

The sardonic grin that spread across his face made my cheeks flame. "Because that feral rage will allow you to take flight whenever you like."

"Huh?"

"That all-consuming bestial need to protect your most precious treasure is exactly the sort of emotional state that is required to achieve flight."

"Then…" I paused to cross my legs, far less gracefully than him, "why are you still so in control of your actions while you're flying?"

"Years of practice," he replied. "And as you'll recall, my actions were far from calm and rational whilst dealing with the Purists after Emma's abduction."

I flinched at the reference to my friend's recent kidnapping, the kidnapping that *my* stupidity had facilitated. "Right."

"Some of it never goes away," he mused in that commanding hushed tone of his.

"Some of *what*?"

"The rage that springs us into action. There are moments when banishing it is all but impossible for even the most practiced of dragons. The key to remaining in control is in learning to suppress the rage and store it away for a future situation where you may use it to your advantage. Channel the fury into your actions and allow that suppressed rage to power your efforts during flight, combat, or interrogation."

"Okay," I muttered, "but how exactly do I do that?"

"That, you must figure out on your own." As he finished his sentence, the Sarrum stood from his chair and headed toward the Waterfall at the far end of the room.

I sat there and watched him like an idiot, until it occurred to me that he meant for me to get off my ass and follow him. Seconds after I got to my feet, he stepped into the Waterfall without looking back or offering a word of explanation.

I hustled to the Waterfall, afraid to let too much time lapse between our exits. If I waited too long, I might transport myself to God-only-knew-where instead of wherever the King expected me to follow him to. The moment I reached the Waterfall, I all but leapt in.

I hopped out in an entirely foreign alternate-universe type environment. Hell, for all I knew it might've been a different planet. It was pitch-dark and cold as hell, the painful artic kind of cold that permeates your bones and sets your teeth chattering the instant it hits you. I tugged the ends of my sleeves down over my hands and wrapped my arms around my torso in an effort to conserve what little body heat I could. Then I turned in slow motion, searching the nightmarish landscape for my badass but incredibly frustrating flight instructor. I couldn't see a damn thing, even with my enhanced dragon night vision. A hushed growl of frustration escaped my throat in a visible mist of frozen breath, the first thing my eyes managed to register.

A chorus of far-off growls answered, like an echo of mine—only *magnified*.

Fuck. What if I hadn't followed the Sarrum through the Waterfall fast enough? Would he be able to locate me if I'd teleported myself to some alternate dimension?

The pack of growling sounds came again.

Yeah, that definitely wasn't just an echo of *my* growl. I was too terrified to have made another sound. Plus, my vocal cords were frozen by a mix of fear and the early stages of hypothermia.

The growls sounded again, closer this time.

Fuck. Fuck. Fuck. Unsure what else to do, I spun around toward the Waterfall to make a coward's retreat.

But the Waterfall wasn't there anymore.

Another chorus of growls sounded, so close that I suspected I could reach out and touch the creatures they'd emanated from—which meant that *they* could touch me.

Shit. What was I supposed to do now? There was a lesson I was supposed to be working on, wasn't there? Something important was about to happen. There was somewhere I needed to be tomorrow...somewhere I had to go. *Damn it.* It was so fucking cold, my brain was beginning to freeze up. *What the fuck was the point of this?*

Channel your rage. The thought hadn't come from an external source, yet the voice that sounded in my head wasn't mine. Still, I knew he wasn't there in the dark with me—whoever *he* was. This was just an echo, a memory of his words. Recent words. It hadn't been long since he'd spoken those words to me. Channel my rage. *What rage?* I was scared out of my wits, but I wasn't mad. I was too cold and petrified to be angry about anything. So, why did the voice that'd echoed in my head tell me to channel my rage? Channel it into *what?* Even if I was furious about something, what the hell was I supposed to channel that fury into?

Flight. Combat. Interrogation.

Right. Thanks, Mr. All-powerful-voice-inside-my-head. There was nobody around to interrogate—except for those growling creatures cloaked in the darkness, but grilling them for information seemed pointless. So…I could probably cross that suggestion off the list. *Combat?* I could try to fight those shapeless growling entities, but why the fuck would I *want* to? Yep, I could strike that option off the list too. So…what did that leave me with? *Flight?* Flying in pitch-darkness didn't seem like the brightest idea, but the voice in my head hadn't given me any other options. So, it was probably time to channel some rage. *Rage over what?* Was there something I was supposed to be angry about?

A vision flashed through my head, as if answering my question—a monstrous black dragon with wings that sparkled like the night sky blanketed by a thousand stars with a beautiful girl in his clutches. *My beautiful girlfriend.* Was that son of a bitch who'd flown off with her here in the dark with me? Maybe I'd taken combat off the table too hastily.

The growling came again, so near that it reverberated inside my head.

Channel my rage. I pictured that bastard flying off with my girlfriend, and a much deeper growl than all of theirs combined rumbled from my throat.

Something took a swipe at me with a claw, or maybe a tooth. Whatever it was, it was razor sharp.

I winced as it sliced through my flesh, and another growl barreled from my throat as I swung a fist to defend myself from my invisible attacker. My fist didn't connect with anything. But a moment later, a pack of arms reached out toward me—more claws, more teeth.

DREAM FRAGMENTS

I howled in pain, a warning for all of them to step the hell back. But the shapeless creatures didn't back off.

Channel your rage.

How the fuck was I supposed to do that? *Channel it into what?*

Something broad and sharp lashed out at me again, slicing a gash across my cheek.

I lifted a hand to my face, and my fingers came away wet and sticky with blood. The vision of that dragon flying off with my girl—*my treasure*—came again as another claw raked across my forehead.

I held onto the image of that girl—*my girl*—as I exhaled, bathing the faceless creatures that surrounded me in fire. I could see the bright orange flames barreling from my mouth, but I still couldn't see my attackers.

I *heard* them though.

Their high-pitched shrieks echoed through the darkness as I took flight. *Holy crap, I was flying.* As soon as I thought it, my body sunk like a stone plunging through the murky depths of a lake. But I thought of that girl and the dragon again and pushed the air behind me with a determined stroke of my wings, like a swimmer propelling himself through water. *That was the trick, damn it.* We're all capable of swimming, but those who can't swim sink because they *believe* they'll sink. I just had to remain confident that I *could* fly, and I'd be able to. Deep in thought as I puzzled that out, I lost focus and my body plummeted down toward those hidden creatures. Okay, so it wasn't just about believing. *Channel your rage.* I thought of that bastard who'd stolen my treasure as I pushed the air behind my wings, and the angrier the image made me, the higher I soared.

I'm not sure how long I flew through the darkness like a giddy kid who'd figured out how to pedal his bike without training wheels. It was long enough for my wings to grow tired and my lungs to become exhausted. *Shit. What now?* There was no Water to take me back to where I'd come from, and no wise powerful teacher to tell me what to do next. So despite my exhaustion, I flew on for what felt like forever. Eventually, my thoughts grew clearer as my wings and my lungs continued to weaken. I remembered who I was, and the mission I was supposed to embark on in the morning, and the King who'd left me to rot here in the darkness. A vision of the Sarrum waving his hand ever so elegantly to summon the Waters popped into my head. I knew I could forget the elegant part. That wasn't happening. I had no doubt about that. But I'd figured out how to fly. Maybe I could stumble onto the Water summoning technique out of shear dumb luck too.

I let myself drift down to the ground that I still couldn't see. I waited a moment to be sure my attackers weren't nearby. Then I waved a hand in the air like a crazy jackass, and…nothing happened. What a shocker that was. So, what was I supposed to do now? *Channel your rage.* Well, I was mildly pissed off that I'd been left here to fumble around in the dark like an idiot. But that wouldn't do. So, I thought of Godric freezing my limbs and taking off with Emma from the clearing, and a monstrous roar barreled from my throat. As I pictured myself tearing Godric apart—like I'd wanted to—I swiped a clawed hand through the darkness and demanded that the Waters make an appearance.

And son of a bitch, *they did*.

I took a deep breath and pictured the great stone hall I'd entered this alternate universe from. Then I stepped in, grinning from ear to ear.

The temperature differential, between the frigid climate I'd exited and the stifling heat in the room I stepped into, robbed the breath from my lungs.

As I sunk to my knees on the stone floor, the Sarrum's voice sounded behind me. "Well, it certainly took you long enough."

But I could hear the grin he was suppressing in the triumphant tone of his voice.

There was an extra spring in my step as I headed down the stone corridor toward the atrium. Although I wouldn't have admitted it to anyone, the proud grin that'd spread across the Sarrum's face after I finally figured out how to fly meant a lot to me. It almost reminded me of the way he looked at Emma—well, minus the adoration, and the desire—just beaming with pride at his prized pupil. I knew I still had a long way to go in my training with the Sarrum, but now I could set out on the mission, confident that I could take flight or summon the Waters if a situation arose where I needed to.

I stopped at the end of the corridor and made a conscious effort to wipe the dorky grin off my face. Then I stepped through the Waterfall into the atrium where Clay had instructed me to meet him. The final phase of my pre-mission training was one last trip down memory lane with my mother's best friend. There wasn't enough time to cover all the details of my mom's story, but Clay was determined to fill me in on the most important parts before we set out for No Man's Land in the morning.

Clay was seated on a bench at the far end of the atrium, smoking a long Tolkien-esque pipe. He looked up with a guilty scowl as I stepped into the room. When he realized it was just me, he shrugged and flashed me a crooked grin. "Didn't see any *no smoking* signs in here."

I let out a laugh as I crossed the room and sat down beside him. "Yeah, it's probably just a given. Don't worry, your secret's safe with me."

Clay's expression grew somber as he tipped the pipe upside down, shook its contents onto the stone floor, and snuffed out the sparks with the heel of his boot. "It's not easy reliving the past," he muttered, "especially the parts we're about to cover. Guess I needed a little synthetic courage to help get me through it."

I did my best to ignore the tears in his eyes to keep myself from tearing up. After all the memories he'd shared with me, I was starting to feel like I actually knew my mother. "I'm not judging."

"Didn't think you would," he muttered with a smirk. Then he dropped his eyes to the pile of ashes on the floor and spread it out a bit more with his foot as he cleared his throat. "We should probably get right to it, since we're kinda working under a deadline tonight."

As I slid closer and extended my arm to him, I couldn't help wondering if I'd feel the effects of whatever mind-altering chemical he'd been smoking.

"It's just tobacco," he muttered, as if reading my mind. "I'm pretty sure the Darkness would kick my ass if he caught me smoking anything else on the palace grounds."

"Isa would kick your ass if she caught you grinding your ashes into the floor."

A hoarse chuckle escaped his throat. "Thanks for the warning. Guess I don't really wanna piss off any creature who doesn't fear the Darkness."

He placed a hand on my arm, and I braced myself for the impending vertigo as the room around us melted away.

As a new room took its place, Clay's gruff voice filled in the gaps in the narrative that we were skipping over due to the time constraints. "The last time we did this, I stopped on the day we went to the Sarrum's law office to ask for protection from the Purists. After Angel told the Darkness she was carrying Godric's child, he drove us to the Sarrum's home in the waking world straightaway."

As soon as Clay mentioned the Talbots' house, I recognized the room I was sitting in. The furniture was different, and the walls were a different color, but the basic layout of the living room in the Talbots' estate was the same.

My mom stepped through the door and smiled at me as she crossed the room and sat down on the couch beside me. We were obviously glossing over a lot of time since the day she and Clay told Benjamin she was carrying Godric's child—*carrying me*. The breezy fabric of her sleeveless maternity shirt was stretched tight across a full round belly. Looking at her up close like this, I could see what a toll the pregnancy was taking on her. Dark circles underscored her eyes, which were much duller than they used to be, and despite how round her belly had become, her face looked thinner and a bit too pale for the sunny weather outside the windows. The monster growing inside her belly was draining the life from her.

That horrific realization brought to mind something the Sarrum said to me the day we first met. *I have the utmost respect for any woman who would endure so much suffering to bring another life into the world.* That's when it hit me. Benjamin had witnessed my mother's suffering, and Isa's, and the suffering of Lord only knew how many other women. I finally grasped why he was so opposed to my relationship with Rose. *This* was what we'd risk by having a physical relationship in the waking world. No wonder Benjamin stood back while some Unsighted man married the love of his life. A pang of guilt gripped me, and not just because of the stress I'd caused Benjamin. *I had done this* to the pretty young girl sitting beside me on the couch, the girl who'd looked so innocent and full of life in that first memory Clay shared with me. She endured all of this agony just to bring me into the world. *Why didn't Clay hate me for that?*

I smiled at her as I wrapped an arm around her, and she snuggled closer and dropped her head to my shoulder.

"The Sarrum put us both up in his home that day," Clay muttered in my ear. "We never set foot back in my apartment. He provided us with all the necessities—

clothes, food, prenatal care for Angel—and most importantly, he provided security. There was only one problem. She only spent half her time in the waking world. In Draumer, Angel was still the Purists' prisoner and we had no clue where they were keeping her. Wherever she was being held, it was heavily warded. The Sarrum had dispersed the royal guard all over the kingdom to look for her, but their search didn't turn anything up, which could mean only one thing. Godric was keeping her concealed in a mirage somewhere. Since I was pretty much on my own in Draumer, I started searching for that demon who approached me in the tavern to tip me off about Godric's plan to impregnate Angel. Turned out, the guy was a customer of mine in the waking world. Our history was what compelled him to risk approaching me in Draumer, but that's a long story. We don't have time to go into all that."

"So," Angel whispered as she tilted her head to look up at me—I mean, *at Clay*—"you really found him?"

"Yeah," Clay's voice muttered from my mouth, "but he doesn't know how to lead us to the mirage where they're keeping you. The Purists blindfolded him when they transported him there after they nabbed you, and they haven't let him outside at all."

"Then what happens now?" she asked in a faint whisper.

"He's gonna help you escape," Clay muttered. "He says there's a small window of opportunity during the changing of the guards, and he's gonna sneak you out of there tonight. Once you get beyond the mirage, the

Sarrum and the royal guard should be able to find you."

Tears filled my mother's eyes as she shook her head. "I don't want them to find me."

I couldn't tell whether it was my shock or Clay's constricting my throat as I whispered, "What're you talking about?"

She flashed me a melancholy grin. "Think about it, Clay. What sort of life would Godric's son have if he grew up in the Sarrum's palace?"

Until she mentioned it, I—that is, *Clay*—hadn't given it much thought. "It'd be a better life than he'd have with Godric."

"But it wouldn't be a normal life," she croaked, her voice thick with tears.

"There's nothing normal about any of this," Clay muttered…

…"The demon did help Angel escape that night," Clay narrated in a gruff whisper as the memory dissolved, "and against my better judgment, I respected her wishes and didn't tell the Sarrum that she'd gotten free. I planned to find her on my own in Draumer, and we figured we could hash the rest of the plan out together once we got somewhere safe. Till then, I told her to get to the fringe as fast as she could. I figured that'd be the safest place for her because the Purists wouldn't expect her to run to Unsighted territory."

A queasiness washed over me as we hovered somewhere between one memory and the next, two disembodied voices floating in a void of nothingness. *How could Clay have been so stupid, leaving my pregnant mother to fend for herself in Draumer?* I reminded myself that this had all occurred in the past, and I wanted to know the rest of her story. I *needed* to know.

"What's happening?" I croaked. "Why aren't we moving to the next memory?" *Was it possible for us to get stuck like this?*

"This next part might feel kinda disorienting," Clay muttered, and I almost thought I detected a note of apology in his gruff whisper, "because the next bunch of memories aren't mine."

The *next part* might feel disorienting? *Every damn bit of this had been disorienting.* "What the hell does that mean?" I muttered. "Whose memories are they, and how did you get them?"

"They're her memories, Charlie. She always meant for me to tell you her story—*your story*—at some point. She wanted you to see it through her eyes," Clay whispered, "only, detached from the physical pain of it..."

Another wave of queasiness washed over me at the mention of my mother's suffering, the suffering *I had caused*. "How is that possible?"

"She shared these memories with me in the waking world," he explained, "so I could show them to you when you grew up, and you could see what happened during her final days."

Her final days. If I hadn't felt so detached from my body, the nausea that those words evoked would've brought my dinner up...

...A new landscape coalesced around me before I could dwell on that thought for too long. The sun was just beginning to chase away the darkness at the dawn of a new day as I—I mean, *my mother*—stumbled from the forest and stepped toward the Water. *I did it.* I made it to the fringe, and nobody had followed me.

I stood still, closed my eyes, and breathed the dew-drenched air deep into my lungs. It had been far too long since I'd breathed fresh air in this world. I opened my eyes as I kicked off my shoes. Tears spilled down my cheeks as I sunk my bare toes in the sand and whispered, "I did it, Clay. I made it to the fringe. Now, I just hope you can find me." I wiped the tears from my cheeks as I stepped toward the Water with a smile on my face, the first smile that'd spread across my face in months.

"I wouldn't wade in there if I were you," a familiar male voice behind me cautioned, startling the hell out of me.

The terror-stricken pounding of my mother's heart confused me, until I realized his voice wasn't familiar to *her*. It was familiar to *me*. A curious mix of her fear and my joy gripped me as I turned toward the voice.

"That Water's cold as hell this early in the morning. You're bound to catch your death of colds if you set foot in it."

My dad looked so young. I couldn't remember him ever looking that youthful. It seemed so odd, not to feel the ache I should've felt as I remembered his final words to eight-year-old me before I ran to the Waters and left him to die. *I love you, Charlie. Keeping you safe has been my life's goal since the day I met your mother. Let me take my last breath knowing I kept my promise to her.* Those words made so much more sense now. But my dad was Unsighted. How did he end up raising me in the waking world?

DREAM FRAGMENTS

Tears stung my eyes—that is, *my mother's eyes*—as I opened my mouth to speak.

My dad froze the instant he noticed the way she was trembling. "Hey now," he murmured in a soft soothing tone that prompted a rush of memories—of him comforting me as he bandaged a cut, or chased an imaginary monster out of my closet in the middle of the night. "It's alright. I'm not going to hurt you."

All of my mother's resolve, everything that she'd been holding back through all those months of captivity, it all crumbled away at the sound of this man's compassionate voice. Somehow, she knew without a doubt that she could trust this man with the kind eyes and the empathetic smile. *She was safe, and she wasn't alone anymore.* For a moment my mother hesitated, frozen where she stood with tears streaming down her cheeks. "Do you live here?"

"For the moment," my dad murmured, his tone soft and gentle. "I don't normally stay in one spot for too long."

This man was a nomad who lived on the fringe. *He was Unsighted.* It would be wrong to confide in him and share everything that she'd been through. But she'd been wronged in so many ways, and this didn't *feel* wrong. Being here on the fringe, talking to this man *felt so right.* To hell with the rules. She didn't owe the Sighted anything...

"After she found your dad," Clay's voice muttered as the scenery dissolved, "she asked me not to come looking for her in Draumer. Against my better judgment, I kept her secret from the Sarrum and Benjamin like she asked me to. We let them believe

Godric still had her, until she realized she needed their help."

...As the world around me solidified, I found myself—or rather, *my mom*—inside a quaint little cabin. From what I could see outside the windows, it looked like the sky was beginning to darken. But judging from all the trees out there, this cabin was tucked deep in the woods, so it might've been brighter beyond the forest. One thing I was sure of, this place wasn't on the Talbots' property in the waking world or within the palace grounds in Draumer. The interior of the cabin was way too rustic to belong to royalty.

A breeze wafted into the cabin's main room as the door opened, and I—that is, *my mom*—shifted on the couch with one hand resting on her big round belly. She smiled at my dad as he shut the door with his free hand, the other hand wrapped around a bundle of wood.

As I watched him carry the wood across the room to the fireplace and add a few pieces to the fire, I felt the baby kick. Although, I didn't want to dwell on that for too long, since that baby was *me*. I was beginning to understand why Clay had stopped to warn me that these memories would be especially disorienting. It wasn't right to feel your fetal-self kicking inside your own swollen belly. Giving that too much thought might make my head explode.

"Thank you, Jack," my mom's voice murmured from my mouth as he sat down beside me.

He responded with the most unabashedly loving grin I'd ever witnessed. I tried to think back to my childhood in the waking world before my dad passed away. I'd been too young to pay much attention to things like that, but I was pretty sure he'd never looked at my mom that way—that is, the woman I grew up believing to be my mom. Like I said, dwelling on that stuff for too long was liable to make my head explode. He placed a reverent hand on my mom's belly. "Is he kicking again?" *This was getting a little too trippy.*

"Yes," she whispered as she sunk against him with her back reclining against his chest, feeling utterly safe and content as his arms wrapped around her. "Jack, we need to talk about what's going to happen after—"

"After you deliver this baby," my dad interrupted, "I'll keep you both safe. That's a promise."

"Jack—"

"Don't go there, Angie," he murmured against my ear. "Everything's gonna be fine."

"Jack, be reasonable," my mom whispered. "I told you, the odds of me surviving this birth—"

"Are twenty percent," he interrupted. "That means there's a solid chance you could pull through this. You keep talking like there's no chance at all of you living to raise this kid. Why don't we focus on that twenty percent chance of a positive outcome?"

"I need to know it's all going to be okay after I'm—"

"I can't," he whispered. "Now that I've met you, I can't fathom a world without you in it."

"But I need to know that if I don't survive…" my mom paused out of habit, expecting him to cut her off like he normally did. When he didn't, she whispered, "I need to know that my baby will be safe no matter what happens."

"I'll keep him safe till my dying breath, Angie," he muttered in a thick whisper. "That's a promise."

"But there's more to it than just raising him in this world."

I felt the bristle of my dad's scruff as he shook his head without taking his cheek from mine—I mean, *hers*. "I still have a hard time wrapping my head around all that *other world* stuff."

"I know," my mom muttered. "I never should've told you about it."

"Why?" he whispered. "Because it's against the rules? So is what that monster did to you. Damn their rules. I'm glad you told me."

"I am too," she whispered. "You're the only one I trust to raise my child the right way."

"You do realize, I don't know the first thing about raising a royal dragon."

"All that matters to me," she whispered, "is that you raise him to be a good person like you."

His scruff brushed against my cheek again as he nodded. "I'll do my absolute best to raise him in a way that'd make you proud."

"But he'll still need a father to raise him in the other world," my mom whispered. "The Sarrum has a law firm there. I spoke to him last week about finding you in the waking world, and reaching out to you to arrange an adoption after…" As her voice trailed off, I realized my mom *wanted* him to cut her off so she wouldn't have to say it.

"And?" my dad prodded in a gentle whisper.

My mom hesitated a few seconds before muttering, "They've located you in the waking world."

"Then why don't they bring you to me now, instead of waiting for…the baby to come?"

"You're Unsighted," my mom muttered. "That wouldn't make any sense to you."

"I believe it would," he murmured. "I'd like to think that on some level, I'd recognize you and realize what you mean to me."

"You're married in the other world," my mom replied in a hoarse whisper.

"But that woman's not my soul mate," my dad replied without missing a beat.

"How can you say that?" my mom muttered. "You don't even know her."

"You're the only one for me," he whispered. "I'm sure of that. I think if I met you in the other world, some part of me would realize we were made for each other."

"It's against the rules to meddle in the lives of the Unsighted like that," my mom whispered.

"Screw their rules," he grumbled.

"I can't," she muttered, choking back tears. "The Sarrum is protecting me from Godric and his followers in the waking world. It wouldn't be safe for me to run off after an Unsighted man who'd think I was insane when I showed up on his doorstep."

"I didn't think you were insane when you showed up on my shore," he reminded her.

"If it was only my life I'd be putting at risk, I would consider it," she whimpered, "but I can't risk this baby's life. The Purists can't get their hands on him. I will not let those monsters raise my son."

"Alright," my dad whispered, tightening his hold on me. "I can respect that, but you have to promise me two things."

"What things?" my mom whispered.

"First, promise me that you'll fight," he whispered. "Don't just assume you've got no shot at surviving this birth. Be strong, and do your damndest to stay here with us."

"What's the second thing?" my mom muttered, knowing full well she had no shot at surviving the birth. This wasn't just any baby in her belly. This child was the son of the dragon who should be sitting on the throne by birthright. This baby's father was the strongest of the strong, but that wasn't the only reason she knew she would die during childbirth. She could feel him draining her. This baby was strong, and he craved all the power and magic he could devour. He'd drain every ounce of it from her when he entered the world because that's what his kind were bred to do.

"Promise me that *when* you survive," my dad whispered, "you'll find me in that other world."

My mom's eyes filled with tears as she nodded, knowing full well she'd never be able to do either of the things he was asking her to...

"Wait," I muttered, my stomach rolling as the atrium reformed around us, "that's not the end."

Clay cleared his throat as he shook his head. "That's all we've got time for tonight."

No, damn it! I needed to see the rest of it! I dropped my eyes to the floor and muttered, "I can't stop there. Give me the cliff notes version of the rest."

When I looked up at him, he was wiping a tear from his cheek. "The Sarrum arranged an adoption after your mom..."

I nodded, so he wouldn't feel obliged to finish that sentence. "How did the Sarrum get that to make sense to my dad?"

A melancholy smile spread across Clay's face. "Remember that memory potion I cooked up for Bob?"

"You gave that to my dad?"

"Your mom did," Clay muttered with a wistful smile. "We worked the potion out together in the waking world, and Isa helped us figure out how to tweak the recipe to things that could be found near the cabin where Angel was hiding. Your dad went out and searched the forest for anything and everything he could find. Your mom told us what he'd collected, and being the brilliant fucking potion-makers that we were, the three of us worked out a concoction that Angel could brew for your dad in that little fireplace in the cabin."

"So he took the potion in Draumer," I muttered, mirroring Clay's grin despite the ache in my chest, "and he remembered my mom in the waking world?"

Clay nodded.

I tried to think back over our time together. *Had my dad ever mentioned Draumer in the waking world?* "How long did my dad's temporary Sight last?"

"Your mom brewed enough potion to last him a year," Clay muttered, "but we lost track of you both after the adoption, so I don't know for certain when he actually ran out."

"How did they get adopting a random stranger's baby to make sense to his wife?" I muttered, a dull ache in my brain reminding me that *his wife* was the woman who raised me as her son.

"They made up some story about Angela being your dad's cousin. Your dad told her the two of them had been thick as thieves as kids, but she'd moved away and they'd lost touch. From what I gathered, his wife wasn't real keen on the idea at first," Clay muttered with an apologetic frown. "But your dad was insistent that he wanted to raise his cousin's baby, and somehow he convinced her to go along with it."

"Well, that explains my mom's detached method of parenting," I muttered. "She never wanted me in the first place."

"She wasn't your mom," Clay muttered. "Your mom loved you with her whole heart. She sacrificed everything to keep you safe. And your dad, biological or not, that man loved your mom more than anything. He never got to tell her that in the waking world, but I was there for the first adoption meeting between him and the Sarrum. Your dad told me he would've done anything for the chance to tell Angel that he'd been right all along. His love for that woman who raised you paled in comparison to his love for your mom. He shared that with me because Angel had asked him to reassure me that you'd be okay with him." Clay stopped to clear his throat before adding, "I would've raised you myself...except, your dad...he was a good man who could bring you up right. I was just a drug dealer."

The sorrow in his eyes made my voice come out in a hoarse whisper, "I appreciate everything you did for my mom."

"Anyway," Clay muttered with a nod, "your dad told me he planned to raise you with every bit of the love he felt for your mom. He said you were a part of her that lived on, and he loved you fiercely for that. I didn't doubt it for a second when he told me he'd love you till his dying breath."

A tear slid down my cheek as I muttered, "He did."

"I know," Clay whispered.

My final moments with my dad flashed through my mind. *I promised your mother that if there ever came a day when we couldn't get away, I'd have you drink this and escape through the Waters.* "That vial of stuff that he poured down my throat before he died," I muttered, blinking back tears, "what was that?" *Bury it, Charlie. Never let them see what you are and never let the Water out of your sight.*

"It was a backup potion that your mom and I came up with," Clay muttered. "It cloaked your magic, burying what you truly were so deep inside you that you couldn't even detect it yourself."

"Did my dad *tell me* that I was a dragon before that night?"

"Yeah," Clay whispered, "he told you everything."

"How could I have forgotten all that?"

"The potion locked those memories away along with everything else," Clay answered in a gruff whisper. "It was safer that way."

"Why didn't anyone think to appoint me a guide in the waking world?" I muttered, reminding myself that resenting the people who'd made those choices wouldn't do me any good now.

"The Sarrum did," Clay muttered. "He appointed two guides to you, but that process was as secretive as your adoption. One of them was the man who owned your dad's company. He was instructed to relocate you and your dad without letting anyone know where they were sending you, not even the Sarrum. The less people who knew the truth, the safer it'd be for you."

"Whoever that guy was," I muttered, "he did a piss poor job."

"He didn't do a piss poor job, Charlie," Clay muttered. "He was tortured and murdered by the Purists when he wouldn't give up your location."

My stomach rolled as I whispered, "Who was the other guide?"

"The housekeeper in England who looked after you while your parents were at work."

Mrs. Bentley, the British housekeeper who'd basically taught me to speak, she was the reason I spoke with a British accent. "She died of a stroke a few months before my dad died…"

"The Purists got to her in Draumer," Clay muttered.

"Why didn't the Sarrum come and get me after all that happened?"

"How would they have explained that to your dad's widow? The Sighted can't do things that make no sense to the Unsighted in the waking world. The King had already bent the rules for you when he set up the adoption. He couldn't go back and undo it, and he couldn't exactly abduct you."

"Well, why didn't he just keep me and raise me in the first place?"

"Because it wasn't what your mom wanted," Clay muttered. "He encouraged her to reconsider, but he respected her choice in the end."

Not sure who to blame for my fucked-up childhood, I shook my head. "He probably would've just shipped me off to be trained by that coldhearted aunt of his who raised Rose."

"Her name is Louise," the Sarrum stated as he stepped from the Waterfall, "and I wouldn't have sent you to her. I was raised by that miserable battle-axe. I would not have condemned you to a fate like that. I offered to raise you as my own here at the palace, but your mother didn't want that for you. She felt that you would be better off with the Unsighted fellow she'd fallen in love with."

"I was your worst enemy's son," I muttered. "Why would you raise me as you own?"

"You are family, Charlie," the King replied as he stepped toward us. "None of us have any say in who fathers us. Fortunately, our lineage does not determine who we will become in the end."

I nodded, completely at a loss for words. Then I thought of Rose. "If your Aunt Louise was so awful, why did you condemn Rose to that fate?"

"That was Isa's choice," he replied as he sat down on the bench beside me. "I urged her to keep her daughter with us so that we might raise her instead, but her grandmother convinced her that wasn't the best course of action. I respected Isa's wishes, and did as she asked."

"You're not at all the man I thought you were," I muttered, "are you?"

A contemplative grin spread across the Sarrum's face. "No, I suppose not."

"Why didn't you tell me all this sooner?"

"It was imperative that we determine where your allegiance would lie first," he replied. "After all, you were consorting with your birth father for the first several months of your training with us."

25

MIA

Tristan and I had been sitting in the kitchen at the house on Sycamore waiting for the others to join us for almost two hours. We'd already polished off our first pot of coffee and were well on our way to finishing a second. It was a good thing Doc planned to sedate us for our mission because with this much caffeine coursing through our bloodstreams, falling asleep naturally would've been almost impossible.

I bit my lip as Tristan stood from the table, carried his mug to the coffeemaker, and poured himself another cup. Downing that much caffeine probably wasn't the best idea, considering how anxious he was to get the mission underway.

I smiled at him as he settled back into his seat across the table from me. "Should I be cutting you off at some point?"

He responded with a preoccupied grin. "We should be taking off for the boss's house by now. Hell, we should be in Draumer setting out for No Man's Land at this point."

I glanced toward the door to the hallway. "I'm sure Nellie and Charlie will convince Bob to join us soon."

"I'm a big fan of the Unsighted knight in Draumer," Tristan muttered, following my gaze as if he hoped the others were about to walk through the door, "but that ornery old bastard upstairs is another story. *Him*, I'd like to dropkick across the house right about now. I'm seriously tempted to go upstairs, throw a burlap sack over his head, toss him in the car and get moving before the day's half over."

"I don't think we've reached that level of desperation yet," I whispered, suppressing a grin. "Besides, I'm pretty sure I heard Brian tell you that was plan X."

Tristan let out a chuckle with a hint of a growl to it. "Then Brian should be the one sitting here waiting for the old bastard to cooperate."

I grinned at him then glanced down at my coffee cup, toying with the idea of getting up for another refill.

"I'm alright with proceeding to plan X now," Benjamin chimed in as he and Isa strolled into the kitchen and headed toward the focal point of the room. He kissed her cheek, then opened the cupboard above the coffeemaker and took out two cups.

"What a shock," Isa teased as she took one of the cups from his hand.

"Well, that's two in favor of moving to plan X. What do you say, ladies?" Tristan murmured in his silkiest voice. "Shall we put it to a vote?"

Isa scowled at Tristan as she sat down beside him, cradling her coffee in her hands. "Be patient with Bob. You'll be old and senile someday too, you know."

"I've got no problem with him being old or senile," Tristan grumbled. "I'm just tired of him acting like a stubborn jackass."

"He can't help that either," Isa whispered, as Benjamin sat down next to me.

"That's a really convenient excuse," Tristan grumbled. "But are we absolutely sure he's not just putting on an act, so he can get away with whatever the hell he feels like doing?"

"Right," Isa muttered, narrowing her eyes at Tristan. "I'm sure Bob jumped for joy when that bullet lodged in his head because he'd be able to piss people off without consequences."

"Whatever," Tristan grumbled. "No matter what the reason is, he's holding up the whole damn mission. I'll be giving that knight an earful when we get to Draumer."

Benjamin glared at Tristan as he downed the last sip of his coffee and sat his empty cup on the table. "Are you gonna bitch like this the entire mission?"

"What's it to you?" Tristan muttered. "You won't be there to hear it."

"No, I won't," Benjamin agreed, his tone a bit more menacing than usual. "But since you're in charge of this show, I expect you to suck it up and stop acting like an asshole."

"Sorry," Tristan muttered as he pushed his chair back from the table. "I've been sitting here twiddling my thumbs, running through scenarios of everything that could possibly go wrong for hours. Guess I'm just anxious to stop overthinking things and get moving."

"You've got this," Benjamin assured him in a gentler tone—well, gentler for Benjamin. "I wouldn't have put you in charge of this mission if I wasn't sure you were ready to lead it."

Tristan smiled at the Darkness as he stood up from his chair. "Thanks. I appreciate the vote of confidence." I cringed as he crossed the room with his cup in hand and stared at the coffeepot for a second, as if he were contemplating another refill. Instead, he rinsed his cup out in the sink and stuck it in the dishwasher.

Benjamin opened his mouth to respond, but the sound of the front door opening stopped him. We all sat in silence, listening as the front door closed and two sets of footsteps echoed down the hall as they moved toward the kitchen.

Doc greeted us with a pleasant smile as he stepped in the room. "Good morning, everyone. It's a lovely day to begin a mission, wouldn't you say?"

"Sure," Tristan muttered. "If we can ever get Mr. Sunshine upstairs to calm down enough to hop in the car."

"Yeah. Sorry about that," Clay muttered as he followed Doc into the kitchen. "My meeting with Charlie ran a little longer than I thought it would last night. I meant to go back and give Bob the potion before he left Draumer, but I didn't get a chance to."

"Yeah, we noticed," Tristan grumbled. "I'd be happy to run upstairs and knock him out, so you can meet up with him in Draumer and give him the potion now."

"Nellie and I just put him in front of the television," Charlie whispered as he walked in the room and headed straight for the coffeemaker. "He should be out in no time."

You know that expression *a watched pot never boils?* Well, it turns out that a watched cranky old man never drifts off to sleep. With nothing else to do but wait, we'd all migrated into the living room. Then we just sat there and watched Bob, while he sat on the couch watching television for one of the longest hours of my life. By the time he finally did fall asleep, it was a miracle any of us were still conscious.

As soon as Bob's snoring confirmed that he was sound asleep, Nellie snuck the remote from his slumbering grasp and turned down the volume as Clay passed through the Waters to give him the potion in Draumer. The rest of us continued to sit there watching Bob's slumbering body, curious to see what would happen when he woke up.

A loud snort from Bob cut through the silent tension in the room like a gunshot, giving my heart a jolt.

All eyes in the room fixed on the old man on the couch as he rubbed a hand over the stubble on his face, blinked the sleep from his eyes, and looked around the room at the expectant faces all staring at him. "Must be a slow day, if you assholes've got nothin better to do than sit around starin at me. I mean, I know I'm beautiful but get a fuckin life."

A muffled sob escaped Nellie's throat. "Bob, is the potion working?"

Bob leaned back and narrowed his eyes at the old woman sitting next to him. "What the fuck are ya—"

"Give it a minute," Clay muttered under his breath.

Doc stood from his chair, crossed the room, and sat down on the coffee table in front of Bob.

Instead of cursing at him for blocking his view of the television, Bob blinked his eyes a few more times as he glanced around the room at his anxious spectators. "I apologize for holding things up," he muttered, his voice a strange mix of the old man's gruff tone and the knight from the royal guard's polite manner of speaking.

"It's quite alright," Doc murmured as he moved an index finger slowly across Bob's visual field. A satisfied grin spread across his face as the old man's eyes followed it. "After all, this is a rather monumental change for you."

Bob nodded as he turned toward the old woman seated beside him on the couch.

Nellie tensed as their eyes met, bracing herself for what her knight in shining armor would make of her as his two separate worlds collided. I couldn't say that I blamed her. The wrinkled, frizzy-haired old woman on the couch was a far cry from her lovely young red-headed self in Draumer. I could relate to that. My true form in Draumer was a hideous featureless monstrosity. When Tristan first told me that he'd known I was a shape-shifter all along, I was floored that he was even speaking to me.

"Nellie?" Bob whispered as he took her wrinkled hand in his. "That is you, isn't it?"

"Yes," she whispered as a tear slid down her cheek, "are you disappointed?"

The old man glanced down at their joined hands and stared, transfixed by the sight of his own age-spotted hand for a moment. "Of course not," he whispered as his eyes returned to hers. "You're every bit as beautiful as you are in Draumer."

"That potion must've messed with your eyesight," Nellie muttered as her cheeks flushed with color.

"I can see just fine," Bob murmured as he placed a shaky hand on her cheek and brushed away the tear with his thumb.

"This is touching," Benjamin's deep voice interjected, "but we've got to get to the boss's house. You two can continue your lovefest in the car."

26

TRISTAN

I tried to focus on the road and the feel of Mia's hand beneath mine as I drove toward the boss's house, but it was almost impossible to tune out the old couple in the backseat. As I cranked up the music to drown out the melodrama playing out behind me, I thanked my lucky stars that I was up front driving the car. Poor Charlie was stuck in the backseat next to the wrinkled pair of lovebirds adjusting to this new twist in their dynamic. I felt sorry for him, sitting back there with no escape from their emotional outpouring. Don't get me wrong. I was happy for the old couple, but this wasn't the time for distractions.

Each time I flinched at a car merging into traffic or changing lanes up ahead, I kicked myself for drinking all that coffee while we were waiting for Bob. The caffeine wasn't helping my nerves, which had already been pretty frayed. The closer we'd come to the start of this mission, the more confident Mia had grown in her ability to defend herself, and for good reason. There wasn't a doubt in my mind that she could hold her own if we ended up in a battle. Mia was ready, and I was glad that she was. But as her dependence on me lessened, I'd found myself facing my own demons—demons that were best left buried in the past.

I looked over at Mia in the passenger seat and winked at her, and she smiled and squeezed my hand. Something in that sweet smile of hers tugged at my heartstrings in a way that only one other creature ever had, but this sure as hell wasn't the time to be reminiscing about her. Maybe Benjamin's faith in my readiness to lead this mission was misplaced. *No.* Even if that was the case, there was no way Brian would've agreed to it if I wasn't ready—unless Brian was too preoccupied with his own demons to notice that mine had begun surfacing. *Damn it.*

I needed to get my head in the game before we set out for No Man's Land. Unfortunately, my mind was determined to drift back to the past. As I slipped the car into cruise control, my thoughts wandered to that first day at my new high school...

...I stepped away from the lunch counter and headed toward the tables with my plastic tray in hand, surveying the layout in the cafeteria. It was the same stereotypical groupings of students that you'd find in any other school cafeteria.

As I passed the entitled-princess table, a blue-eyed blond in a skintight designer skirt motioned toward the empty seat next to hers.

I grinned at her but kept walking. That's when I spotted the girl from homeroom that the asshole next to me had been picking on—the one who accepted her backpack from me after I scooped its contents off the floor, and then left without even telling me her name. She was sitting all alone at a table in the far corner of the room.

I kept my eyes on the girl who was inexplicably immune to my charm as I headed toward her, ignoring the waving hands and flirtatious invites to join other tables. She sat with her head down and her posture hunched, eating her lunch in silence.

When I reached her table, I sat my tray down across from hers. "Mind if I join you?"

She looked up, her dark eyes narrowing as she appraised me with an unreadable expression on her face, but she didn't answer. Since she didn't outright tell me to get lost, I decided to interpret her silence as an invitation to sit down.

She shook her head as she watched me settle into the chair across from her. "You're at the wrong table."

"Come on, give the new guy a break," I murmured, cranking my charm up a notch to help break the ice. "I haven't got a right table because I don't have any friends to sit with yet."

As her face reddened at my words, my first thought was that I'd cranked the charm up too much. Then I noticed the tears in her eyes. "Why don't you go sit with the cheerleaders and jocks?" she croaked in a timid whisper. "They all look like they're dying to be your new best friend."

Confused by her tears, I frowned at her as I searched her eyes. "I'd rather make friends with you."

"Just...don't," she muttered in a timid, almost pleading whisper. "You don't have to make a fool of the class loser for the cool kids to like you. They'll accept you because of your pretty face."

Too stunned to come up with a response, I sat there and stared at her with my mouth hanging open as she gathered up her things and stood from the table.

Without another word, she walked away, stopping just long enough to toss her half-eaten lunch in the trash. Then she left the cafeteria without looking back once.

I stood up from the table and abandoned my untouched lunch. Ignoring the hushed comments and giggles from the cheerleaders, I followed the girl whose name I still didn't know out the door. I stepped out into the hallway just in time to see her turn a corner and quickened my pace to catch up to her.

She heard me coming, yanked open the closest door and slipped in the room without looking back at me.

I reached the door a few seconds later and followed her in.

"You can't be in here," she hissed.

I glanced at the rows of lockers and benches behind her and realized I was in the girls' locker room. "Then come out and talk to me."

She crossed her arms over her chest and growled, "Why are you messing with me?"

"What the hell did I do to make you think I was messing with you?"

"You talked to me," she muttered as her eyes filled with tears.

Floored by her tears, I took a deep breath before whispering, "Okay?"

She blinked back the tears, then rolled her eyes and shook her head. "Guys who look like you don't make friends with girls like me, especially not on their first day at a new school."

"Says who?" I muttered, more than a little taken aback. It was one thing for her to be unaffected by my charm, but this girl flat out hated my guts—which pissed me off, since she didn't know a damn thing about me.

"Just leave me alone," she muttered as she walked past me and headed for the door.

Too stubborn and confused to let her leave on that note, I took hold of her arm to get her to turn around and talk to me.

She spun around to face me, yanking her arm free and recoiling as if I'd hauled off and punched her.

The raw terror in her widened eyes hurt worse than any hit I'd ever taken in a fight. It was like staring into the eyes of my seven-year-old self in a mirror. "I'm sorry," I muttered, taking a step back from her as I fought back tears of my own. "I didn't mean to scare you."

"You didn't..." she choked on a sob as her voice died off, unable to finish the sentence. Something in her eyes had softened, and I could tell she felt it too—that gut-wrenching feeling, like she was looking in a mirror as she caught a glimpse of the unguarded pain in my eyes.

I shook my head and took another step back.

But she took a tentative step toward me, wiping a tear from her cheek as she muttered, "My name is Nina, by the way."

The air in my lungs escaped me in a pent-up rush. It felt like I'd been holding that breath for years. "I think we started off on the wrong foot, Nina," I muttered, blinking the sorrow from my eyes as I took a half-step toward her. "What do you say we start over?"

She let out a sniff then nodded as she sat down on the nearest bench.

"It's nice to meet you, Nina," I whispered as I sat down next to her, transfixed by the light in her eyes...

...A hollered, "The fuck's goin on?" from the backseat snapped my focus back to the present.

Shit. I didn't recall Clay saying anything about the potion's effects being spotty after the first dose.

"We're driving to the Sarrum's house," Charlie replied in a nonplussed tone that suggested this sort of outburst was nothing new to him. "Remember, Bob?"

"What in the fuck are you talkin about?" Bob growled. "Listen, pretty boy, you better pull this fuckin car over before…" I caught a glimpse of him shaking his head in the rearview mirror as I pulled off to the side of the road. "What the fuck's happenin?"

"We're safe, Bob," Nellie crooned in a singsong voice, like she was soothing a fussy infant. "Everything is okay. We can trust these people."

Bob rubbed a hand over the stubble on his face as his eyes met mine in the rearview mirror. "If you lay a hand on us, you fuckin pervert," he muttered, "I'll beat you to death with my fuckin cane."

"You don't even have a cane," Charlie reminded him.

"Then I'll pistol whip the deviant bastard…" Bob muttered, confusion clouding his eyes as he took in his surroundings.

"As fun as that sounds," I murmured, doing my best to hide my concern at his relapse into Unsightedness so soon after he took the potion, "I'm gonna get back on the road now. And if I hear so much as another peep from the backseat, we're gonna go to plan X." Maybe I should've tried a little harder to suppress my irritation, but we'd wasted too much time waiting around for him already.

"Plan X?" Bob muttered.

"I'll give you that one because you're confused," I growled as I merged back into traffic, "but if you make another fucking sound, you're not gonna like what comes next."

27

GODRIC

A tired sigh escaped me as I sat down in the armchair beside the window of my childhood bedroom. Dealing with the witless bunch of minions I was currently forced to rely on was exhausting. This had seemed the natural place to escape to when I headed upstairs. *How could I have forgotten why I avoided this room?*

I was unraveling, and I had only myself to blame for it. I'd set the process in motion as soon as I finished creating this mirage, when I sat down in the garden and revisited a conversation I'd had with Lilly in that very same spot. But this was the room I had been dreading visiting, the room where it'd all begun to go wrong. As much as that pained me, it was still a memory of my Lilly. Those memories were all I had left of her. Pleasant or agonizing, I couldn't bear to let a single moment we'd spent together fade from my memory.

An ache flared in my chest as my eyes drifted to the bedroom door. Would it have made a difference if I'd never gone on that trip to Vienna all those years ago? That was a question I'd never get an answer to, a question I couldn't bear to ponder...

...A contented grin played at the corners of my mouth as I opened the door to my bedroom and breathed in my sister's intoxicating scent. I had only been gone for three weeks, yet it felt like a lifetime since I'd seen her.

I stepped in the room and my grin widened at the sight of my nineteen-year-old sister, curled up so small and childlike on my bed. Overcome with a sudden swell of emotion, I wanted more than anything to believe that she had chosen to nap on my bed because she missed the comforting familiarity of my scent as desperately as I'd missed hers. My steps were slow and deliberate as I moved toward the bed, imagining her joyful expression upon waking to find me home two weeks early.

It wasn't until I rounded the bed that I noticed the tearstains on her cheeks. Conflicting emotions warred within me. I wanted to wake her and comfort her, but for all I knew she hadn't slept well. Perhaps she needed the rest. Something was definitely off because I couldn't sense the emotions that'd prompted her tears. She was my greatest treasure. I had always instinctually known exactly what she was feeling.

As I stood there staring at her slumbering face, entirely at a loss as to what she needed, she whimpered in her sleep.

Desperate to know what was troubling her, I sat down on the edge of my bed and touched a hand to her cheek. "Lilly?"

She gasped and bolted upright, her heart racing as her eyes locked with mine. "Henry?" she whispered. "Are you really here?"

It was such an odd thing to ask, and the realization that it was me that'd woken her wasn't steadying her heart rate like it normally would. "Yes," *I whispered.* "I concluded my business at the convention early, so I could come home and surprise you."

A tear slid down her cheek as she glanced toward the door. "Did father know you were coming back early?"

"No," *I murmured, brushing the tear from her cheek with my thumb.* "I didn't want to risk him spoiling the surprise."

"I thought I might never see you again," *she whimpered as she wrapped her arms around my neck and buried her face against my collar.*

"Why on earth would you think that?" *I muttered, pulling back to look her in the eye.* "I wasn't due to come home for another two weeks."

She swallowed back a sob and rasped, "I would've been gone by then."

Those words, combined with her tears and the pained expression on her face iced the blood in my veins. "What are you talking about?" *I murmured, cupping her tear-stained cheek in my palm.*

"The Graysons are arriving tomorrow," *she whispered as more tears spilled down her cheeks.* "I'm supposed to go with them when they return home. Father arranged a marriage between me and Phillip Grayson."

Flames flared in my visual field, bathing my vision in a wash of azure fire as the pounding of my heart displaced all other sounds. "What?"

"He planned for it to be done before you returned home from Vienna," *she whispered, her blue eyes reflecting the flames that danced in mine.*

The taste of bile filled my mouth at the thought of coming home to find her gone. "Why on earth would he do such a thing? What does he stand to gain from this..." *I couldn't even bring myself to voice the word.*

"I don't know," she muttered as her eyes dropped to her lap. "He said he's doing this for your benefit."

A feral growl rumbled in my throat. "How could the loss of you ever benefit me?" The flames in my eyes had grown so intense that I could barely see Lilly's face, as if she were already slipping away from me. Panic gripped me at the thought. She was mine—the one thing in my life that was pure and true—my treasure. How dare he plot to take her from me?

Fear flickered in my sister's eyes as she watched my composure unravel. "I don't know," she replied in a trembling whisper.

I kissed the top of her head and wrapped my arms around her, terrified that it was my fury that'd frightened her. "You are safe, Lilly," I whispered against her ear. "I promised you that I would always keep you safe, and that is a vow I will never break."

She hugged me back with all the strength she possessed. And I breathed a sigh of relief as she pressed her cheek against mine and whispered, "Don't let them take me, Henry. Please."

I tightened my hold on her and pressed my cheek a bit harder against hers as I whispered, "I swear to you, I will stop this."

"How?" she whispered, breathing the word against my skin.

I cradled the back of her head in my palm, wanting nothing more than to keep her there like that forever, the rest of the world be damned. Another sob escaped her as I stroked a hand over her hair. I straightened and held her beautiful face in my hands for a moment, drinking in every delicate feature of this fair creature I'd never done anything good enough to deserve. There was nothing I wouldn't do to keep her by my side. I lowered my head,

DREAM FRAGMENTS

pressed my lips to her forehead, and lingered there for a moment as I planted a kiss on her porcelain flesh. Then I leaned back, took her hands in mine, and whispered, "Lock the door as soon as I leave this room, and don't come out until I return."

Her small hands trembled in mine as she searched my eyes. "You're frightening me."

"You needn't ever fear me," I murmured. "You are the sister of the future King, Lilly. There is no need for you to fear anything, ever. I am going to fix this, I promise you."

She nodded as I stood from the bed, her eyes still locked with mine as they filled with fresh tears.

I felt my heart stutter as I stood there watching her tremble with fear. "I'll return as soon as I can."

"Alright," she whispered as she watched me step backward toward the door, her eyes never straying from mine.

I opened the door and stepped into the hall with a determined sigh. "Lock this door," I whispered as I started to pull it shut, "and don't open it for anyone but me."

I waited until I heard her footsteps approach the door, then I pulled it shut and stood frozen as I listened to her turn the lock. Dropping my forehead to the door, I whispered, "I promise you, Lilly. No one will ever take you from me."

A haze of sapphire flames erupted in my visual field as I turned and marched toward the stairs...

...Tears streamed down my cheeks as I stood from the chair and moved toward the bed, my heart throbbing at the memory of those promises I had made to my sweet sister—*all of them lies*. Although I had no way of knowing back then that it would turn out as it did, every promise I'd ever made her had corroded into lies.

"I promise you, Lilly," I whispered as I sat down on the bed where I'd unwittingly lied to her all those years ago, "my old heart will not rest until I make them pay for what they did to us."

A low growl escaped me as I stood back up and moved to the window. It offered a perfect view of the patio, where I'd rushed from the house to confront our father. *Had Lilly watched it happen?* In all these years, that thought had never occurred to me.

I wiped the tears from my cheeks as I recalled the details of my volatile exchange with our father, wondering what Lilly had thought of me if she watched it all play out...

...My heart hammered in my chest as I stormed out the back door.

Father was seated in a chair on the patio, eyes fixed on the glass of liquor in his hand. When he heard me barreling toward him—smoke billowing from my flared nostrils, teeth bared—he looked up and grinned at me as if he hadn't a care in the world. "Welcome home."

I hardly felt my feet connect with the patio as I closed the distance between us, wrenched the glass from his hand and let it smash against the brick floor. The shattering sound brought a wicked grin to my face as I yanked the old man to his feet by the collar of his shirt. His brittle bones would fragment just as easily as that glass, but would their shattering resonate with the same satisfying clarity? "You miserable selfish son of a bitch, what the hell were you thinking?"

My father's grin widened as I released his collar. "I was thinking of you, Henry. Lilly's departure is for your own good."

Maddened by his cavalier tone, I growled, "What the hell are you talking about?"

Something in my voice made the smile slip from his face. "People have been talking, Henry. It's a popular topic of conversation amongst the Sighted, the future Sarrum and the sister he loves more than any brother ought to love his sibling."

"Then they're all mental," *I muttered*. "No rational soul would judge a man for the depth of his love for a family member."

"Come now, Henry," *my father murmured, the smug grin returning to his face as he took a step back from me.* "You stormed out here to lay it all out on the table, so let's be honest."

Rage stoked the fire within me as I narrowed my eyes at him. "What the hell are you getting at?"

"Don't play stupid with me, son," *he growled as a wisp of smoke escaped his flared nostrils*. "I watched the two of you grow up together. Do you think for one second that I'll believe you've never noticed the adoring way she looks at you, the way she has ALWAYS looked at you, as if her entire world revolves around you?"

"Of course she looked at me as if I was everything," *I spat back*. "I WAS everything to her! You abandoned her and left me to raise her when I was no more than a child myself."

My father's eyes widened at my words. "It isn't one-sided, Henry. I see the way you look at her, your gaze lingering on her body for just a little too long. There's a hunger that flickers in your eyes when you think no one is watching."

Maddened by his implications, I let my fist fly toward his face, knocking him to the patio floor. Rage colored my vision in flickering shades of blue as I stood over him. "You are a sick pathetic old fool," *I growled*. "I will not *allow you to pervert my love for Lilly, the one pure thing in my life."*

"This isn't just about what I think, Henry," he muttered as he wiped the blood from his mouth. "Everyone sees it, and it won't do to have that sort of rumor circulating when you become King. I'm doing you a favor by removing your sister from the picture."

Mad with rage, I lifted my foot and stomped on his chest, barely able to see the look on his face through the flames as his ribs splintered. But I heard the sound, just as brittle as I'd suspected it would be. "Did you honestly think I would allow that to happen?"

The instant I lifted my foot off his chest, he pushed himself to his feet, awkwardly hunched and hugging his ribs. "I don't need your permission to arrange a marriage for my daughter, Henry."

"I am the future Sarrum of Draumer," I growled.

"Yes, but I am your father," he replied in a venomous whisper, "and until you are crowned, you have no authority to rule over me. As the head of this household, my decisions are to be carried out by this family without question."

"Then I suppose there's only one solution," I snarled as I wrapped my hands around his throat.

His expression was defiant and furious at first, but as my grip tightened, his eyes widened in shock. When he realized I had no intention of stopping, he began to struggle against my hold. But we both knew I'd surpassed his strength years ago.

He was a stubborn old dragon, I'll give him that. It felt as if he fought the inevitable forever, clawing at my arms and face, further bruising his own neck as he struggled against my grip.

A lifetime of abuse at his hands flashed through my mind as I loosened my hold, allowing him a quick breath before tightening it again, drawing out the inevitable so that he'd suffer at my hands as I had suffered at his all those years. I'd endured countless episodes of abuse at his hands over the years, but he had gone too far this time. Threatening Lilly's well-being was unforgivable.

When there was no fight left in him, his eyes pleaded with me as he mentally reached out, begging for mercy.

"You never showed us any mercy," I growled. "Why on earth would I show it to you now?"

I'm afraid the end was rather anticlimactic. He just sort of deflated as the light drained from his eyes. When a dragon mother dies during childbirth, the newborn dragon instinctually devours its mother's magic as the light leaves her. After all this wicked man had put us through, I figured he owed me as much. So I locked eyes with him and watched the light fade from his eyes as I drained the life from him, filling my lungs with every ounce of magic he possessed. After I'd taken all that he had to give, I let my father's useless carcass drop to the patio floor.

A muffled gasp was the first indication that my actions had been witnessed. Realizing that his cover had been blown, my father's shadow stepped into the light. Despite his advancing years, my father's shadow was still a fearsome man. He held my gaze, his expression stoic as he stepped toward me.

"Hello, Idris," I murmured as I straightened my tie.

"Henry," my father's shadow replied with a dip of his head.

"It's unfortunate that you witnessed that," I muttered with a remorseless grin. "Where exactly do we go from here?"

"My bonded soul is dead," my father's shadow replied. "I will honor my bond with him by aiding the son who now possesses his magic however he wishes me to." A frown spread across his face as he shook his head. "I watched you grow up, Henry. He was never a father to you. You and your sister deserved better."

There was so much sincerity in his eyes that his words nearly moved me to tears.

"I am sorry that I couldn't stop him from hurting you as a child," Idris muttered. "If you feel that I deserve to suffer the same fate as your father, I won't fight it."

I shook my head, then cleared my throat. "I suppose I could use a shadow of my own."

Without another word, the shadow stepped toward me and pulled me into a hug. Tears rolled down my cheeks as we stood there in that embrace, exchanging more love in that moment than my father had expressed in a lifetime...

...I shook my head as the memory faded. There was no stopping this now that I'd opened the floodgates. The rest of the memories would come whether I wanted them to or not.

I dropped back into the armchair as the past reclaimed me...

...I doubt I'd been asleep for more than an hour when the faint sound of my doorknob turning roused me. Since I was still away meeting with the royal counsel in Draumer, the opportunity to slip back to the waking world and spend more time with Lilly felt like a gift I didn't deserve.

I leaned across my bed and switched on the light on my bedside table. "Lilly?"

She stepped in the room, dressed in a thin white nightgown, hugging herself to combat the chill in the air. "I'm sorry I woke you," she whispered as she shut the door.

As her bare feet stepped toward my bed, I sat up and smiled at her. Although, I couldn't help fearing what she thought of me now, after what I'd done. "It's fine," I whispered. "I couldn't really sleep anyway."

She inched a bit closer to my bed, her eyes questioning and her movements hesitant. A draft in the room caused her to shiver in her thin gown as she nodded.

Troubled by the fact that I still couldn't sense her emotions, I shook my head. "You'll catch a cold standing there like that. Why don't you come sit down and share my blankets?"

The hesitance in her stance as she pulled the covers back broke my heart. Normally she would've jumped under the blankets straightaway without feeling the need to wait for an invitation. I don't think she caught more than a glimpse of my bare leg before dropping the blanket and looking up at me. "You're not wearing anything."

"If it bothers you," I whispered, puzzled by my inability to sense the feelings behind her words, "grab my pajama bottoms off the chair and toss them to me."

"It doesn't bother me," she whispered as she slid beneath the blankets, careful to leave plenty of space between her body and mine.

I lowered myself to a reclining position with one arm propping me partially upright. "So you couldn't sleep?"

"I drifted off for a bit," she whispered, "but when I woke up, I wasn't sure whether what happened today was real. So I tiptoed to Father's room and found it empty." Tears filled her eyes as she shook her head. "Then this awful thought occurred to me, that you might be gone too. I didn't mean to wake you. I just wanted to peek in and reassure myself that you were still here."

I dug my fingernails into my palms to keep my eyes from tearing as I whispered, "I'd never leave without you."

A tear slid down her cheek as she dropped her eyes to the blankets.

I felt an overwhelming need to pull her into my arms and comfort her, but I was too afraid that I was the cause of her tears. "Please don't hate me," I whispered, my heart aching at the thought of losing her because of what I'd done.

"I don't hate you," she whispered without lifting her eyes from the blankets. "I just…"

"What is it?" I muttered, extending a hand toward hers, but drawing it back without touching her. "Please talk to me, Lilly. I need to know what you're thinking. You just…what? Finish your sentence. Please."

"I just wish that you weren't my brother," she sobbed, turning her back to me as she slid out from under the covers and started to stand from the bed.

I lunged toward her and took hold of her arms so she'd sit back down, fearing that if she left the room like this I might lose her forever. Despite the searing pain burning a hole through my insides because of what she'd just said, I couldn't let her go. Not like this. "I'm so sorry I frightened you," I whispered against her ear. "I did what I had to do to keep you safe. There was nothing I wouldn't have done to protect you from that fate."

"I don't blame you for that," she muttered, tilting her head in my direction without actually turning to look at me. "I know you did it for me, and I love you for it."

"But you still wish I wasn't your brother," I muttered, trying desperately to keep the bitterness that those words evoked from darkening my tone. I couldn't afford to do anything that might push her further away.

"Yes," she whispered.

"If my actions today didn't cause you to feel that way," I muttered, cringing at the bitterness I couldn't keep from

my tone, "what did I do to make you regret being my sister?"

"You love me more than anyone else ever will," she whispered, tilting her head a bit farther in my direction, "more than I'd ever want any other person to love me."

"And why does that upset you?" I muttered, hating the sorrow in her voice.

"I'm going to grow old all alone," she whispered. "There will never be anyone for me to turn to for comfort when I wake up frightened in the middle of the night."

"You'll always have me," I whispered in her ear. "I have no intention of moving to the palace without you."

"I know," she muttered, "but Louise Talbot will be lying beside you at night."

"She will never mean more to me than you."

"But I'll be lying in an empty bed in your palace," she muttered, "untouched by anyone ever."

I took a deep breath before asking, "Did you want to marry Phillip?"

"No," she muttered, "of course not."

"Then...you wish to marry another man?"

She shook her head. "You'll hate me if I say anything more."

"I could never hate you," I replied, my voice firm as I slid closer and wrapped my arms around her.

A tear slid down her cheek and dropped to my forearm as she sat there, rigidly resisting my hug without saying a word.

I stared at her tear on my skin, afraid to move as I whispered, "Talk to me, Lilly. There is nothing you could ever say that would make me feel differently about you. Tell me what it is that you want."

A sob escaped her as she squeezed her eyes shut. "When I said that I wished you weren't my brother, I didn't mean that I hated you. I meant that I wished..." her words died off as she spun toward me, and the look in her eyes stopped my heart.

My God, she was beautiful. Tears filled my eyes as the realization of what she was trying to tell me sunk in.

In that instant, with our eyes locked, all the feelings I'd never allowed myself to process swelled within me. The fact that our father had been right all along should have sent me racing from the room. Instead, I drew her into my arms and wept...

...I wanted to remain in that one perfect moment of clarity until I withered and died, but it was imperative that I keep my fury primed and ready for the fight ahead. So I stood from the chair and sat back down on the bed as my thoughts pushed forward.

Idris had taken care of contacting the Sighted coroner and paying him generously to report that our father's cause of death had been a massive heart attack. Alas, my poor father had been alone in the garden when it happened, and no one found him in time to revive him. When the Graysons arrived the next day, I informed them that their arrangement with my father would regrettably have to be terminated. After all, a wedding would hardly be appropriate whilst my dear sister was in mourning.

It took the Talbots less than a week to send a messenger to our house to inform us that the Sarrum had fallen ill and he was unlikely to make a full recovery. According to their messenger, my intended bride, Louise Talbot, had conveniently contracted the same mysterious ailment. Although she had recovered, the illness had rendered her infertile. Since our union could no longer produce an heir to the throne, the

Talbots declared that the only viable solution was to wed Louise's younger brother, Alexander, to my sister. The bearer of this appalling news had been instructed to transport Lilly to the Talbots' home straightaway...

...Fury seeped from every pore of my body as the elf on our doorstep stood there waiting for us to comply with his orders. Smoke billowed from my nostrils as I stepped closer to him.

He took a few steps back and muttered, "You understand that I have been ordered to bring Miss Godric back to the Talbots' estate with me, Master Godric."

"What I UNDERSTAND," I growled, "is that YOU are expendable."

Heart thudding, he took another step backward toward the car he'd come in. "Sir?"

I moved toward him at the unhurried pace of a predator who has no doubt he can outrun his prey. "Do you honestly believe they expected us to bow down and comply with these orders they instructed you to deliver?"

The fool's eyes widened as he let out a stuttering breath. "They sent me to..."

I ignored Lilly's hand on my arm as I moved closer to the bearer of this catastrophic news. "Do you think for one second that they assumed we would calmly accept this news you've delivered? If they truly meant to restrain my fury and abduct my sister today, do you really think they would have left the task up to just one elf?"

The pathetic sod just shook his head.

"You were meant to relay the information," I snarled in his face, "so that after I have torn you to shreds, the message will sink in before they send a troop of soldiers to our house to collect my sister."

The details grew hazy after that, obscured by the flames and his screams...

...I begged Lilly to consider fleeing with me, but I couldn't convince her that there was no other option before the royal guard showed up on our doorstep.

They intended to take her alone.

I fought them of course, but when they threatened to make a full inquiry into our father's death if we continued to resist, Lilly agreed to go willingly—under the condition that her brother be allowed to accompany her. My options after that were to stand down and watch them take her away, or go with her.

Had there been the slightest opportunity for us to escape after that, I would have risked everything to get her out of there. But one dragon, no matter how powerful and driven by rage, was no match for the entire royal guard.

28

CHARLIE

It'd taken us almost an hour to calm Bob down enough to get him to lie down on the hospital bed that would be his resting place for the duration of our mission. Doc said he suspected Clay's potion was affecting Bob differently because of the holes in his memory caused by the gunshot wound he'd sustained rescuing Addison and her brother from the men who abducted them all those years ago. Bob kept waffling—remembering both worlds, forgetting one, then the other—and I didn't like the idea of us setting out for No Man's Land with him in that condition. But it wasn't up to me. They'd all agreed it was best not to waste any more time. Even Bob agreed during his lucid moments.

"Charlie?" Isa murmured, pulling me from my thoughts as she stepped into the hallway and motioned for me to stand up from my chair. "Are you ready?"

I flashed her a half-assed attempt at a smile as I stood and followed her into the grand ballroom. "Ready as I'll ever be."

I'd never been one to give a crap about room decor, but even I was impressed by the monstrous crystal chandeliers dangling from the decorative high ceiling in the massive room. They caught the light from every source and sparkled like diamonds, throwing splashes of color throughout the room. Whatever type of wood the perfectly polished floor and decorative trim were made of, it looked expensive as hell. If I had to guess, I'd say the curtains that adorned the large windows around the room were made of silk, and if there were different grades of silk, this was definitely the top-of-the-line stuff. The hospital beds and medical equipment lined up in neat rows in the center of the room looked entirely out of place within the grandeur of this space meant for hosting decadent galas.

My footsteps seemed to echo louder than they should as I followed Isa across the room, feeling rather voyeuristic as I scanned the faces of the members of our party who were already sedated. Nellie had been the first to go under to prove to Bob that there was nothing to fear. Remembering just enough about the other world to understand that he needed to cooperate in order to go along and watch out for his soul mate, Bob had grudgingly consented to be the second to go under.

Tristan grinned at me from across the room where he and the Sarrum stood talking. When we arrived at the house, Tristan had insisted on going last so he could oversee his entire team's sedation.

I smiled back at Tristan, then glanced at the patient Doc was attending to. For a second, I was confused by the unfamiliar face in the bed next to Bob's until I realized the unconscious man must be Melvin, Pip's alter ego in the waking world. I'm not sure what exactly I'd expected Melvin Wise to look like, but it wasn't this guy. He was younger than I'd imagined he would be, and he looked so *normal*. Apart from a bit of scruff—no doubt due to the long flight he'd taken to get to the Sarrum's house—he looked altogether clean-cut and respectable. The nerdy glasses Doc was carefully removing from his face made it easy to picture him as a teacher, or an accountant, or some other profession that was clever and good with numbers.

Rose and Addison's beds were side by side in the row behind Nellie, Bob and Pip. I grinned at the peaceful expression on Rose's sleeping face and felt a pang of remorse over not having wished her well before she left for the boss's house earlier that morning. Then I realized that was ridiculous since she'd be waiting for me at the palace in Draumer.

Isa stopped beside an empty bed in the row after Rose and Addison's. Since everyone else was already unconscious and accounted for, I assumed the other two unoccupied beds in the row were for Mia and Tristan.

I frowned at Isa as I took the hospital gown she held out to me. "Is this really necessary? Can't I just wear my own clothes?"

"It is necessary," Doc replied as he approached the two of us, "for reasons you would probably prefer not to think too much about." He chuckled softly in that jovial manner of his at the quizzical expression on my face. "There are certain matters of bodily function that must be attended to in the unconscious patient, but we'll take care of all that after you are sedated."

"You're right," I muttered. "I don't want to think about it. So, am I just supposed to strip down and change into this in the middle of the ballroom?"

"There's a powder room through the double doors at the far end of the room," Isa murmured as she gestured in that direction. "You can change in there and come out when you're ready."

"I suppose it's too late to change my mind about all of this," I muttered.

"I'm afraid so," Doc replied softly. "But you can rest assured that we respect our patients' privacy, which is why we are attending to you one at a time."

I glanced across the room at Tristan and the Sarrum.

"Trust me," Doc chuckled as he followed my gaze, "the Sarrum has no interest in observing any of the medical proceedings. He's simply here to see you off."

As if on cue—which it probably was, considering his heightened hearing—the King ended his conversation with Tristan and headed across the room toward my bed. "Having second thoughts?" he asked as he reached us.

"Me?" I muttered with a shake of my head. "Nope, never. I love wearing hospital gowns and getting catheterized for no medically necessary reason. That's how I roll."

"There may be no medical reason," the Sarrum replied, suppressing a grin, "but there is a dire reason for this mission."

"Right," I muttered, nodding to excuse myself as I set off for the bathroom with my hospital-patient garb in hand.

I changed as fast as I could and left my discarded clothing on the bench in the room, hoping that was the proper etiquette for stripping and donning an open-assed hospital gown to strut through a ballroom in.

Keeping my crew socks on as a quiet act of defiance, I stepped out of the bathroom and made my way back to my bed with the back of the gown clasped in one hand to keep from mooning the King of the whole fucking Dream World.

"I'm seriously questioning my life choices at the moment," I muttered as I hopped onto the bed as gracefully as I could while being sure to keep the gown closed in the back.

The Sarrum grinned at me as he settled into a chair beside my bed that hadn't been there when I left the room. "Are you really?"

"No, not really," I muttered. "I get why all this medical stuff is necessary. It's just..." I let out a sigh as I swung my legs up onto the bed and covered them with the blankets. "Do you really think I'm ready for this?"

"I have no doubt that you are," he replied without a trace of humor in his tone or expression.

"So," I muttered, looking up at Doc as I lay back against the pillow, "what happens now?"

"Now," the Sarrum murmured, "you set out on this venture like the royal dragon you are."

I turned my head and narrowed my eyes at him. "Right, and what is it about wearing an open-assed hospital gown that screams *royalty* to you?"

"The needs of the body must be tended to whilst you are otherwise occupied in Draumer," David replied in a disciplinary tone that made my cheeks burn. "What happens to your body while you are in this medically induced coma should be of no concern to you."

"Medically induced coma," I muttered. "Awesome. That makes me feel loads better about all of this."

"Are you quite done?" the King asked, leaning back in his chair.

"Yeah," I muttered, wondering why Doc hadn't poked or prodded me with anything yet. "I guess I am."

"Then I suggest you open a portal to the great hall where the others are waiting for you," the Sarrum murmured.

"First of all, you know I can't do that," I muttered, "and second, wouldn't that expend too much energy?"

"To answer your first statement," the Sarrum replied with a grin, "I know that you are perfectly capable of summoning the Waters and forming a temporary portal to your intended destination. As to your second concern, you won't miss the energy expended whilst you're trekking through the Dark Forest, and it will replenish in plenty of time for any situation that might require your full strength."

"Alright," I muttered, "so how do I form a portal?"

"Confidence is key in these matters," the King murmured as he motioned for Doc to give us some space. "The Water creatures will obey any command given by a royal dragon, as long as it's delivered forcefully with the proper amount of threat implied."

"Fabulous." I knew next to nothing about the Water creatures. We'd touched on them during my training, but only enough for me to know they were temperamental buggers that most creatures were incapable of seeing or even sensing. I had only seen one once, while whooshing through the portal Godric used to pull me to his mirage, back before I knew who he really was. "I'm lying here like a chump with my ass hanging out of this super stylish hospital gown. That's sure to command their respect." When David narrowed his eyes at me, I shrugged. "Sure. Why the hell not?" I snapped my fingers, and nothing happened.

"You are more powerful than all of the Water creatures put together," the Sarrum murmured. "Now, own that power and try again."

Right. Own my bare-assed-gown-wearing power. I thought of Godric and all the hurt he'd caused the people I cared about. That son of a bitch was my birth father. As much as I despised him, there was no denying that he was a powerful dragon, and his royal blood coursed through my veins. I would gladly own the power I inherited from him to help take him down. I closed my eyes and thought back to the way I felt when I drank his blood wine, and the way I felt when he called to me inside the house where he was holding Emma and Nellie hostage. My blood recognized that I was his offspring, and that wasn't something to suppress. That power and magic was my birthright. I was the son of Henry Fucking Godric, the royal dragon who'd been slated to be the King of Draumer.

I drew a deep breath without opening my eyes, and I focused on the royal blood flowing through my veins. I felt its strength and power as that familiar warm tingling sensation flowed through me. Instead of resisting it like I had in the past, I embraced it and let it super-charge every molecule of my being. When I opened my eyes, the ballroom was obscured by the haze of orange flames that flared in my visual field. I grinned at my cousin seated at my bedside as I snapped my fingers, and the Waters immediately appeared before us.

The Sarrum stood and motioned for me to do the same, so I did. But I couldn't quite tell whether our bodies were really standing, or if we'd crossed over into the realm of souls. I figured it was probably the latter, considering we'd fall on our faces if we left the waking world with our bodies standing upright. As the Sarrum's eyes met mine, his furrowed brow expressed how trivial that question was at the moment.

Instead of asking for an answer, I nodded. "What now?"

"Now," he replied with a satisfied nod, "you part the Waters and we enter the great hall of the palace."

Sure, why not? I flicked my wrist toward the wall of Water before us in an offhand manner that mimicked the Sarrum's blasé uber-confident technique.

As the Waters began to part, I bit my lip to keep from giggling like a giddy kid who'd just figured out how to operate a new toy. The gap closed a bit, no doubt sensing my childish reaction to its compliance. But I breathed in deep, felt the fire ignite within me and exhaled a puff of smoke through my flared nostrils as I gave my wrist another casual flick. This time, I pictured the great hall of the palace as the Water shifted at my command. Fire rushed through my veins as I started walking through the portal I'd created.

A proud grin spread across the Sarrum's face as he walked beside me. Actually, we more *sauntered* than walked, two bad-ass royals who had nothing to fear and no doubt that the Water creatures would cower in their presence.

As we stepped out into the great hall, Brian's voice sounded behind me. "They grow up so fast."

Rose smiled at me as I walked up to her and put an arm around her shoulders.

Despite my display of bad-assery, Benjamin's booming voice startled the crap out of me. "Consider that your last gesture of affection for the duration, dragon. From here on out, you'll need to stay in character. You never know where the Purists might have eyes."

I cringed at his words, but hopefully Rose didn't notice. It was a sore subject for the two of us. Rose had wanted to consummate our relationship in the waking world before we set off on the mission, but I was too afraid to take the risk. At the start of our relationship, it had been my fear of Benjamin that'd *kept it in my pants* in the waking world, as he so romantically put it. I wasn't afraid of the Darkness anymore, but as that deterrent had subsided over time another had taken its place. Learning about the difficulties of dragon pregnancies during my lessons had scared the crap out of me. And after experiencing some of my mom's pregnancy through Clay's memories, the thought of taking that risk had been too terrifying to even debate with Rose after I got back from my final session with Clay. So instead of starting a physical relationship on our last night together in the waking world for who knew how long, Rose and I had spent our last bit of free time arguing.

I wasn't just being stubborn and unreasonable like she insisted I was. Honestly, I'd even discussed it with

Benjamin at one point because he'd spent most of his adult life with his soul mate married to another man. In Draumer they had been a couple all along, but they didn't begin a physical relationship in the waking world until the threat of an accidental pregnancy was no longer an issue for Isa. Benjamin said it'd been an easy decision for him. Isa had already been lucky enough to survive one dragon pregnancy. He'd been beside her and watched her suffer, and there was no way he was going to play Russian roulette with her life a second time.

"Sorry about last night," I whispered in Rose's ear.

"Are you?" she muttered as she shrugged off my arm.

The fact that these were our last moments together as a couple for as long as this mission would last made the sting of her rejection twice as painful, but I suppose I deserved it. My self-restraint had made her feel rejected on plenty of occasions. I knew that for a fact because she was my greatest treasure. I could sense what she was feeling.

Before I could answer Rose, Brian called us all over to where he stood with the Sarrum and Benjamin. I let out a tired sigh as I nodded and headed toward Brian.

Rose kept her distance from me as we moved toward the Waterfall entrance to the great hall.

"We have a few things to say before you all head out," Brian announced, his eyes stopping on each of us who were going on the mission. "First of all, like Benjamin said, you need to remain in character the entire time you're out there. The occasional telepathic conversation should be fine as long as there's no one close enough to pick up on unintentional changes in your facial expressions, but any gestures of affection are out of the question. They could be seen by eyes that you aren't aware are watching you."

Benjamin nodded in agreement as Brian finished speaking. "I'll be escorting you all out of the palace under the cover of shadow and walking you far enough so that prying eyes will have no reason to assume you've come from the palace. Once we've traveled far enough, I'll retract my shadow to cover only myself and walk back here alone. That way nobody will be aware that a group has set out from the palace."

The Sarrum cleared his throat the instant Benjamin stopped speaking. "I would like to thank each and every one of you for volunteering for this mission. We are all in your debt. For those of you who have lingering concerns about your readiness for this," he murmured, without shifting his gaze to me, "I want you to know that I have no doubt that every one of you is qualified and adequately prepared for this task."

It was such a general statement that I couldn't help wondering if I wasn't the only one who had last minute doubts.

29

MIA

The Sarrum was obviously talking about me when he mentioned that some of us were having doubts about our readiness for the mission, but it was kind of him to keep his statement vague rather than single me out. I'd felt so confident and certain that I could do this as I neared the end of my training, but now that we were about to follow Benjamin out of the palace and venture into the Dark Forest, I felt far less sure of myself. It wasn't the forest that frightened me. I was a creature of Darkness. Slinking through the depths of the Dark Forest had always been a favorite pastime of mine, but we were going back to the Purists' meeting place. Of course this wasn't the same physical location, or the same group of creatures. The Sarrum had destroyed all of them right along with the cabin they'd kept me in. But this was the same organization, the same slavers' auction, and the same crimes perpetrated by the cruelest monsters.

As much as I'd tried to hide it, Tristan had sensed my hesitation. That's why he told Doc he wanted to be the last one to go under. He said he wanted to oversee the sedation of every member of his team. I'm sure that was true, but I knew I was the main reason he insisted on going last. Submitting to sedation and every physical violation it entailed was a terrifying concept for me. The prospect of having no control over what would be done to my body felt a little too much like being shackled to that bed in the Purists' cabin.

It was easy to admit my fears to Tristan. He seemed to be at his strongest when he knew I was relying on his strength. Helping me through this was the perfect distraction from the worries that'd been weighing him down.

I smiled to myself as I pictured the way he'd stood at my bedside, holding my hand while I slipped through the Waters. He had kissed my forehead and promised he'd stay until they got me all situated, then he would meet me in Draumer.

Almost as if reading my thoughts, Tristan gave my hand a squeeze as we lined up behind Benjamin.

I took a deep breath, then shifted into the shape of a girl on the talk show we'd watched while waiting for old Bob to fall asleep. Tristan, Addison and I had discussed different forms I could take for the mission the day before. I couldn't bear to pose as a fairy. The princess was the last fairy I'd morphed into, so there were too many nightmares associated with that form. Plus, we already had one fairy. Nellie was the fairy in our group, and Addison was an elf. Since Rose would be concealing her dragon form by posing as a human, we decided I might as well do the same. I smiled at Tristan, testing out my new face. "What do you think?"

"I think I like your real face better," he whispered as we moved toward the Waterfall entrance to the great hall.

I considered reminding him that my real face was the face of a featureless demon, but I decided against it and grinned at him instead. There wasn't any time for a discussion.

Charlie and Rose were the first to follow Benjamin through the Waterfall. Bob, Pip and Nellie stepped through after them with Addison following close behind.

Tristan kissed my cheek and whispered, "I love you." Then he stepped through, still holding onto my hand.

I followed him in stunned silence. He'd never said those words to me before, and he hadn't even given me a chance to respond. *How* did he love me—as a friend, like a sister, or something more?

I shook my head as I emerged from the Waterfall entrance to the Dragon King's lair. There would be no opportunity to discuss what he'd meant for God only knew how long. "I love you too," I muttered in Tristan's ear as we all huddled close together.

We waded out of the pool of Water at the base of the Waterfall as one entity, all of us cloaked beneath Benjamin's shadow. The silence was deafening as I glanced at the rock ledge high above us. A pair of pitch-black eyes blinked at me in the darkness, and a horrifying pang of doubt gripped me. Had Tristan really said that? *What if I'd misheard him?*

I cast a sideways glance at Tristan, and the grin on his face put all my fears to rest. *Thank God.*

We'd been walking in silence for hours, maybe even days. It was difficult to keep track of time in the Dark Forest. The whispering of the dryads—the spirits who inhabited the trees—was enough to drive you insane. They projected their voices inside your head to threaten, beg for help, and warn you to turn back before it was too late to save yourself. Normally, I wasn't bothered by them. In fact, I'd befriended quite a few dryads in my day. They were usually more than willing to provide shelter within a hollow in their tree trunk. Once you got used to their strange means of communication, they were actually pretty good company. Their discouraging words were just a means of defense against souls who might otherwise cut down their trees. Since they had no way of knowing which creatures meant to harm their tree, they did their best to frighten off anyone who happened by. Despite my familiarity with the ways of the Dark Forest and the creatures who inhabited it, even I was beginning to question my sanity by the time Benjamin signaled for us to stop moving.

We all eyed each other in silence as the Darkness retracted his shadow, covering only himself for the return journey to the palace. For a while we just stood there staring in the direction Benjamin was headed, despite the fact that none of us could see or sense him now that we were outside his protective bubble. The forest seemed a thousand times more ominous without Benjamin. The whispering of the dryads grew louder, and their words of warning became Darker and far more disturbing.

"Let's rest here for a bit," Tristan growled, his harsh tone making it clear this wasn't up for debate. It might've made me cringe if I hadn't known it was an act. A slaver taking his captives to auction wouldn't speak kindly to them or give them any say in their course of action.

Addison took hold of my hand and Nellie wrapped her arms around the two of us, a mother figure offering a bit of comfort to her fellow captives. Rose kept her distance from the three of us, eyes alert as she watched for any signs of life that might be hidden nearby. All of us had our roles to play.

Bob scrounged up some wood and started a fire. Then we all sat in silence for a long time, listening to the whispering of the dryads, hoping they were the only creatures nearby, but too afraid that they weren't to risk even a telepathic conversation. When the whispering got to be too much, Bob put out the fire and we all stood up and started walking again without any of us saying a word.

It went on like that for days. There were moments when I forgot we were acting and I mourned my freedom, fearing what would happen when we reached the slavers' auction. Whenever I remembered the truth, I prayed that at least one member of our group would be able to keep a clear mind. We hiked till our feet throbbed, rested till the whispering of the dryads nearly drove us mad, then we repeated the process over and over again.

I kept it together for a good long while, at least I thought a lot of time had passed. It was equally possible that we were only hours into our journey.

However long it had been, the journey felt pointless and I just wanted to go home, wherever that was.

30

TRISTAN

This was a mistake. This entire venture had been a massive mistake. It had been a long time since I'd hiked through the Dark Forest, long enough for me to have forgotten what it did to your mind. *What the hell was I doing?* I didn't need to take captives. Creatures came to me willingly, but I didn't sell them to others for money. *This was all wrong.*

I had no idea how long it had been since we last stopped to rest, but it felt like it'd been ages. Without uttering a syllable, I signaled for us to take a break. As we settled down for a rest, I blinked my eyes and looked at the faces of the creatures I was traveling with. My eyes lingered on a cute young girl, but that was just her façade. Inside, she was something else—a changeling—a friend, maybe more than just a friend. I focused on her face as we all sat in silence, until my thoughts began to wander…

…I would've married Nina. Young as we were, there wasn't a doubt in my mind that she was the one for me. If

only I had told her that, maybe it might've made a difference. It might've given her something to hold on to.

I tugged the hood of my jacket up to keep the rain off my face as I trudged across the muddy cemetery. The gray sky and dismal weather seemed fitting. Everything good had left this world right along with her. Why hadn't Nina called me before swallowing those pills? Why hadn't I been enough to keep her from taking her own life? Those years that we'd spent together were the best years of my life. Nina was my first love, and I'd wanted her to be my only love.

I stood at a distance during the funeral service instead of sitting down with the others. None of their words would make a difference to me. I actually did try to listen for a while, but everything the minister said just pissed me off. So I walked away from the service, away from Nina, away from the best thing that'd ever happened to me. My whore of a mother had been right. Our kind weren't made for meaningful relationships, so I vowed right then and there never to be in one again.

I got drunker than I'd ever been in my life that night, and I woke in the morning next to an elf whose name I couldn't have recalled if my life depended on it. The rest of my day in the waking world was a blur that I stumbled through with a hangover so massive I swore I'd never drink again.

How ironic was it that I tended bar in my other life? There was no avoiding the bar scene in Draumer, but at least I was on the sober side of the counter at The Dragon's Lair.

I was heading out back to grab some supplies when I heard my brother's voice call out, "Need a hand?"

I turned around and shot him a grin. "Looking good, big brother."

He wrapped his arms around me and pulled me into a hug. "You too, bud." He tightened the hug as he whispered, "I'm so sorry about Nina."

I shrugged free from his hold and started toward the door to the stockroom. "I appreciate the sentiment, but I don't feel like talking about that tonight. If that's why you came, you wasted a trip."

"I came because I've got a job offer for you," Brian murmured as he fell into step beside me.

"I already have a job," I muttered as I pulled the door to the stockroom open.

"This is a job in the waking world," Brian whispered as he followed me into the room and closed the door behind him, "and I'm not leaving till you at least hear me out. This opportunity is too good to pass up. In fact if you say no, I may have to kick your ass."

Despite my irritation, I couldn't help grinning at that. "Yeah? I'd like to see you try. So, what is this dream job?"

"I'm going to work for the Sarrum," Brian murmured with a grin that suggested he had no doubt he could kick my ass and felt no need to prove it, "and I want you to come with me."

"Uh huh," I muttered, turning to look him in the eye. "Just how many shots did you down before you came looking for me?"

Brian didn't shy away from the eye contact. He just grinned and muttered, "He's offered to pay our way through law school, Tristan."

I shook my head, then turned my back to him and started grabbing supplies from the shelves. "Why the hell would he do that?"

"Because he needs someone to guard his wife-to-be while she's going to college," Brian murmured as he stepped up beside me.

"Fuck you," I muttered. *"Why the hell would the Sarrum want a couple of incubi to guard his future bride?"*

"I'm not gonna leave you alone till you agree to come meet her," Brian muttered without answering my question...

...I couldn't remember if I'd ever thanked my big brother for changing the course of my life that day.

I blinked my eyes into focus as my thoughts returned to the present. How long had we been sitting down to rest? My eyes had been glued to Mia the entire time my thoughts had drifted. She centered me. Everything felt in focus again. I remembered the mission, and that it was up to me to watch out for this group and see to it that nothing happened to any of them. Nobody was gonna get hurt on my watch ever again.

Mia tilted her head as she stared back at me, as if she was trying to remember who I was. She was going to get through this. I would get her through this. There was no other option.

We should probably get moving again. My eyes were on Mia, but the thought was directed toward all of them. I needed to make sure everyone was still on track. The forest had a way of messing with your mind.

All right, Charlie replied mentally as he muttered aloud, "Let's get moving."

I took a moment to study each member of the group, waiting until I saw the recognition in their eyes. With some, it took longer than others.

As we stood up to start moving, my eyes were on Bob. Something in the Unsighted knight's stare troubled me.

"The fuck you lookin at, pretty boy?" young Bob grumbled as he hoisted his pack on his back.

The senile old man's manner of speech sounded so odd rolling off the tongue of the noble young warrior in front of me. "We're in this together, Bob," I muttered. "Remember?"

"I don't know…" young Bob's eyes glazed over as he took in his surroundings. "Where in the fuck are we?"

"Keep it down," Pip muttered from Bob's shirt pocket.

Thanks to Charlie's dragon reflexes, he managed to pluck Pip from Bob's pocket a second before Bob could flick him away like an unwanted piece of pocket lint.

Pip's widened eyes were fixed on Bob as he whispered, "Thanks, Charlie."

"The fuck is that thing?" Bob muttered as his eyes locked with his tiny sidekick's.

"Man," Pip muttered as Charlie tucked him in his own shirt pocket, "that's just hurtful."

Bob shook his head as he searched the eyes of the other members of our group.

"It's alright, Bob," Nellie crooned as his eyes met hers.

We can't be having this conversation out loud, I reminded everyone, hoping to God Bob's memory would fill in the gaps and not get us all killed before we even left the Dark Forest.

"Fuck," Bob muttered as he frowned at Pip. "I'm sorry I…"

"Whatever," Pip muttered, dropping his eyes to the rim of Charlie's pocket. "Let's just get moving."

"Please forgive—"

"If it's all the same to you," Pip interrupted without meeting Bob's eyes, "I'm gonna hitch a ride in Charlie's pocket for a while."

We should get moving before we draw too much attention to ourselves, Addison reminded us.

Bob's eyes glazed over again as he turned toward the elf from his past. "How—"

The rest of the old knight's sentence died on his lips as the whispering of the dryads grew louder, as if they were trying to break the tension.

"Let's move," I growled. With that, I started moving without waiting to see if any of them would follow. We needed to get back in character before this conversation got us all killed.

You don't belong here, the dryads whispered inside my head.

I couldn't tell if they were speaking to all of us or just me, but it didn't matter. There was nothing to do but keep walking.

The inhabitants of No Man's Land will destroy you, the voices whispered in my head.

I grimaced and kept walking, thankful that at least I could hear the rest of my team falling into step behind me.

Or perhaps you'll destroy each other before you even get there. Your minds are weak and your spirits are broken.

Just keep walking. I wasn't sure if I meant to encourage the team or just myself. Either way, there was nothing to do but keep moving forward.

You can't save them, incubus.

A growl of frustration rumbled in my throat as I reminded myself to ignore their words.

You couldn't save Nina, and you won't be able to save her either.

I tuned their whispering out as best I could and prayed that the rest of my team could fight off whatever demons the dryads were attempting to resurrect in their minds.

You don't deserve them, incubus. You have no right to seek happiness. They're all going to die because of your selfish attempt to redeem yourself.

31

CHARLIE

We'd been walking for days without a break, at least it felt like it'd been days. I considered myself a pretty strong-willed creature but after this much time in the forest, I was starting to feel like my mind was as full of holes as Bob's.

I shook my head and focused on moving forward, following the footsteps of the incubus in front of me. *Tristan.* His name was Tristan, and he was the one leading this mission. Our reason for traipsing through the forest for days on end escaped me at the moment. I just hoped to God our minds would clear once we left the Dark Forest, but I wasn't holding my breath for that to happen. A place called *No Man's Land* didn't exactly conjure images of sunshine and rainbows.

Too lost in my muddled thoughts to pay attention to where I was stepping, I tripped on a root sticking up out of the dirt and stumbled forward.

Pip's grip on my shirt pocket tightened as I fell back into step with the group. "Watch your step, big guy," he muttered. "Don't forget, you're carrying precious cargo down here."

I looked down at him and muttered, "Sorry." A second later, I stumbled forward again, ramming Rose in the back with an elbow as I tried to catch my balance.

She turned and shot me a death glare that made my blood run cold.

"Sorry," I muttered, glancing down at my feet to escape the fire in her eyes.

The root had somehow managed to wrap itself around my ankle, but the rest of our group was still trudging ahead. "Uh, guys," I muttered, "this tree's got my foot."

Tristan stopped dead in his tracks and turned back toward me, and the rest of them did the same.

"Easy," he muttered under his breath as he inched toward me. When he reached me, he knelt down and gripped the root as I struggled to yank my foot free, but the root kept tightening around my ankle.

"What the fuck's happening?" I squeaked a few octaves higher than I meant to.

"Hold still," Tristan muttered, tightening his grip on the root as it continued to wrap around my leg.

"Is this a dryad?" I asked in a panicked whisper.

"No," Tristan muttered, "dryads just whisper harmless threats. They don't do things like this."

The instant he finished speaking, the root started rising up out of the ground, pulling my leg right along with it. Frozen with shock, my eyes widened in horror as it flipped me upside down and lifted me off the ground with poor Pip hanging on to my pocket for dear life. The higher it rose with me in its grip, the more the roots resembled fingers, as if a great gnarled hand was rising up out of the dirt.

"What the fuck is happening?" I squeaked in a borderline hysterical pitch.

"Relax," Tristan growled through gritted teeth as he grabbed ahold of my arm.

I grabbed his arm with both hands and held on for dear life. "Easy for you to say!"

"STOP YOUR NOISE," a deep booming voice grumbled from the darkness above.

I craned my neck to peer up through the leaves at the pitch-black sky. "What the—"

The root-hand shook me so violently that finishing my sentence was impossible. "STOP YOUR SQUAWKING, YOU PUNY FOUL-MOUTHED CREATURE!" the voice rumbled from the treetops.

I tried to suck in a breath as it lifted me higher, tugging me out of Tristan's iron grip like it was nothing. "Sorry," I squeaked in the calmest voice I could muster in my panicked state.

To my relief, the shaking stopped. "WHY HAVE YOU DISTURBED MY SLEEP, INSECT?"

Insect? "Who am I talking to?" I muttered, hoping the question wouldn't provoke the root-hand to shake me again.

"I WILL ASK THE QUESTIONS," the voice growled, giving me a forceful shake to emphasize its words.

"Yeah," I muttered, "sure…of course."

"WHAT ARE YOU DOING IN MY TERRITORY?"

"We didn't know this was your territory," I muttered, "whoever you are."

The tree-hand tightened its vice grip on my leg and gave me another shake. "THAT IS NO EXCUSE!"

"Sorry," I whimpered.

And the shaking stopped.

I took a deep breath as I debated what to say to keep this tree-monster from shaking me to death, but I was at a loss. *Why wasn't anybody on the ground trying to help me out of this?*

"THEY HAVE NOT DISTURBED MY SLUMBER," the voice growled. "YOU HAVE."

Spectacular. On top of everything else, this thing could read my thoughts. Unsure what else to do, or what the hell I'd done to piss this thing off, I just nodded.

"SPEAK UP," the voice grumbled.

"Well," I muttered in the most diplomatic voice I could manage while dangling upside down like a piñata, "which is it?"

"WHICH IS WHAT?"

"I beg your pardon, almighty tree-voice," I muttered, "but which is it? Am I supposed to shut up or speak louder? I'm not sure how I can do both, and I'd really like to avoid doing anything that provokes you to shake me like a ragdoll."

"DO YOU THINK YOU'RE FUNNY, INSECT?"

A thousand smartass responses raced through my head as I opened my mouth, but the look on Tristan's face convinced me to shut my mouth without voicing any of them.

"We are deeply sorry for disturbing you, gatekeeper," Tristan murmured in his silkiest voice.

The root-hand loosened its grip on me ever-so-slightly at the sound of Tristan's voice. I held my breath, and hoped like hell its grip wouldn't slack enough to drop me on my head.

"WHY HAVE YOU WOKEN ME?" the voice demanded in a thunderous growl.

"We did not intend to," Tristan practically purred, laying the charm on so thick that I think we were all beginning to fall under his spell. "We are merely passing through on our way to No Man's Land."

"WHAT BUSINESS HAVE YOU THERE?" the voice boomed, tightening its grip on my ankle again.

"No business," Tristan crooned, "just pleasure."

"YOU DARE DISTURB MY REST TO SATISFY YOUR CARNAL DESIRES?"

"Begging your pardon," Tristan purred, "but we didn't realize you were sleeping here. If you unhand my friend, we will be on our way. I promise you, we will not disturb you ever again."

"WHY SHOULD I RELEASE THIS INSECT WITHOUT EXACTING ANY PUNISHMENT?"

Because he's of royal blood, Tristan replied, his telepathic voice no less seductive than his spoken.

I am? Oh yeah, right. I was a dragon, cousin to the Sarrum of Draumer, and son of the would-be-king. I closed my eyes and focused on the warmth of Godric's blood coursing through my veins. It was time to own that power. "That's right," I growled, "so unhand me at once."

At that, the root-hand opened and let me drop. It took me a couple pounding heartbeats to remember that I could fly. I unmasked and took flight an instant before my head hit the ground. Curious to see the face of this tree-bully, I flew up toward the treetops.

"YOU DO NOT FRIGHTEN ME, DRAGON," the rasping voice boomed.

It took a minute for my brain to process what I was seeing. The two large knots high up on the tree's trunk were this thing's eyes, and the giant hole below was its gaping mouth. Whatever this tree-creature was, it was enormous. My wings froze at the sight, and I dropped a few feet before reminding myself that I was a royal dragon. "You don't scare me either, tree-man."

A branch swung forward, swatting me like a flyswatter smacking a bug. "YOU ARE LITTLE MORE THAN A NUISANCE TO ME, DRAGON."

A fire raged in my belly as I flew closer to him. "What are you?"

"I AM A BEING MUCH OLDER THAN YOU AND YOUR KIND," the gaping tree mouth grumbled, "AND I WILL BE HERE LONG AFTER YOU ARE GONE."

A puff of smoke billowed from my nostrils. "Unless there's a forest fire."

The eyes of the tree-creature darkened as he narrowed them at me. "YOU DARE THREATEN ME?"

Shit. Okay, maybe I had overplayed my hand. It was probably time to cut my losses and get the hell out of there before this thing rammed a branch through my heart. "Um, no."

"MY KIND DOES NOT BOW TO YOU, DRAGON. SOME DEMONS ARE BEYOND YOUR KIN'S DOMAIN. OUT OF RESPECT FOR YOUR MORE INTELLIGENT ELDERS, I WILL SPARE THE LIVES OF YOU AND YOUR FRIENDS. HOWEVER, TRESSPASS HERE AGAIN, AND YOU WILL NOT FIND ME SO FORGIVING."

"Fair enough," I muttered, slowing my wing beats to descend. I'd seen more than enough of this creepy-ass tree's face.

The tree-demon caught me in its gnarled fist, tightening its hold as it wrapped around me. "IF IT WERE NOT FOR YOUR COUSIN, I WOULD DEVOUR YOUR SOUL AND GRIND THE BONES OF YOUR COMPANIONS TO DUST."

"Noted," I croaked as the wooden hand constricted my ribcage.

Apparently satisfied with my response, the tree-demon nodded. Then it erupted in an inferno of pitch-black flames, polluting the air above us with thick Dark smoke.

I could feel my blood boiling as I stared into the black flames in the demon's hollow eyes. Its smoke filled my lungs, singeing my insides and hardening like tar. I had come so far from where I started out. Now it was all going to end without me ever proving myself to the Sarrum, living up to my full potential and helping him take down my asshole birth father.

As the smoke began to cloud my thoughts, the demon whispered, "I DO NOT FEAR FOREST FIRES, INSECT."

Unable to voice a response with my lungs full of tar, I answered in thought. *Noted.*

As the branch-hand lowered me to my petrified traveling companions, I nodded. *I apologize for disturbing your sleep, sir.*

It deposited me on the ground in my human form, despite the fact that I hadn't intentionally unmasked.

As I sucked in a breath and stared up at the tree that no longer looked alive in any way, a tiny voice muttered from my shirt pocket, "I've hitched a ride with you long enough. I'll take my chances with Bob's Swiss cheese memory. Put me back in his pocket."

32

EMMA

I leaned forward in the chair at Charlie's bedside and took his limp hand in mine. I knew he couldn't feel it, but it made me feel like I was doing something to support him. His furrowed brow and twitching mouth suggested things weren't going well at the moment. I felt so useless sitting at home while they were all risking their lives on this mission.

Doc smiled at me as he walked past Charlie's bed with his arms full of medical supplies. "They are all capable warriors, Princess. I have no doubt that they will return home safely."

I gave Charlie's hand a squeeze as I smiled at the witchdoctor. "I just wish I could be doing something a little more useful."

As Doc crossed the room to shelve the supplies he was carrying, I looked down at Charlie's sleeping face. His expression seemed a bit more relaxed. Hopefully whatever difficulty had furrowed his brow was behind them now. I gave his hand another squeeze and whispered, "Wish I could be there to help, Charlie."

A shuddering gasp from the other end of the room made Doc drop everything in his hands to the floor. "I'm going to inform the Sarrum that Pip's awake," he hollered as he raced to the door.

Heart pounding, I let go of Charlie's hand and rushed toward Pip's bed.

He bolted upright, breathing in great heaving gasps, his pupils far too dilated for the sunlit room. Confusion clouded his eyes as I reached his bedside.

I took his hand and smiled at him with just a touch of dazzle, hoping it'd help calm his nerves. "You're safe here, Pip." When he responded with a quizzical frown, I whispered, "Sorry, I suppose I should call you Melvin in this world."

"Mel is fine," he muttered, already looking calmer than he had a moment ago.

"I'm Emma," I murmured.

"I know who you are, Princess." He glanced down at our joined hands and winced as David and Doc entered the room.

"It's fine, Mel," I whispered, letting go of his hand as I grinned at David. "I was only offering a bit of comfort."

"I appreciate the sentiment," he muttered, eyes glued to my husband as he and Doc approached us, "but I'd prefer to keep my heart in my chest."

"You needn't fear me," David murmured as he reached the bed. "Tell us what you came back to report."

"Right…" Mel blinked a few times, then nodded his thanks as Doc handed him his glasses. He expelled a tired sigh as he put them on, then muttered, "Charlie just pissed off a giant demon tree."

David's stoic expression showed no trace of worry as he nodded. "So you've reached the gatekeepers. You are making good progress." When Mel responded with a blank stare, David smiled. "You did not wake up screaming, so I assume the gatekeeper allowed all of you to pass through unharmed."

"Yeah, I guess so," Mel muttered. "I kinda passed out in Bob's pocket after the giant tree...uh, I mean the *gatekeeper* let go of Charlie."

"Those venerable creatures are the gatekeepers between No Man's Land and the Dark and Light realms," David explained with a patient smile.

"So," Mel muttered, "we made it past the gatekeeper?"

"I suppose you did," David agreed, "since you're still breathing."

Mel's eyes fixed on something in the distance as he nodded. "The gatekeepers guard both sides of No Man's Land," he muttered, more to himself than to any of us. "Does that mean we'll have to get past them on the other side to reach the Forest of Light?"

"No need," David murmured, smiling at me. "We will journey to the Forest of Light. You just focus on reaching that tavern in No Man's Land and accompanying Ezekiel to the Purists' meeting place."

Mel let out a sigh of relief. "Alright, boss." Dropping his head back against the pillow, he added, "Thanks."

"Godspeed," David replied with a nod.

At that, Mel closed his eyes and entered the Waters.

A mischievous grin spread across David's face as he held a hand out to me. "Do you feel up to a trip, my dear?"

I shot him a dazzling smile as I took his hand. "I wouldn't miss it for the world."

33

DAVID

A radiant smile spread across Emma's face as we entered the courtyard side by side. She looked stunning in her shimmering snow-white gown, such a stark contrast to my no-nonsense all black ensemble. "The sunglasses are an interesting touch," she whispered, tracing a fingertip along the frame of the dark glasses in my hand. "Why would you ever want to hide those eyes of yours?"

A wicked grin curved my lips, conveying my desire to delay our departure for an hour or two. Unfortunately, the time for pleasurable delays had passed. "It's best to keep my eyes covered in the Light Forest," I murmured, touching a hand to her cheek. "The inhabitants there are nothing like you."

She raised an eyebrow as she tilted her head toward my palm. "How do you mean?"

"The Light creatures will fear the fire in my eyes," I murmured, tracing a thumb over her bottom lip.

"Then they're all fools," Emma whispered. "They don't know what they're missing."

I placed a hand on the small of her back with a deep-throated chuckle as we started across the courtyard. "They have good reason to fear me. You are the only Light creature who has no need to."

"I don't buy that for a second," she whispered as we reached the Waterfall. "You wouldn't harm them any more than you would harm me."

I winked at her then slipped on the sunglasses. "I would be far less forgiving of their transgressions." With that, I stepped into the Water.

As I stepped out into a meadow in the Light realm, the blinding brilliance of the sun rendered my Dark eyes useless. Thankfully, my ears could more than compensate.

My wife stepped out an instant after me, a quiet gasp escaping her lips as she took in her surroundings.

Although I still couldn't see, I could hear enough to appreciate her reaction. Songbirds called out to one another across the vast expanse of open space. Unlike the melancholy tunes of the night birds in the Dark Forest, their melody was a joyous celebration of life. A warm breeze blew across the meadow, caressing blades of spring grass and the petals of a wide array of wildflowers, no doubt in every color of the rainbow. However, more than any other sensation, I felt my wife's guilt for having teased me about the sunglasses now that my primary reason for donning them was apparent.

I took her hand in mine. *Do not feel bad for a moment, Princess. My feelings are not so easily hurt.*

Her joy washed over me like an ocean wave, saturating all of my senses for a moment.

I blinked my eyes as the scenery began to come into focus. "Do you regret having missed out on this all your life?"

She frowned at me as if I had lost my mind. "This is nice, but it doesn't hold a candle to our clearing."

I touched a hand to her cheek, staving off my own guilt for having denied her all of this.

She took my hand from her cheek and kissed it, then tugged me forward. "You're being ridiculous."

I lowered my mouth to her ear as I stepped up beside her. "Do you suppose I would let any other Light creature speak to me that way?"

"I don't care about any other Light creatures," she muttered as we reached the crest of a hill.

Creatures of Light were splashing about in the lake down below, some clothed in gauzy garments that clung to their wet bodies, others immodestly soaking in the sunlight without a stich of clothing on. Their playful laughter added another gleeful element to the songbirds' melody. Slender female creatures with shimmering wings hovered just above the surface of the lake, their bare feet skimming the surface as they flitted about between the creatures playing in the water. Some of the swimmers were human in appearance. Others displayed brilliantly colored mermaid tails that glinted in the sunlight as they dove beneath the surface.

I glanced at my wife beside me, expecting to see a flicker of despondence in her expression.

Instead, she raised an eyebrow. "No, I do *not* regret missing out on spending my adult life frolicking in the Water like a child."

"Fair enough," I murmured. "As I said before, you are not like these other creatures."

The steel of an elven blade poked me square in the back, rudely interrupting our conversation as a highborn male voice demanded, "How did you get here, Dark creature?"

Emma bit her lip as she looked up at me.

I let her hand slip from mine as I turned to face the elf without shying away from his blade. Instead, I glanced downward as he prodded my chest with it. "I would be careful with that toy of yours. You wouldn't want to hurt yourself."

A huff of indignation hissed from the lips of the pointy-eared young man holding the sword. His facial features were so delicate that they bordered on effeminate, and he was dressed in an utterly garish violet garment that did nothing to accentuate his masculinity. "How dare you?"

"How dare I *what*?"

"Do you realize who you are speaking to?" the boy demanded.

"No, I do not," I murmured as I took a step toward him, moving the tip of his blade right along with me, "nor do I care."

The boy let out another huff as he prodded my chest with the blade.

"You know," I whispered as I took another step toward him, no longer amused by his manner of greeting us, "a threat is only as effective as the threat-maker's resolve to follow through."

Unable to control his temper, the elf pulled his arm back and jabbed his sword at my chest with the full

DREAM FRAGMENTS

force of his weight as he hollered, "You are trespassing here, demon."

The boy's eyes widened as the blade crumpled against my chest like tinfoil. He released the hilt of his sword with a yelp of alarm as the blade began to melt and watched in horror as it dripped to the ground in a molten heap of silver.

"What are you?" he muttered as he took a step back.

I removed my sunglasses as I advanced toward him, the sting from the Light well worth it. I couldn't help grinning at the look of shock on his face as he stared, transfixed by the flames in my eyes. "I am the Sarrum, you dolt, and I have come to speak with your Queen."

The boy dropped to his knees and lowered his head toward the ground as he muttered, "Then...is this our Princess beside you, my King?"

"You can call me Emma," my wife replied as she stepped beside me.

"Not if you value your life," I interjected.

The boy dropped his head so close to the ground that he practically kissed the dirt. "I would be honored to take you to my Queen, Sarrum."

"Please do," I murmured. "I am anxious to ask her if this is how her border patrol greets all Dark creatures who venture into her territory."

"Sir?" he muttered, wincing as he looked up at me.

"Any Dark creature whom the gatekeepers have allowed to pass into the Light poses no more threat to your kind than you do," I replied. "Yet, you greet me to your territory with the blade of your sword. Is this how my guards ought to welcome a Light creature who ventures into the Darkness?"

"No, Sarrum," he whimpered as his eyes filled with tears. "Please forgive me."

"I'm not an especially forgiving man," I snarled. "So I suggest you remain alert to properly greet visitors to this realm whilst on duty in the future, rather than wandering off to ogle the sunbathers."

"Yes, Sarrum," he sniveled, his voice little more than a whisper.

I shook my head in disgust at his spinelessness. "You do realize that you have made an attempt on the life of the Sarrum of Draumer, don't you?"

The color drained from the boy's face as he whispered, "Sir?"

"I could execute you on the spot for your actions."

Fear leaked from every pore of the elf's body as tears streamed down his cheeks.

"Welcome another Dark creature into the Light with the tip of your sword, and I shall relieve you of your cold heart," I murmured. "Do I make myself clear?"

"Yes, Sarrum," he whimpered, wiping the snot from his nose with a shirtsleeve as he bowed his head.

I winked at Emma, then slipped my sunglasses back on. "Lead us to your Queen. You have wasted enough of my time."

My wife gave me a disapproving frown as the elf stood with his shoulders hunched and his teary eyes averted.

"Yes, Sarrum," the boy muttered as he started walking, hunched over like an old man.

I grinned at my bride as we fell into step behind him. *Don't give me that look, Princess. Had he greeted us properly and inquired about our intentions in a polite manner, there would be no need for me to scold him.*

Emma narrowed her eyes at me as I took her hand. *Didn't you overdo it a bit?*

I flashed her a wicked grin as we followed the elf onto a well-lit path through a forest of pure white trees and fragrant flowers. *Not at all. On the contrary, I think you have made me soft. There was a time when I would have gutted our guide for greeting me like that.*

She shook her head. *If you insist on calling him out for his transgressions, you could've at least said something about that hideous purple outfit he's wearing.*

I suppressed a chuckle as I pulled her close and kissed her forehead. *I'll keep that in mind for the future.*

34

CHARLIE

None of us had said a word since the demon-tree granted us passage into No Man's Land. Pip was back in Bob's pocket, and I was pretty sure he was still pissed at me, but that might've been all in my head. The paranoia in this wasteland was palpable. Something in the fog-dense air messed with your mind.

No Man's Land definitely lived up to its name. The terrain was more wide-open than the Dark Forest, which just made you feel all the more vulnerable. The air was thick with grayish-brown clouds, giving the whole atmosphere a dismal polluted feel. Huge fissures zigzagged through the bone-dry ground without a single blade of grass, or even so much as a weed. We did pass the occasional tree, but they were all leafless and rotting. A sparse scattering of buildings dotted the barren landscape. Some were nothing more than slapped-together shacks, and others were massive buildings that looked like they might've been grand a few thousand years ago. I wouldn't have set foot in any of those buildings—big or small—because the whole place had the feel of a post-apocalyptic wasteland, where zombies or radiation-mutated marauders could be hiding behind every door. Like I said, this place made you paranoid. As if all of that wasn't creepy enough, the skeletal remains of massive creatures also dotted the barren landscape. Many of them looked alarmingly similar in shape to a dragon's frame, but I tried not to dwell on that.

As we trudged in silence through this nightmarish landscape, I found myself longing for the ominous whispering of the dryads in the Dark Forest. No Man's Land appeared to go on forever in every direction. *How will we ever reach the Light Forest?*

Pip hopped to attention in Bob's pocket. *Oh yeah. I forgot to mention, we don't have to go on to the Forest of Light. The Sarrum said they've got that covered. We just have to make it to Hell's Gate.*

"Awesome. That sounds like a much cheerier place," I muttered under my breath as I waved a hand to swat at a mosquito that seemed intent on buzzing in my ear.

The bug buzzed off to avoid my hand but flew back the instant I lowered it. "Turn back before it's too late," a tiny voice buzzed in my ear.

I stopped moving and glanced at the faces of my travel companions. Most of them responded with quizzical frowns, but Pip and Tristan seemed to have similar reactions. "Did you just hear something speak?" I whispered.

"Go home," the voice buzzed in my ear, "or you'll all die a horrible death."

I lifted my hand to swat the talking mosquito away again.

"No!" Pip shrieked before my hand connected with it.

I froze with my hand in the air. "Why?"

"Look closer," Pip whispered. As soon as he said it, one of the mosquitos flew into Bob's pocket beside him.

I was about to say *I told you so* but as I stepped closer, I realized why Pip had stopped me. It wasn't a bug at all. The buzzing creature looked like a tiny woman with dragonfly wings. No one would accuse this bug-sized woman of being beautiful. Her face was withered and grayish, and so were her wings.

"What are you?" I muttered.

She scowled at me then crossed her arms over her chest as she turned to Pip. "Get out of here before you all lose your lives."

"What's your name?" Pip whispered.

"Turn back," buzzed the insect-woman hovering by my ear.

"What are these things?" I whispered as I turned to Tristan.

"They're imps," he muttered, extending a finger and grinning when one of the tiny winged women landed on it. "For the most part, they're harmless."

The imp on Tristan's hand blinked up at him without saying a word.

"Why ain't she tellin you to get lost, pretty boy?" Bob muttered as he peered down at the thing in his pocket beside Pip.

"What woman has ever told an incubus to get lost?" I muttered as I stood at the ready, just in case this hybrid version of young and old Bob lost it again and decided to evict both passengers from his pocket. "Why should these things be any different?" An image of Tristan charming the imp housekeeper who worked for the Talbots while Isa was in a coma popped into my head, and I shuddered. I was about to ask why the hell he'd flirt with something so ugly, but then I remembered Mia was a faceless changeling, *before* sticking my foot in my mouth for once.

"Go back," the imp buzzed in my ear.

But the one on Tristan's finger just stood there in a daze, blinking up at his beautiful face.

"Is that all they can say?" I whispered.

"No," Tristan muttered, "but these poor creatures seem to be in shock. I think they're trying to warn us away from something."

"Awesome," Pip muttered as he stared into the dull beady eyes of the little lady beside him. "That's just awesome."

"Can we take you somewhere safe?" Tristan asked the tiny hag perched on his finger.

Her widened eyes continued to study every perfect detail of his face as she shook her head. "Not safe."

"Right, this place isn't safe," Tristan murmured. "But can we take you somewhere else?"

"Nowhere is safe," the tiny creature whimpered. Then she nodded to her friends and they all flew off, leaving us with our mouths hanging open.

"Well," Bob muttered under his breath, "that was real fuckin comfortin."

God help me, I was starting to like hybrid-Bob. If you asked me, he was the best of both worlds. He had the bravery of the noble warrior in Draumer and the foul mouth of the old guy I'd found so entertaining during my stay at the facility. "Yeah," I muttered, squinting at the massive skeleton splayed out across the scorched ground in the distance, "I can't wait to see what we run into next."

35

TRISTAN

I think we'd all hoped the spottiness of our memories would recede after we left the Dark Forest. Unfortunately No Man's Land was just as bad, if not worse. It felt like we'd been walking through this wasteland in silence for ages. It was killing me that I couldn't talk to the members of my team like I normally would, especially Mia. I was dying to know how she was holding up. Was she regretting this whole venture? Because I was sure as hell starting to. *Some leader I was.*

I couldn't stand the fact that the men had been doing all of what little talking we'd done on this trip. Mia, Addison, Nellie, and Rose had to stay in character, and captive slaves wouldn't take part in their captors' conversations. We'd all known that going into this, but the reality of it was almost unbearable. Who the hell wanted to listen to a bunch of guys bitching about their dire circumstances? Women brought comfort and hope to a conversation, and we needed a whole lot of both at this point. I was dying to turn around, apologize to every member of the team, and lead them all back to the palace.

As we trekked across this scorched wasteland, I couldn't help wondering what the hell had happened to it. Who knew? Maybe this was how it'd always looked. I suppose that'd make sense. The place was sort of a purgatory between the hellish Dark Forest and the heavenly Forest of Light. What dwelt between those two extremes? Nothingness, and No Man's Land was exactly that—neither good nor bad—just a whole lot of nothing.

I was getting close to losing my mind by the time we heard the first hint of music in the distance. I looked at the others, hoping it wasn't just my imagination playing tricks on me. But they'd all heard it. I could tell by the looks of relief on their faces. The music wasn't soothing or beautiful. It wasn't even pleasant to listen to, but it was something besides the deafening silence and nothingness of this wasteland, and that made it pretty damn wonderful.

As we picked up our pace and headed toward the source of the discordant tune, I hoped to God this was the tavern we were looking for. If it wasn't Hell's Gate, we could be walking straight into a trap. For all we knew, this could be what those imps were trying to warn us about. But what other choice did we have than to press on?

As we moved closer and the music grew louder, a shabby-looking building appeared up ahead, and I mean that literally. The place took shape out of nowhere as we approached, almost as if this establishment only existed for those who were looking for it. The magic behind that sort of camouflage was sensible. What better place for outlaws to congregate, than a hole-in-the-wall dive bar that didn't exist unless you were seeking it out?

The tavern was constructed out of a combination of rough stone and rotting lumber. The floorboards on the front porch looked like they'd crumble beneath the weight of a few heavy patrons, and the skulls of various creatures were tacked to the wooden posts that held up the sagging porch roof. As we moved closer, the stench in the air made me wonder if those skulls had been recently severed from the heads of the creatures they'd belonged to. *Hell's Gate* was painted in peeling red letters across a wooden sign, dangling from the one remaining chain that hadn't completely rusted through.

I steeled my nerves as we neared the bouncer standing by the porch steps. He was a hefty bald-headed demon whose bulging muscles were somewhat obscured beneath a solid layer of blubber. This guy had clearly never missed a meal in his life, but you sure as hell wouldn't dare tease him about it. He looked like a mix of troll and sorrow, with maybe a bit of ogre thrown in for good measure.

The bouncer pushed himself up from his leaning stance against the porch and grimaced at us, displaying a mouthful of pointed teeth that looked about as well cared for as the building he guarded. His beady black eyes narrowed as he sized up the women in our group in a way that made me want to knock his rotten teeth in, but I restrained the impulse and reminded myself to stay in character. "Stick your property in the shed out back before you go inside," the bouncer grunted with a nod toward the females in our group.

I stepped closer, planting myself between him and the women. "That's not happening. They stay with us."

"The fuck they do," the bouncer grunted as he puffed out his chest.

As I was debating whether to start a fight or charm him, a deep voice called out, "Hey, asshole. Who the hell do you think you're talking to?" Zeke scowled at the bouncer as he ducked his head to clear the doorway and stepped out onto the porch. "This is my brother. I invited him to meet me here, and you're making me out to be a bad host. I sure as shit don't appreciate that."

The bouncer let out a gulp as he watched my half-incubus-half-giant friend cross the porch and descend the steps that creaked in protest under his weight. The members of my party looked equally unsure what to make of this terrifyingly beautiful creature.

"Hey, Zeke," I murmured as he pulled me into a rib-crushing bear hug. "It's been a long time."

"Too long," he grumbled, dropping the hug. He shoved the bouncer aside as his eyes traveled over the members of my team. The wide grin that spread across his face managed to reassure my group while simultaneously convincing the bouncer that he was sizing up the merchandise. "Put these women at the table next to mine," he demanded in a grizzly-bearish growl as he turned to the bouncer. "My brother's a smart guy. He knows better than to trust your ugly crew to keep their hands off his property while he's inside."

The bouncer bared his stained teeth at my friend but didn't voice a response.

"Tell me I'm wrong," Zeke growled as he bent down and stuck his face in the bouncer's. "I dare you."

The bouncer's puffed chest deflated as he shook his head and took a step back.

A shit-eating grin spread across Zeke's face as he placed a heavy hand on the bouncer's shoulder, visibly weighing him down a few inches. Then he turned his back to all of us and started up the porch steps. "Well," he growled without looking back, "what are you waiting for?"

All of us, including the bouncer, shrugged. Then we followed him up the steps and into the tavern.

36

MIA

A shiver raced down my spine as we followed Tristan's friend up the porch steps of the tavern. My body had gone rigid the instant that bouncer eyed us like pieces of meat and told Tristan to stick us in the shed out back. Too many demons had looked at me that way while I was tied to that bed in the Purists' cabin. Volunteering to go on this mission had been a huge mistake.

I knew the gigantic half-incubus we were following into Hell's Gate was an old friend of Tristan's, but it was still hard not to fear him. There was no denying that he was gorgeous and charming, but charm didn't work on me anymore, and the sheer size of this guy was terrifying. He could snap us all in half like twigs if he wanted to. I had to keep reminding myself that Zeke was on our side as I watched him cross the porch and enter the tavern.

As I followed Addison across the threshold, the ripe stench of a stagnant room full of sweaty demons engulfed me. I had to make a conscious effort not to gag as I watched Rose and Nellie file in after me. The interior of Hell's Gate made me feel as if we'd burrowed deep inside the belly of a cave. The windowless dome-ceilinged main room was constructed of rough stone with a dirt floor, and the lighting was so dim that I felt the need to reach out and take Nellie's hand. I told myself I did it because she was a creature of Light and she might not be able to see, but that wasn't the only reason I was gripping her hand.

Following Tristan's lead, we stood by the door and watched as Zeke crossed the room and approached a group of demons sitting at a table littered with empty bottles. He flashed them a charming grin and struck up a conversation with the biggest guy at the table. We were too far away to hear what he said, but the demon smashed his mug down on the table and shook his head as he growled something back. Zeke just kept on grinning as he yanked the muscular demon out of his chair and lifted him until his feet were dangling above the floor.

As Zeke made quick work of clearing the rest of the demons from the table, my eyes drifted to the source of the music that'd lured us to the tavern. A sinewy slack-jawed demon with yellow eyes and spindly fingers was seated at a grimy piano that sounded like it hadn't been tuned in decades. The melody he was playing was a bit off-key, but the tune was delicate and lovely. It was almost like listening to a music box with worn-out batteries that no longer played quite right. Although it sounded like a chorus of chain-smokers were belting out the lyrics to the melancholy tune, it was actually just one demon—a pestilent—seated on top of the piano. It was a bizarre performance to witness, a heart-wrenching harmony, sung just a bit out of sync by a chorus of voices all emanating from one creature whose body was entirely composed of buzzing insects. You'd think a floor show like that would be painful to listen to, but I found it beautiful in an eerie unnerving sort of way. Then again, I was a creature of Darkness. When I glanced at Nellie, the grimace on her face suggested she wasn't equally impressed.

My eyes kept drifting back to the entertainers as we followed Tristan across the room and sat down at the table Zeke had emptied and dragged beside his booth. The other females joined me at the table while the men slid into the booth with Zeke. As we were settling in, an apron-clad sorrow rushed over, muttering curses under his breath as he cleared the empty bottles from the table Zeke had secured for us.

I turned my attention back to the floor show across the room. There was so much sorrow in the singer's rasping voices that I found myself fighting back tears. I tuned out the rest of our surroundings and focused on the vocalist, so moved by his performance that I couldn't help fantasizing about ditching this whole mission and sneaking off with him. A creature with that much raw emotion in his voice couldn't possibly be dangerous. As he sang, his gaze drifted in our direction. When his eyes locked with mine, something in his tortured stare told me that he wasn't there by choice. I wanted to ask Tristan to help me save him, but I knew that wouldn't be possible. We each had our roles to play, and I was playing a helpless victim—a role I was all too familiar with. Unable to bear the agony in the pestilent's eyes, I dropped my gaze to the table.

Swept up in a sea of nightmarish memories, I missed everything that was said until Zeke's deep voice spoke inside my head. *I apologize for sticking you at a separate table, ladies. These ugly bastards aren't exactly big on women's rights.*

We knew that coming into this situation, Addison replied telepathically. *We're just thankful you were able to convince them to let us come inside.*

There was a note of amusement in Zeke's telepathic voice as he replied, *I can be pretty convincing when I want to be.*

I looked up at the giant-incubus, and he grinned at me as he spoke inside my head again. Although, this time the thought was only directed at me. *So, you are the creature who has captured Tristan's heart. Rest assured, I would lay down my life to keep the woman my brother loves safe from harm. Nobody's going to hurt any of you on my watch.*

I blinked at him a few times, wondering if I'd imagined those words.

But Zeke winked at me, assuring me that he'd said what I thought he had. Then he turned his attention to Pip. "Tristan said he'd be traveling with two and a half hunters. You must be the half."

Pip stared up at Zeke with his mouth hanging open, as if he couldn't quite decide whether to drool over him or stab him with a fork.

Zeke let out a great big belly laugh. "You're a feisty half-man by the looks of it. If you ask me, your valiance counts a hundredfold compared to these warriors who are so much larger than you. I admire your bravery, little man."

"Thanks...I think," Pip muttered as he blushed a deep shade of pink.

Charlie cleared his throat, drawing the giant's attention away from Pip. "Zeke, you called Tristan your brother. Are you two actually brothers?"

"Not by blood," Tristan murmured, grinning at Zeke, "but we grew up together at a camp on the outskirts of the Dark Forest."

Charlie nodded as his eyes darted from Tristan to Zeke. "Why do I get the feeling you're not talking about a summer camp with arts and crafts, and singing around a campfire?"

Zeke let out a deep-throated chuckle as he reached across the table and patted Charlie on the cheek. "You're adorable."

Charlie's cheeks flushed with color as he muttered, "Uh, thanks."

Shaking his head at the giant-incubus, Tristan murmured, "So, do we have a destination to head to?"

"Sure do," Zeke whispered. "Unfortunately, we've also got some company for the journey."

37

GODRIC

I'd been spending the majority of my time alone in the replica of my childhood bedroom since the day I inadvertently slipped in to escape the noise. It was easier to lose myself in the past when there were no moronic demons around to disrupt my train of thought. There was nothing to do now but revisit the remainder of my days with my sister. Pleasant or painful, I couldn't prevent the rest of the memories from flooding back.

I dropped my head against the headrest of the chair by the window that I'd been sitting in for the past hour. Then I closed my eyes and pictured my Lilly's face. With each memory I recalled, her features grew sharper. In fact, there were moments when the image seemed so real that I had to resist the urge to reach out and touch her.

She was such a strong creature. No one had ever given her enough credit for that. Not only did she gracefully play the hand she'd been dealt, but she did it all with a smile on her face. I could never forgive myself for being so weak that she'd felt the need to put on a brave face for me...

...The ache in my heart nearly incapacitated me as I approached the door to the bedchamber where Lilly was getting ready for the ceremony. I steeled my nerves, knocked on the door, and couldn't help frowning when Louise Talbot opened it. There truly were no limits to the Talbots' cruelty. Asking the woman who ought to be preparing for her own nuptials to tend to her replacement was a whole new level of sadism, even for them.

Louise forced a smile as she widened the opening. "Hello, Henry."

I nodded and forced a smile of my own. "Louise."

"You aren't supposed to see the bride before the ceremony," Louise muttered.

I bit my tongue to stop myself from commenting on the ridiculousness of her statement. Was she so in denial that she'd convinced herself the two of us were still the ones about to wed? "That only applies to the groom," I whispered. "Since our father is no longer with us, I have come to walk my sister down the aisle."

"Oh," Louise muttered as her eyes grew distant.

I had no idea what this woman was thinking or feeling. No matter how things had turned out for the two of us, I doubt I ever would have. Louise Talbot was no treasure to me.

"Henry?" Lilly called out from inside the room.

I pushed past Louise and watched her slink out the door. Then I shut the door behind her, turned, and got my first look at Lilly.

My God, she was breathtaking. Her hair was pinned up in elegant curls. Massive jewels crowned her head, dripped from her earlobes, and circled her slender neck; but her veil and gown were magnificent in their simplicity.

The gauzy white fabric cascaded down her slender frame, hugging each perfect curve and shimmering with each slight movement.

I blinked the tears from my eyes and grinned at her. "You look stunning."

"Thank you," she whispered as she tilted her chin up and blinked her eyes to keep her tears from ruining her makeup. The makeup was unnecessary. My sister was a fresh-faced creature of pure beauty. Painting her face merely obscured her natural perfection.

"Are you ready?" I whispered, extending an arm to her.

"No," she muttered. "But I don't really have any other options, do I?"

I crossed the distance between us, and a whimper escaped her throat as I kissed her forehead and wrapped my arms around her. "I am so sorry I failed you, Lilly."

She shook her head as she pulled back from my arms. "You didn't fail me, Henry. None of this is your fault."

"I promised to always keep you safe," I muttered in a rough whisper.

"You're still here," she murmured, reaching up to touch my cheek. "I know how much this is killing you. You were supposed to be the next Sarrum. The title doesn't rightfully belong to Alexander."

I opened my mouth to respond, but I couldn't seem to find my voice.

"But you're still here, Henry," she muttered. "As much as this is killing you, you haven't left my side. That means everything to me. I couldn't bear any of this without you."

"You'll never have to," I murmured.

She smiled at me as she took my arm. "I know."

We drew a collective breath then left the room arm in arm to march toward her death sentence...

...When the minister declared them husband and wife, I felt my heart fracture within my chest. Each celebratory moment I observed from the shadows that day deepened the cuts. Each monumental event in her marriage detached me a bit further from everyone but her. I became a useless husk of my former self. All I could offer my sister was my presence in her life, my shoulder to cry on, and my company to help her pass the time...

...After Alexander kissed my sister's cheek and said his goodbyes, I allowed some time to pass before excusing myself from the room.

My sister's husband hadn't left the grounds yet. His car was still parked in the drive, but it took me a while to locate him in the garden.

My approach was clearly lacking in stealth because he smiled when he heard me coming. "What can I do for you, Henry?"

"You can tell me why you feel it necessary to go off on another business trip so soon after returning from the last," I growled. "Can you not at least pretend to love my sister?"

The jovial grin slipped from his face. "I DO love her, you fool."

"Fine way you have of showing it," I snarled.

"Really?" he growled as he stepped toward me. "She is my dearest treasure, Henry. I am perfectly attuned to her wants and needs. So why do you suppose I go on so many trips?"

His answer was so unexpected that I found myself at a loss for words.

"What she wants most, is to spend time with you," he growled under his breath. "I am not the soul Lilly treasures, but you knew that already." He waited a

moment for me to respond. When I didn't, he muttered, "I leave to give her time alone with you."

I'm not sure I managed any response at all before he stormed off to his car and drove away...

...It was only a few business trips after that when the heart I already knew to be damaged was broken beyond repair...

...It was a lovely spring day. Lilly and I had decided to get out and enjoy the sunshine by bringing a picnic lunch to the lake.

Her food still sat untouched in front of her. She pushed it aside and smiled at me, but there was a reluctance to her expression. I hadn't seen anything like it since the night she came to my room and confessed how she felt about me.

"What is it?" I murmured, shoving the rest of my lunch aside and taking her hand in mine. "Something has been troubling you all day. Talk to me, Lilly."

Her eyes drifted to the lake and for several moments, we sat there in silence while she worked up the courage to speak. Finally, she brushed a tear from her cheek and turned toward me. "You're going to be an uncle."

Blue flames obscured every trace of our surroundings as I muttered, "No."

"I should've run away with you the day that first messenger came to our house and informed us that I was to wed Alexander," she muttered.

The fear in her voice doused the flames within me. She needed me to be strong for her now. I pulled her into my arms and tightened my hold when she dropped her head to my shoulder and burst into tears. "You're tough," I whispered in her ear. "You can survive this."

She shook her head without lifting it from my shoulder. "He's too strong. I can feel it already, Henry. I won't be around to raise this child."

There was nothing I could do or say to fix this, so I held her in my arms and wept with her...

...Perhaps it was love that kept Alexander away on business for the majority of my sister's difficult pregnancy. Although, I suspected it was cowardice. It was easier to convince yourself that everything would turn out fine when you remained at a distance.

I, on the other hand, was there for every agonizing second of the pregnancy that plagued my sweet Lilly. I stood by her, held her hand and kept her company, and watched helplessly whilst that monster in her belly slowly drained the life from her...

...Lilly was only two weeks shy of her due date when Alexander decided to take off for Brazil. I had held my tongue on all the other trips because I wanted her all to myself, but he was the cause of her demise. He ought to at least be man enough to stay and watch what his love had done to her.

I was waiting for him in his study when he came in to collect his things for the trip.

"We've already had this conversation," he muttered as he entered the room.

"You don't deserve her," I snarled. "Are you not even man enough to stand by her and witness the damage you've done?"

He shook his head as he walked to his desk and unlocked the top drawer. "Neither of you want me here, Henry. So why do you fault me for leaving?"

"Because, you stupid son of a bitch," I snarled as I stood from the couch, "you did this to her. How can you

claim to love her and run away when she needs you the most?"

"She has never needed me," he growled. "It's always been you!"

"That's a rather convenient excuse," I snarled. "But if you are not man enough to stand by her now, don't you dare come back after she's gone!"

"I am the Sarrum," he growled as he stepped out from behind his desk. "Have you forgotten that? You are only here because I allow it, because she wants you here and I want to please her."

A maniacal burst of laughter sprang from my mouth. "Please her? You've sentenced her to death."

38

EMMA

The longer they kept us waiting in the Fairy Queen's sitting room, the less patient David and I became. I'd never met this woman, but I disliked her already. The Light kingdom wasn't so far removed from the Dark that she had no knowledge of the war that was brewing. Keeping us waiting just to make herself feel important was childish and petty.

I dropped my head to David's shoulder and sunk against the warmth of his solid frame as his arm wrapped around me. For lack of anything else to do, I perused our surroundings for the umpteenth time. The gleaming white marble structure they'd seated us in was open to the elements, allowing the occupants to enjoy the clear blue sky, the brilliance of the sunlight, and all the fairytale splendor of this sickeningly sweet kingdom. Maybe it was the fact that David's blood inked my skin that made all this frivolity turn my stomach, or maybe I'd just spent too much time living in Darkness to appreciate the Light. Either way, it irritated me that they hadn't seated us in an enclosed area where my husband wouldn't need to shade his eyes.

"You do realize this is all for your benefit," David murmured in my ear.

"For me?" I whispered, tilting my head to look up at him and loving the fact that his brilliant blue eyes weren't hidden from me at this angle. "Why?"

"The Fairy Queen is obsessively jealous of you," he murmured. "The throne that she occupies is rightfully yours. However, you have attained a far more covetable title. She is well aware of how inferior she is to you, so she wants to make herself feel important in your presence."

"She's wasting precious time," I whispered.

A grin of adoration spread across my husband's face. "You were raised to be a practical creature, Princess. These Light souls are far too concerned with their own self-worth to worry about wasting anyone else's time."

I shot him a dazzling smile, a subtle attempt to ease his impatience. "Have I thanked you lately for rescuing me from all of this?"

Before David could respond with anything more than a throaty chuckle, an entourage of dainty creatures with sparkling wings and whimsically impractical outfits in every color of the rainbow came flitting into the open-air sitting room. The last to enter was a waifish fairy whose pale pink wings resembled the dew-drenched petals of a rose. As she stepped toward us, I couldn't help wondering how much time it'd taken to make her gown. The silk had been dyed an identical shade of pink to match her wings, and the tiny gems adorning the fabric caught the sunlight and glistened like perfectly placed drops of dew. "Please rise for the Queen," she instructed in a lilting voice.

As I lifted my head from David's shoulder, he tightened his hold on me and murmured, "Don't you dare."

A giggle that I couldn't entirely suppress drew the rose-petal fairy's attention to me as I whispered, "Trust me, it didn't even cross my mind."

The raven-haired fairy Queen glared at me as she sashayed into the room, but she hoisted the many jeweled layers of her gown, climbed the steps of her marble throne and sat down without commenting on my laughter.

"Perhaps I should visit your realm more often," David mused as he turned toward the rose-petal fairy.

Her pale cheeks flushed with color as she raised a quizzical eyebrow.

A wicked grin spread across David's face, deepening the fairy's blush as he murmured, "Do you not intend to introduce your guests to the room?"

The fairy squinted as she looked the two of us over. "I don't..."

My husband slipped off his sunglasses, and she gasped and dropped to her knees the instant his flame-filled eyes met hers.

The rest of the Queen's entourage did the same the moment they realized who he was.

But the Queen responded with a loud huff as she crossed her arms over her chest. "What brings you here today, Sarrum?"

"I am still waiting for a proper greeting," David replied as he put his sunglasses back on. "Perhaps I should reinstate the practice of stationing members of the royal guard within your realm to give the Light creatures a refresher course in the hierarchy of the kingdoms."

The fairy Queen frowned as she uncrossed her arms. "I do apologize, Sarrum. Of course, we are happy to welcome you and your wife to the Light realm."

"*My wife?*" David echoed in a Darker tone. "I do not recall that being the proper way to address your Queen."

A few of the Light creatures kneeling before us looked over their shoulders at the fairy Queen, suggesting they actually *could* use a lesson in the hierarchy within the realms.

"*My wife,*" David growled, addressing his words to the Queen's subjects, "is the rightful Queen of the Light realm. The Queen whom you bow to only sits on that throne because *my wife* reigns over all realms alongside me. All souls of the Light, Dark and In-Between realms kneel before my bride."

"Is that why you've popped in for a visit," the fairy Queen grumbled, "to test our manners?"

"No," David replied. "You know exactly why we have come."

One of the smaller kneeling creatures peered up at me as he whispered, "Why?"

"Our way of life is under siege," David replied matter-of-factly. "Surely you have at least heard of the Purists?"

"Godric's supporters," another kneeling fairy muttered with a nod.

"Yes," David murmured. "They are preparing to attempt a hostile takeover. If they were to succeed, all realms would suffer the consequences."

"So," the fairy Queen muttered as she gripped the arms of her throne, "you've come seeking soldiers to fight for you?"

"How much respect do you suppose Godric and his followers would show the creatures of the Light realm?" David asked. "He thinks them almost as worthless as the Unsighted."

"How dare you?" the fairy Queen squealed as she stood from her throne.

"How dare I *what*?" David growled as he stood up and stepped toward her. "Consider what a change in Sarrum would mean for your realm? Would you have me forget you and leave you defenseless if Godric were to win this war? Because he and his supporters certainly won't forget that you are here. They already capture and sell Light creatures who happen to cross their paths into slavery. Is this of no concern to you?"

"None of that will happen," the Queen grumbled, although her eyes looked less certain.

"This is ridiculous," I snarled as I stood and moved to my husband's side. "If you can't set aside your bruised ego and do what's best for your realm, perhaps I should take my rightful place on that throne."

The fairy Queen let out the least intimidating growl I'd ever heard as she took to the air and hovered above the steps of her throne. "How dare you! You're nothing but the Sarrum's wingless little plaything!"

For the first time in history, storm clouds darkened the sky above the Light realm, and every creature within earshot screamed as a deafening crack of thunder shook the ground. Then my husband unmasked to his dragon form, causing several of the Light creatures to lose consciousness.

The fairy Queen dropped to the ground and knelt with the others as the Dragon King stepped toward her. "I apologize," she whimpered.

"I'm afraid that's not good enough," I replied as I moved to my husband's side. "You are not worthy of my throne."

39

CHARLIE

I thought things were tense when we started out on this mission, but as we trudged through No Man's Land with our new traveling companions, I found myself longing for the uncomfortable silences we shared back then. Unfortunately, there was no way to avoid including them on this leg of our journey. Zeke would've raised suspicions if he turned down their offer to lead us to the Purists' new headquarters. After what happened at their last meeting place, Godric's followers weren't taking chances by sharing the location of the new spot in writing, or even saying it out loud. If you wanted to get there, you had to use the buddy system and go with someone who knew the way and was willing to vouch for you. Although our dim-witted guides were too paranoid to tell us their names, they were apparently perfectly comfortable leading us straight to the Purists' top secret hideout. The dipshit twins might have been outlaws, but they weren't exactly mastermind criminals.

DREAM FRAGMENTS

Our new travel buddies were a couple of beefy Cyclopes with major hygiene issues. Compared to these two, Pip smelled like a fucking rose garden. Since neither Cyclops would divulge his name, we'd taken to calling them Curly and Moe. Following the one-eyed stooges through the vast expanse of wasteland was frustrating as hell because they had about as much depth perception as they had brains. Every so often, whichever of us was closest to them would have to grab their arms to stop them from stumbling over or crashing into something they'd misjudged their distance from. As miserable as I was with this new arrangement, I had no right to complain because it was much worse for the women in our group. Now that the moron twins were with us, we didn't dare say anything at all out of character. Even telepathic conversation would've posed too great a risk because despite how dumb the average Cyclops was, their telepathic abilities were actually quite keen.

I couldn't even begin to guess how long we'd been following them because the sun never rose or set in No Man's Land. The sky was always the same dingy hopeless shade of yellowish-gray. And aside from Pip, no one in our core group needed sleep—although, we now had to waste time pretending to whenever the Cyclopes needed rest—so there was no accurate way to keep track of our days and nights.

Desperate to break up the monotony for a while, I dropped back in line to walk next to Zeke. "So, how exactly did you and our two guides meet?"

A sly grin spread across Zeke's devilishly handsome face as he glanced at the two stooges up ahead. "Curly and Moe stumbled upon me while I was pillaging a band of scavengers in the Dark Forest."

Tristan shook his head to scold us for chatting without turning around to look at us. My eyes drifted toward him as I muttered, "And?"

"And we struck up a deal," Zeke continued, paying no attention to Tristan's silent scolding.

Tristan glared at us over his shoulder, and I gave him an apologetic shrug as I whispered, "Why?"

"Well, they snuck up on me, intending to gut me and take the spoils I'd rightfully plundered," Zeke murmured in a deep sultry tone that made me feel the need to dig my nails into my palms and remind myself that I wasn't gay. "But when they got a closer look at the sixteen freshly-killed ogre corpses I was ransacking, they thought better of it and decided to offer me a deal instead."

Painfully aware that Zeke's devilish grin was making my cheeks burn, I cleared my throat. "What was the deal?"

Zeke's smile widened as he winked at me, letting me know that my blushing hadn't gone unnoticed. "I let them take a share of the loot in exchange for directions to the next slavers' auction."

"Huh," I muttered in a throaty rasp.

Since I couldn't control my body's reaction to the giant-incubus, and that was all I could think to say, we fell back into a tense silence.

As best I could tell, it was only a few hours after that when we caught our first glimpse of the new meeting place in the distance up ahead. I could sense the apprehension of every member of our team as the realization that we'd finally reached our destination began to sink in. If it'd just been us, I couldn't help wondering if we would've turned tail and headed back to the palace to share the location instead of marching straight into enemy headquarters. But it wasn't just us, and we had no way to discuss what came next in private.

With each step we took toward the dilapidated cement structure that served as the Purists' new headquarters, my thoughts muddied and the stifling humidity intensified. Maybe it was just my imagination, but I could've sworn the sky was also darkening. Curious whether I was the only one feeling the effects, I stole a few sideways glances at the other members of our group. Everyone but Rose wore a vacant expression, their hair matted with sweat as they tugged at their damp clothing, as if the conditions were bothering them far more than they bothered the two of us. Despite the brain fog and the sweltering heat, we pressed on.

When Bob let out a muffled grunt, I turned toward the young knight and grimaced at the bewildered expression on his normally stoic face. If this place was affecting my nearly impenetrable dragon brain, I could only imagine how bad it must've been for him. A second after that thought occurred to me, it was lost in the ever-thickening fog that was clouding my mind.

"What the fuck's wrong with the air round here?" hybrid-Bob muttered.

Curly stopped walking and grabbed Moe's arm so he'd do the same.

The rest of us followed suit, and we all turned our attention to Bob as Curly rolled his bloodshot eye at him. "It's just the warding around the place. If that's bothering ya, you ain't gonna last long inside."

"Nah, I'm good." As he shook his head, Bob cast a sideways glance at Nellie. She and Addison were the members of our party who were most likely to be affected by the Dark magic warding the building because they were both creatures of Light.

Committed to playing her role, Nellie dropped her gaze to the ground and responded to Bob's unspoken concern with a barely perceptible shake of her head.

There was no more discussion among any of us as we crossed the rest of the distance between us and the Purists' hideout. With every step, I found it more difficult to recall why we were heading toward such an undesirable place. As I squinted and tried my damdest to clear the brain fog, a memory washed over me, displacing everything else. The weirdest part was that the memory wasn't *mine*...

...Gut-wrenching screams echoed through the room as a gentle ocean breeze caressed the curtains of the open windows, making them billow inward. Despite the fresh air wafting in, the air in the room tasted stale.

I squeezed Clay's hand as another scream drowned out the comforting lull of the ocean waves. Disoriented as I was, it took me a few seconds to grasp that the sound had come from me. The crippling pain was making it almost impossible to see or think straight. All I could do was scream at the top of my lungs and squeeze my friend's hand until it subsided.

My scream died off as the pain began to ebb, and Clay placed a cool washcloth on my forehead while the doctor spoke to me in a thick Scottish accent. But I passed out from exhaustion before I could decipher the meaning of his words. This had been going on for a day and a half. My energy was so zapped by this point that I drifted off the moment each contraction subsided and didn't regain consciousness until the next one hit.

I lifted my head off the couch in the cabin in the woods and blinked my surroundings into focus.

"You're doing great." Jack smiled at me as he drew me into his arms. "You're gonna beat this."

I tried to smile back, but it was a weak attempt. I was too drained to put on a brave face at this point. "How would you know how I'm doing?" I muttered as my eyes drooped shut. "You aren't there."

The moment I opened my eyes, the pained expression on Jack's face made me regret those words. "I'd be there if I could, Angie. You don't know how much I wish you'd come and got me in the waking world before this started. I should be the one holding your hand in that other world."

"Clay is taking good care of me," I muttered.

"I don't doubt that," Jack whispered, "but it should be me beside the woman I love. I'd do anything to be there helping you through this."

I bit my lip and squeezed my eyes shut, praying that he'd listen to reason now.

"No, Angie," he whispered, shaking his head as I looked up at him. "I can't."

"You didn't even let me say it," I whimpered.

The faint smile on his lips did nothing to downplay the agony in his eyes. "I didn't want you to feel like you had to," he muttered. "I know what you're gonna say. How the hell can you expect me to leave you here, Angie?"

"We have no way of knowing when this baby will come," I muttered, "or how long it'll be before he drifts off to sleep and enters the Waters for the first time."

"*Then we might have lots of time left that we could be spending together,*" *he croaked.*

"*Jack,*" *I pleaded, squeezing his hand,* "*we might only have minutes. I love you with all my heart, and I know you're still rooting for me to pull through this. But that's not—*"

"*Don't say that,*" *he interrupted.* "*If you don't keep a positive attitude, you've got no shot at beating this.*"

"*This isn't something to beat,*" *I whispered.* "*This is my son, and I know in my gut that I won't survive his birth. Please don't let me die worrying that you didn't get to the Waters in time.*"

Jack tipped his head back and blinked at the ceiling as he shook his head. "*This is insane.*"

"*I know it feels that way,*" *I whispered.* "*I'm sorry I dragged you into all this.*"

"*Don't be sorry,*" *Jack muttered, dropping his eyes to mine as a tear slid down his cheek.* "*You're the love of my life, Angie. There's nothing I wouldn't do for you. I just…*"

"*What?*"

"*I can't leave you alone,*" *he croaked in a hoarse whisper as he wiped another tear from his cheek.* "*How am I supposed to walk out that door and go sit by the Water, while I know you're in here taking your last breaths? What the hell kind of man would leave the woman he loves to die alone?*"

Tears streamed down my cheeks as I whispered, "*I won't be alone. Clay will be there with me in the waking world till the end. That's where I'll take my last breath. But when my baby emerges from the Waters for the very first time, I need you to be there. I need you to convince the storks that you are the father of my child, because you are the father I choose. I'm trusting you to do what I'll never be able to. It's time to let me go and start being a father to my baby. Please, Jack."*

He let out a sob as he hugged me tight. "Promise me you won't stop fighting for your life," he whispered in my ear, "and that you'll come find me in the waking world after you've given birth to that baby. Because you and I are gonna live happily after ever, Angie. I'm sure of it."

"Jack..."

"Promise me," he whispered as he tightened his hold on me.

"I promise," I muttered. "I love you, Jack. I'll love you till my dying breath. Now, please go fight for my baby."

The warmth of his tear dripped down my cheek as he croaked, "I'll go get him, and I'll see you soon." With that, he stood up and smiled at me. There was so much hope and strength in that smile. He truly believed I could beat this.

I grabbed his hand, pulled him closer and kissed his lips for the last time. Then I forced a smile and nodded. "See you soon." Then I watched the man I loved cross the room and walk out the door, knowing full well I'd never set eyes on him again. I choked back a sob and pressed a hand to my broken heart, comforted by the knowledge that my baby would be safe with him.

Then a tidal wave of pain swept over me, wrenching me from the Dream...

...I sucked in a breath as the present re-solidified around me. *What the fuck was that?* It felt identical to the memories Clay had shared with me, but this wasn't a memory he'd shared. This memory was new to me. Even though it'd come out of nowhere, there wasn't a doubt in my mind that I'd just witnessed my mother's final moments in Draumer.

40

GODRIC

Too agitated to sit still and endure any more memories of my sister's demise, I paced the dining room floor of my childhood home. It was too early for other souls in the house to be awake. However, I had little interest in returning to the waking world. Back there, I was nothing but a decrepit old man; but here in Draumer, I was one of the most powerful creatures in existence. Reminding myself of that seemed crucial at this juncture. The time for mourning the past and wallowing in self-pity was over. The game board had been set, and all the pieces would soon be in play. This was the beginning of the end for David Talbot. His reign was all but over. He just wasn't aware of it yet.

"You always did prefer this world to the waking world," Louise murmured as she entered the room, cradling a cup of tea in her hands.

I turned toward her with a contemplative frown. "Why on earth wouldn't I?"

"Well," she muttered, stalling for time as she searched for the right words, "things haven't exactly gone your way here in Draumer."

Despite all the reasons I had not to smile, a wicked grin spread across my face. Louise's cautious tone confirmed what I'd already suspected. She still feared me. Perhaps that shouldn't have thrilled me, but it did. Love was a feeling long dead to me. Fear was the only sensation still capable of arousing me—others' fear of course, not my own. There was nothing left for me to fear. "That is all about to change, Louise."

"I hope you're right," she muttered, dropping her eyes to the cup in her hands. "It'd be just my luck to choose the wrong side in all this." The moment the words left her lips, she looked up at me with widened eyes.

I held her gaze as I stepped toward her, thrilling at the scent of fear permeating from her pores as her heart rate quickened. "You chose your side a long time ago, Louise."

"I know," she muttered as she set her cup down on the dining room table. "Still, I've spent most of my life pretending to be on their side."

"Yes," I murmured as I stepped closer, "you've played your part well. I shall not forget that when I take the throne."

She wove her fingers together and squeezed them to still her trembling hands. "Have I played my part well enough to be crowned your Queen?"

My grin widened at her tenacity. "Do you wish to be Queen so desperately that you would wed a man who terrifies you?"

"Yes," she replied without hesitating to consider the question, "that crown was always supposed to be mine."

"Indeed, it was," I murmured, tucking a strand of hair behind her ear and thrilling at the way she trembled at the contact. "And what of your fear of me?"

A rush of breath escaped her in a thready exhalation. "It's not an entirely unpleasant sensation."

I cocked my head to one side as I studied her expression. This woman's wants and needs were a complete mystery to me. "No?"

"I'm the sterile old spinster of the Talbot family, Henry…" Her voice died off as she realized her mistake. I no longer answered to that name, and it infuriated me when people forgot that. "Forgive me, Sarrum. Old habits die hard."

A thrill coursed through me, hearing my ex-intended address me by my rightful title. "Sterilizing you was an unforgivable offense, Louise."

Fear flickered in her eyes, but her lips parted in anticipation as I closed the gap between us. How serendipitous that her fear seemed to thrill her just as much as it did me. "Did no man ever touch you?" I rasped as I leaned toward her.

Too timid in these unfamiliar waters to voice a response, she swallowed and shook her head.

"Well, I suppose that's one wrong we must remedy straightaway," I murmured, touching my forehead to hers.

Although I still couldn't sense her desires, the rapid rise and fall of her chest was a telltale sign. She feared me, but the possibility of my touch excited her.

I gripped her by the waist and pinned her against the table like a predator pouncing on his prey.

Flames danced in her eyes as I lifted her to the tabletop, and her gaze shifted to the open door across the room.

"I suspect everyone else is still asleep," I rasped as I followed her gaze.

She exhaled a breathy sigh. "I don't care either way."

The air was so saturated with the scent of her fear that I could all but taste the adrenaline coursing through her veins. Maddened by a need I had quelled for far too long, I pulled up the hem of her dress as she reached for my belt buckle.

As the last layers of cloth and lace were torn away in an animalistic flurry of groping hands, she looked up at me. Inexperienced as she was, the uncertainty in her eyes might've caused a kinder man to hesitate. But the last of my compassion had dried up long ago, the day my sister drew her final breath. Instead of slowing to allow her to acclimate, I barreled forward with raw bestial greed.

A guttural moan escaped her throat as her arms wrapped around me, pulling me closer, the fire in her eyes confirming that my actions aligned perfectly with her desires. Perhaps I could sense her needs more than I cared to admit.

Our feral cries echoed through the room as conscious intent succumbed to bestial instinct, and we melded into a mindless bundle of exposed nerves and tangled limbs, channeling two lifetimes' worth of frustration into a carnal explosion of rage-driven lust.

As our breathing slowed, I dropped my head to her shoulder and found myself fighting an inexplicable urge to weep.

41

DAVID

I despised this plan with every fiber of my being. How in God's name did she expect me to wage war when I had no idea how she was doing? I contributed little to the conversation, staring at the Waterfall entrance at the far end of the great hall whilst Emma discussed her intentions with Benjamin and Brian. Distant as my thoughts were, it took me a moment to realize they were waiting for a response from me.

I looked from face to face, their expectant expressions awaiting the answer to a question I'd paid no attention to. "I'm afraid my thoughts drifted for a moment," I muttered. "Could you repeat the question?"

Benjamin's brow furrowed as he replied, "Do you want both of us to accompany the Queen to the Light realm?"

"Yes," I muttered as my eyes drifted to my wife. "If Emma is to remain in the Light realm without me, I want my strongest warriors by her side."

"This won't be forever, David," Emma whispered as she took my hand. "I'll come back to the palace as soon as we've won this war. I promise you, I can do this."

"I do not doubt your abilities in the slightest," I muttered as I gave her hand a squeeze. "However, the Light realm's army will require a great deal of training in order to be capable of holding their own in battle against the Purists."

"We're going to pay the old commander of the Light regiment a visit as soon as we get there," Brian assured me. "That self-proclaimed Fairy Queen who's been presiding over the Light realm dismissed him when she first took power because she considered it pointless to spend so much time training soldiers. With the commander's help, along with the help of all the soldiers she strong-armed into retirement when she claimed the throne, I'm confident that we can whip their army into shape in time."

I nodded as I turned to Benjamin. "You will terrify the Light creatures."

"I don't intend to make myself visible to the majority of them," my shadow replied. "But I'll be there in the shadows, glued to the Light Queen's side in case she needs me." A grin spread across his face as his gaze shifted to Emma. "It feels strange calling you that, but it also feels right. I'm pretty sure you're the only one capable of bringing about the necessary changes in the Light realm."

Emma smiled at the pair of them. "With the two of you by my side, I have no doubt we can do this."

"And how am I to function with no knowledge of how my treasure is doing?" I growled. "Losing you all but destroyed me the last time."

"I had no idea who *or what* we were last time, David," Emma murmured. "Do you think for one second that I won't be doing everything in my power to help end this war so I can come home to you?"

"And who will rule the Light after you depart?" I muttered. "Certainly not that incompetent fairy who took charge in your absence."

"I'll have plenty of time to find a suitable replacement while I'm there," Emma murmured. "I have no intention of leaving you permanently, David, but I need to know you'll be alright in my absence. If you aren't at your best, then all will be lost. But if you trust that I'm a competent monarch—and focus on the fact that you'll have me back at your side after you defeat Godric—you'll be unbeatable because you'll be fighting your way to me."

I smiled at her as I touched a hand to her cheek. "Who taught you to be so wise and fearless?"

She tilted her head, leaning into my touch as she whispered, "I'm afraid you have yourself to blame for that."

"Well, not to boast," I murmured, "but I did a marvelous job. I fear the Light realm will fight to keep you after this conflict has ended. Then I shall have no choice but to battle them to retrieve you."

"The Light realm doesn't get a say in that decision," Emma murmured. "I'd burn that realm to ash if that's what it took to make my way back to you."

"I don't doubt it," I muttered, grinning at her reference to the promise I'd made to her. *I would burn both worlds to ash to still time for us if you asked me to.* "Take whatever members of the royal guard you would like to accompany you to the Light realm, and teach them to fight like I taught you to."

She grinned at me as she wrapped her arms around my neck. "I wouldn't dream of doing anything less. Benjamin and Brian will be more than enough. You'll need the rest of your soldiers to fight the Purists because the majority of this war will be fought in the Darkness."

"Unless Godric gets wind of the fact that my Queen has taken her rightful place as ruler of the Light realm," I muttered. "He is well aware that hurting you would incapacitate me."

"We'll be discreet," she whispered, "and he'll be none the wiser. This is a chance we need to take if we want the Light army to stand with us."

"Whatever you need, my Queen," I whispered, "ask and you shall receive it. You have my undying support."

She nodded and kissed my cheek, then headed off to prepare for the trip.

"If it comes down to a choice between winning the battle, or protecting my wife," I whispered to Benjamin and Brian as I watched her walk away, "I trust you will make the right decision."

Both of them nodded as Benjamin replied, "Her safety will be our top priority, Sarrum."

"That's not good enough," I muttered as I watched Emma exit the room through the nearest Waterfall. "Her safety must be your only priority."

"Then it will be," Brian agreed. "Neither of us would ever allow anything to happen to her, Sarrum. We'd both lay down our lives for her without hesitation."

42

TRISTAN

It took a conscious effort to keep my breathing steady as we closed the distance between us and the crumbling cement structure the Cyclopes were leading us toward. It wasn't just the sweltering heat, or the darkening sky, or the warding around the building that had me on edge. It was the fact that we'd accomplished what our team had set out to do. We found the Purists' new meeting place. Now all we had to do was make it through the warding and keep it together long enough to gather some information that would make this mission worthwhile.

The demon standing guard at the front door eyed us warily as our group approached. Aside from the ragged scar marring the right side of his face from forehead to jaw, it was easy to imagine his exquisitely sculpted features gracing the pages of GQ. An Armani suit would've looked just as spectacular on him as the black leather and partial armor getup that adorned his well-toned body. Unruly dark locks added a savage quality to the demon's bad boy look, and pitch-black eyes kicked his animalistic appeal up a few more notches. The scar that snaked down the side of his face puckered as he grinned at us, displaying a mouthful of razor-sharp teeth that pretty much decimated his modeling career potential. As he crossed his arms over his broad chest, I couldn't help noticing the length of his pointed fingernails. Beneath his battle-ready ensemble, his feet were bare and his toenails were also long and pointed—making them look more like claws than human nails.

Since they were still leading the way, Curly and Moe reached the guard first. Moe grinned at him and spoke in a hushed growl that made it impossible to catch his words.

The demonic doorman's grin widened as he sauntered toward the rest of us, looking each of us over like he was sizing up his dinner options. It was all I could do to suppress the urge to run my sword through him as his dark eyes undressed the women in our group. As if reading my thoughts, he wrapped a hand around the decorative hilt of his sword as he spoke to Moe in an incomprehensible demonic growl. Then he moved back to the door, opened it and ushered the two Cyclopes inside.

When he motioned for the rest of us to follow them, Zeke and Charlie took the lead while I hung back and waited for the other members of our team to go inside. Addison was the last to step through the doorway. But when I moved to follow her, the demon pressed his palm against my chest.

Every muscle in my body tensed as I fought the overwhelming urge to reach for my sword. "Is there a problem?"

"Yes, actually there is a big fucking problem," he snarled in a thick demonic accent as he swung his foot back and kicked the door shut, cutting me off from the rest of my team.

"So," I murmured, making a deliberate effort to look uninterested, "what is it?"

He flashed a wicked grin, and the whiteness of his razor-sharp incisors glinted in the waning light. "You are not welcome here, incubus."

I locked eyes with him as I leaned closer, forcing his palm back with my chest. "Why the hell not?"

He took his hand off my chest to trace a pointed fingernail along the length of the scar that snaked down the side of his face. "You see this?"

"Yeah, it's pretty hard to miss," I murmured. And although I knew exactly what he was getting at, I asked, "What about it?"

"Your brother gave me this," he snarled, tucking a few tangled locks of hair behind his ear to emphasize his one glaring imperfection. "I can't let you enter without returning the favor."

"I've never seen you before," I replied with a shrug. "Why in the hell do you think you know who my brother is?"

"Blood magic in the warding alerts me when a relative of one of our captives shows up."

This wasn't news to me, but I feigned a surprised scowl. "You've definitely got the wrong guy. My brother was never anybody's captive."

"No, I don't suppose he was," the demon snarled. "But he stole my merchandise, and he sliced my face when I tried to stop him."

"You're bat shit crazy," I murmured. "My only brother is that gorgeous big fella you just let inside."

As the demon grabbed a fistful of my shirt, the door swung open behind him. I'd never been happier to see Zeke than I was in that instant. He glared at the clawed hand gripping my shirt and growled, "What the fuck's the hold up?"

"Your pretty friend and I were just having a little chat," the demon replied without taking his eyes off me. "He was begging me to book a private room, so we could get nice and intimate later tonight."

"Bullshit," Zeke growled without batting an eye, "my brother's got better taste than that."

The demon grinned as his gaze shifted to Zeke. His eyes lingered on my friend, sizing him up for a few heartbeats before he released my shirt. "We'll see."

"Listen, asshole," Zeke growled. Behind him, I could see Charlie and Bob inching toward the door. "If you've got a problem with my brother, we can take our business elsewhere. And I'll be sure to tell every fucking demon I meet that the auction's new doorman is driving customers away with petty threats. How do you suppose Godric would react to that?"

"Godric doesn't give a fuck about our festivities," the demon scoffed.

"Maybe not," Zeke agreed, dropping his voice to a menacing whisper, "but he'd definitely give a fuck about you making the new headquarters an undesirable place that his supporters are gonna think twice about frequenting."

"Go inside then," the demon snarled, baring his razor-sharp teeth at Zeke. "I'll square things with the pretty one later. One way or another, he owes me a pound of flesh."

"Can't wait," I murmured with a wink.

Frustrated that Zeke had bullied him into letting me go, and even more frustrated that he was aroused by both of us, the demon growled at me as he stepped back.

Never one to shy away from a threat, I grinned and blew him a kiss.

He lunged toward me with his clawed hands raised, but Zeke caught him by the collar and yanked him back. "Stand down or we're outta here, and I'm spreading the word that you're driving away potential converts to the Purists' cause."

As Zeke released him, the demon fixed me in the death glare to end all death glares and motioned for us to go inside.

I stepped in after Zeke and closed the door in the demon's sneering face.

Zeke shook his head as we moved into the main room. *We aren't exactly off to a great start, brother.*

I grinned at him. *I know, but it's probably best to play this out for now. Our only other option is to fight our way back outside.*

Zeke patted my cheek with a deep-throated chuckle. *Something tells me fighting might be our only option outta here.*

Let's give it a while and see how this pans out. I glanced around the cavernous room we'd stepped into. It didn't have any comfortable furnishings like the cabin in the woods that'd served as the Purists' previous meeting place. This place was far more utilitarian, and we were sorely outnumbered. The room was packed so tight that it was practically standing room only.

While our attention was focused on the door-demon's threats, the women in our group had been herded toward the other captives. I caught sight of Mia as a lanky demon with a wicked underbite was leading her across the room by the arm. Instead of the fear I expected to see in her eyes, she met my gaze with a look of steadfast determination.

I wanted to get closer and find out how she was holding up, but Zeke led me further away toward a group of traders huddled together in conversation. Charlie and Bob fell into step beside me, but their eyes remained glued to the females we'd brought to this ungodly place.

The traders' conversation died off as we approached, and Zeke greeted them with a mischievous grin as he wrapped an arm around me. "My brother and his friends have come as my guests, fellas. They're interested in doing some business tonight."

The bulkiest demon narrowed his yellow eyes at us as he knocked back the rest of the drink in his hand. I didn't even want to hazard a guess at the ingredients of the chunky blood-red mixture. "What've they brought to trade?"

"Four females," Zeke muttered as his eyes darted to the women across the room.

"Well then," the fat demon replied as he followed my friend's gaze, "maybe I should go inspect the merchandise they brought."

"I already did," Zeke growled, "and I plan to buy all of them."

The fat one's lip curled upward at that. "Then what good are these traders to us?"

"We're also looking to do some buying," I murmured, lacing my words with a hefty dose of charm.

The fat demon studied me with emotionless eyes for a few pounding heartbeats before cracking a smile. "Well then, go get a drink and make yourselves at home. The bidding starts later tonight. Until then, feel free to look around and sample the merchandise."

I could feel every member of my group cringe internally at that, but none of us let our poker faces waver. "Don't mind if I do," I murmured as my eyes wandered over the captives standing beside the women from our group. It was all I could do to keep from vomiting at the thought of what these monsters did to their victims. *Mia had been one of those victims*, but I forced myself to block that out. If I let my thoughts go there, playing it cool would be impossible. How the hell Zeke could stomach this over and over again, I'd never know. But the world was a better place because of it. My giant-incubus brother had rescued more captives than any Purists' raid had ever taken, and Zeke housed all the Unsighted souls he rescued in his home, hidden safely within a mirage.

"Come, my friends," Zeke murmured, clamping a hand on my shoulder to lessen the tension I knew he could sense. "Let's go make ourselves at home."

I should've stayed vigilant. But as Zeke swept me along with his muscular arm around my shoulders, my thoughts drifted to the past...

...A stream of hushed curses sprang from my mouth as I mopped up the rancid puddle of sick that some

sloshed-off-his-ass troll had left beside his table before stumbling out the front door of The Dragon's Lair. I'd spent more than a few days questioning my life choices lately, and this was definitely one of those days. I glanced up at the bar, and a sympathetic smile spread across Aubrey's face as she winked at me.

I smiled back and blew her a kiss to show there were no hard feelings. She'd won two out of three games of rock-paper-scissors fair and square.

Something behind me captured Aubrey's attention, and her eyes widened in disbelief.

I turned to look over my shoulder and watched the crowd part as Zeke made his way across the room toward me. My half-giant-half-incubus brother and I weren't family by blood, but the two of us had grown up together in Draumer at the same camp for Sighted orphans. Most of us at the camp weren't actually orphans in the true sense of the word. Our parents had just never claimed us. Some of us ended up there because we'd been born to Unsighted parents; others, because our Sighted parent didn't want to be burdened with a child. Zeke and I had been watching each other's backs for as long as I could remember. Under normal circumstances, I would've greeted my old friend with a beaming grin, but something was off about him. Zeke wasn't sauntering toward me with his usual confident swagger. You could practically see the cloud of gloom hanging over him.

My gaze drifted back to Aubrey as I propped the mop in my hands against the table.

She nodded, wordlessly agreeing to finish the job so I could devote my attention to my surprise visitor.

Zeke grinned at me as he reached the table, but it was a superficial formality that didn't reach his eyes. "Hey, brother."

"Hey," I whispered, greeting him with a big bear hug.

He cleared his throat, ending the hug with uncharacteristic abruptness. Then his gaze dropped to the half-mopped up mess on the floor, but he didn't waste time mentioning it—which was also out of character for him. Normally, any opportunity to bust my balls would've been too tempting for him to pass up. His eyes swept over the room as he whispered, "Can we talk someplace private?"

"Yeah, of course." I started toward the bar, and he fell into step beside me without another word.

Aubrey was stepping out from behind the bar as we reached it. I grinned at her and kissed the top of her head. "I owe you one, sweetheart."

A faint smile curved her lips as she looked up at Zeke. "Maybe you could introduce me to this magnificent beast when he's a little less sullen."

Despite the storm cloud hanging over him, Zeke grinned at her and outstretched his hand. "I'm Ezekiel Gaumond," he murmured in a seductive rasp as she placed her hand in his, "and you must be the lovely Aubrey I've heard so much about."

She answered him with a throaty chuckle. "Well, your drinks are on the house tonight, big fella."

He lifted her hand to his lips and planted a tender kiss on her knuckles. "Gorgeous and gracious. Now I see why Tristan's so fond of you."

"You boys are a dangerous combo," Aubrey chuckled. "You better get out of here before I forget all about that mess on the floor."

I bent and kissed her cheek. "You're an angel."

"And don't you forget it," she whispered as she gave me a playful shove. "Now get."

As she started toward the mess, I motioned for Zeke to follow me to the door that led out back.

He followed me down the hall to the conference room in silence. In fact, neither of us said a word until after we were seated and I'd poured us both a drink.

I grinned at him as I handed him one of the glasses. "What brings you here, brother?"

He took the drink from my hand with an appreciative nod and downed most of it in one swig before answering. "I need your help, Tristan."

"Whatever you need," I muttered, topping off his drink. "Name it."

A muscle in his jaw twitched as he shook his head. "Davina, my Unsighted sister, is lying in a hospital bed in the waking world because she swallowed a bottleful of pills yesterday. When I asked her why she did it, she told me she feels like everything's wrong with the world but she has no idea why. So, her Sighted doctor and I went looking for her in this world. Turns out, her settlement on the fringe was attacked by a group of hunters a couple nights ago. They carted her and most of the others from her settlement off to a slavers' auction, and I can't get anywhere near the fucking place."

I swallowed back the queasiness that his words evoked. "Why not?"

"The Purists ward their fucking buildings with blood magic." Zeke glanced down at the glass in his hand and gulped down its contents before growling, "Any relative of a captive who shows up at the door is executed on the spot. I need to find somebody who can pose as a buyer and get inside to bust her outta there."

"Just tell me where to go," I muttered. "I'll be there in a heartbeat."

"Too risky," he whispered, absently tracing a finger around the rim of his empty glass. "There are too many souls who know you and I are basically kin."

"Shit," I muttered, tilting my head to stare up at the ceiling. "Then why don't I ask my brother, Brian?"

The muscle in Zeke's jaw twitched again. "Why would your brother help me, Tristan? He doesn't approve of a damn thing about me."

I sat up a little straighter and polished off my drink before whispering, "Can you blame him? You work for the fucking Purists."

"It's just a job," he muttered in a hoarse whisper.

"Not in Brian's book." I dropped my eyes to our empty glasses and refilled them both. "There's no such thing as a gray area for my big brother. He lives his life in black and white, which is why I think he'd agree to help. I'm pretty sure he'd be willing to overlook his distaste for you and your wicked ways to save an innocent soul."

"If Brian gets Davina out of there, I'll devote the rest of my damn life to doing good," Zeke muttered as his eyes filled with tears. "I'll fucking do anything he asks me to if he saves my baby sister."

"Let's go find him," I whispered, blinking the tears from my eyes.

43

CHARLIE

I'm not exactly sure how I expected things to go once we made it to the Purists' meeting place, but I sure as hell hadn't pictured anything like this. This felt a little too much like standing in the middle of a lions' den, slathered in meat drippings while mingling with a drink in your hand. It wasn't until that particular visual popped into my head that it occurred to me, our plan wasn't really all that well thought out. What were we supposed to do in a scenario like this? Stand around making small talk until some filthy demon decided to drag a member of our team off to a private room to *sample the merchandise?* The taste of vomit crept up my throat at the thought. This was all so fucked up, and I had no way of knowing if anyone in our group had the vaguest idea where to go from here. In all the years I'd spent locked away in mental facilities with nobody believing a word I said, I had never felt this trapped. Lives were at stake here, and not just our lives. If it was just my safety we were putting at risk, I would've been okay with keeping up this charade. But it was Rose, Nellie, Mia, and Addison's safety we were risking. I knew enough about these auctions to know that not all the *merchandise* survived the *sampling* these monsters subjected them to. In their perverse minds, the death of a victim or two was nothing more than an acceptable business loss.

As we made our way toward the makeshift bar in the corner of the room, I was seriously considering grabbing Rose and bolting for the exit.

"What the hell's this?" Bob grumbled beside me. "Where in the fuck are we?"

"Shit," Tristan muttered under his breath.

"You," Bob growled as he glared at Tristan. "What the fuck're you doin here, pretty boy? Did you fuckin drug me and drag me here?"

I put a hand on hybrid-Bob's shoulder to pull his attention away from Tristan. "We're all friends here, Bob."

"Charlie?" Bob muttered as he turned toward me and searched my eyes.

"Yeah, Bob," I whispered, "it's me. Listen, you've gotta trust me and keep your voice down in here. I know you're having trouble remembering this, but we've got a job to do. If you don't keep it down, you'll be putting Nellie in danger."

"Nellie?" Bob muttered as his brow furrowed with confusion. "Did that bastard drag her here too?"

Hanging back to keep out of Bob's line of sight, Tristan shook his head. *Careful, Charlie. You're pretty much the only one he trusts right now. I'm not sure clueing him in to the fact that Nellie is being held captive across the room is the best move.*

I kept my eyes glued to Bob as I replied, *Then what should I tell him?*

Try to reorient him to the here and now, Pip suggested from Bob's shirt pocket. *Remind him what's really going on.*

Worried that Bob might freak out if he noticed the tiny creature watching him from the pocket of his shirt, I stepped closer and waited for signs that I should relocate Pip to my pocket before his hybrid-minded partner tossed him out. "Bob, we came here together to gather intel," I whispered. "Remember?"

"I'm not…" Bob muttered as his vacant eyes searched the room. He might've forgotten our mission, but he recognized the love of his life the instant he caught sight of her standing with the captives across the room. "Nellie's over there. Why in the fuck are we just standin here like a bunch of assholes?"

As he started toward Nellie, I grabbed his arm. "You can't charge over there, Bob. That could get a lot of people hurt. You need to trust me and play along right now, okay?"

"No," Bob grunted, "that ain't okay at all. Unhand me, kid, or I'll cut your fuckin hand off."

I tightened my grip on Bob's arm as my eyes locked with Tristan's. *Is it time to cut our losses and fight our way outta here?*

To my surprise, Tristan shook his head. *Try to subdue him. I want to hang on for as long as we can.*

The taste of vomit rose up my throat again as my eyes darted to the women who'd come on this mission with us. *Why?*

Because these auctions aren't always just for pleasure, Zeke chimed in. *The higher-ups sometimes meet here to conduct business before the bidding starts. We should try to keep this up long enough to see if any high-ranking Purists make an appearance.*

Pip's eyes widened as he looked up at Tristan. *Is that really worth the risk?*

An apologetic frown spread across Tristan's face as his eyes dropped to Bob's mini sidekick. *If Godric or one of his key players shows up, it sure as hell will be.*

I let out a tired sigh as my gaze shifted to Rose on the other side of the room. *Do you really think that's worth putting the women we came here with at risk?* If this all went horribly wrong, Rose and I would never get the chance to kiss and make up. Why the hell had I been so damn stubborn on our last night together?

Tristan's confident stance wilted at my words, but it only took him a second to regain his composure. *Do you think that doesn't worry me, Charlie? I'd never forgive myself if anything happened to Mia, but they all knew what they were signing up for when they volunteered to go on this mission. Besides, they're not exactly helpless creatures. They're all fierce warriors.*

"This is nuts," Bob grumbled as he tugged his arm free from my hold. "What in the fuck are we doin standin around here?"

Bob's outburst was loud enough to draw the attention of the yellow-eyed demon who'd invited us to make ourselves at home. He puffed out his broad chest as he headed toward us with his eyes glued to Bob.

"Keep it down," I muttered. "That demon who's headed our way is getting suspicious. I don't think you want to find out what he'll do to Nellie and the others if he realizes why we're here."

"Why the fuck are we here?" Bob demanded as the demon stepped up to us.

"Yes," the demon snarled, "why are you here?"

"I think this pretty boy drugged us to get us here," Bob muttered.

The demon narrowed his eyes at Bob. "Is that so?"

"He's a dementia patient in the waking world," Tristan explained without missing a beat. "Sometimes he gets confused about which world he's in. When that happens, he goes into one of these fits."

"Then this probably isn't the place for the old geezer," yellow-eyes mused. "Does this look like a nursing home to you boys?"

"Who the fuck're you callin a geezer, ya snot-nosed punk?" Bob shouted as he charged toward him. "I'll kick your flabby ass any day of the week."

Tristan grabbed Bob's arm and yanked him back in line with us. "Cool it, grandpa."

"I ain't your fuckin grandpa," Bob growled.

"Get him out of here before I lose my patience," yellow-eyes snarled.

"Who's gonna make us?" Zeke asked in a booming growl that drew every eye in the room to our standoff.

The demon sneered at him. "There goes the last of my patience."

"Then we'll show ourselves out," Tristan murmured in his silkiest voice.

Yellow-eyes licked his lips as his focus shifted to Tristan. "I think maybe you should stay, *pretty boy*."

My stomach dropped as the demon guards across the room grabbed ahold of the captives, including the ones from our team. Rose's eyes met mine as a stocky demon locked his arms around her in a death grip and started tugging her toward the door behind him.

I felt the fire ignite within me as my nostrils twitched with a maddening need to expel a warning plume of smoke. If these Purists realized I was a dragon, things would escalate fast. So I drew a deep breath and reminded myself that Rose was a dragon too. I knew she was more than capable of defending herself, but that didn't stop my dragon instincts from screaming at me to burn everything that stood between us to get to her.

Despite the fact that Bob had just accused Tristan of drugging and kidnapping him, the charge in the air between yellow-eyes and the rest of us seemed to make him reconsider who to align himself with. "I don't think so, numb nuts," he growled at yellow-eyes. "Nobody threatens the pretty boy but me."

"Dementia patient or not," the yellow-eyed demon snarled, "you have overstayed your welcome, old man."

For a disoriented hybrid-Sighted dementia patient, Bob's reflexes were lightning fast, or maybe it was the fact that nobody expected him to get violent that caught us all off guard. Whatever the reason, none of us reacted fast enough to stop Bob from drawing his sword and running its blade through the yellow-eyed demon's chest.

The demon stared at Bob through widened eyes as he pressed his palms to his chest with blood gurgling from his mouth and dripping down his chin. When the scrawny demon behind the bar noticed the blood spilling from yellow-eye's mouth and oozing between his fingers, he started shouting.

Then all hell broke loose.

The scar-faced guard who'd stopped us outside the entrance to the building came rushing in seconds after the commotion started. The demonic doorman headed straight for Tristan, but the rest of us were too busy fighting off the demons rushing toward us to notice that something had immobilized the leader of our team.

44

MIA

I probably should've been terrified to be back among the Purists' captives—and I was, until they went after Tristan. Something was wrong. He wasn't even trying to defend himself, let alone protect the members of his team. My chest tightened as the demon who'd grabbed me when Bob started yelling pulled me toward the door behind us. I knew what horrors lurked behind the doors in places like this, and I'd rather die a fiery death than ever revisit that sort of hell. Terrified as I was, I'm not sure how I had the state of mind to glance over at Tristan. But the instant I caught sight of him, I recognized the vacant expression on his face. I'd seen it on the face that stared back at me in the mirror more times than I cared to admit. Tristan's mind had reverted to past horrors. Those traumatic moments he couldn't quite bring himself to share with me had swallowed him up again.

As the demon dragged me farther away, I watched Tristan's focus return to the present. Then his body went rigid. The only explanation I could think of was that a creature somewhere in this building possessed the power to immobilize his victims the way Godric could. My heart hammered in my chest as my eyes scanned the room, desperate to locate Tristan's hidden assailant.

When the scar-faced demon who guarded the entrance to the building rushed inside, there wasn't a doubt in my mind that he was headed for Tristan. I'd witnessed enough of their exchange out front to know that demon had a problem with him for some reason. With two attackers closing in on him, while he was powerless to defend himself, Tristan's life was in danger.

The thought of a life without Tristan made my throat constrict, and I forgot all about the danger I was in. All those extra self-defense lessens Addison had given me during our training came to mind, and I recalled the advice she so often repeated. *Use your greatest strengths to best your enemies.* Skilled as I'd become with every weapon Tristan and Brian introduced me to, I had no weapon to use at the moment, but that didn't matter. My skill with those weapons had never been my greatest strength. The identity I'd been ashamed of all my life—the faceless creature who could morph into any form—*that* was my greatest strength. It took the horror of seeing the soul I loved in mortal danger to force me to accept that. As the demon dragged me away from Tristan, I was finally able to revisit those memories I'd worked so hard to suppress.

I let my body go limp as the demon yanked the door open, tugged me inside the room and shut us in alone together. As he dragged me across the floor, I looked up at him and smiled.

"You won't be smiling for long," he sneered as his fat fingers dug into the flesh of my upper arms.

"I could say the same to you," I whispered.

"I think you've lost your mind, little one," he muttered as he tugged me toward the stained mattress against the far wall.

The instant I let those buried memories surface, I felt my eyes turn black. "Actually, I've never felt saner," I replied in a voice cold as ice, *her voice*. I expected my vision to fail me in the dimly lit room, but I could see clear as day with those pitch-black eyes. Nightmarish images of the blond shadow whose sweet-talking mate lured me to the Purists' cabin in the woods flickered through my mind, and Payne's cruel laughter tumbled from my lips as I took her form.

The demon released me with a startled shriek and shrunk back in horror, and a sadistic smile spread across my face as I stood up and watched him cower beneath me.

As I turned and headed for the door, I thanked the heavens that Payne had chosen to bind herself to me. A shadow and the soul she bound herself to were capable of sharing certain abilities and in her greed for more power, Payne had bound us together to acquire the ability to shape-shift. Her bone-chilling voice echoed in my head as I recalled how she'd reasoned aloud that it was worth the commitment because I would soon be dead, but she'd retain the skill I'd given without consent. How ironic it was that she was now dead, and I possessed the power to save the man I loved thanks to her actions.

As I pulled the door open, instinct told me there was no need to raise my voice to quiet the chaos in the main room. I just propelled the fear I could now project out into the crowded meeting room. In this new form, it felt as natural as breathing.

Silence devoured every decibel of sound as every eye in the room fixed on me, and a wicked grin spread across my face. "I leave you naughty children alone for a little while, and this is the madness you descend into?"

"You're...supposed to be dead," the guard holding onto Rose muttered.

"I'm afraid the reports of my death were greatly exaggerated," I replied in an ice-cold whisper that sent a collective shiver rippling through the room.

"How did you survive that fire in the cabin in the woods?" the demon holding Nellie's arm rasped.

A coy smile curved my full lips as I channeled a hefty dose of fear toward the demons across the room who were closing in on Tristan. "I was never in that fire."

"How is that possible?" Nellie's captor whispered as he inched away from me.

"That girl we used to trick the Sarrum was a changeling, you dolt," I murmured as I stepped into the room. "After we all finished with her, I slipped into her room and bound myself to her. Then I forced her to take my form while I took hers, and I took her place on that bed. The Sarrum never rescued that broken changeling. It was me that the incubus carried from the cabin minutes before the Dragon King set fire to it, and I've been with them this entire time."

I strolled toward Tristan at a predatory pace, the same way Payne had approached me in that cabin in the woods. "The incubus is mine. If you've so much as bruised my new plaything's perfect flesh, I'll make you hurt more than you ever imagined possible." I projected a hefty dose of fear toward the scar-faced demon, and he let out an agonized shriek as he fell back from Tristan. As for the anonymous demon who'd immobilized Tristan, I could only hope that my performance would convince him to stand down too. "You incompetent morons have put me in a terrible position. How am I supposed to return to the palace and gather more information for Godric now that you've blown my cover?"

"You have our sincerest apologies, Payne," the demon with the scarred face whimpered. "We won't breathe a word of your true identity to anyone."

I felt my eyes darken as I crippled him with the largest dose of fear yet.

"Please," he whimpered, "I've got a family to provide for in the waking world."

"They're better off without you." As I spoke the words, I felt the scarred demon's heart give out. I just prayed his death would be enough to deter Tristan's hidden attacker.

"You can't kill all of us," muttered a skeletal creature a few feet away from me.

I broke his neck with a snap of my fingers, without even turning to look at him. "Nothing motivates me to accomplish something more than being told that I can't do it."

The silence in the room was deafening as I stepped up to Tristan. I held my hand out to him, hoping the spell that'd immobilized him had been dropped. His gorgeous green eyes locked with mine as he reached up, took my hand and let me tug him to his feet.

I put my hands on either side of his face and planted a rough kiss on his lips. "You belong to me, incubus."

The expression on Tristan's face was unreadable. For several pounding heartbeats, I feared I might've taken this too far, until his hand squeezed mine.

I let out an icy chuckle as I surveyed the panic-stricken faces in the room. The absolute fearlessness and power that I felt in Payne's form was such an intoxicating change of pace from my own weakness. I found myself toying with the idea of keeping the charade up long enough to get face-to-face with Godric.

Unfortunately, fate had other plans.

45

CHARLIE

I'm ashamed to admit I lost focus after the fighting broke out at the Purists' meeting place. At the worst possible moment—when all our lives were at risk—my thoughts drifted to another memory that wasn't mine…

…As the pain wrenched me back to the waking world, I opened my eyes and found Clay sitting at my bedside holding my hand. "I did it," I muttered in a thready whisper of my mother's voice. "I convinced Jack to leave the cabin and go wait for my baby by the Waters."

Clay blinked the tears from his bloodshot eyes as he forced a somber smile. "I knew you could get him to do the right thing when the time came."

"Speaking of time," I whispered, squeezing my eyes shut, "I don't have much time left, do I?"

There was a moment of silence before Clay muttered, "Who knows? Maybe you can beat this."

But when I opened my eyes to scowl at him, the tortured look on his face suggested he didn't think I had a snowball's chance in hell. I shook my head without lifting it from the pillow because I couldn't muster the strength.

"Let's not spend our final minutes lying to each other, alright?"

"Alright," he agreed as he brushed a tear from my cheek with his thumb. *"What the hell am I gonna do without you, Angel?"*

"You're gonna turn your whole life around after I'm gone," I whispered with a faint smile. *"You'll meet a cute guy, settle down, adopt a couple kids, and make a living selling life insurance or something equally boring that you won't mind doing because it'll put food on your family's table."*

He let out a rough chuckle as he squeezed my hand. "Is that right?"

"Yeah, it is," I whispered, fixing my gaze on the ceiling to hold back the tears that threatened to spill if I looked him in the eye. *"I'm sure of it. You're gonna live a happy life, Clay."*

He lifted our joined hands to his mouth and planted a tender kiss on the back of mine. "I don't know how that's gonna be possible after my sunshine is gone."

"I think somewhere deep inside," I muttered as I lowered my eyes to his, *"you always knew it was gonna end like this."*

A perplexed frown spread across his face as he leaned closer, tilting his ear toward my mouth as if he thought he'd misheard me. "What are you talking about?"

"You must've sensed I'd be watching over you one day," I whispered, *"because you've been calling me Angel since the day we met."*

A tear slid down his cheek as he muttered, "If I knew my words had that much power, I would've called you a permanent pain in my ass."

"I'm gonna be a permanent pain in your ass," I whispered. "I plan on haunting you for the rest of your life."

A faint smile curved his lips. "Promise?"

A tidal wave of pain enveloped me, worse than any contraction that'd come before it, and I choked back a scream as the world around us blurred.

"Breath through it, Angel," Clay whispered.

But I knew him better than I'd ever known anyone, and I could tell a part of him hoped that this was the end because he couldn't stand to watch me suffer like this...

...As my mother's memory ebbed and the world around me reappeared, I was shocked to find that the fighting had already stopped. A few lifeless demons lay strewn across the floor, and a female shadow was standing next to Tristan with a smug smile on her beautiful face. I could've sworn I heard one of the demons across the room call her *Payne* as he growled at her in a thick demonic dialect.

I studied Tristan through narrowed eyes. If the shadow who had tortured Mia in unspeakable ways was standing right beside him, why wasn't he running his sword through her heart? *And how the hell was she still breathing?* "How..." The rest of the words died in my throat as my eyes drifted across the room to Rose. That filthy demon still had his hands on her. My heart hammered in my chest as I watched the son of a bitch lower his head to whisper something in her ear.

It was hard to be sure at this distance, but I could've sworn her eyes darkened as the heat of his breath assaulted her ear. Rose nodded and muttered something back, her posture and facial expression subservient as she continued to play her role.

When the demon released her, I had to fight the impulse to rush to her and pull her into my arms. I had no idea what was going on at this point. Any move I chose to make might drive things in the wrong direction. It felt like I'd missed some pivotal stuff while my mind was stuck in the past, reliving my mother's final moments.

Every muscle in my body tensed as I watched Rose make her way across the room to us. When she reached us, she met my eyes with a faint hint of a smile on her lips as she tucked herself between me and Bob. For that brief hopeful moment, I let myself entertain the notion that things might turn out okay.

When Rose reached over and plucked Pip from Bob's pocket, I figured her dragon instincts sensed that Pip wasn't safe there in his partner's muddle-headed state. What happened next was so horrific that it took my brain far too long to process what I'd witnessed.

For as long as I live, I doubt I'll ever be able to erase the image of Rose snapping Pip's neck like a twig from my mind. Her eyes were so cold when she did it, as if it was nothing.

Bob let out an agonized cry as he snatched his sidekick's limp body from her hands.

Unfazed by Bob's anguish, Rose turned and pointed at the shadow standing beside Tristan. "That isn't Payne," she announced at the top of her lungs, her hollow voice utterly devoid of emotion. "It's just the changeling in Payne's form." Tears swam in Rose's eyes as she turned to me. *Join me, Charlie. You were always meant to stand beside your father. I can't do this without you.*

The pounding of my heart echoed in my head as conflicting emotions warred within me, immobilizing me. What the hell was I supposed to do? Protect the woman I treasured with all my heart—*the woman I'd just watched murder our friend*—or save the rest of my team from the horde of Purists that were closing in on us? I turned to look at Bob, and the pained expression on his face as he cradled our lifeless friend in his hands made the decision for me.

I felt my heart fracture as I turned back to Rose and searched her pleading eyes for a logical explanation. Was it remorse that filled those chocolate brown eyes with tears? *No.* As much as my injured heart wanted to believe that was true, my instincts told me otherwise. Desperate as I was to come up with a justifiable reason for what I'd watched her do, I knew there wasn't one. *How could there be?* Pip was selfless and kind. Small as he was, he'd risked his life to save Bob and the rest of us on more than one occasion. That tiny heart of his was pure gold, and *Rose stopped it from beating* like it meant nothing to her.

The fracture in my heart deepened as I unmasked and took dragon form.

The instant the Purists realized what I was, the room erupted into chaos.

I swept Bob, Tristan, Mia, and Zeke into my wings to pull them out of harm's way. And in the midst of the free-for-all that followed, Addison and Nellie managed to fight their way free from the demons holding onto them. My heart raced as I watched them battle their way through the crowd to reach us. The instant they were close enough, I scooped them into my wings with the others. Still desperate to believe this was all some catastrophic misunderstanding, or medically-induced-coma hallucination, I turned toward the woman I treasured more than anything.

As Rose unmasked to her dragon form, my heart stuttered. Senseless and pathetic as it was, the scent of sugar cookies, and honey, and freshly mowed grass started leaking from my pores at the sight of her.

Her delicious floral scent bled through the air in response, assaulting my nostrils in the most intoxicating way as she closed in on us alongside the Purists.

Baffled that my body could still react to her this way, and crushed by everything I'd witnessed, I forced myself to think back to my final lesson with the Sarrum. Then I focused on summoning the Waters like I did that night in the Darkness.

A perfect circular Water portal formed in front of us at my silent command, but there was no time to dwell on the accomplishment. As the Purists rushed toward us, I drew everyone inside my wings into the portal with me.

Rose and the others lunged for the opening, and my eyes locked with hers as I willed it shut. The hurt in those violet flame-filled eyes hit me like a punch to the gut as the Waters sealed us off from the rest of the world.

The silence inside the tunnel of Water was eerily absolute as I reverted to human form. For a long while, we all just stood there staring at the tiny lifeless body cradled in Bob's hands.

Addison was the first to find her voice. "We don't have any way to call for help now," she muttered without taking her eyes off the fallen member of our team. "Pip was the only one who could go back to the waking world to tell the others what was happening and bring back help."

"Won't they wake us all up once they realize Pip's heart isn't beating?" Nellie asked in a hoarse whisper.

"No," Tristan muttered. "They wouldn't dare bring us back with no idea what's happening here. If they pulled one of us away at the wrong moment, others could die because of their disappearance."

"What about Zeke?" Nellie muttered as she placed her hands beneath Bob's as if the gesture could lessen her soul mate's burden. "Can't he go back to the waking world, pick up a phone and let the Sarrum know what's happened?"

"I'm sedated too," Zeke muttered with a shake of his head. "I've got my own doc keeping me under."

I dropped my eyes to my feet because it hurt too much to look at Pip cradled in Bob and Nellie's hands. "So, we're stuck here?"

"Yeah," Addison whispered as she placed a hand on her childhood knight-in-shining-armor's shoulder, "and we need to get out of the Waters before Rose and the Purists find a way to follow us here."

I swallowed the lump in my throat as I looked up at her. "If we can't get back to the waking world, where exactly am I supposed to open a portal to?"

"Hold onto my hand," Zeke murmured as he held it out to me, "and take us to the place I'm picturing."

I turned to Tristan with a raised eyebrow, wordlessly asking whether he approved.

"I trust Zeke with all our lives," Tristan muttered with a nod. "And if you knew him like I did, you would too."

As I took Zeke's hand, the image of Rose snapping Pip's neck flashed through my mind, turning my stomach and making my head swim.

"We need to get moving, Charlie," Tristan whispered. "They're gonna find a way to follow us through the Waters soon."

I focused on the far end of the tunnel with a nod. Then I concentrated on opening a portal and commanding the Waters to take us wherever Zeke meant to go. For several unsteady breaths, we all just stood there waiting. In fact, nothing happened for so long that I was amazed the others weren't freaking out. I was beginning to worry we might be trapped in the tunnel forever, but I couldn't let the Waters sense my lack of confidence. So I pictured the elegant way the Sarrum always commanded the Waters with a nonchalant wave of his hand. Nostrils twitching from the effort, I waved my hand through the air.

But nothing happened.

It wasn't until faint sounds began to emanate from the end of the tunnel we'd entered that I realized what I was doing wrong. I needed to channel my rage into forcing the Waters to obey my command. So I pictured the callous look on Rose's face when she snapped Pip's neck…the look in Bob's eyes as he stared at his sidekick's body, trying to process what she'd done…the uncertainty in Rose's eyes as she closed in on us with the Purists—at least, I wanted to believe it was uncertainty that'd misted her eyes when she reached out to me with that telepathic plea. *Join me, Charlie. You were always meant to stand beside your father. I can't do this without you.*

DREAM FRAGMENTS

The portal that opened at the far end of the tunnel seemed miles away. As the sounds coming from the direction we'd entered grew louder, we started racing for the opening. This sloppy exit didn't exactly rival the Sarrum's graceful command of the Waters, but I was more than happy to settle for a clumsy retreat that took us all safely wherever Zeke had led us.

When we reached the opening, I let the others rush out first. If my tunnel didn't hold up, I wasn't about to risk anyone else's life longer than my own.

My descent was anything but graceful as I toppled from the portal onto sweet spring grass after the rest of my team. The instant I was clear of it, the Water portal vanished.

I stood up and brushed off my clothes as I took in our surroundings. The stark contrast between wherever we were now and the soundless tunnel we'd just exited was disorienting. The sun was shining in a clear blue sky, songbirds chirped from their perches in lush green treetops, and a grand country home stood a short distance away.

Without any discussion, we all started toward the house. As we got closer, a grin spread across Zeke's face at the sight of the four young women chatting on the front porch. The smallest one stood up from her dainty perch on the side railing and grinned at Zeke as she skipped down the steps.

Her beauty took my breath away, enough to make me forget all about the horrors we'd left behind. The battle that'd broken out at the Purists' meeting place ...Pip's murder...Rose's heart-wrenching betrayal...all of it melted away as I watched her move toward us with her long dark curls blowing in the breeze. There was a sultry smokiness in her dark brown eyes that could hypnotize a man, enough to keep him standing and staring till his pounding heart gave out. As we moved closer, the petal soft appearance of her full pink lips filled me with a desperate desire to crush my mouth against hers. She was dressed in a no-frills pink sundress, but there was no need to adorn her body with fancy clothes. That simple piece of pink cloth draped from her body, clinging to each exquisite curve with such perfection that she looked more like a masterpiece carved out of marble than a living, breathing woman.

As I watched her run into Zeke's open arms and throw her arms around his neck with an affectionate grin, a raging desire to knock him aside and take his place flared inside me. "Hey, big brother," she murmured in a voice like liquid silk.

The fire in my belly subsided a bit when I realized they were siblings, and my brain managed to regain a modicum of control. *Zeke was half incubus.* Judging by my reaction to her, I would bet every cent I'd ever earn that his sister was Tristan's female equivalent—a full-blooded succubus.

When Tristan elbowed me, it took a serious effort to peel my eyes away from Zeke's sister. "Davina is Zeke's baby sister," he murmured, "and in case you haven't got enough blood flowing to your brain to figure it out, she's a pure succubus."

"Yeah," I muttered as my gaze returned to her, "I got that. Thanks."

"Don't get too doe-eyed over her," Tristan murmured as we moved closer. "You don't wanna see Zeke go into protective big brother mode."

"I don't know," I whispered, peeling my eyes away from Davina just long enough to glance at her gigantic brother's bulging muscles. "It might be worth getting torn limb from limb."

"She's also hopelessly hung up on someone else," Tristan murmured as we reached the Greek-godlike siblings.

Davina greeted Tristan with a beaming smile. "And how is that someone else?"

"Good," Tristan muttered. "Sorry to drop in unannounced."

"You're family, Tristan," she murmured. "You know you're always welcome here."

She took a moment to greet each one of us with a welcoming smile, and my cheeks flamed when her eyes met mine. Without thinking, I turned to get a look at Pip's reaction to Davina's charm—partly out of habit, and partly because my brain wasn't doing much of the thinking. The sight of our friend's lifeless body in Bob's hands was enough to sober me out of my lust-drunken state.

"Everyone," Zeke murmured in a somber tone, respectful of our recent loss, "this is my baby sister, Davina."

"Hello," she murmured, her delicious voice smooth as silk.

"Davina," Zeke whispered as he gestured toward each of us, "meet Charlie, Addison, Mia, Nellie, and Bob."

Bob stepped up beside me as Zeke introduced him, and Davina covered her mouth with her hand at the sight of Pip's motionless body. Tears filled her eyes as she looked up at Bob. "Does your friend need medical attention?"

"No," Bob replied in a hoarse whisper, "I'm afraid he didn't make it out alive."

"I'm so sorry," Davina muttered as a tear slid down her cheek. "Why don't you all come inside? You look like you could use some rest."

46

TRISTAN

The six remaining members of our team were fed, we freshened up, and we got some rest at Zeke's safe house hidden within a mirage in the middle of nowhere. I doubt that brief respite lasted more than a few hours, but it was difficult to gage the passage of time in Draumer. However long we'd been recuperating from our losses and brainstorming about how to proceed, it felt like ages since we'd stumbled from Charlie's Water portal onto the sweet spring grass of Zeke's safe haven.

We were sitting on the front porch, watching the sun set over the tiny grave we'd buried our fallen friend in. Having just finished an impromptu memorial service for Pip, none of us felt much like talking. So we sat and stared at the sky, each of us lost in our own dismal thoughts.

Charlie was seated across the porch from me with his eyes glued to Zeke's kid sister. I wanted to break him free from the hypnotic effect of Davina's charm, but I didn't because my reasons for wanting him to snap out of it were selfish. Charlie was a royal dragon. He was the strongest remaining member of our team, and I wanted him focused enough to participate in the strategic discussion we needed to have in the immediate future.

Thankfully, we had Zeke with us now. I didn't doubt for a second that he'd have my back no matter what. That gave me a lot of comfort, but it also made me feel guilty as hell. He'd risked the safety of his mirage and all the refugees he sheltered within it by bringing us there. It'd been a heat of the moment decision because he knew we were goners without an escape plan, but I saw the regret on his face every time he looked at one of the Unsighted souls he'd rescued. We couldn't afford to overstay our welcome. We needed to determine our next move before the Purists figured out how to follow us to Zeke's mirage.

The sky was beginning to darken and there was a chill to the evening air, but the vibe inside the house was too cheery for us. We didn't begrudge the refugees their fun. We were just too distraught to take part in it.

Mia caught my eye from her seat beside Charlie. I winked at her, and she flashed me a knowing grin. It felt good to be able to express affection without worrying it might blow our cover, and it was amazing to witness the change in Mia. I understood why she'd suppressed what she was capable of doing because of Payne's actions. Those memories were still too raw and painful for her to dwell on, but she'd let them surface in spite of that in order to save the rest of us. She was so damn powerful now that I wasn't even sure I could take her in a fight, not that I'd ever have any need to find out.

Mia blushed at our extended eye contact as she dropped her eyes to the porch floor. Proud as I was of what she'd done for us, I was glad she'd reverted to her waking world form after we reached Zeke's mirage. It was too disturbing to interact with her in Payne's form. Talking to Mia while staring into the eyes of the woman who'd broken her felt so wrong that it turned my stomach.

Nellie, Bob and Addison sat huddled together by the porch steps. Both women had their heads resting on Bob's shoulders, and he had an arm wrapped around each of them. He'd get through this with their help, but it was gonna take some time. Thank God the effects of that damn potion Clay had given him finally seemed to have worn off. All things considered, I probably should've been more patient with him while he was struggling with that. Once again, I found myself questioning Brian and Benjamin's faith in my readiness to lead this mission. *What would they say if they could see us now?*

"Well, aren't you a sorry bunch, sitting out here in the dark," Zeke murmured as he stepped out the front door to join us on the porch.

I shook my head as he sat down on the bench beside Davina. "The darkness suits our current mood."

A burst of feminine laughter wafted through the screen door from inside the house, making us both smile.

"Yeah, I see what you mean," Zeke murmured. Davina shivered at the cold and he wrapped an arm around her and kissed the top of her head as she dropped it to his shoulder. "They all deserve to be happy though. They've been through a hell of a lot."

"I know," I muttered, grinning at Mia as she looked up at me.

"You were a total badass with those Purists, Mia," Zeke murmured. "I've got mad respect for you."

"Thanks," Mia muttered in a meek tone that didn't mesh with her badass actions earlier in the day.

"So," Charlie muttered, peeling his eyes away from Davina to focus on me, "where do we go from here?"

"That's what we need to figure out," I whispered with a shrug.

"I still can't wrap my head around what Rose did," Charlie muttered, squeezing his eyes shut. "Did you—"

A deafening crack of thunder interrupted him midsentence, and a blinding burst of light lit the sky. On edge as we'd already been, we were all on our feet in an instant.

"What the fuck was that?" Bob muttered.

"We've got company," Zeke growled as he moved toward the railing to get a better look at the sky in the distance. He'd barely finished his sentence before racing inside.

Zeke's words to the Unsighted refugees he housed were muffled by the door, but there was no mistaking the urgency in his deep voice. While the rest of us gathered our weapons and marched down the porch steps, we could hear the commotion his words instigated inside the house.

Less than a minute later, Zeke stepped out onto the porch with a sword in hand. He scowled at Davina as he moved toward her. "Get inside, and help protect the others."

"I want to help *you*," she muttered.

"It'll help me a hell of a lot to know you're safely barricaded inside," Zeke growled.

Davina let out a startled gasp as a massive silver-scaled dragon crested the hill in the distance with an army of demons behind her. "There are too many of them."

"We'll handle it," Zeke growled as he gave her a firm shove toward the door to the house without taking his eyes off of Rose and the band of Purists advancing toward us. "Now, get the fuck inside."

"She's right," Addison muttered under her breath as she drew her sword. "There are too many of them." She shook her head, then turned to Bob and kissed his cheek. "It'll be an honor to go out battling beside you."

I wanted to offer them some words of encouragement, but Davina and Addison were right.

We couldn't beat these odds.

47

EMMA

It took us a day and a half to reach the homestead of the former commander of the Light regiment on foot. Treacherous as the journey through the foothills was, it was a necessary trek because traveling through the Waters was too risky. The Purists would be watching for any unusual movement throughout the realms, and we didn't want to do anything that might tip them off to the fact that I had taken my rightful place as ruler of the Light realm.

As Brian knocked on the front door of the weathered stone cottage perched high on a hilltop overlooking the Waters, I couldn't help feeling like a solicitor showing up unannounced on the commander's doorstep. I knew next to nothing about this man who'd commanded the Light Queen's army till the usurper who took my throne dismissed him, but it didn't exactly sound like they'd parted on good terms. So it was quite possible that this visit would end with his abrupt dismissal of us as soon as he answered the door.

Brian scowled at the closed door as he knocked a second time, a bit louder than the first. "I hope this wasn't a massive waste of time."

"It wasn't," Benji's deep voice murmured beside me.

Cloaked in Darkness as he was, Benjamin's hushed voice sent a shiver down my spine. "What are you basing that on?"

"Commander Mackendrick's actions," Benji muttered. "If he no longer cared about protecting the Light creatures, he wouldn't have stayed in this realm after the imposter Queen dismissed him."

I frowned in Benjamin's general direction. "Where else would he go?"

Before he could answer, the heavy oak door began to creak open.

I suppose it was foolish of me to expect an old man to answer the door since plenty of creatures chose to retain their younger appearances in Draumer as they aged. Still, I have to admit the handsome middle-aged man who opened the door took me by surprise. Beneath his furrowed brow, his eyes were the same breathtaking shade of blue as the Waters at the base of the hill. His wavy hair and reddish-brown beard were neatly trimmed, and he was dressed in a freshly pressed outfit—complete with a button-down shirt and vest—as if he'd been expecting to entertain guests.

The commander looked Brian up and down, appraising him with those keen blue eyes. Then his gaze shifted to me, and a grin spread across his face as if we were old friends and he was delighted to find me at his door. His stare lingered a moment before he shook his head and extended a hand. "Forgive me, my

Queen," he murmured in a charming Scottish accent that made me instantly fond of him. "Where are my manners this evening? It's lovely to meet you."

Dopey American that I was, I couldn't help grinning at his accent as I took his hand. "You act as if you were expecting me."

He lifted my hand to his mouth with unbroken eye contact and planted a chaste kiss on the back of it like a perfect gentleman. "I was expecting you, my dear." With that, he released my hand and turned his attention to Brian, extending his hand to him.

"I'm Brian Mason," Brian muttered as they exchanged a firm handshake, "and that's an awfully familiar way to address your Queen, don't you think?"

An utterly endearing grin spread across the commander's face as his gaze returned to me. "I do apologize if I've offended you," he murmured as he opened the door a bit wider and welcomed us in with a wave of his hand. "I feel as if you and I are old friends."

"You didn't offend me," I murmured as I stepped inside with Brian.

The commander nodded then turned his attention toward the door and waited for Benjamin to enter before closing it, as if he could see him perfectly fine. "Won't you all come in?" he muttered as he headed down the hall.

We followed him into a quaint sitting room with a massive picture window that overlooked the Waters at the base of the hill. Following the commander's lead, I settled onto the opposite end of the sofa from him. Benji and Brian took the easy chairs on either side of the sofa that were angled to facilitate conversation while providing a glimpse of the spectacular view.

Again, the commander grinned at me as if I were a long-lost friend. Odd as that should have seemed, I couldn't help feeling like it was true. "Can I offer you anything?" he murmured. "Water, tea, or wine perhaps?"

"No, thank you," I replied, mesmerized by the oceanic blue of his eyes. "I apologize, but I don't know your first name. How should I address you?"

"Commander Lochlan Mackendrick at your service," he replied with a polite nod. Then his gaze shifted to the chair to his left that appeared to be empty. "Would you care to make an appearance, Darkness? It's got to be rather lonely lurking in the shadows all the time."

"Actually," Benjamin replied, letting the Darkness slip away as he leaned back in his seat, "I prefer the shadows. This realm is a bit too bright for my taste."

A knowing grin spread across Lochlan's face. "You get used to it after a time."

"You say that as if you know how he feels, Lochlan," I mused.

"I do indeed, my Queen," he murmured, grinning as his eyes met mine. "I am not a creature of Light like yourself. And please, call me Loch. Lochlan is a bit formal for my liking."

"I'll call you Loch if you stop calling me Queen," I agreed. "My name is Emma Talbot."

"But of course, I knew that already," Loch replied. "I'll gladly call you Emma, as long as your bodyguards don't get too bent out of shape over it."

An unintentional chuckle slipped from my mouth. Everything that this man said sounded charming in his thick Scottish brogue. "They answer to me, Loch. They'll only get bent out of shape if I ask them to."

Loch's grin widened at that. "Alright, Emma it is then."

"You said you aren't a creature of Light," I replied, shifting sideways to face him straight on. "I know I'm new to this realm, but it seems a bit unusual to have a Dark creature in command of the Light army."

He shifted toward me, mirroring my movement. "It's no more unusual than a fairy Queen who's wed to the Sarrum of Draumer, the Darkest creature in existence."

"Fair enough," I muttered. "So, how exactly did you end up commanding the Light regiment if you aren't a creature of Light?"

"That's a very long story, but the short of it is that I'm an absolute mutt," he replied, "every bit as unusual as a fairy Queen who grew up in the heart of the Darkness. My mum was a creature of Light, but my dad was a creature of pure Darkness."

"If you don't mind me asking," I murmured, "what sort of creatures were they?"

His eyes brightened at the question, like surface water reflecting rays of sunlight. "You do realize that's quite an inappropriate question to ask someone you've only just met?"

"I guess curiosity got the better of me," I muttered, cheeks burning as I dropped my eyes to the couch cushions. "I apologize if I offended you by asking."

"You didn't offend me in the slightest," he replied, lowering his head just enough to catch my eye. "Your grandmother asked me the exact same question the first time we met."

Embarrassed that I'd made such a basic blunder and grateful that he didn't seem put off by it, I bit my lip and waited for him to continue.

"My mum was a mermaid," he muttered with a far-off look in his eye, "and my dad was a dragon. Darkness being the dominant trait, that makes me a Dark creature with an unusual fondness for the Light."

"Half mermaid and half dragon," I muttered, "that's an interesting mix."

He let out a boisterous chuckle. "*Interesting*, that's a polite way of saying strange. There's no need to sugar coat it on my account. I know I'm an odd duck."

"I take it you know why I've come here," I murmured, suppressing a grin.

"I certainly have my suspicions," he replied. As I watched him talk, it suddenly occurred to me why I found him so endearing. I'd been bombarded by the ridiculous frivolities of Light creatures since my arrival. It made perfect sense that I'd feel a fondness for this charming man with a dragon's heart beating within his chest. "I suspected you'd be paying me a visit at some point."

"So, you heard that I'd taken my rightful place on the throne?"

"No," he admitted, "but with all the goings on in this world, it was only a matter of time before the rightful Queen returned to us."

"We've never met before," I whispered, searching his eyes because a part of me felt like we had. "So, how could you presume to know how I'd react to world events?"

"Your grandmother, the last true Queen of this realm, was very dear to me," he murmured as his gaze drifted to the window. "Perhaps it was more of a hope that you'd follow in her footsteps and stand up for your people."

"My grandmother was the one who appointed you as commander of her army, wasn't she?"

That mesmerizing brightness flashed in his eyes again. "That she was. Although if she hadn't, I suspect I still would've found my way here somehow."

"Why?"

"Because the Queen was the love of my life, my dear."

That was a response I hadn't expected. "Wasn't she married to an Unsighted man?"

"Yes, she was in the waking world," he muttered. "Marrying a Sighted man was out of the question for her since it was her duty to provide the Light realm with the next fairy monarch. If she had wed a Sighted man, she would have given birth to a dragon child. The only way to produce an heir with pure fairy blood was to marry an Unsighted male fairy."

"I guess I never really gave that much thought," I muttered. "I'm sorry."

"Don't be," he replied, placing his hand on top of mine. "That's just the way of things, isn't it?"

"But my grandmother didn't give birth to a Sighted child."

"No, she did not," he agreed, "but her son married a fairy bride, and they produced the purest fairy this world has ever seen."

I couldn't help blushing at the way he was grinning at me.

"Forgive me for staring," he whispered, "but you look so much like her."

"I never got to meet her," I muttered.

"She passed before your time," he replied with a nod, "but she would've been so proud of you."

"How can you say that? You don't know anything about me."

"That's not quite true. I've kept tabs on you from afar."

"We need to prepare our troops for war," I murmured without preamble. "Would you consider resuming your post as commander of the Light regiment?"

"I was afraid you'd never ask," he replied. "It would be my honor to command your troops. When do I start?"

Before I could answer, Brian jumped to his feet. "Davina's in trouble," he growled under his breath. "I'm guessing somebody managed to follow Zeke back to their mirage."

"Shit," Benji snarled as his eyes fixed on me. "We can't leave the Queen's side."

"You most certainly can," Loch murmured as the two of us stood from the couch. "She'll be perfectly safe with me. I will tear any beast who even looks at her wrong limb from limb."

Benjamin and Brian exchanged a worried glance, but there was no time to waste hashing out security details.

"Go," I ordered, heart racing at the thought of what horrors might've caused Davina to call out to Brian after all these years. "If the Purists followed the team to

Zeke's safe haven, they'll need all the help they can get."

48

DAVID

The tension in the great hall of the palace was palpable, and for good reason. It had been decades since the heads of all the royal dragon families had assembled in one place like this. All that spitfire and venom in one room was a recipe for catastrophic disaster—or rather, it would've been had the reason for our meeting not been so dire. As it was, recent events had set all of us on edge. First there was the abduction of my Aunt Louise—my father's elder sister—who'd played an integral role in the upbringing of countless dragon children, including myself and Isa's daughter, Rose. Then there was the unexplained sudden death of Melvin Wise, the smallest member of the royal guard.

"Why don't you pull the rest of the team you sent to gather intelligence back to the waking world?" Alberto Torres asked as he stroked a hand over his graying beard. Although he was small in stature for a male in human form, the soft-spoken head of the

Ecuadorian clan was a fearsome warrior and an admirable, levelheaded patriarch.

A low growl rumbled in Isa's throat as she leaned forward in her seat to my right. "Because we have no idea what's going on with them in this world. Pulling them back at the wrong moment could get them all killed."

"So we lose a few foot soldiers," Percival Weston chimed in with a shrug. The lanky head of the American clan crossed his arms over his chest and stretched out his long legs, crossing them at the ankles as he slouched in his seat. "That's an acceptable loss if it keeps them from getting captured and spilling secrets to the enemy." Weston was a hotheaded patriarch who lacked any semblance of strategic intelligence. Isa had always disliked him, and he certainly wasn't winning any favor with her now.

"Like hell it is, Weston," Isa snarled. "My daughter is on that mission. Would you be so quick to sacrifice the team if your only daughter were among them?"

"So dramatic," Weston murmured, his patronizing tone dripping with sarcasm as he rolled his eyes. "Yeah, I would sacrifice my daughter for the greater good."

"If your daughter is anything like you, I would also consider that an acceptable loss," Falen retorted in an even tone that didn't mesh with the glare he shot Weston. The head of the Irish clan, who preferred to be addressed by his surname only, was a no-nonsense patriarch who put the needs of his people ahead of his own and a skilled military strategist who didn't waste time mincing words. He was even less fond of Weston than Isa was, and he wasn't afraid to show it.

"How dare you?" Weston grumbled, although he looked more amused than offended.

"This is getting us nowhere," I murmured, my voice silencing all peripheral chatter. "Does anyone have any viable suggestions to offer?"

Demetri, our head dungeon keeper, straightened in his seat to my left as he cleared his throat. "I could assemble a search party and go looking for them."

I dismissed the idea with a shake of my head. "I am not about to blindly dispatch a second team to search for the first when we have no idea what fate has befallen them."

"What does your Queen have to say about all of this?" Carter interjected. Due to his mother's recent death, the patriarch of the Drake family from New Brunswick was now the youngest head of family among us. He was also inarguably the most pleasing to the eye. The aesthetic perfection of the dark-haired dragon's facial features and physique in human form had sparked many a rumor that the blood flowing through his veins was not entirely pure. Well aware of the whispered accusations that his biological father was an incubus, and not the pure-blooded dragon his mother was married to, the young dragon was eager to prove himself a worthy member of our counsel.

"*My* Queen?" I growled as I fixed Carter in my flame-filled gaze. "Don't you mean *our* Queen?"

"Of course, Sarrum," he muttered, his posture wilting under the weight of my stare. "My apologies. Where is *our* Queen today?"

"That is not your concern," I replied, my clipped tone making it clear the whereabouts of my wife was not up for further discussion.

"We are getting off track," Adisa piped in. The matriarch of the Osei family from Ghana let her gaze linger on the younger dragon's physical perfection for a moment before her eyes locked with mine. "We came here because it is time to stop standing idly by while the Purists wreak havoc all over Draumer. Now is the time for all of us to join forces, track that son of a bitch and his followers down, and wipe the whole lot of them off the face of this world."

"Well said, Adisa," I agreed with a nod. "All available warriors from each house—"

Zeke's safe house has been compromised, boss, Brian's voice echoed inside my head, cutting me off midsentence.

All eyes in the room fixed on me as I responded telepathically. *Can you still track her after all this time?*

Yeah, boss. Benjamin and I are headed there now.

Rage obscured my vision in a blaze of blue flames. *Do you mean to tell me you've left the Queen unguarded?*

No, Commander Mackendrick is with her. He's agreed to return to his former post.

I tightened my grip on the arms of my throne, suppressing the fury within. *Then she is in good hands. Report to the great hall, and we shall accompany you to the mirage.*

I'd barely finished the thought when Brian and Benjamin stepped from the nearest Waterfall.

Every set of eyes in the great hall shifted to the warriors who had joined us.

"We've got a lead on where they are," I announced as everyone sprang to their feet. "All who are willing and able are welcome to follow and lend a hand in whatever battle awaits us there."

DREAM FRAGMENTS

All but a few of the oldest dragons fell into step behind me, and we followed Brian through the Waters without further discussion.

I exited the Waters immediately after Brian. But instead of stepping out onto the sweet meadow grass that normally blanketed the safe haven, scorched earth crumbled beneath my feet.

The carnage was widespread within the tattered remnants of Ezekiel's mirage. Many of the Unsighted souls he'd so painstakingly rescued lay slaughtered on the ground. Others were banded together, fighting the Purists for all their worth. In the thick of things, six members of Tristan's team fought for their lives and the lives of the Unsighted amongst them.

As the royals who'd accompanied us branched out to aid those in need of assistance, Benjamin and Isa's eyes searched the haphazard horde of souls for their daughter.

Not far from where we stood, Bob, Nellie and Addison were fighting to protect the Unsighted souls huddled between them. Blood spattered Tristan and Ezekiel's handsome faces as they plowed through the enemy forces, striking some down and charming others to turn their blades on themselves. Mia had assumed the form of Payne, the female shadow who'd tortured her after forcing her to take Emma's likeness at the Purists' cabin in the woods. Shocking as her choice of forms was, it was nothing compared to the realization that she was crippling demons right and left with the projection of shadow's fear. However, amidst all this destruction, there was no time to ponder the revelation that Payne must have bound herself to Mia before I tore the flesh from her bones.

Isa's cry of alarm rose above all other sounds in the mirage, drawing my attention to Charlie and Rose. Both of their bodies were bloody and charred, and they appeared to be locked in a battle to the death. Rose stilled for a moment at the sound of her mother's cry. Had it been any other foe he was battling, Charlie would've delivered the death blow whilst she was distracted.

But this was Rose.

Charlie met my eyes from across the battlefield, his body frozen with indecision and his grief palpable even at a distance.

As I rushed toward them, Rose blinked her eyes and surveyed the extensive carnage around her. Then she called back her troops, and every Purist who was able fled through the Waters with her. Had it been anyone other than Rose leading the enemy forces, I would have followed. But I would not harm Isa's daughter.

This was not her fault.

49

GODRIC

An aching emptiness robbed the breath from my lungs as I pulled the door open and stepped inside my sister's childhood bedroom. The best years of my life had been spent within the walls of this house, and many of my fondest memories were of ending the day seated on Lilly's bed reading her bedtime stories.

I crossed the room, picked up the book of fairytales on her nightstand, and sat down on her bed. *What had possessed me to read her these inane stories?* All of them ended the same, with the innocent young girl marrying her Prince Charming and living happily ever after in some gleaming castle.

My Lilly's tale had ended quite differently...

...Heart racing, I sprang from the car and hurried toward the front door of the Talbots' estate. That meeting had been an absolute farce. The Light Queen never had any intention of collaborating with me to overthrow Alexander Talbot's rule. There was only one reason why she would've invited me to her office under such false pretenses. The Talbots had asked her to.

Flames blurred my vision as I neared the door. I would slaughter every one of them if I was too late to return to Lilly's side. Alexander, her pathetic excuse for a husband, was still out of the country on business. If my sister had gone into labor in my absence, she'd have been all alone. My stomach roiled at the thought as I wrenched the front door open and raced toward her bedroom.

It only took me seconds to reach the room, barge in, and find it unoccupied.

As I stepped out into the hall, a maid strolled past me whistling a cheery tune as if everything were just as it ought to be.

Infuriated by her nonchalance in the midst of my panic, I grabbed her by the arms and spun her toward me. "Where is my sister?"

She responded with a blank stare, but I could feel her heart pounding as the color drained from her face.

I tightened my grip on her arms and ignored her resultant yelp. "Answer me," I snarled, "or I will rip your throat out with my teeth right here and now in the waking world."

She let out a whimper and dropped her gaze to the floor as she muttered, "They moved her."

I shook her until she lifted her panic-stricken eyes to meet mine. "Moved her where?"

"The guesthouse," she replied in a feeble whisper.

She collapsed to the floor the instant I released her, but I didn't give a damn about her.

Smoke billowed from my nostrils as I raced through the house and exited through the back door.

I had only taken a few steps toward the guesthouse when the door swung open. Frozen where I stood, I watched with my heart in my throat as a parade of staff came pouring out. The Talbots' family physician was the first to exit, his jaw clenched and his eyes cast downward. A woman in white stepped out after him, hugging a bundle of blankets to her chest as if they contained the most precious treasure in the world.

My stomach dropped at the sight.

I couldn't say for certain who came out after her, but my nausea intensified with each set of slumped shoulders and mournful expression that passed through that doorway.

When the last of them had vanished, I headed toward the house at the sluggish sort of pace that propels you forward in a nightmare where it feels as if your feet are cemented to the ground. I was desperate to reach that building, but terrified of what I would find inside. Perhaps it would all turn out fine. Lilly could be in there resting whilst some kindhearted nurse watched over her.

Tears spilled down my cheeks as I reached the door. I couldn't feel her. There was no heartbeat... no rush of emotions at the birth of her child... no exhaustion. There was nothing at all to suggest that my sister still drew breath. All I felt was the gaping hole within me that grew larger with each passing second.

I reached out and gripped the doorknob with a trembling hand, but I couldn't bring myself to turn it. In this moment, horrific as it was, there was a miniscule chance that my sister's heart was still beating. After all, there had been a few occasions in the past when I couldn't sense her wants or feel the beating of her heart. As long as that door remained shut, there was still a possibility that my sweet Lilly was in there resting peacefully.

That gut-wrenching moment seemed to stretch to eternity as the black hole in my chest swallowed everything good that'd ever dwelt within me. I finally grasped how our father felt when he lost our mother. Despite all my hatred for him, I could empathize with his grief now.

Tears streamed down my cheeks as I dropped my forehead to the door and prayed to a God that I didn't believe in to let me find her alive. I didn't care that the Talbots had stolen my crown and stripped me of my rightful title. Nothing else mattered as long as my sister still drew breath. I had promised to keep her safe. If they'd broken that promise, I would devote every last breath in my body to making them pay for what they'd done to her.

When I had no tears left to shed, I straightened and dried my cheeks. If Lilly was still alive in there, I didn't want her to see me acting so weak. I took a deep breath and squared my shoulders. Then I opened the door.

She looked so small and pale, lying in that bed all alone. The sight of her brought to mind all those nights that I'd read her one of those sadistic fairytales that led young girls to believe this was something to aspire to. This was how my sister's fairytale had always been destined to end.

I held my breath, clinging to the foolish notion that perhaps she was merely resting, as I moved toward her.

I sat down on the bed beside her motionless body and took her small hand in mine. It was stone cold—and yet, my mind refused to accept the truth. I pressed my ear to her chest, desperate to detect some hint of life. There was no rise and fall of her chest, no faint sound of breath, no heartbeat.

She was gone.

The one good thing in my life that was pure and true had been stolen from me, and they'd left her here all alone like some discarded eggshell. That was all she'd ever been to them, a dragon's egg to incubate their future King until he grew strong enough to rip the shell apart and claw his way into this world. The Talbots had their precious heir to the throne now.

And I had nothing.

I had vowed to keep Lilly safe since the day she was born, and they'd trampled that vow. I wouldn't rest until all of them paid for what they'd done to her.

As I kissed her pale cheek, I felt what little was left of my heart shatter. Its jagged shards tore at my insides as I stood from the bed, walked to the door, and stepped outside.

Then I marched toward the house, guided by the faint beat of a tiny heart that echoed the sound of my Lilly's...

..."My King," a demonic voice muttered behind me.

I dried the tears from my cheeks before standing to turn toward him. This unfortunate sod had no idea that he was about to become the recipient of all my fury.

When I turned, Rose Salazar Talbot was standing just inside the door beside Louise. Her hair was wild, her chest was heaving, and her cheeks were streaked with a mixture of dried blood and tears. Rose stepped toward me, holding my gaze as she muttered, "I couldn't convince your son to join me."

Overcome with the grief my sister's bedroom had just rekindled, I met Rose halfway across the room and drew her into my arms. Then I maneuvered us both to Lilly's bed. Rose sat down beside me, dropped her head to my chest, and burst into tears.

I tightened my hold on her and stroked a hand over the disheveled locks of her hair, matted with my son's blood. "He'll change his mind, Rose."

She tilted her head and looked up at me with desperation in her eyes. "How can you be so sure of that?"

"He treasures you above all else, my dear," I murmured as I wiped the blood and tearstains from her cheeks. "Eventually, he will have no choice but to fight his way to you. And when he is ready to accept his destiny, we will welcome him with open arms."

50

CHARLIE

The Sarrum stood beside the porch steps of what was left of Zeke's house, and everyone from our side of the skirmish who was still able to stand was gathered around him. They were discussing how to proceed with the war and where everyone should go after they left the mirage. I sat cross-legged on the ground no more than a few feet away, too numb to register a word of what was said.

Smoke scorched its way up my throat and billowed from my nostrils in an angry plume as I surveyed the remains of Zeke's safe haven. My surroundings were somewhat obscured by the haze of orange flames blazing in my visual field. But from what I could tell, the lush prairie landscape that'd greeted us when we first arrived now resembled the burnt remnants of a warzone—which, I suppose it basically was. Everything seemed so out of focus now. I hadn't been able to see or think straight since I watched Rose flee the mirage with the Purists.

How could I have been so stupid *again*? This whole war had started because I let Godric dupe me into sneaking him into Emma's mirage, where he kidnapped her right out from under the Sarrum's nose. You'd think I would have learned my lesson after that, but apparently I hadn't learned a fucking thing. I turned right around and fell in love with Godric's puppet. If I'd been thinking with my head instead of my heart, maybe I would've sensed what Rose was up to before she snapped Pip's neck. *Had any of it ever been real?* Or had she just been playing us all the entire time?

My eyes drifted back to the survivors who stood huddled around the Sarrum. They were starting to disband now, but I stayed seated on the ground like the useless lump that I was. I didn't know what the plan of attack was, and I didn't much care anymore. They were better off without me. I was a liability, a sucker, and a coward. I had an opportunity to take Rose down when Isa's scream distracted her, but I couldn't bring myself to do it. Honestly, if the Sarrum hadn't shown up with reinforcements, I probably would've let Rose destroy me because the alternative was too unthinkable.

Water portals were being formed and creatures were exiting the mirage through them, but I was too busy wallowing in self-pity to pay attention to who was headed where.

"It's time for us to take our leave now, Charlie."

I looked up and blinked the Sarrum's face into focus. Until he spoke, I hadn't noticed we were the only two souls left in the mirage. "Okay," I muttered as I got to my feet.

He formed a portal with an elegant flick of his wrist, and I stepped in after him without either of us saying a word.

I followed him down the short tunnel of Water and stepped out onto a balcony at the palace. We headed toward a group of chairs by the railing with plush black velvet cushions in pristine condition, despite the fact that they didn't look like they'd hold up well outdoors. The Sarrum settled into one of the chairs, and I followed his lead and dropped into the one beside it.

As we sat there in silence, my eyes drifted to the Waterfall entrance to the palace down below, and I cursed the day the Sarrum's wife first walked through that door at the facility. None of this would be happening if the two of us had never become friends. *I wish I'd never set eyes on Emma Talbot.*

"You don't mean that," David murmured.

I lifted my eyes to his face without really seeing his features. He was just a dark silhouette against the backdrop of an even darker sky. Even the night sounds of the forest seemed muted, as if Rose had stolen every bit of life from the landscape I'd once found so enchanting. "What happened to everybody else?" I asked in a hollow whisper.

"Tristan and Mia are here at the palace," he murmured with a raised eyebrow that suggested I should already know the answer to my question, "as are Benjamin and Isa."

A lump formed in my throat as I nodded. "What about Davina and Zeke, and all those Unsighted souls who were under his protection?"

David exhaled a tired sigh as he shifted in his seat. "They have relocated to the Light realm where they shall be kept safe for the duration of this war."

"After everything that hasn't gone according to plan, how can you be so sure that they'll be safe there?"

A muscle in his jaw tensed as a blaze of sapphire flames filled his eyes. An instant later, he suppressed the fury and regained composure. "Emma has taken her rightful place as Queen of the Light realm. Brian is there with her, as are Bob, Nellie, and Addison. I have no doubt that Ezekiel will help defend their borders and keep the refugees safe, and the commander of the Light regiment is immensely capable. They are all in good hands."

"How can you stand to be apart from Emma?"

"I can't," he admitted in a hoarse whisper, "but this is how it must be for the time being."

Tears filled my eyes as I muttered, "How could I have been such an idiot?"

The Sarrum shook his head. "We all trusted Rose, Charlie."

"But I'm the one who *fell in love* with a traitor," I muttered.

"None of this was her fault."

I squeezed my eyes shut as that horrific image of Rose ending Pip's life sprang to mind for the umpteenth time. "How can you say that? She snapped Pip's neck like it was nothing, and I watched her kill too many Unsighted souls to count while I was trying to get to her in Zeke's mirage."

"This was not your fault either."

"I should've killed Rose when Isa distracted her," I muttered, "but I couldn't bring myself to do it."

"Of course you couldn't," he replied with a sorrowful smile. "She is your greatest treasure."

I nodded because I didn't know what else to say.

"I realize this is difficult," he murmured, "but I need you to pull yourself together and move past it now."

I let out a humorless chuckle as I raked a hand through the clumps of blood and dirt caked in my hair. "Why?"

"Because you and I are going to end this war," he murmured. "If we eliminate Godric, I believe we can save Rose and all the other dragons Louise Talbot poisoned with his blood."

My stomach dropped at his words. "How do you know Louise poisoned them? Did you *know* this was going to happen?"

"Not until quite recently," he replied matter-of-factly. "I had my suspicions when Louise was taken from her home, but you'd already set out on your mission by then. Pulling any of you back to the waking world to warn you would've posed too great a risk, especially since it was merely a hunch. We knew nothing for certain until Rose turned on you and sided with the Purists."

That nightmarish image of Pip's final moment reared its ugly head again, and I dug my fingernails into the palms of my hands to banish it from my mind. "Do you really think we can save Rose?"

"I do."

Something he'd said earlier suddenly clicked. "Why did you say *you and I* are going to end this war?"

"I believe Godric has poisoned the mind of every dragon Louise covertly administered his blood to. She played a vital role in the upbringing of many of the royals, and there is no way to know for certain how many she infected with his venomous intent. Every dragon she tainted will be loyal to him once he calls them to action. They will turn on us on the battlefield and answer only to his blood."

"So…"

"You have always been the answer, Charlie," he murmured. "Godric's blood flows through *your* veins. If we eliminate the would-be-king, regardless of whether or not they're under the sway of his blood, the Purists will follow you because *you* are his heir."

"Uh huh," I muttered, "and what exactly does that mean?"

"It means that the throne must go to you."

Maybe I'd lost more blood than I realized because I must've heard him wrong. "What?"

He leaned forward, tilted his head, and narrowed his eyes at me like he was inspecting me for a head injury. "I intend to name you as my successor to the throne."

I tried to do a mental recap of the battle in Zeke's mirage. *Did I hit my head hard enough to cause a concussion at some point?* "Aren't you supposed to *father* the next Dragon King?"

"The old ways of controlling the royal gene pool through arranged marriages and carefully orchestrated pregnancies is barbaric and antiquated. I never intended to father my successor," he murmured, leaning back against the velvet cushions of his chair.

"I think Doc should probably check me for a concussion, or give me a blood transfusion or something," I muttered, "because I'm pretty sure I'm hallucinating." *Maybe I'd wake up back at the facility and discover that none of this had ever been real.*

"I'm afraid we no longer have the luxury of easing you into this," David murmured. "Benjamin and I had hoped that given enough time and training, your true nature would emerge on its own. Although I had begun to suspect that you'd require some assistance to reach your full potential, it seemed unwise to force the transformation before you set off on the mission. As I'm sure you'll recall, your first flying lesson proved that you were unable to remain rational and in control of your behavior when your dragon-instincts took center stage. I couldn't risk your id taking control whilst you were undercover in enemy territory. Fully adjusting to your new reality is going to be a painful and difficult process, but now that you've returned to the palace—and Benjamin and I will be nearby to keep you in check—we cannot afford to wait any longer. You have always been the solution to this war, Charlie. Once you accept that, we can begin to train you properly as the royal you are. It's time to open your eyes, so that you may embrace what you are truly capable of."

Yeah, I'd definitely lost the last scraps of my sanity. "Open my eyes?"

"You have been stumbling around blindly in the Dark for too long," David replied. "It is high time that we remove the blinders from your eyes."

I wasn't sure whether this improbable turn of events should make me feel excited or terrified. "How?"

"Stand up," he murmured as he stood from his chair.

I stood up beside him, squeezed my eyes shut, and did my best not to flinch when he placed a hand on either side of my head. I could almost feel his eyebrow raise as his fiery gaze burrowed into me. *Right, open my eyes.*

I expected him to level me with his customary you're-a-dumbass scowl as I opened my eyes. Instead, he smiled at me.

Warmth seeped into me from his hands, and an involuntary grin spread across my face.

"**Wake, Dragon**," the Sarrum commanded in a monstrous growl, both aloud and inside my head. He wasn't speaking English, but I understood every word of the demonic dialect I had never heard before, as clearly as if I'd spoken it all my life. "**The time to hide has ended. Open your eyes, and assume your rightful place in this world.**"

A blinding ache flared inside my head, distant hoof beats and monstrous shrieks echoed in my ears, and the world around me blurred…

…There were tears in my father's eyes. "Bury it, Charlie. Never let them see what you are, and never let the Water out of your sight."

I wanted to act brave and make my father proud, but I couldn't stop the tears from falling. How could I leave him behind?

"Promise me," he whispered. "Promise me you'll keep it hidden."

I shook my head. "Let me stay with you."

He choked back a sob as he pulled a little blue vial from his coat pocket. "Drink it," he muttered as he pressed the vial into my hand, "and stay hidden."

"We can both jump in the Water," I whispered, tears streaming down my cheeks. "We can get away together."

A tear slid down my father's cheek as he shook his head. "I love you, Charlie. Never forget how much I loved you. I promised your mother that if there ever came a day when we couldn't get away, I'd have you drink this and escape through the Waters."

"I don't understand." Heart in my throat, I ignored the hoof beats that shook the ground beneath our feet and the unholy shrieks echoing from the forest. "Why can't you jump out of here with me?"

He sighed and hugged me to his chest. "We'd just come back to this same spot tomorrow, and they'd be waiting for us. There's no escape for me, Charlie. Not this time. But if I stay behind, you can wake wherever you want tomorrow. Just remember to concentrate on staying away from here. The Waters will listen to you, Charlie. And if I get away, I promise I'll find you." He grabbed the vial from my hand, uncorked it, and poured it down my throat, and I was too terrified and confused to fight it.

A deafening chorus of shrieks rose from the forest, and my heart froze. The heavy flapping sounds of monstrous wings filled the air and giant hoof beats shook the ground so hard that my teeth chattered.

"Go!" My father gave me a shove toward the Waters.

But I shook my head, refusing to budge.

"I love you, Charlie. Keeping you safe has been my life's goal since the day I met your mother. Let me take my last breath knowing I kept my promise to her."

I should've argued, but a monstrous growl just inside the trees spooked me, and I ran to the Waters and left my father to die...

...A thunderous roar shook the entire castle, and it took me a moment to realize the sound had come from me.

"Your mother was a clever woman," David murmured as he released my head from his hands. "She concocted a potion to mask your true nature in the event that your father could no longer keep you hidden. After you fled through the Waters, they had no way to track you when you returned to Draumer."

I was trying to focus on the Sarrum's words, but there was too much going on around us. The breezeless air had given way to a violent wind that was whistling in my ears with relentless force, and the sounds emanating from the Dark Forest were no longer hushed. Every chirp, buzz, and rustling leaf had become a deafening distraction. On top of that, countless voices echoed from all around us. "I was only eight," I muttered, a clap of thunder drowning out the words as I spoke them.

"And yet, you managed to make it to adulthood on your own," David mused in an ear-splitting growl.

The beating of his heart, and my heart, and too many other heartbeats to count hammered in my ears.

This is all my fault. If I'd been brave enough to ignore my grandmother's advice and raise Rose myself, this would never have happened.

I took a few steps back from David as I looked around for Isa. *Where was her voice coming from?*

David crossed his arms over his chest and grinned at me. "You are hearing her thoughts from inside the palace."

"I've never picked up a stray thought from Isa or anyone else at the palace," I roared, although I'd

DREAM FRAGMENTS

meant to whisper. "Is she too upset to guard her thoughts after what happened with Rose today?"

"There is no guarding anything from a dragon," David replied in a thunderous roar.

I squinted at him—his relaxed posture, the casual way his mouth formed the words. This didn't look like the stance of a monster growling at the top of his lungs.

"I am whispering," David's voice thundered, "as are you. Your hearing is far more acute than you are accustomed to. It will take some time, but you will get used to it."

"What did…" The sound of my own booming voice echoing inside my head was making it difficult to focus and voice my thoughts. "What the hell did you do to me?"

"I set free what has been buried deep inside you for far too long."

The night sounds emanating from the forest…all those beating hearts…the thoughts of creatures who were nowhere to be seen, howling inside my head…it was all too overwhelming to process. "Well, it's too much," I roared as I stepped toward him. "Bury it back wherever you found it."

Another clap of thunder sounded, shaking the floor beneath our feet. A second later, the sky opened up and rain began to pelt us with relentless force.

"Why is it raining?" I roared as a burst of lightning lit the sky. "I thought it never stormed here."

"Storms are not a natural phenomenon in Draumer," David agreed in a deafening whisper. "They are the byproduct of a dragon's emotions."

"Are you telling me *I'm* doing this?"

A grin spread across his face as he nodded. "I am."

"Well," I roared, punctuating the word with an unintentional clap of thunder, "how do I *undo* it?"

"Tell it to stop," he replied matter-of-factly, like he was instructing me to perform a simple task any idiot was capable of.

I narrowed my eyes at him.

And his grin widened as he shrugged his shoulders.

"Stop," I muttered, expecting nothing to happen like it normally did whenever I tried something dragonish for the first time.

But it *did* stop, *all of it.* The wind died off. The rain stopped falling. Only the deafening sounds of life emanating from the forest and the palace remained.

I'd been bracing myself against the gale winds without giving it any thought. Their instantaneous disappearance knocked me off balance, and I landed on my ass with nothing but the stone floor of the balcony to break my fall. I let out a monstrous roar, too loud for my human mouth to produce.

"What the hell's happening?" I muttered as I sat up and leaned against the railing.

"You just need to give it time," David replied.

"What difference will time make?"

"It will come and go for a while, but eventually you'll figure out how to tune out the extraneous sounds," he replied as he joined me on the floor, "just as your mind tuned out unnecessary stimuli in your previous form."

I glanced down at my human body, then looked up at him. "I'm not in my dragon form."

"There is no other form," David replied. "How you appear to yourself and others is of no consequence. You are always dragon."

"Okay..."

"Focus on tuning out the extraneous sounds."

As he spoke, I shut my eyes and concentrated on tuning out everything but his voice.

"Good," he murmured, his volume less overpowering than it'd seemed a moment ago.

I drew a trembling breath, and exhaled an unsteady blast of steam. Then I opened my eyes and raked a hand through my hair as I stared at my cousin. A smoky blue haze hovered in the air around him like a full-body halo.

"Your Sight is much keener now," he murmured. "A masked creature will no longer be able to hide his true nature from you."

"But you still look human to me."

"Yes, but you see the edges of the deception now."

"Is that what the haze around you is?"

"It is," David murmured as he slid closer to lean against the railing beside me.

"What else is different?" I muttered.

"Everything will be different now," he replied with a grin. "The world around you will bend to your will. If you do not like the night, you can simply turn it to day."

"Wait...what?"

He let out a thunderous chuckle. "Try it."

"How?" I muttered. "Is it like using the clapper, or something? Do I just clap my hands and—"

The instant I clapped, the endless night sky turned clear blue and sunlight lit the Dark Forest bright as day. A chorus of snarling, and growling, and furious howls rose from the forest below.

A grin of amusement tugged at the corners of David's mouth as he snapped his fingers. The absolute darkness returned, and the complaining died off. "Dark creatures do not appreciate the light."

"Right," I muttered. "Guess I should save that party trick for another time." Just for the hell of it, I snapped my fingers and willed the rain to start up again.

A burst of lightning lit the night sky, followed by a crack of thunder as the rain began to pour.

A few seconds later, a chorus of howling complaints rose up from the forest.

I didn't snap my fingers. I just *thought* that I wanted it to stop.

And it did.

I couldn't stop myself from laughing out loud.

David raised an eyebrow, but his grin was downright playful. "Enjoying yourself?"

"Yeah," I chuckled. "I really am."

"Well, I'm afraid it's time to stop the child's play and begin your training." With that, he stood, unmasked to his dragon form and took flight.

As I watched him soar through the air, I felt no hint of the fear that'd weighted me to the ground in the past. The concept of flying seemed as logical as walking. I pushed myself to my feet, drew a deep breath and felt the fire in my lungs. *I was made to fly.* It seemed so obvious now. I wasn't sure how I'd missed it before.

My thunderous laughter echoed through the night as I took flight and chased after the Sarrum. I had never felt so alive. I took it all back. *I couldn't be happier that fate brought me and Emma together back at the facility.*

David hung back, hovering in midair until I caught up to him. "Fate had nothing to do with it," he growled as we flew through the air side by side.

"What do you mean?"

"Think about it," he murmured as we soared above the treetops. "Do you honestly believe it was coincidence that Godric's son, his ex-wife, and his arch-enemy's soul mate all ended up at the same facility?"

I'd never given it any thought, but when he put it like that, it did sound impossible. "I guess I never really thought about it," I muttered.

"Godric has followers everywhere," David mused. "He orchestrated both your and Nellie's placement at the facility, so he could keep tabs on everything that he felt belonged to him. Then he orchestrated the committal of my dearest treasure to the same location, striking where I was vulnerable. None of it was coincidence or fate. He meant to set all of it in motion. I must admit, he managed to stay several moves ahead of me for quite some time. However, the tables are about to turn. It is time for us to cripple Henry Godric, deliver the death blow, and rid both worlds of his malevolence."

The Sarrum's words were enough to sober the dopey grin off my face. *What the hell was I doing, acting like a kid playing with a new toy while Rose was under that psycho's influence?* "It doesn't matter that Godric started it," I growled. "You and I are going to finish it."

The grin that spread across my cousin's monstrous face chilled me to the bone, even in my dragon form. "Now, *that* we may chalk up to fate."

If you'd told me the day I first set eyes on Emma back at the facility, that this was my fate, I would've laughed you out of the room.

But as I soared above the Dark Forest next to the Dragon King, I knew in my heart that ending Godric and bringing order to Draumer had always been my destiny.

Keep reading for an excerpt from
Book Five of the Dream Waters Series

Excerpt from Book Five of the Dream Waters Series:

CHARLIE

I sat in a booth near the back of the pub, nursing my single malt with Benjamin cloaked in shadow beside me. Under normal circumstances, I might have been pissed that the man we were there to meet was almost an hour late. I was pretty sure Benjamin was close to using up the last of what little patience he had, but I was enjoying myself too much to care. It wasn't every day that I got to fly to Glasgow for a top secret meeting with the commander of an allied kingdom's army.

I swirled the drink in my glass as I leaned back against the booth's buttery leather upholstery, content to sit and people watch until the commander showed up. Meeting with the commander of the Light army in Draumer would've raised too many eyebrows. It also would've been obvious that something was up if the Sarrum had been the one to fly to Scotland and meet with Commander Mackendrick. Despite the fact that I was Godric's son, I was still enough of a nobody in the waking world to take off on a red-eye flight to Scotland under a fictitious name with a top-notch fake passport without anyone questioning what I was up to. Benjamin had flown to Germany five days earlier on a private jet. After that, he'd made his way to the hotel in Glasgow where I was staying almost entirely under the cover of shadow.

After a day of sightseeing with Benjamin cloaked in shadow beside me, we'd arrived at The Fox's Den Pub and Scullery promptly at six o'clock when our meeting was set to begin. Now the minute hand was inching its way toward seven o'clock, and the commander had yet to make an appearance.

"Exactly how long do you want to sit here like a jackass waiting for Mackendrick to show?" Benjamin grumbled under his breath.

"I've got nowhere else to be," I whispered, hoping no one would notice me conversing with myself. "Come on, where's your sense of adventure?"

"Schlepping around as your shadow all day isn't exactly my idea of an adventure," he muttered.

"I love you too, Benji," I whispered with a smirk, knowing full well he wouldn't draw attention to our table by raising his voice at me for addressing him by the nickname only Isa, Rose, and Emma were permitted to use.

"You know," he muttered a bit closer to my ear, "I could dump your body in Loch Ness and nobody would ever be the wiser."

"Yeah?" I whispered. "And what would you tell the boss?"

"That you fell out of the boat on our tour of the loch," Benjamin murmured, "and despite all my efforts to save you, you disappeared never to be seen again."

The Darkness in his tone sent a shiver down my spine. "Sounds like you've given that story a lot of thought."

"A shadow has to pass the time somehow while he's following you around all day like an asshole."

The bell above the front door jingled, announcing the arrival of a new customer before I could think of a clever comeback.

The middle-aged man who stepped inside was wearing one of those caps that old Irishmen always wear, and he was dressed in a stylish wool pea-coat over a shirt and tie. His reddish-brown hair and beard were impeccably groomed, and he carried himself with an air of confidence that commanded respect. Despite appearing to be in perfect health, and walking with steady purposeful strides, his left hand gripped a cane that he wasn't using.

He nodded and flashed the bartender a charming grin, then ordered a drink.

Lazily slouched in touristy people-watching mode, it caught me off guard when the bartender nodded and pointed to our table as he handed the man his drink. The man's charming grin widened as he tipped his cap and said something that made the bartender let out a great big belly laugh.

"Who the hell is this guy?" I muttered under my breath. The man we were waiting for had been appointed commander of the Light army by Emma's grandmother. I wasn't pissed to be kept waiting, but to be kept waiting only to have some other stooge show up on the commander's behalf was just plain rude. Benjamin and I had traveled around the globe to meet with Mackendrick. But he couldn't be bothered to drive a few hours to speak with us himself?

"That's him," Benjamin whispered.

"That's *who*?" I muttered as the commander's delegate approached our table.

"The name's Mackendrick," the man replied, his charming grin widening as he held his hand out for a handshake. As he and I shook hands, his gaze shifted to Benjamin. "Sorry to keep you fellas waiting for so long. The traffic is murder this time of day."

I turned my head to see if Benjamin had slipped out of the shadows, but my dragon eyes could barely detect the Darkness's blurry outline. *How the hell could this guy see him?* "Are you here on your grandfather's behalf?" I muttered as Mackendrick Junior slid into his side of the booth across the table from us.

The twinkle in his eye as he chuckled made it almost impossible to be annoyed with him. Junior was too damn charming to dislike. "No," he replied in a lowered voice, leaning over the table. "I am the fellow you came here to meet."

I sat my drink down on the table and leaned forward, studying him through narrowed eyes. "*You* were the love of *Emma's grandmother's* life? Your plastic surgeon must be one hell of a miracle worker."

He chuckled again as he shook his head. Then he turned his attention to the man cloaked in darkness beside me. "You didn't prep him very well for this meeting, did you, shadow?"

"I didn't want to detract from his grand adventure," Benjamin muttered.

There was a hint of disapproval in the commander's stare as he eyed my invisible friend for a moment without commenting on his response. Then Mackendrick turned his attention back to me. "Why don't you ask that selfish child whom you work for to give you a history lesson when you get back home?"

Selfish child? "Huh?" It wasn't exactly an eloquent response, but I was at a loss.

"David," Mackendrick replied, spitting the name from his mouth as if it were a piece of rancid meat.

"David Talbot?" I muttered. "Am I missing something?"

"Apparently," he replied with a forced grin. "But this isn't exactly the time or place for a history lesson now, is it?"

"Did we come here to talk civilly or just do a bunch of male posturing and name-calling?" Benjamin inquired in a hushed growl.

"The boy takes offense at someone standing in for me when he is only here because David doesn't dare meet me face-to-face?"

"Wait," I muttered, "what's happening here?"

Mackendrick slid to the edge of the bench on his side of the booth. "I'm afraid you've wasted a trip, Mister...?"

"Oliver," I replied, "Charlie Oliver."

He was just starting to rise from his seat when I said my name. As soon as he heard it, he sat back down. "Henry Godric's boy?"

"I'm afraid so," I muttered, "but I hope you don't hold that against me."

"Godric never broke a promise to us," Mackendrick muttered. "The same cannot be said of David Talbot."

"What did my boss do to piss you off so much?"

"That is a discussion for another time," he replied softly, "in another world."